Just Say It

Tessa Barrie

Cover design: Deb Sutton

This book is a work of fiction

My sincere thanks to:

Adrienne Dines who, with the late Barbara Large, rekindled my passion for creative writing.

Pippa Houghton for putting up with my bad moods and histrionics after the entire manuscript disappeared into the ether, on more than one occasion.

Pat Stanley for the constant chivvying and belief that I could do it.

Deb Sutton, who 'held my hand' throughout the whole self-publishing process, delivering tough love and teaching me so much.

Contents

Turning Forty

Hangover Saturday

Mother v Daughter: Round One

Wasted Day

Carpe Diem

1963 – 1977

Earliest Memories

Learning the Hard Way

Blame It on the Mother

Bonding

Time to Get Tough

The Truth is Out

Mother v Daughter: Round Two

Eighteen

Enter Henry Stage Left

The Ultimate Betrayal

Getting Back in Touch

New Beginnings

Into Exile

The Truth About Henry

Luck be an Iron Lady

Escape to London

Stellar

Agony Aunt

The Spark of a Flame

Fisticuffs at Fanny's

Katzenjammer

The Feeling Never Dies

Moving On

Bloodletting

Double Disloyalty

Charred Remains

Lisa Dear

Finty Follow Up

Life-Changing Decision

Starting Over

Taking It Slow

Christmas Day

The Surprise Visit

A New Millennium

Emotional Overload

Saying Goodbye

Arthur's Revenge

Going the Wrong Way

Pernod in Paris

Contentment

Forebears

Marriageable Material

Footloose

Loose Ends

Closing In

Tying the Knot

Settling In

Living a Lie

New Life

The Rutherford Legacy

Commitment

About the author

Turning Forty

It was almost the end of the year, a century, a millennium, and what a decade it had been. The Cold War was over, Nelson Mandela was free at last, and the Internet was changing the way everyone worked and lived their lives. It was also Lisa Grant's fortieth birthday.

Leading up to this significant milestone, she hadn't been sleeping well. She'd been having nightmares about many things, but particularly the recurring dream about turning sixty, not forty. She would wake up in a cold sweat, arms flailing around in the air and screaming, 'there's been some mistake! My mother's only fifty-nine!' She didn't identify with being forty. She wasn't ready to be middle-aged. There were so many loose ends from the last thirty-nine years she needed to tie up first.

She'd been in a hurry to get home because her oldest friend, Adele, had arranged a birthday meal just down the road in the picturesque market town of Cirencester. Adele always said she was late for everything, and she was right. As a self-confessed workaholic, Lisa would always be the last one out of the office every evening, but she couldn't be late, not tonight. Now, standing in front of the wood-warped front door of the charming but dank Cotswold stone cottage she was renting, the bloody thing refused to open. Flummoxed and panting after several abortive attempts, she psyched herself up for one final superhuman effort to get in. Letting loose a stream of expletives, she mustered the strength of a prop forward, launched herself at the door, and shouldered her way inside.

Once in the stark hallway, the all-pervading smell of mould engulfed her. Turning on the light, she bent to pick up a small pile of post that had arrived through the letterbox. The Portuguese postmark on a birthday card from her father reminded her that a bottle of Mont das Uvas Pinot Grigio was chilling in the fridge. She headed to the kitchen, a glass before going out should lift her flagging joire de vivre. As she walked, her boots created an echo as they connected with the ancient limestone flooring that ran throughout the ground floor. The stone flags contributed to the constant chill inside the cottage, as they had been doing for over four hundred years. The Cotswold stone two up, two down, was impossible to heat, and black mould streaked across the walls both upstairs and down, and despite regular scrubbing with bleach, it never went away. Lisa had been putting off telling her lecherous landlord that the smell of damp was getting worse, but she had to call him and say he could come anytime while she was at work, because she didn't want a repeat of his last visit when he arrived unannounced.

Late home from work, as usual, she'd asked Adele round for a meal, and had just run a bath. She was about to get in when the doorbell rang. Craning her head, she looked out of the bathroom window and, although a cascade of Golden Shower roses obscured her view of the drive, she was certain it was Adele, so opened the window and shouted, 'Hi, gorgeous, I'm in the bath, grab a glass of wine and come on up.'

Lowering herself into the bath, she heard the front door open and close. She thought it was odd that Adele hadn't parried with something along the lines of 'what is it you have never understood about leaving work on time?' It was only the sound of laboured breathing and heavy clumping coming up the stairs that made her realise that it probably wasn't the petite Adele.

'Della?' She panicked, leaping out of the bath, and wrapping a towel around her, just as Quentin Fernsby, aka lecherous landlord, appeared at the open bathroom door, holding a glass of Pinot Grigio in his hand, his glazed eyes out on stalks.

He seemed to have lost control of his mouth, his bottom lip flopping open. He licked it before slurring the words, 'I'm here to fix your shower head.'

'Quentin! What a surprise! I thought you were Adele; she'll be here any second now.' Sidling past him, she made it into her bedroom and locked the door just as Adele arrived.

After that unfortunate episode, Lisa asked him to replace the strip light in the bathroom, which he still hadn't done. He could do it when he inspected the mould and sort out the front door at the same time. On the plus side, she only paid a peppercorn rent, and her financial situation was dire.

She ran the tips of her fingers across the top of the old night storage heater in the kitchen. It had only just come on, so she would keep her coat on a little longer; there was no point in lighting the fire in the living room as she was going out. Opening the fridge, she took out the bottle of wine and poured herself a glass. Taking a sip, she savoured the taste on her tongue for a few seconds before swallowing and exhaling the words, 'Thank God it's Friday.'

Sifting through the post, she added anything official looking to the stash behind the biscuit barrel on a shelf of the distressed kitchen dresser. The answerphone on the shelf below was winking at her, so she pressed play… 'Happy birthday, Li! Just to say my darling husband has volunteered to be our chauffeur tonight, so we'll be round at 7.45 to pick you up. So, you better get your skates on. Look forward to seeing you later.' Adele knew her better than anybody. After twenty-nine years and everything life had thrown at them, the pinkie promises they made to each other aged eleven had stood the test of time. She glanced at her watch. It was 7.15 p.m., just enough time to open her cards.

She walked through to the sitting room and slumped into an armchair. Its springs protested loudly beneath its threadbare upholstery. It was just one of the time-worn pieces of furniture that came with the rental. She put her glass down and looked at the birthday cards on her lap. No doubt the wordings would be along the lines of the carefully chosen card from her co-workers, which she had opened while at work. It featured the numbers four and zero together, in large Technicolor font, splattered with glitter and the words, *I may be forty, but I feel like a twenty-year-old when I wake up every morning. Unfortunately, there's never one around.* Ouch! What did she expect from her much younger colleagues?

There were six cards, the handwriting giving away who had sent them. Lisa shuffled them into the order she wanted to open them and started with the person with whom she had the weakest emotional tie. The card was so typical of her mother, Elizabeth. A stately home with acres of manicured gardens. She opened the card and gasped when a cheque fell out. Elizabeth's idea of a birthday present for her only child since she reached puberty had always been seductive lingerie. Encouraging her daughter to dress to please men was all part of Elizabeth's plan to find Lisa a wealthy husband. A strategy that spectacularly backfired when a seventeen-year-old Lisa, wearing Doc Martens and dungarees, vented her pent-up emotions. 'Why do you always talk such bloody rubbish, Mother?'

Maybe, now that Lisa was forty, her impossible mother had finally got the message. Had it seeped into her dense grey matter that Lisa was never going to be a mollycoddled kept woman like her? Or, as Elizabeth would more succinctly put it, 'marriageable material', but it was a shock, her mother had never given her money before, which might have been something to do with Lisa's teenage mantra, 'I could never call myself a strong, independent woman if I can't fend for myself,' but, she had never been strapped for cash before. Those halcyon, carefree days might seem like an eternity ago, but it was only three years since she was enjoying the benefits of her high-flying job in London. Was that why her mother had chosen to send her money now? Was she feeling a tinge of guilt? Unlikely, even if it was due to her mother's negligence, she found herself in this unsatisfactory situation. Remorse or guilt were not words found in Elizabeth's vocabulary. That aside, Lisa could never forgive her mother for her ultimate betrayal. She also blamed Elizabeth for the loss of the two most important things in her life. Yet, despite her mother's atrocious behaviour over the years, Lisa had never been able to sever their umbilical tie. She kept her distance, but Elizabeth was always there niggling into her subconscious.

Picking up the cheque, she couldn't read either the writing or the figures. Elizabeth hated parting with money, so her handwriting shrivelled on cheques. Lisa would need her new prescription glasses to decipher her mother's tiny scrawl. Through gritted teeth, she had parted with a substantial amount of cash to buy her first pair of glasses for reading and computer work. She had been irritated by the Eyes4You poster girl, Diane Keaton. Thirteen years older than Lisa and rocking the bespectacled look. Youthful, intellectual, and ridiculously sexy. After trying on most of the frames, Lisa gave up trying to find a pair that didn't make her look like a nerdy Seven Dwarfs Doc. Fumbling around in the depths of her cavernous handbag, she pulled out a Kit-Kat wrapper. Digging deeper, she found a Starburst organically combusting right at the bottom. No glasses, frustrated, she ran her fingers through her hair and found them. She put them on and scanned her mother's cheque. £400. She was shocked. It was a very generous present, but what was her mother's rationale? £10 for every year Lisa had been on the planet? She couldn't help thinking Elizabeth must have an ulterior motive.

Reservoirs of choppy water had flowed under the bridge between them, taking some of the best bits of Lisa's life with it, along with the flotsam and jetsam. She should ring her mother to thank her for her cheque – given the size of it – but she wasn't going to be riled, not on her birthday. Especially not on her fortieth birthday. Elizabeth never failed to strike a nerve. Putting the wine glass to her lips, Lisa tipped her head back and drained the rest of the glass. She would ring her mother in the morning.

Hangover Saturday

The phone started ringing, and Lisa's head gingerly ventured out from under the covers, blinking her eyes open. There had been mornings like this before, since acquiring a love of wine, when her first-waking thought was *never, ever again.* She flung out her hand to grab the phone and silence its intense ear-splitting ring tone. 'Hello!'

'Morning. I'm just checking to make sure you're still alive.' Adele's breathy whisper was barely audible.

'Well, I think it's probably too early to tell if I'm alive or not, but thank you for checking. It's just as well I don't have to go anywhere, for two days.'

'I honestly don't think I've felt this bad since the day after your twenty-first birthday. I won't be up for much today. My darling husband has volunteered to take Josh and Amy out for the day while I spend a decadent day in bed binge-watching *Cold Feet* videos, but it was a fun evening, wasn't it? I have to say the highlight for me was you, quoting from your book.'

Squeezing her eyes together, Lisa glimpsed a vague image of herself standing on a chair and spouting what, in hindsight, was a bit of a monologue.

'I despair of my daughter! If only she had gone to finishing school, as I wanted her to, wedding bells would have rung years ago, and I would have been a grandmother by now. Not that I look remotely old enough to be the mother of the bride, let alone a grandmother. Forty, for goodness sake and no husband. How absolutely dreadful. How

could this possibly happen to a daughter of mine?' The thought of having a forty-year-old daughter did not sit comfortably with Cynthia, especially a forty-year-old unmarried one. She squirmed inwardly, turning up her stinky fish nose and pursing her lips. Spinster of the Parish. It would have been so easy for me to find Katie a wealthy husband years ago when she was still slim and quite pretty, but the silly girl was never interested. Trying to find her a husband now she's forty will be a challenge, if not impossible.'

'I did, didn't I?'

'I haven't seen you so pumped about anything for a very long time.'

'Pumped?'

'Indeed, you were. You had the entre restaurant in hysterics.'

Lisa opened her mouth and a breathy moan escaped her lips.

'Oh, God.'

'Well, it's a tiny restaurant, Li, it's easy to hear what your neighbours are saying, and somebody's got to provide the cabaret.'

'Stop! I can see the headline in the *Standard* now, *Forty-year-old Cirencester Piss Pot Writes Book About Her Mother.* I suppose I told everybody in my best Elizabeth-Goldsworthy-Grant-Foghorn-Leghorn voice as well?'

'You did, and you sounded *just* like your mother! You were so funny when you regaled the scene about your mother's attempts to marry you off to The Right Honourable Digby Dishwater! The bit where he says, *'come on, Nell Gwynn! Show me your oranges,'* as he moved in for a kiss, and you responded by bawling, get off me, you old letch! My mother is more your age than I am!'

'Oh, God, Della, please tell me I didn't refer to him by his real name. He only lives down the road. Why didn't you shut me up?'

'No, you didn't, and as for shutting you up, when you're in an alcohol-induced-full-flow-mode, that's impossible. Connie was begging you to join GADS by the end of the evening.'

'GADS?'

'The Gloucestershire Amateur Dramatic Society. Anyway, I'm excited about your book, and it's such a great title. *They Always Look at the Mother First.* I love it! Inspired or what? You really couldn't make up a character like your mother, the Ice Queen, could you? She reminds me of Cersei Lannister in that George RR Martin book you bought me for my birthday.'

'The Game of Thrones… Hmm, she was one, Cersei. A narcissist, and a sociopath.'

'What is it they say about truth being stranger than fiction? That would be your mother.'

'She pushes the grounds of credulity for sure. Although, I'm not convinced anybody would want to read a book about the relationship between a narcissist mother and her daughter…' She stopped and took a deep breath. '… whose dysfunctional upbringing left her with a deep-rooted fear of committing to a long-term relationship in her adult life. Phew! That was a mouthful! Especially with a hangover.'

'Well, I would!'

'And I would be gutted if you didn't, but it just might not be everybody's cup of tea, that's all.'

'But it's got all the essential ingredients. Sex, drugs, and rock-and-roll, all sewn together with a thread of deceit and a smattering of adultery, topped off with a dollop of heartache and pain. So, Bob's your uncle and Fanny's your aunt, Li, you could well have a bestseller on your hands. And what about TV Rights? Move over, Alexis Carrington, and bring on Cynthia Baskerville-Clifford, and you know what? I can see Joan Collins bringing out the worst in your mother.' Adele always buoyed her up.

'I wish I had your faith, Della.'

'You're a good writer, Li, and you never give yourself enough credit. Even the first draft of your book all those years ago made Jack laugh, which is a major accomplishment as he's always up to his eyeballs in stuffy old historical tomes.'

At the mention of Jack's name, Lisa's cheeks flushed; even after eighteen years, she still felt uncomfortable talking to Adele about her brother. 'But you know what? Finishing the book has been a little trip down therapy lane for me. Anyway, thank you so much for organising last night. It was a great evening. It's always good to see everybody letting their hair down.'

'That's what friends are for, and it was great to see you so upbeat about life again. Sorry, gonna have to go, I think I'm going to be sick…' The line went dead.

Lisa put the phone down. 'So much for being a pair of responsible forty-year-olds. I'm feeling pretty ropey myself.'

Getting out of bed, she went to the bathroom and filled a glass with water. Plopping two Alka Seltzers in, she sat on the bed watching the effervescent tablets dissolve before swilling the contents in one. She wasn't ready to face the day yet, so she got back into bed.

Her head was thumping, and the feeling of nausea washed through her in waves. Three years ago, she had returned to Gloucestershire, naively believing she could salvage what was left of Silkwoods, the family home, her home, as her father had put the house in her name after she was born.

Silkwoods was originally built as a farmhouse during the early 1600s and, three years ago, it was still widely known as a 'historical treasure', as well as being one of the finest manor houses in the country. It had survived, relatively unscathed, for hundreds of years, after it avoided total annihilation by Oliver Cromwell's rampaging armies, as the dense woodland surrounding the estate cloaked the house from potential marauders. Until 1997, when it succumbed to her mother's mind-blowing carelessness, after she 'accidentally' set fire to it.

Massaging her temples, trying to make the headache go away, she recalled her mother's confession after the event. 'Now… and I don't want you to be cross, Lisa, dear, because these things do happen, but I'm afraid I forgot to pay the insurance premium.' Lisa, rendered speechless, as her mother droned on about how devastated she was about the incineration of her Giorgio Armani suits, which she had meant to take to London. Her whinging monologue finally coming to an end, with the tragic conclusion that she was going to wear the blue one at Ascot. By that time the words *'Forgotten to pay the insurance premium'* had drilled their way into Lisa's scrambled brain. Her mother was very fortunate that she had divulged this information over the phone. Had she delivered the news face to face, Lisa might not have been accountable for her actions. 'But these things don't *just happen…*' Lisa screamed down the phone, but her mother had already hung up. 'Except when you are involved!' she added miserably.

On day one of her restoration attempt, she marched into what used to be the large Tudor entrance hall bubbling over with blitz spirit. Wearing blue overalls, wellington boots and a pair of yellow Marigold rubber gloves, her heart sank as she surveyed the wreckage. The once impressive Jacobean staircase had gone, piles of powdery cinders, the only reminder of where it stood. Looking up through a gaping hole in the roof which, for hundreds of years, was supported by the original curved beam ceiling, she watched a skein of ducks flying about three thousand feet overhead and burst into tears.

The odds were stacked against her from the start, and as the months passed, she did what she could but quickly bled her savings dry. Restoration is an expensive business and restoring Silkwoods to its historical treasure status, had been little more than a pipedream. Rummaging through its charred remains had only stirred up unsettling memories of her dysfunctional childhood, but at least it had galvanised her into finishing the book, and provided her with a climactic, towering inferno, ending.

Her eyelids felt heavy as her thoughts began to fade, slipping into darkness, letting go of consciousness. Rolling over into the foetal position, one last thought flickered through her cerebrum; she needed to get out of her self-dug rut, then drifted into a deep, REM sleep.

Mother v Daughter: Round One

'Knock, knock!'

Elizabeth swept into Lisa's bedroom, rapping her knuckles lightly on the Peter Frampton poster stuck to the inside of the door, before checking her recently manicured nails for any signs of damage.

'Have you ever heard of knocking *before* you come in, Mother?' Eyes riveted to her typewriter; her voice was edged with chilly sarcasm. 'I could have been stark-bollock naked.'

'What a ghastly expression! Anyway, I did knock!'

'Yes, but only *after* you'd let yourself in. There is a difference.'

'Oh, for goodness sake, Lisa, I'm your mother; I've seen you naked before.'

'Yes, Mother, I believe you did, once, on the day I was born.'

'What are you doing?'

'Something you would never understand, I'm working.'

Her mother's eyes narrowed as she peered over her daughter's shoulder and read. *Honeysuckle has long been associated with various superstitions. For example, if it was planted around the entrance of the house, it could prevent witches from entering the home.* 'I didn't know you were interested in plants, or old wives' tales come to that.'

Lisa sucked air in, then exhaled the words. 'There are a lot of things you don't know about me, Mother. *The Standard* asked me to write a piece about the wildflowers of the Churn Valley, and I have a deadline to meet so, if you don't mind, can whatever it is wait?'

'No, it can't, I'm afraid.' Elizabeth opened Lisa's wardrobe and peered in. 'Your wardrobe is sadly lacking, Lisa, dear, and I'm going back to London tomorrow. It's high time you and I went clothes shopping, and this afternoon would suit me.'

'Lacking? Just in case you hadn't noticed, I've been away at boarding school for the last six years, I haven't had a chance to unpack my trunk yet,' but her mother wasn't listening as she flicked through the sparse content of Lisa's wardrobe.

'We need to buy you dresses, stockings, and fun things like that. It's wonderful being a woman, Lisa, dressing to please men, and making yourself look as good as you possibly can all the time.' Lisa suddenly felt acutely nauseous.

'Dressing to please men? Mother, I have no wish to dress to please men! And I like the contents of my wardrobe.'

'But you're much too old to be lounging around in jeans all the time. We need to buy you some makeup as well. You could look quite attractive if you made a bit of an effort.'

'Mother! I'm seventeen. I don't feel the need to slather myself with makeup, and I feel comfortable wearing jeans. We live on a farm, remember?'

'Yes, I'm more than aware of that. The stench of decaying organic matter is a constant reminder that one is surrounded by hundreds of cows. However, just because we live in the country doesn't give us carte blanche to let our looks go to pot and wander around looking like a yokel chewing on a piece of straw. One must make sure that one looks good *all* the time. Especially me, I can't afford to walk around looking like that!' Exasperated, Elizabeth outstretched both arms in Lisa's direction.

'Prospective husbands always look at the *mother* first, you know.'

Lisa turned her head slowly to look up at her mother, trying not to laugh. It was true. Her mother was not only self-absorbed and arrogant, but also completely mad.

'Where did you get those ghastly Hillbilly dungarees and labourer's boots from anyway?'

'I borrowed the Levi dungarees, and the *Doc Marten* boots from Adele. They are very expensive, and I absolutely love them!'

'Who is Adele?'

Lisa rolled her eyes. 'Adele is my best friend, and she has been for the last six years! Her parents have brought me home from school on many occasions, and I've been to stay with them loads of times.'

'Well, both you and your friend need educating on haute couture. You're going to have to buck your ideas up, Lisa. You'll never find yourself a husband if you always look like you've just fallen off the back of a hay cart. Anyway, you know I've had your name down at the Debutantes House since before you were born?'

'Have you now?' Lisa felt her hackles rise as she struggled to stay calm.

'And you will, of course, remember that I graduated as Debutante of the Year in 1958?' Elizabeth ran her hands down both sides of her body, from her breasts to her hips.

'Ah, yes. Debutante of the Year, a prestigious title one receives in recognition of all one's hard work learning how to pour cups of tea and developing one's upper class pronunciation, so you sound just like your namesake, Her Majesty the Queen.' Then, forcing the timbre of her voice up a couple of notches and clenching her nostrils, she continued. 'I don't think you will ever let one forget that one's efforts were rewarded with such a distinguished title during one's esteemed youth. Now, Mama, where is one's non sequitur leading one?'

'I spoke to the headmistress at the Debutantes House this morning, and they are looking forward to welcoming you in September. I will be an impossibly hard act to follow, but it will be such a wonderful experience for you and…'

'Mother! I can assure you, the very last thing on my mind is following in *your* footsteps and becoming the nubile upper-cruster for 1977.'

'What did you say?'

'I think you heard me perfectly well, Mother. Let me put it another way, I have no intention of going to fucking finishing school and, to coin one of your favourite phrases, that's the end of it.'

'Dear God, Lisa! All that money I spent on your education at a school for young ladies, and you come home with a vocabulary reserved for railroad navvies! However well you say you did there, it clearly hasn't made a lady of you. So, a year at the Debutantes House will sort you out!'

'Is that right? Well, it's not going to happen. I worked my arse off at school to achieve good O and A-level results. A stroke of luck, I think, was what you said when I told you what my A-level results were. You were very wrong. It was down to hard work and gritty determination. Not that you will ever know what it is like to work, let alone hard! So, I've no intention of wasting all those years I spent studying to be sent away to be taught how to pour a bloody cup of tea! I taught myself how to do that years ago, thank you very much!' Her mother's face scrunched into her '*nobody ever dares to disagree with me*' look, such was the unswayable confidence she had in herself. She could never be wrong. However, warped her self-opinionated views were.

'Why on Earth wouldn't you want to go to finishing school? You'd automatically be launched into high society, meet all the right people and be snapped up by a highly eligible bachelor, so you'll never have to contemplate looking for a ghastly job.'

Her mother's condescending tone was fanning the flame of Lisa's emotional fire. She had a great deal to get off her chest and now seemed like the perfect opportunity, as Elizabeth seemed intent on pushing all her inflammatory buttons. After seventeen years, the dam that had suppressed the emotional chaos stored inside Lisa's head was about to burst. Her heart was pumping, and her bubbling anger rising.

'But I *want* to get a job, Mother! If you had spent any time with me during the last seventeen years, you would know that going to finishing school would be the very last place on Earth I would want to go. If, at any stage of my life, you had taken even the remotest interest in me and what I wanted to do with my life, you would know that following in your footsteps and becoming debutante of the bloody year is never going to happen! We don't live in the dark ages anymore, Mother. Gone are the days when women were dragged off by their hair to become good little house-fraus. Or, in your case, Lady of the Bloody Manor, women are free to make their own choices, intellectually, culturally and politically.'

'Lisa! I simply don't understand you. You could have any man you wanted once you graduated; it would be such a good start in life for you.'

'You might have thought that snaring a husband was a good start in life for you, but it's not for me. I don't want a man!'

'Oh, dear God, Lisa! You're not a lesbian, are you? 'Life is difficult enough, Lisa, without being a les…'

Gritting her teeth. She let the remark slip, but she had every intention of getting back to it. The dam breached.

'For once in your life, Mother, just shut up and listen!' As Elizabeth sat down unsteadily with a disgruntled huff, Lisa got to her feet to continue her tirade. 'I'm not looking for a man because I don't need a man to define me, and anyway, as you said, anybody interested in me will be checking you out first, and that will really put them off!'

'Lisa, how simply dare you!'

'Oh, I dare, Mother! Right now, I'm looking for a job, a J-O-B, job. A good start in life for me, Lisa Grant, not Elizabeth Goldsworthy or Goldsworthy-Grant, whatever it is you call yourself these days, would be to get a job. I have never, not for one moment, had any ambition to become debutante of the sodding year, and the very last thing I want to be is a stay-at-home wife. Well, you would agree with me on that one, wouldn't you, Mother? Because you were never at home, were you? So, forget it, I have no intention of going to fucking finishing school!'

'Lisa! You disappoint me, and you are so uncouth!'

'Uncouth? If you think that telling you what *I* want to do with the rest of *my* life is uncouth, then I give up. I'm going to be a journalist, and you can't stop me. You remember my English teacher, Mr Barraclough, don't you? No! Of course, you don't because you never actually came to my bloody school, did you? Not once! It was Jim, Nellie, and Arthur who always supported me on sports and presentation days. Most of the girls assumed both my parents were dead. Quite honestly, you both might as well have been. Coln Castle is the borstal of the south for young ladies. You have no idea how cold it was at night and how bloody awful the food was. I was so unhappy during my first term, until Adele and her family took me under their wing. I was bullied initially. Did you know that? No, of course, you don't, because you've never asked me how I was, let alone whether or not I was bullied!' The nucleus of the rant was about to burst and expel large quantities of bottled-up putrefied emotional shrapnel all over her mother. 'Not only was I bullied during my first term, but that's when I found out the truth about my father.'

Wasted Day

Lisa woke up panting. Her heart pounding after another unsettling dream.

'Is it normal to have recurring dreams? Especially when they are always about your mother. Perhaps I should see someone about them?' She looked at her watch. It was 5.00 p.m. 'Oh, God, what a waste of a day! You're a disgrace, Lisa Grant!'

After a long, luxurious soak in the bath, she stepped out onto the soft, anti-slip bathmat, catching a glimpse of herself in the floor to ceiling mirror. In her soporific hangover state, she hadn't noticed when getting in the bath that her lecherous landlord had let himself in to replace the strip light while she had been entertaining fellow diners at the Bella Pasta. Her immediate reaction was, *'Thank goodness I wasn't here,'* but it was only when she focussed on her reflected image, butt naked and dripping soapy bathwater, that the effects of the powerful fluorescent lighting hit home.

'When did all *that* happen?'

Even through thick steam, the full-length mirror was unforgiving. Her bottom jaw hung open as she stared at the sagging spectacle in front of her. The last time she had scrutinised her naked reflection, everything had been pert and where it should be. She cupped her hands under her breasts and pushed them up slightly. Then, as she let them go, gravity deemed that the only route for them was south. From pert to prolapsed in such a short space of time! Why hadn't she been paying closer attention?

'No wonder nobody fancies you anymore, Lisa Grant! Nobody likes saggy tits, especially forty-year-old saggy tits and especially yours!' With the soundtrack from *Hair* playing in her head, she remembered having been inspired by those liberated ladies of the Swinging Sixties, who threw all caution and their nipples to the wind when they made a bonfire of their bras.

'I might have been inspired then, but that inspiration is having a serious knock-on effect now. Quadragenarian - the age of pear-shaped and saggy. I might not *feel* forty but, sure as hell, every sagging bloody inch of me smacks of middle-aged spread! And underneath all the flab, I expect my bloody ovaries are like withered prunes!'

She moved closer to the mirror to inspect her face while rubbing her fist against the steamed-up glass to clear a larger area of visibility. Fluorescent lighting is a killer - it leaves nothing to the imagination. Things had appeared on her skin. Blemishes? Age spots? Whatever they were, she did not like the look of them.

Her straight, split-ended hair fell unevenly onto her damp shoulders. She hooked the bedraggled strands behind her ears and applied pressure to her frown lines with the tips of her fingers, as if trying to iron out the furrows. Pulling down her bottom eyelids, two bloodshot eyeballs stared back at her, fleetingly reminding her of her old governess, Miss Laverty. She slid her fingers down her nose. It looked bigger - quite a lot bigger, then across her cheeks and down to her chin.

'Bloody hell! I'm growing a sodding beard!'

Grabbing a towel, she tried to cover everything up, tugging at the corners, but there was at least a two-inch gap. Making a mental note to buy a couple of bath *sheets,* as opposed to *towels,* she put on a dressing gown instead, tying the cord aggressively round the love-handled potato sack that used to be her waist, and went downstairs to make a cup of coffee.

Her birthday cards were on the kitchen table. She looked at them all again before putting them up on the mantelpiece above the fireplace.

Happy Birthday, Lisa! And here's to many, many more! As dear Albert would have said, 'few are those who see with their own eyes and feel with their own hearts.' You are one of those people, Lisa, and I feel very lucky to have had you as a step-daughter for thirty-four years. With love, Arthur.

She scrunched up her nose, attempting to stifle a tear, but several slipped down her cheeks. Arthur had been a wonderful stepfather - she was the lucky one.

She put her mother's cheque in her purse, which reminded her that she needed to ring Elizabeth to thank her. Absent-mindedly dialling the number of her bête noire, she wondered if, now she'd reached the dizzy heights of a quadragenarian, would she be able to keep her cool during all future conversations with Elizabeth?

'Hay-low! Belgravia 888492. Jeremy Jermayne speaking.' The voice of her mother's string-of-pump-water lover for over forty years warbled its way down the line. Lisa had always found his educated accent and uneven sing-song tone annoying, and it hadn't improved with age.

'Hi Jeremy, it's Lisa!'

'Hello, Sweet Pea, how are you?'

She bristled. Calling her Sweet Pea was another irritation. She should say something, but she knew she never would. Since the Jack debacle, hurting other people was something she avoided doing at all costs. 'Well, not too bad, all things considered, thank you, Jeremy. How are you?' She instantly regretted asking the question as, like her mother, it would trigger a monologue.

'I'm as handsome and as rrrrravishing as ever!' His words came out in a characteristic, narcissistic rush. Lisa imagined him clicking his heels together as he said it; another of his irritating habits. Jeremy and her mother were a perfect match in narcissist heaven. 'Your mother just can't keep her hands off me! *Grrrrow,*' he warbled.

Lisa cringed and rolled her eyes. They were both knocking sixty and still at it like a pair of rabbits, but quickly dismissed the pique-loaded thought from her mind.

'Anyway, happy birthday for yesterday, Sweet Pea. I expect you would like to speak to your fond mama, who is looking particularly rrrrrravishing herself today.'

'Out of the way, Jeremy! Lisa, dear! I thought you must have forgotten about your poor old mother. I thought you might have called me yesterday.'

'Ah, yes, sorry, Mother. *For God's sake! Why am I apologising?* I was very late home from work, so it was a very tight turn around before I went out again.'

'How does it feel to be forty? It makes me feel positively ancient!'

'Age is but a number. *Why did I say that? Age equals old.* But thank you so much for the cheque. It was extremely generous of you.'

'Well, I thought you could buy yourself some decent clothes and perhaps do something with your hair.'

'*Of course, the ulterior motive. I should have realised.* Do something? With my hair? *Why bother saying anything?*' Her hungover body tightened as she waited for the expected acerbic verbal assault.

'Colour it, perm it, to give it some body at least. It was looking horribly straggly when I last saw you.' The tone of Elizabeth's voice lowered towards the end of her sentence as if she'd announced the death of a close friend.

'*Don't let her piss you off!* I quite like my hair right now,' she fibbed, crossing her fingers as she spoke – a little foible she'd carried with her since childhood. Lying was her mother's most unsavoury trait. A trait Lisa wanted to disassociate herself from. *Get a grip! You are forty, and this conversation has gone far enough.* 'I'll look forward to taking myself shopping, Mother. Thank you again for your extremely generous present.'

But Elizabeth hadn't quite finished. 'And when you buy yourself some decent clothes, dear, buy a bigger size. Buy a dress. Not jeans, they don't suit you. People with big bottoms shouldn't wear jeans.'

'I can't believe you just said that, Mother!'

'Well, you've been piling it on for some time now. It can happen when one gets older, not to me, of course, but one has to keep a close eye on these things, Lisa, dear, otherwise you'll be the size of a house before you know it. What did you do last night?'

'I went out for a meal to Bella Italia.'

'Goodness! I hope you didn't eat any pasta?'

A wave of guilt swept over her as her mind flashed back to the particularly delicious spaghetti bolognaise she had consumed the previous night.

'An extra grande portion for the birthday girl with the compliments of the chef.' Mario had said, as he sprinkled a very generous amount of Parmesan cheese on the top of the Pisa-esque mound of pasta.

'I hope you had a steak, with a salad, it was your birthday, after all.' Her mother continued. 'It's worth remembering that one can always eat well when one eats out, without consuming thousands of calories of carbohydrates. Who did you go with?'

'Adele and a few other girlfriends. She organised everything, which was very kind of her.'

'Oh, no men at all?'

'No, Mother. No men… at all.'

'Oh, I see… how funny… no men.'

Sensing that her mother was about to go down that well-trodden are-you-quite-sure-you're-not-a-lesbian route, it was time to wind up the conversation. 'Well, thank you again, Mother, for the very generous present, but I must go. I'm just about to go for a run,' she crossed her fingers, 'I'll speak to you soon.'

Relieved to get that conversation out of the way and while muttering under her breath, 'rather straggly… hope you didn't eat any pasta, no men at all… oh I see… how funny…' She rang her father.

'Olá, Pai!'

'Hello to you too!'

'What are you up to?'

'It's a glorious day here in the Algarve. We've just come back from a long, leisurely lunch at Antonio's.'

'Thank you for the card and the airline ticket, it's very generous of you, and I can't wait to see you both at Christmas.'

'It's our pleasure, and we can't wait to see you. We miss you so much. Henry's booked on the same flight. Have you heard from him?'

'No, but I'm sure I will, soon…'

'How are you? How's the job?' Will picked up on her hesitation, as a deep sigh puffed its way down the phone.

'I can do the job standing on my head, but here's the thing, I don't want to be doing it at all. I have nothing in common with any of the people I work with. They are all so much younger than me for a kick-off, and I don't want to write about state-of-the-art public lavatories or the blurb for catalogues anymore. I want to go back to writing about people and the good things they do for their fellow human beings like I used to at *Focal Point.* It was my dream job, but I know I can't blame anyone but myself for leaving.'

'You can't *blame* yourself.'

'I think I can, Dad. I may try and swing the blame on Mother dearest because she was responsible for the fire at Silkwoods, but I was the one that made the ridiculous decision to give up my job. I have no idea what was going through my mind at the time. Both you and Arthur told me not to, but I believed I could restore Silkwoods to its former glory, on my own. It was a stupid thing to do and, I bled myself dry financially after twenty years of building up a nest egg. Anyway, I need to change my job, but there's nothing around here, job or otherwise, not for me anyway.'

'We'd love you to come here, Lisa, you know that. You can be involved with the vineyard as much, or as little, as you want - and you can write to your heart's content. You know we converted the old Schist house with you in mind so you can be independent of the old fogies.'

'I feel like a bit of an old fogie myself, these days.'

'Don't be so ridiculous! You said you would set up a website for us. And the wine tastings, of course, you've already proved yourself to be a brilliant host when we left you in charge last Easter.'

'Like father, like daughter, eh? You've always been the host with the most, so it must be in my genes!'

'You're a chip off the old block for sure, and you coped brilliantly. Tommy and I felt completely relaxed about taking time out to go on a busman's holiday to Stellenbosch. And what about you hosting writers' retreats at the vineyard? I seem to remember you were going to speak to your old friend Finty. You said she was working as a literary agent now and that she might be up to co-hosting a retreat with you.'

'I haven't forgotten. I've sent Finty a copy of my book, but I haven't spoken to her yet. I'm sure I will, hear from her soon, even if she isn't interested in the book. I've been giving my life some serious thought since I last saw you so, by the time I see you at Christmas, I will have a concrete plan.'

'Sounds good to me. What did you do last night?'

'I went to *Bella Pasta* with Adele *et al.* So, I confess, I feel very ropey, and I've had a completely wasted day.'

'You're only forty once, Lisa.'

'I know, and it's just as well. Adele said she hadn't felt as bad since the day after my twenty-first.'

'Oh dear, and what a memorable evening that was! Please give Adele my love and tell her we're looking forward to having them all to stay again.'

'Will do. I'd better go, dad. I need to eke out what is left of my wasted day, and thank you again for the ticket. Love you!'

'Love you more.'

Carpe Diem

The following morning, Lisa was sitting in front of her Dell Dimension computer at 7.00 a.m. The Dell, together with the printer and fax machine, was the reason for her current overdraft. She'd agreed to take on some freelance work again, so would need state-of-the-art-technology, and managed to convince herself it was money well spent, even though she'd had to borrow it from the bank. She was speculating to accumulate. Taking a sip of coffee, she opened her emails.

FROM: Sweeting, Darla - Summer House Press

SUBJECT: They Always Look at the Mother First

Dear Lisa

Thank you for sending us your novel, They Always Look at the Mother First, which we read with interest.

You establish a pleasingly light and incredibly readable tone in the opening. Your description of Cynthia Baskerville-Clifford's daughter, Katie, and the way she sees the world already marks her out as a character the reader will want to invest in.

From reading the synopsis, it does sound like there is an awful lot going on, and it's worth making sure that characters are properly developed for readers to identify with them, especially as the situations they find themselves in become more complex.

Make sure you amuse, rather than bludgeon, the reader with witty lines - less is definitely more when it comes to comic writing. I also wondered whether the title might be a bit on-the-nose? Otherwise, this is a good beginning, but unfortunately, it's not what we at Summer House Press are currently looking for.

Best of luck with your writing.

Kind regards, Darla Sweeting, MA

P.S. I remember you when you were writing for Focal Point. I was still at school, but you were a great inspiration.

'Still at school, eh? Well, I can assure you my characters are properly developed. They've been in the making for forty years, before you were born, but at least you bothered to reply!'

FROM: Wilde, Jack

SUBJECT: Thanks to modern medical advances such as antibiotics, nasal spray, and Diet Coke, it has become routine for people in the civilised world to pass the age of 40, sometimes more than once - Dave Barry Turns 40.

As you are a self-confessed quote freak, I thought you would enjoy that one. If you haven't read the book, you need to. You would love it. Anyway, Happy Birthday, Li, and I hope you have a good night tonight and A doesn't get you too pissed. I will be back in the UK for Christmas and the New Year, so will see you at A&M's Millennium party, when I look forward to wishing you a Happy New Year. Jack x

P.S. After forty-two years on this planet, I cannot believe that I have never taken time out to watch one single sunrise, so I thought the Millennium sunrise would be a poignant and inspirational one to watch and I'm hoping you might watch it with me?

Lisa started blowing hot and cold, which surely couldn't still be attributed to yesterday's hangover but, hopefully, it wasn't anything to do with the menopause either. Every time she thought about Jack, visions of the curly raven-haired, adorable children they might have had together, flashed into her mind. She had treated Jack so shoddily, but he hadn't behaved with a great deal of maturity either. He only realised he had been an idiot after marrying the boring Brenda, or the tart-in-law, as Adele referred to her. Jack never forgot Lisa's birthday and always sent her Christmas cards, or an email, which made her feel guilty, as she never reciprocated, but she consoled herself with the thought that his wife would not approve of her husband's ex sending him greetings cards and, watching the millennium sunrise, á deux, would surely be grounds for divorce?

It had been eighteen years since she had ended their relationship, and New Year's Eve would be the first time she had seen him since watching him stride away from her up the Champ de Mars. It was too late for many things, including an apology. She wasn't sure how she was going to handle seeing him again, but she hoped it would be with the maturity of a forty-year-old.

FROM: Collins, Rory

SUBJECT: HAPPY BIRTHDAY

Hey Lisa! Fond memories of Les Miserables and your birthday! I can't believe it was quite so long ago. What are you up to? You still haven't responded to my last email! I think about you a lot, Li, so it would be good to catch up properly next time I am in the UK. In the meantime, have a great day and hope to hear from you SOON!! RXX

Lisa felt the dehydrated skin on her cheeks flush. Rory, sex-God on steroids.

'I can't believe I first met him fourteen years ago; it doesn't seem like it,' she thought, recalling the memory. Finty had organised seats for the opening of *Les Miserables* at the Barbican Arts Centre as a surprise for her birthday, and Rory was there. Thanks to *Focal Point,* Lisa had seen all the brilliant musicals running in the West End at the time, apart from *Les Mis,* and was so excited to see it and its star-studded cast which included Colm Wilkinson as Valjean and Alun Armstrong as the scurrilous Thénardier. She had been so swept away by the performance, she'd bawled her eyes out during much of it, and left the theatre with mascara trails running down her chin. *Les Mis* had made its mark as her favourite musical of all time, and she'd seen it umpteen times since.

Finty had warned Lisa about Rory's reputation of racking up trophy notches on his bedpost, or anybody else's, including Finty's as it turned out but, attracted to his rugged good looks, she'd invited him back to her flat after the performance. Her mascara trails didn't put him off, as he agreed.

Everything about Rory was so different from Jack, who was so steady, so adorably straight, and loving. Rory was wild, reckless, and rampant. After snorting a few rails – she'd never told Adele, as she would not have approved – he racked up several notches on her bedpost. It wasn't a memory, hazy, as it was, that she was particularly proud of. It was just great, mind-blowing sex, with no ties. She had set an alarm for 6 a.m., she had two hours sleep, waking up with numbness and a foul taste in the back of her mouth, took a quick shower, before kicking Rory out and was sitting at her desk by 7.30 a.m. Exhausted, but functioning as, hangover be damned, she churned out her review of *Les Mis*.

They were, loosely, together on, but mostly off, for about six years, although he only came home to roost about fifty percent of the time. She was the one who never wanted any ties but then, of course, neither did he. By the time she had him reasonably house-trained, and he was keeping more than just a toothbrush at her flat, he drifted off one morning and never came back. His rugged good looks came with a guarantee to provide great bed-rattling sex but, unfortunately, the sex didn't make up for the fact he was a complete and utter shit.

FROM: Cahoon, Henry

SUBJECT: HAPPY BIRTHDAY

Dear Li! I'm so sorry I haven't even managed to get a card in the post to you. I know, I'm hopeless, but I have been up to my arse in sheep dip all week. I'll give you a ring next week and perhaps we can go out for a meal together? My treat. All love, H XXXXX

Dear Henry. As disorganised as ever. But as step-brothers go, and despite her misguided teenage lust for him, he was one of her closest friends.

Her desk was surrounded by boxes of years-worth of interviews and reviews she had written while working for *Inside Gloucestershire, Stellar* and *Focal Point*. Bending down, she patted one of the boxes affectionately. She had loved her job with Focal Point, interviewing the great and the good, but there would have been no Focal Point if it hadn't been for her chance meeting with Margaret Thatcher, when she was only nineteen. Who would have thought it? Lisa, with her left of centre views, was once inspired by the leader of the Conservative Party. Her interview with Maggie was responsible for her first big break in journalism. She so admired strong women and in Maggie she had found the ultimate Iron Lady of the Seventies, apart from Gloria Steinem, but she was American.

She flicked through the contents of the box, pausing to take out her Maggie interview. She liked looking at it. She was very proud of it. ***Margaret Thatcher: Conviction Politician***. It was hermetically sealed inside a freezer bag, along with the hand-written letter she had received from The Right Honourable lady shortly after it was published.

Dear Lisa. You are to be applauded. I was most impressed with your article in Inside Gloucestershire, given that we spent such a short time together and I am sure you will find yourself outside Gloucestershire in no time at all as, I have no doubt, you will be snapped up by one of the major publications before erelong. And remember, disciplining yourself to do what you know is right and important, although difficult, is the highroad to self-esteem and personal satisfaction. I admire and respect the perseverance shown by one so young. Keep challenging yourself, Lisa, and your perseverance will see you through. With every good wish, Margaret

Thatcher.

She exhaled heavily and put the document back in the box. The Right Honourable Lady's words had come back to haunt her. It was time to start challenging herself again. She pulled out the first draft copy of *They Always Look at The Mother First* and ran her fingers across the first page - ***Chapter One: Narcissistic Heaven.*** It was smeared with traces of nineteen-year-old Vesta chicken curry and a coffee cup ring mark; tell-tale signs of burning the candle at both ends at the flat in Notting Hill. Having finished writing the book she had put on hold after her career took off, she felt a sense of pride, as well as relief. Forty years of being the butt of Elizabeth's demeaning comments had taken their toll and finishing it with almost another twenty years of new material to write about had been very satisfying.

The scars of her dysfunctional childhood had affected her adult life in many ways, including her inability to commit to a long-term relationship. Writing a spoof about her life, loosely disguised as fiction, was the only way she felt she could eyeball the ghosts from her past and revisit her mother's appalling behaviour. She had channelled her inner child and eyeballed a few demons, and rounded everything up with, what she hoped was the nous of a quadragenarian, but it had only scratched the surface of the underlying problem - her mother. Despite their differences, she'd always believed there must be a deep-seated reason why her mother had always been incapable of showing love, or even showing a modicum of affection.

'Some sort of childhood trauma, maybe?' she thought. Opening her desk drawer, she pulled out a scratched and battered Waller and Hartley Milady Toffee tin and spread its contents across her desk. A few black and white photographs of people she could only hazard a guess at who they were, and the faded, musty-smelling envelope with the words *Lizzie's birth certificate,* scrawled across the front in uneducated, childish handwriting.

She remembered the day she first stumbled across the tin and its curious contents in the attic when still a child. Growing up as an only child, the attic at Silkwoods had been a source of fascination, her secret place. A treasure trove, full of dusty old boxes and trunks containing all manner of unexplained treasures, including old-fashioned women's clothes, an army uniform, and various bric-à-brac. The attic was somewhere she could lose herself for hours under the ancient rafters, with its hidden gem, a priest hole. The perfect place to hide, when needing to escape from her mother. She'd found the tin whilst rummaging through a trunk of old linen. She smiled, visualising her childhood-self trying to work out who the people in the photographs might be.

A grumpy-looking man with a huge moustache, wearing a funny black hat that reminded her of one of Nellie's pudding basins. His trousers were too big around the tops of his legs and too tight around his calves. He had a gun tucked under his arm, like the one in her father's office, which she had never seen him use. The grumpy man was standing in front of a small cottage. Next to him was a smiling young man whose arm was around the shoulders of a young woman, who she thought looked a bit like her mother, holding a baby in her arms. Another photo was of the same young man with an older couple. Both men wore white bows around their necks, which made her laugh. The stern-looking woman had a dead white fox draped around her shoulders, which made her shudder. Unable to work out who they were, she had lost interest and put them away.

She stumbled across the tin again when she was eighteen, shortly after she'd found out about her mother's ultimate betrayal. In a highly charged emotional state, she'd been too shocked and angry to do anything about them at the time, so she blotted them out, just like she had done with all the other traumatic events in her life. Archiving them to the back of her mind. Fortunately, during one of her last visits to Silkwoods before the fire, she'd felt compelled to go into the attic to see if they were still there, believing they were worth further investigation. They were. She had planned to take copies and put the originals back in the tin, then thought, 'they've been sitting there for years, why bother to put them back?' Now she was glad she had the originals, as they were going to be crucial to her search.

Lisa learned very early in her life that asking her mother anything about her family was a subject best avoided, as it always struck a nerve. Nobody knew anything about Elizabeth's early years, including her two husbands, and long-term lover, Jeremy. All *anybody* knew about her was from the time she arrived in London, as a blushing debutante in 1957 was that she was the Granddaughter of Viscount Rutherford, who her mother described as a *grumpy old sod* who lived in a stately home somewhere in Cambridge, so no love lost between Elizabeth and her only known relative.

The birth certificate gave the name of Elizabeth's mother, but not her father. Elizabeth, with all her airs and graces, was illegitimate? A fact, although unimportant to Lisa, would be a stigma Elizabeth would want to strike from her noble pedigree. She held the grainy photograph of the young woman with the baby close to her face.

'Is that little scrap you, Mother? Why did you shut your family out of your life when you came to London and married my father?'

Picking up the photograph of the two men wearing white ties, and the woman wearing the abominable white fox fur stole, she turned it over. The words *Nichols & Sons, Photographers and Frame Makers, St. Mary's Passage, Cambridge,* were stamped on the back. There was also a precious handwritten clue; *The Servant's Ball, Ditton Hall, July 1939.*

Having finished retracing her own life from as far back as she could remember, an overwhelming urge to discover more about her mother's past swept through her. She owed it to herself. If she was ever going to sort out her own life and make a fresh start, she needed to break the negative emotional hold her mother had over her.

'Carpe diem! Seize the day, Lisa Grant. It's time to really get to know your mother.' She opened Google search.

1963 – 1997

Earliest Memories

As someone who had recurring dreams about growing up at Silkwoods, recalling her very first childhood memory was harder than Lisa first thought it would be. A blurred, flashing image of herself giggling, while running along a path in Clifferdine Woods surrounded by a carpet of bluebells. It seemed familiar, albeit a little surreal.

Growing up on a farm in the heart of rural Gloucestershire during the Sixties, wasn't all bad. Silkwoods nestled comfortably into a hillside, the River Churn darting and bubbling its way through the lush green pastures and woodland that surrounded the house. An idyllic, picture-postcard setting during the summer months, although a bloody nightmare to get in and out of when it snowed like hell in the winter.

Silkwoods was widely known as a historical treasure, having received a mention in the Doomsday book. Originally built as a farmhouse, it was extended over the years, including the magnificent 19th-century loggia which overlooked the lake, home to lapwings, greylag geese, and the occasional otter. Its rambling, barn-like qualities with priest holes in both the attic and the fireplace in the morning room, served as a vacuum for the wind to whistle through the entire house, whichever way it blew. The wooden floorboards, some as old as the house, creaked and groaned when being walked on and the limestone slab flooring, which covered most of the ground floor, added to the chill. So, it was never a warm house.

Her father told her that the Cotswolds experienced one of its worst winters after she was born and, despite having installed a Potterton central heating boiler earlier that year, it failed to cope, given the size of most of the rooms, and despite large open fires in the living rooms being stoked throughout the day, her mother had insisted on wearing a plush sheepskin coat in the house. Lisa imagined her mother would have felt trapped, because during most winters the steep incline down to the house from the main road was glazed with ice and impassable for weeks, which would have made it impossible for Elizabeth to access her lifeline, Kemble Station, her escape from what she always referred to as the stagnating countryside.

Memories of her mother during her very early years were few, but there were many of her father. Organising Easter egg hunts in the garden, playing Pooh Sticks together in Clifferdine Woods on a bridge crossing the River Churn. Taking her for walks around the farm, proudly carrying her on his shoulders, introducing her to his much-loved polo ponies, Dairy Shorthorn cattle, and Border Leicester sheep. Riding bareback around the woods, her father's arm wrapped tightly around her, her short little legs straddling the withers of her paternal grandfather's much-loved and bomb-proof cob, the thirty-year-old, Badger. Every night Will would read to her, and their favourite stories were about Winnie-the-Pooh, but Will had composed a verse himself which always before turning out the light, which they recited together before Will turned out the light. If we ever need to part, I'll take you with me in my heart, so when I close my eyes at night, I'll think of you and feel alright.

'Goodnight, my gorgeous girl, sleep tight.'

The housekeeper at Silkwoods, Nellie, was Lisa's first memory of a maternal role model, who was the salt of the Gloucestershire earth. A self-taught and excellent cook, with a well-rounded body giving away that she sampled a little too much of her own fantastic cooking. Above all, she had a heart of gold.

Her first, relatively unblurred, memory of Elizabeth was when her father tried encouraging her to spend the morning with them both.

'Elizabeth, Lisa and I are going to see the bluebells in Clifferdine Woods this morning, they're really quite magnificent this year. They have to be seen to be believed. I could drive you both there in the new Land Rover.'

'Oh, yes, I love Daddy's new 'drover'!' Lisa had sat down on the floor in the boot room, to pull on her wellies. 'Please, come with us, Mummy,' while wondering if her mother's dress and matching cropped jacket was the best outfit to go for a ride in the 'drover.'

'Mummy's very busy, Lisa, dear, but you go ahead and pop your wellies on.'

'Okay, Mummy.'

'Do I have to, Will?' Elizabeth hissed. 'I was planning to go shopping this morning, and I've arranged to meet Daphne Scott for lunch at one o'clock…' Looking back, her father had looked irritated, no doubt trying to curb his frustration, because he'd hissed into Elizabeth's ear.

'Just for once Elizabeth, please try and show a bit of interest in your child and what she would like to do! I know you're never going to grow to love country life, but an acceptance of it would be something. Lisa would love it if the three of us went together, wouldn't you Lisa?' She'd nodded enthusiastically, 'and we can check on the newborn lambs in the Priest's Field on the way there.

'Oh, yes, please, Daddy!'

'The lambs will melt your heart, Elizabeth, well, they would melt most people's. I sometimes think yours is made of stone!' Lisa remembered feeling surprised because she'd never seen her father cross, or snappy, before.

'Perhaps Nellie would like to cook one!' Elizabeth parried.

'Mummy!' The first time Lisa remembered expressing shock.

'Alright, I'll come!' As a child, she would not have picked up on the dull, uninterested tone in her mother's voice, but it was a resonance she would become familiar with over the years.

'Whee! Mummy's coming with us to see the bluebells! Please can you help me, Daddy?' She was still sitting on the floor trying to pull on her wellies, and Will knelt down to help her.

'As long as you can get me back here by midday, Will. One cannot allow oneself to be late, it's horribly bad form. I'll just have to go shopping after lunch.' As Elizabeth gingerly pulled on a wellington boot, her body stiffened as she felt something squirm beneath her toes and she exhaled a high-pitched screech.

'Will! There's something alive in here! Get it out!' Lisa got to her feet, and as Will pulled the boot off, a field mouse dropped to the floor and scuttled out of the back door into the shrubbery, and Lisa had squealed with laughter.

'It was only a mouse, silly Mummy!'

Elizabeth leant against a wall, gasping for breath, and trying to regain her composure.

'It might be only a mouse and highly amusing to you, Lisa, dear, but rodents are nasty, dirty little things and spread ghastly diseases. I'm sorry, but you can stuff your bloody country life, the pair of you! It just doesn't suit one. I simply cannot stand it. There are creatures waddling around everywhere! The next thing is, I'm going to find rodent droppings in my lingerie drawer. I'm going back to London to find a degree of sophisticated normality!' Elizabeth swept out of the room, slamming the door behind her.

Will looked down at Lisa, concerned her mother's outburst might have upset her, but she was still giggling.

'Silly, silly, Mummy, it was only a tiny, baby mouse! Come on, Daddy! I'll race you to the 'drover'!'

When Elizabeth was in London, Will and Lisa saw a great deal of Thomas, who helped exercise the polo ponies. Sometimes Thomas would stay for a drink or an evening meal.

'Lisa, I would like you to meet my very good friend, Thomas Cahoon. He lives the other side of Clifferdine Woods, and he has two boys who are a little bit older than you.'

'Hello, Mr Cahoo.'

'Hello, Lisa, I'm so happy to finally meet you. Oh, and why don't you call me Thomas? Your Daddy's told me a lot about you. And, as he's very kindly asked me to stay for supper, would you like me to read you a bedtime story?

Lisa thought about it for a moment. 'Oh, yes please, I would like that, but only Daddy is allowed to read my favourite stories about Pooh Bear and Piglet, but I like the one about Orlando the Marmalade cat.'

'Orlando it is then.'

A second maternal role model came into Lisa's life after Will employed a nanny. At twenty-two, Eileen Fisher was the same age as Elizabeth, but a complete natural with children, warm and bubbly, with a light-hearted sense of humour. 'Hello, Lisa. My name is Eileen, and I've come all the way from Galway, County Clare, which is in Ireland, so you and I can be the best of friends and go on wonderful adventures together.'

Lisa remembered her four-year-old face glowing with excitement.

Eileen reached out her hand. 'Come on then! There's no better time to start than now. How about you introduce me to all the animals on the farm?'

It was love at first sight.

Learning the Hard Way

Lisa was still enjoying the honeymoon period with Eileen when, on one of her mother's rare visits to Silkwoods, she summoned Lisa to the sitting room.

'I have some exciting news for you, Lisa, dear. You know your little friends, Julia and Charlotte, who live just down the road?'

'Yes.' Lisa responded, hopefully. Perhaps there was a party in the offing.

'Well, they will be coming here every morning during the week.'

'Oh, good. To play?'

'Oh, no! Goodness me, Lisa, dear,' Elizabeth scoffed, 'life isn't just about *playing* all the time. Julia and Charlotte will be coming here to learn.'

'To learn? Eileen teaches me lots.'

'Eileen? Good heavens no, we employ Eileen to wash and dress you, Miss Laverty…'

'Miss Lavatory?'

'Laverty! Not Lavatory! Lisa, dear, don't you dare start calling her Miss Lavatory, Miss Laverty is a governess who has been teaching Lord Davenport's children, so she is used to teaching very polite and well-behaved children.'

'Governess?'

'Yes, a proper teacher, and she is coming here to teach the three of you. Isn't that splendid news?'

Lisa wasn't so sure. 'But Eileen teaches me new things every day.'

'Lisa, dear, Eileen is not a teacher, Miss Laverty is, and she will be here on Monday morning at 9.00 a.m. sharp.'

Lisa shared her Miss Lavatory joke with Julia and Charlotte, who thought the re-christening was hilarious, but they all stopped laughing when they met her for the first time, as Lisa told Eileen and Nellie when she was having tea later that day.

'Her eyes are all funny.' Lisa was concerned, half-heartedly dipping a bread soldier into her boiled egg. 'There are red stripes on the white bits in her eyes. She looks a bit like *Kaa* in *The Jungle Book*.'

'You've only met her once, Lisa, I'm sure everything will be fine when you get to know her properly. Isn't that right, Nellie? I'm sure she's a lovely lady,' but Lisa hadn't quite finished.

'She's got red lines on her face too and a big thing on her cheek, which jumps up and down when she talks. We can't stop looking at her.'

'Well, you know it's rude to stare, don't you, little darlin'? So, you mustn't. Now, eat up, young lady.'

Lisa nodded her head. 'It's very hard *not* to look at her, Eileen, and she's really old. I think I've had enough to eat, thank you. I don't like her black clothes and she's grumpy as well.'

Eileen winked at Nellie, stifling a laugh. 'I am sure things will get better. Are you sure you've had enough, sweetie?'

Lisa nodded again.

'Okay, you can watch TV for a bit before I take you upstairs for a bath before bed.'

Lisa scampered out of the room singing, 'Ring-a-ring a poo, we'll flush you down the loo, a flush you, a flush you, you're a grumpy old moo!'

'Lisa!' Eileen exclaimed.

Nellie burst out laughing. 'She didn't learn that from me!'

'Nor me, Nellie.'

'And she better not let Lady Muck hear her reciting anything like that, either.'

'I'll speak to her, Nellie. Mind you, from a four-year-old's perspective, Miss Laverty must look a bit like Methuselah, poor woman. With her bloodshot eyes, spider veins and that great big wart on her face. Let God strike me down if I'm lying! Mrs Grant says she's only sixty, but I find that hard to believe. She's very shaky too, which might account for the bloodshot eyes…'

*

A few weeks later, Eileen had just come back from a walk with Lisa and was playing with her in the nursery, when Nellie appeared at the door.

'Lisa's tea's ready, Eileen. Her daddy's caught her a trout!'

'Mmm, lovely!' Lisa jumped to her feet and ran towards the door. 'I'm very hungry today!'

'Not so fast, young lady! What do we do before we eat?'

'We wash our hands!' Lisa chorused. There was a sink in the nursery and, as Lisa scuttled off to wash her hands, she overheard

Eileen talking to Nellie in a half-whisper.

'I'm really worried about little Lisa, Nellie, she hasn't been her usual sparky self for the last few days, and I've started noticing little welts on her legs and hands.'

Nellie gasped. 'I hope that old battle-axe isn't smacking them.'

'So do I! And, sometimes, when the children come out of their lessons in the morning, they all seem subdued, and one or more of them look like they've been crying.'

'I've washed and dried them!' Lisa bounded over, holding her hands out for inspection.

'That's a good girl, 10 out of 10! Now off you go and eat, Nellie and I will be right behind you.'

Lisa ran in the direction of the kitchen, but lingered by the pantry door, out of sight, but in earshot.

'I don't know, Nellie... I'm beginning to think that Lisa's first impressions about Miss Laverty were right. How on earth did a woman like that ever become a governess? She has to be the most disagreeable woman I have ever met.'

'I'm surprised Lisa hasn't said anything. She's such a sensitive little scrap. She didn't hold back after the first morning.'

'Well, that's just it. She seems to have clammed up about Miss Laverty altogether, I've asked Lisa several times about how she got the marks on her hands and legs, but she always says she doesn't know, or she can't remember. I rang Mrs Grant to tell her that I was worried.'

'What did she say?'

Eileen sighed. 'She told me not to be so ridiculous, and that Miss Laverty came with excellent references and then she said, 'I hardly think smacking a child is such cause for concern, Eileen. What better way is there to discipline a naughty child?' I said, Mrs Grant, they're only four! They wouldn't do anything terrible enough to deserve a smacking. Then she hung up on me.'

'You should tell Will, Eileen. That woman hasn't got an ounce of affection for that lovely little scrap. A woman like that should never be allowed to have children. She's had nothing to do with her, not even when she was a baby. I was in the room when Lisa was born. When the midwife wrapped Lisa up and passed her to her mother, Lisa started to cry. Lady Muck showed no interest in holding her. Instead, she held her at arms-length and demanded that the midwife take her away. It's just as well her father is such a lovely man. He adores that little girl.'

'Come on, Nellie, let's go and sit with Lisa.'

Still in earshot, Lisa ran to the kitchen table and quietly sat down. So, being smacked was, okay?

*

The following morning, the windows of Lisa's nursery, which doubled up as a classroom, were flung wide open. Jim was busy muckspreading in the top fields and the aroma periodically wafted into the room.

Lisa was visualising what she and Eileen might do after the boring

Miss Lavatory had gone. A walk by the river, perhaps? Miss Laverty's characteristic drone was reaching acute boredom level. The subject, arithmetic, and Lisa hated arithmetic.

'If you were going shopping…' Miss Laverty looked round the table. Julia and Charlotte were paying attention, but Lisa was resting her head on her forearm on the table, sucking her thumb and fantasising about playing poo sticks. '…which coin would you prefer to take shopping with you, a penny, or a sixpence? Lisa!' Miss Laverty reached for a ruler.

Lisa looked up at her and stared into Kaa-like eyes. The words, 'a penny,' popped out of her mouth, along with a subconscious yawn.

'And why *exactly* would you choose a penny, Lisa?'

Lisa thought about it for a second before absentmindedly responding, 'Because it's bigger!'

Julia and Charlotte sucked in air through their teeth; they both knew Lisa was wrong. It was an unfortunate response as in the pre-decimalisation era, one copper penny, although much bigger than a silver sixpence, was worth five times less.

Looking into Miss Laverty's pulsating bloodshot eyes, the proverbial penny in Lisa's head dropped.

A scowling Miss Laverty stood up, her gnarled face screwed into a tight grimace, wart twitching as she picked up a ruler in her shaking hand and slapped it down onto the back of Lisa's hand. A soft whimper escaped her lips as she tried very hard not to cry, watching the red mark streak across her soft skin. Narrowing her eyes, the pièce de résistance of her very best cross look, she fixed the witch with her stare, took a deep breath, and putting both hands palm down on the table, braced herself.

Miss Laverty lifted the ruler again, a glazed, unhinged look in her bloodshot eyes, and slapped it down onto the back of Lisa's other hand.

This time Lisa let rip a blood-curdling scream, which reverberated around the house. Enough was enough. 'Eileeeeeeeeeen!'

All three children jumped up, instinctively reaching out to hold each other's hands in solidarity as they raced towards the door, screaming Eileen's name.

Still holding hands with Julia and Charlotte, Lisa turned around, drew herself up to her full three-foot seven inches, and bawled at the red-faced, twitching gargoyle. 'I hate you, Miss Lavatory! And my daddy says he hates you too!'

Eileen burst through the door. 'Lisa, whatever is the matter?' Kneeling, Eileen wrapped her arms around the three whimpering children as Lisa pressed her tear-stained face against her shoulder, 'there, there, it's okay. It's okay.'

All three children peered from under their eyelashes as Eileen glowered at Miss Laverty who was sitting staring at the table, the ruler clenched in her shaking hand.

'What *have* you been doing to these children, Miss Laverty? They're absolutely terrified!' Eileen's soothing Irish tone was already making the children feel much better.

Miss Laverty's eyes stayed riveted to the table.

Julia managed the words, 'She hurts us, Eileen,' between jerky sobs. 'Look.' She took Lisa's hands gently in her own, to show Eileen. The ruler-shaped marks imprinted on the back of her hands looked angry and had begun to swell.

Eileen gasped. The force of the impact had created blood-red streaks, which were snaking their way over Lisa's wrists and up her arm. 'Miss Laverty! How *could* you? They are just babies. You should be ashamed of yourself. Come on, girls. Let's go and make Lisa's hands better…' Then, turning to face Miss Laverty, 'and then, we'll go and find Lisa's daddy and see what he has to say about all this.'

*

The following morning, Lisa took to her bed, feigning illness. She couldn't stomach the smell of lavender water or the sight of Miss Laverty for one more nauseating second. 'I feel sick. I don't want to have my lessons today.'

Eileen sat down on the side of her bed, smiling. 'Well, I've got good news for you, Lisa. There won't be any lessons today, or any other day, not with Miss Laverty anyway, because she's gone. Your daddy went to see her last night and told her to go away and never come back. She's gone for good, so you don't need to fret about her anymore.'

'Never, ever?'

'Never ever. You will never see Miss Laverty again!'

Miss Laverty was out of her life for good. Lisa's sickness

miraculously disappeared as she bounced out of bed and threw her arms around Eileen's neck. 'I'm so happy! I love you, Eileen!'

'And I love you too! Little darlin'. Now, it's time for you to get dressed and have your breakfast, then we'll go for a walk by the river, and we'll see how many plants and wildlife we can see.'

Eileen took over Lisa's education. She was a quick learner, and by the time she was five, she could name all the flowers in the garden and the plants that grew along the riverbank. As well as all the wildlife, insects, and birds on the estate. She loved to read, and she quickly found out she loved to write as well. Seeing her words come alive on the page gave her a thrill and a powerful sense of achievement. A passion that would grow stronger with each year that passed.

Blame It on the Mother

On one of the rare occasions Elizabeth was at home, she took Lisa and Eileen to Cheltenham to buy Lisa a new pair of shoes. While Lisa was trying on various pairs, supervised by Eileen, Elizabeth kept her distance but, like a hawk, she was taking a keen interest in what was going on.

'Now, Lisa, I can see you dancing in that pair later!' Eileen teased, prompting the sales assistant to ask, 'Why don't you tell your mummy which pair you like the best.'

Lisa pointed at the pair of bright red Start Rite shoes on her feet, and looking directly at Eileen said, 'I like these best, Mummy. Can we take them?' Which was Elizabeth's cue to pounce. Towering over Lisa, who knew she had said the wrong thing, as she felt her naturally rosy cheeks burn.

'Why, Lisa, dear, I wonder who on Earth you will be calling Mummy next? We'll take those, thank you,' and pointed to the black pair.

*

'Where are you going, Eileen?'

'I'm going to see your Mummy.'

'Why?'

'I'm going to ask her if she is going to be at home for your birthday. I'll be back by the time you finish your drawing.'

Will was away playing polo at Cowdray Park, so Eileen approached Elizabeth with a degree of caution, knowing she hadn't taken the 'mistaken mummy' moment during the shoe-buying episode too well. 'Good morning, Mrs Grant. How are you today?'

'Busy, Eileen. Will this take long? Because I'm having my hair done in Cirencester in an hour, and I need to change before I go out.'

'I was just wondering if you were going to be home for Lisa's sixth birthday in October?' She tactfully left out the part about Nellie having told her that Elizabeth had never been around for any of Lisa's birthdays.

'Eileen! I know perfectly well when *my* daughter's birthday is! I'm the one who gave birth to her, and what an agonising experience that was, so I am very unlikely to forget about it. So, you don't have to remind me when it is! And, whether I am going to be here, or not, is absolutely none of your business.'

'But, Mrs Grant, it was just that Lisa wanted to…'

'Enough, Eileen! I draw the line at a member of my staff telling me what to do!'

'But I only…'

'I will not stand for insubordination, Eileen, and you've stepped out of line too many times for my liking.'

'What?'

'My husband might think you are mama miraculosa, but he isn't here. Lisa only needs one mother to organise her life, and that is me! So, I would like you to leave right now.'

'But Mrs Grant please, I…'

'Just go!'

'I'll go and explain things to little Lisa…' Eileen's voice quivered with shock.

'You'll do no such thing!' Elizabeth snapped. 'You will leave this house immediately. Go and pack your things! Do not go and see Lisa. There is no need for you to explain anything to *my* daughter! I will be writing you a glowing reference, which I will forward to you in due course. Now go!'

Elizabeth stood waiting by the sitting room window until, with a satisfied smile, she watched a tearful Eileen scuttle down the drive with clothes hanging out of her hastily packed suitcase.

Lisa finished her drawing and got up to find Eileen and found a tearful Nellie sitting at the kitchen table.

'Ah, Lisa, luvvie. I've just seen Eileen, who sends you lots and lots of love, but she has to go away, and she's ever so upset about it.'

Lisa's bottom lip started to tremble. Her body felt like it had been taken over by a flutter of butterflies. 'Go away? For how long, Nellie?'

'For a long time, luvvie.' Nellie tried to contain her own tears but gave up when Lisa's face crumpled, and her eyes shed a waterfall of silent tears.

'Forever, you mean?'

'Oh, my duck, come here…' Nellie got up and clasped Lisa to her ample midriff. 'There, there now.'

'Whatever is the matter with her?' They both jumped as Elizabeth strode into the room.

'Lisa's understandably upset about Eileen going, Mrs Grant.'

'Oh, for goodness sake, Lisa, what a performance. It's high time you grew up!' There was a shocked silence, broken by the choking sound of Lisa sobbing into Nellie's midriff. 'Lisa, that's quite enough! Now go upstairs and do whatever it is you do before you have your supper.'

Elizabeth's snapped instruction made Lisa spin away from Nellie, and to the surprise of both women, started screaming at her mother. 'Why did Eileen go? Did you make her go?'

Elizabeth was shocked, arching an eyebrow, then frowned as she gathered her thoughts. Being balled at by a red-faced child was a first. 'It was time, Lisa. You are very nearly six, you don't need a nanny anymore.'

But Lisa wasn't going to let it drop. 'You told her to go, didn't you?' She squeezed her eyes together as she had done with Miss Laverty. 'Why can't *you* go away? Everything is better when you're not here!'

'Well, Lisa, dear, if that's how you feel, you can go to your bedroom right now and stay there for the rest of the day, which will save Nellie a job because you won't be having any supper tonight.' And turning to Nellie, 'I cannot believe I gave birth to such a rude daughter. My husband made a huge mistake sacking Miss Laverty. This child needs to go to school.'

'I hate you!' Lisa screeched, deliberately crashing into Elizabeth's side as she ran out of the room. She ran up the Jacobean wooden staircase and tripped halfway up, falling heavily on both knees. Picking herself up, she ran to Eileen's room and looked around. The bed was stripped of sheets, the cupboards and shelves bare; all trace of Eileen had gone. Curling up on the bare mattress, clutching her bruised knees, she cried herself to sleep.

For a long time after Eileen left, if Lisa was missing, she could be found curled up on the bed where Eileen used to sleep, sucking her thumb.

While still struggling to cope with the loss of Eileen, Elizabeth arranged for Lisa to start at a school about five miles away from Silkwoods that took pupils from five to eleven years of age. Lisa felt sure that all teachers would be like Miss Laverty, but found out much to her relief, that they were more like Eileen and learning new things was fun. Life got even better when she started making new friends.

'Your daughter has an excellent grasp of the English language, Mr Grant,' the headmistress told Will when he picked her up from school one day. 'She is quite the little storyteller too. She enjoys writing them and reading them to her classmates. There are some very happy little bunnies in Lisa's year. I particularly like her story called *Pooh Sticks Bridge*, you feature in that one, I believe.'

Towards the end of the summer term, Will dropped Lisa at school, as he always did. Instead of blowing her a kiss and waving before he drove away, he got out of the car. 'Piglet?'

'Yes, Pooh.'

'Can I have a hug?'

'You can, if you catch me a trout for my supper from the stream in the Hundred Acre Wood.'

'It could be arranged.'

'Then you may give me a hug!'

Will knelt in front of her, hugged her tightly, and whispered in her ear, 'you are my world, my universe, my moon and stars.'

Lisa squealed with delight. 'Daddy, you're being silly!' A handbell started ringing; classes would start in ten minutes. 'You have to let me go now, Pooh.'

He moved his head back, holding her at arm's length. 'I love you, so much, Piglet.'

'I know you do, Pooh, and I love you too.'

'Love you more, Piglet.'

Lisa giggled, wrapping her arms around his neck, before running after her classmates into the building shouting 'I'm looking forward to eating my trout!'

Later that day, Lisa rushed through the school gates to find Jim waiting for her. When they arrived home, she went through to the kitchen to find Nellie, who was sitting at the kitchen table, resting her head in her hands. 'Hello, Nellie. Are you tired?' She pressed her soft cheek against Nellie's. 'Poor Nellie, you work so hard.'

Nellie sighed, slipping her arm around Lisa's waist and pulling her close. 'Hello, my duck.'

'Daddy said he was going to catch me a trout for my supper, did he? I'm starving!'

'No, your daddy told me to tell you he was very sorry, but he hadn't got time to go fishing today.'

'Oh, never mind. I expect he'll catch me one tomorrow.'

'Lisa, your mummy's at home, she wants to see you now.'

'But I've got homework, and I'm going to do it now, with you Nellie.'

'I'll do your homework with you later, but your Mummy needs to see you now.'

Lisa pulled a face and hung her satchel up on the back of a kitchen chair. 'Oh, alright then,' and wandered off in the direction of the sitting room.

Her mother was on the telephone, the tone of her voice was irritated and impatient. 'I just want to screw him for every penny he's got! Am I clear? And I'm hoping I can count on you to make sure that happens.' She looked up as Lisa walked through the door. 'I have to go, Sidney,' she snapped, 'I have a visitor.' The expression on her face was unnerving as she slammed down the phone. 'Come in, Lisa, dear, and sit down over there.' She pointed to an armchair directly opposite her.

Lisa, obediently, sat down. Her brown divided school skirt exposing her iodine-smeared grazed knees, scuffed earlier that day after a fall on the tarmacked school playground. Lisa watched her mother take a deep breath and run her hands lightly over her flipped bob.

Elizabeth exhaled and looked at her daughter, frowning. 'There's something I need to tell you, Lisa, dear. I'm afraid your father and I have irreconcilable differences.'

What on Earth were irreconcilable differences? Lisa wondered, guessing they weren't good.

'So, he won't be living here anymore.' Elizabeth finished her sentence with a nod of the head.

'Why not, where's he going?'

'He is going to live in Portugal, dear,' her mother said, curtly. 'With, er, a friend of his.'

'Why?' Lisa felt her face flush and started to cry.

'Oh, for goodness sake, Lisa! These things happen with grown-ups all the time. You can go and see him if you like.'

'When can I go, and why Porkogul? What's wrong with living here?'

'Because he, er,' her mother seemed distracted by Lisa's feet sliding from side to side across the parquet flooring, and with each slide the rubber soles of her school shoes created a prolonged, stuttering squeak.

'Because what?' Lisa whined. 'When's he coming home?'

'Stop squeaking!' Elizabeth bellowed, which made Lisa sit bolt upright. 'Because Portugal is where your father has decided to live, so he won't be coming home, and that is the end of it. I'm sure you'll get used to not having him around, Lisa, and Portugal is not a million miles away. Perhaps you can go and stay with him for Christmas or something, I'm sure he will be in touch.'

Lisa knew Portugal was in Europe, and she had never been out of Gloucestershire. It seemed like a very long way away, but she could count though. It would be over three months before she saw her father again. A very long time.

Elizabeth droned on, 'I expect the weather will be warmer in Portugal in December. It will be warmer than it is here, anyway.'

Lisa's sniffles became shoulder-heaving sobs. 'I want my daddy!'

'Enough!' Her mother shouted, getting to her feet, and waving an irritated hand in the air. 'One cannot have what one always wants.' Lisa's audience was over. 'Run along now, Nellie will have your supper ready soon.'

With her shoulders hunched, Lisa shuffled towards the door, deliberately scuffing the rubber soles of her shoes to make a staggering squeak with each step across the parquet flooring. As she left the room, she felt her mother's glower burn into her back.

'Come on, my dove, eat up for your auntie Nellie.'

Lisa pursed her lips and shook her head. 'I'm not hungry, Nellie, thank you.' She loved Nellie cooking for her, but it was poached eggs on toast, not her promised trout, and the person who promised to catch it for her, like Eileen, had gone away.

'I expect you to eat a good breakfast before you go to school tomorrow, mind. Come on, let's go upstairs, it's time for you to have your bath and get ready for bed.'

Bath time was usually fun, but despite Nellie's reassuring tone and gentle coaxing, Lisa had little to say. The shock of her father leaving, without saying goodbye or catching the trout he had promised her, was sinking in. After her bath, she put on her pyjamas and sat down on the side of her bed. Nellie turned the bedside light on and sat down beside her, putting both arms around her shoulders, drawing her close. Lisa nestled into Nellie's side and slid both her arms around her midriff. A few silent minutes of comforting affection in Nellie's arms made her feel a little better.

'You can watch TV for a bit if you like, Lisa lovie?'

Lisa thought about it for a few seconds before slowly pulling away from Nellie. 'No, I think I'm going to read my book. The one Daddy bought me.'

'All right, my duck, you do that.' Nellie tucked her into bed, leaning over to kiss her on the forehead before handing her the book on the bedside table, *Now We Are Six* by A. A. Milne. 'I'll come back and turn your light off in a bit.'

Her mother was on the first train back to London the following morning, and Lisa was delighted to hear that Jim and Nellie were moving into Silkwoods with their two teenage children. Elizabeth returned, briefly before Christmas, for a long weekend.

'I thought I was going to Porkogul for Christmas?'

Elizabeth was arranging her collection of scarves at the furthest end of her walk-in wardrobe, and the sound of Lisa's voice made her jump. 'Lisa, dear, you startled me. Portugal? Ah, well, I thought that might have been an option, but I haven't heard anything from your father, so I assume it's not convenient for him. From what I understand, they're living in a bit of a hovel out there.'

'Hovel?'

'Yes, it's a bit of a pigsty.'

'Pigsty?'

'Well, no, um, he's bought a house which needs a lot of work doing to it.'

'Oh… will you be here for Christmas?'

'I don't think so, Lisa dear. Mummy has a very busy life in London, and my poor friend Jeremy Jermayne is going to be on his own over Christmas, coping with his elderly mother. His wife went to Australia on business, and she's decided to spend the Christmas break there with her long-lost cousins. So, I thought, helping my dear friend Jeremy and his mother celebrate Christmas, would be a charitable thing to do. And, I have been asked to so many grown-up Christmas parties in London which are just not suitable for children.'

Lisa went to Eileen's old room to process the Christmas agenda. Her father hadn't been in touch with her since the day he left. He hadn't sent her a birthday card, and now she wasn't going to be spending Christmas with him either. Sitting on the side of the bed, something she had never felt before began bubbling up inside her. Sliding off the bed, she ran down to the boot room and picked up her father's shepherd's crook. Running out into the garden, she used the staff as a machete to decapitate the thriving plants in her mother's prized autumnal herbaceous border.

When Christmas Day arrived, Jim and Nellie made a fuss of her, and she'd played games with their children. She had a great time without either of her parents being around.

'I'm much better off without either of them,' she thought, as she opened the presents from her mother, all neatly wrapped up in Harrods packaging. A pale blue, frilly party dress, black patent leather shoes and matching handbag, just what every fashionable farm-living six-year-old needed for country life.

She put her mother's presents to one side and opened the gift from Jim and Nellie. It was a child's typewriter. Like the dress, it was pale blue, with white keys. In awe, she ran her fingers lightly across its smooth surface. She couldn't have wished for anything better. She jumped up and ran over to Nellie. 'It is the bestest present ever!'

'We thought it would be good for all those stories you have been writing.'

'I love it! I will write a special story, just for you and Jim!'

'That would be lovely, my darlin'! We'll look forward to that. Oh, I have another parcel for you, Lisa, from America,' Nellie announced with a degree of knowing satisfaction.

'America? For me?' Lisa sat cross-legged on the floor, clutching the box with a white envelope taped to the top. She had absolutely no idea who it could be from until she ripped open the envelope and a letter fell out.

Dearest Lisa… I have been writing to you regularly since I left. Unfortunately, every letter I sent you came back to me, 'return to sender'. So, I decided to send your Christmas present care of Nellie;

I should have done that before. I was so very sorry that I had to leave you, but your mummy wasn't very pleased with me, and she wouldn't let me say goodbye to you, and I am sorry for that. I'm getting used to New York now. It was a bit of a shock at first after Silkwoods. Apart from Central Park, there are no wide-open spaces. I miss our walks together very much. You would love the bookshops here, and the toyshops…

'It's from Eileen…' Lisa looked up at Nellie in disbelief. 'She hasn't forgotten me.'

'Lisa, my duck… Eileen would never forget you.'

Towards the end of the day, her mother rang to wish Lisa a happy Christmas. There was music, and the sounds of a party going on in the background. 'I hope the dress fits you, Lisa, dear. If it doesn't, I will change it. And I thought the patent leather shoes were just you.' Lisa was looking down at her bare feet as her mother spoke, wiggling her toes. Even at six, she knew that black patent shoes were never going to be her.

'Yes, they are very nice, Mother. Thank you.' It was a bit of a fib, so she crossed her fingers as she said it. What she wanted to say was she had a letter and presents from Eileen, and Jim and Nellie had given her the best present ever. But she didn't, she just said, 'I've had a lovely day. I hope you are having fun too with Mr Jermayne, and his mother.'

As in the past, Lisa barely noticed her mother wasn't around. She preferred it that way. Every time she came home, ripples of uneasiness flooded through the household. Lisa kept herself busy, throwing herself into her schoolwork and making time to write stories and poems.

Children have an innate ability to accept and adapt to change. Lisa was an expert at occupying herself. She discovered her father's LP collection in the sitting room, spending many hours developing her love of music, particularly the musical theatre. She knew all the songs from the shows *My Fair Lady*, *The King and I,* and *West Side Story*, but her favourite musical was *South Pacific*. She knew Nellie Forbush's part inside out, keen to perform her version of *Honey Bun* to any available audience.

As the months passed, Lisa blotted out the things that troubled her most and was enjoying life with Jim and Nellie in the role of surrogate parents. One evening, whilst watching her favourite TV programme, Blue Peter, with Nellie, they heard the front door slam.

'Hello! We're home! Is anybody around?' It was her mother's shrill voice.

Lisa jumped up. 'We?' she said, excitedly looking at Nellie. 'We? Is Daddy back?' She ran into the hall and stopped abruptly.

'Oh, hello, Lisa, dear.' Her mother, unemotional as ever, was peeling off a pair of leather gloves. Next to her was a much older man in a wheelchair, his legs covered in a tartan blanket. 'This is Mr Goldsworthy, Lisa, dear, your stepfather.'

'Hello.' His voice sounded hoarse but friendly enough. 'I've heard a great deal about you, Lisa, and I'm looking forward to getting to know you.' The way he talked was strange. He was talking English, but he didn't sound English. 'Your mother tells me you enjoy writing stories, well, I will enjoy reading them.' A wheezy chuckle followed his comment, which turned into a coughing fit.

'Oh, Arthur dear, are you alright?' Her mother attempted to show concern. 'I will organise refreshments as soon as possible.' Nellie was standing next to Lisa, her jaw disengaged and struggling to tie her apron around her ample waist. 'Nellie! Mr Goldsworthy and I would like to dine at 7.45 p.m. Please, could you make up the bed in Mr Grant's old office downstairs and ask Jim to serve us drinks in the drawing room, now.' Elizabeth was gesturing towards the room that had always been known as the sitting room.

'Yes, Mrs Grant… er, Mrs Goldsworthy. In the er, drawing room. I'll tell Jim; they should have finished milking by now.'

Bonding

After divorcing Will, and back on the marriage market, Elizabeth started hosting parties for London's elite, in what she called her *little flat in Mayfair*. The same property that was described by the estate agent as '*a sumptuous three-bedroomed apartment with an enormous sitting room, perfect for entertaining on a grand scale.*' Throwing lavish soirees was an integral part of her plan to find another husband. They provided her with the ideal opportunity to showcase her beauty and flaunt her charm in the comfort of her own home. Her exaggerated catwalk-walk and seductive pout, along with her well-publicised divorce spoils, left a trail of panting, red-blooded males strewn in her wake. The marriage proposals flooded in, but she turned them all down because they didn't have a bank account quite the size of Arthur Goldsworthy's.

She was introduced to Arthur, the UK's most eligible American bachelor, by mutual friends. Elizabeth had done her homework. She had a good idea of Arthur's net worth before she gave him her well-rehearsed, struggling single-mother monologue. Nobody was more surprised than Arthur when Elizabeth accepted his marriage proposal, but if he'd thought that a much younger wife would look after him, he was wrong. Elizabeth employed a live-in carer before they left the registry office. Elizabeth and Arthur were an inappropriate pairing in the eyes of many. Not least because of the gaping twenty-five-year age gap between them.

At the start of their married life, Arthur travelled back and forth to

London with Elizabeth, until he realised that, unlike his young wife, he enjoyed being at Silkwoods. Elizabeth was contrite when he told her he wished to spend more time in the country, while inwardly breathing a sigh of relief. Her life was her own once more. Hours of unlimited me-time beckoned.

'There is so much that needs doing around the place, Elizabeth, and spending more time at Silkwoods will give Lisa and me more time to bond.'

'I don't think my daughter knows how to bond, Arthur, dear.' Elizabeth mumbled under her breath.

'Well, Elizabeth, it would give me enormous pleasure to show her how.'

Arthur threw himself into renovating the house, starting with installing new bathrooms, as well as a new kitchen, with gadgets, much to Nellie's delight.

'Oh, Mr Goldsworthy, I wonder what Mrs Beeton would have said about the Kenwood Chef?'

Once Arthur had worked his entrepreneurial magic on the interior of the house, he turned his attention to the farm. Elizabeth had sold the polo ponies, and the sheep after Will left, so Arthur applied his money-making skills to dairy farming. He increased the size of the Silkwoods herd, and built a state-of-the-art milking parlour, as well as modernising all the farm buildings, taking great pride in being the only American dairy farmer in Gloucestershire.

*

Contrary to what Elizabeth thought, Lisa made it easy for Arthur to bond with her. Initially she followed him around like a puppy, driven by her insatiable curiosity. She wanted to get to know her disabled stepfather, as much as he was determined to bond with her. He was a very knowledgeable, well-read man with an Oxford degree in economics. His one true passion was reading, which he did voraciously, encouraging Lisa to do the same, and she needed little encouragement. To her delight, he moved his library of books from Belgravia to Silkwoods.

'Now, Lisa, you and I can be bookworms together!'

Lisa's first achievement in the literary world was writing a poem about one of the Blue Peter dogs. Her prize was the much-coveted Blue Peter badge, which she proudly wore every day. She read the poem to both Jim and Nellie so many times, they knew it by heart. So, in the absence of any other audience, she read it to her stepfather.

'You know what, Lisa?' he said, his steely grey eyes twinkling. 'I love having you read to me.' So it became a habit. She read everything to him, books from his library, newspapers, as well as stories she had written.

Lisa was intuitive in many ways, and as the years rolled by she identified the adults in her life that she could trust, which did not include either of her parents. She was yet to find out exactly why her father had vanished from her life without saying goodbye, and she was still angry with him for leaving. She'd had no communication from Will in four years, so she was glad that she hadn't gone to see him in Portugal that first Christmas. Her mother never tried to persuade her, fobbing her off with the glib comment, 'he can't even remember when your birthday is, and he's never once asked how you are.' Before hastily adding, 'not that I am aware of anyway.'

Time to Get Tough

The years that followed were the most stable of Lisa's childhood. Arthur and Nellie always made her feel special and loved, doing everything they could to create some semblance of normality. She saw very little of her mother, which she considered a relief. When Elizabeth was at home, Lisa always felt chastised for no other reason than for being herself.

She tried not to think about her father, but it wasn't easy. He had told her so many times how much he loved her but, if he'd really loved her, he wouldn't have gone away. She'd told Will that she loved him too, and she'd said it because she did, but she would be more careful next time if she felt she needed to say those words. Perhaps it would be better not to say 'I love you' to anybody, ever again, but however hard she tried to blot out her father-related thoughts, he was always there just before she drifted off to sleep. When she closed her eyes, she could hear him whispering the words, '*if we ever need to part, I'll take you with me in my heart, so when I close my eyes at night, I'll think of you and feel alright.*'

As Lisa and her friends enjoyed the long, lazy days of summer 1969, they were getting excited about starting senior school together in September. But, for Lisa, it was not to be. On one of her mother's rare visits to Silkwoods, she summoned Lisa to the drawing room and told her that she would be starting boarding school in the autumn term.

'I went away to boarding school when I was eight,' her mother was upbeat. 'And you're ten now, so it's high time you went.'

75

The words, 'but I don't want to go anywhere,' whinged their way out of Lisa's mouth, accompanied by an emphatic stamp of her right foot.

'You will be eleven very soon, and your teacher tells me that you are very bright for your age. Just like your mother.' Elizabeth guffawed at her own joke, which failed to amuse Lisa, then proceeded to deliver another well-prepared, rambling monologue about how boarding school would be the making of her. 'After seven years at boarding school, you will go to the Debutantes House in London, and from there we will find you an ideal husband. Someone who will provide you with financial security for life, so you'll never have to find a terrible job. And remember, Lisa, dear, all prospective husbands always look at the mother first.'

Lisa was listening, clinging on to the pertinent points, but her mother could well have been talking Chinese. 'But I don't want a husband, and I don't want to go away!' She stood in front of her mother, pouting with her hands on her hips.

'Petulance really doesn't suit you, Lisa, dear. It's all arranged, you are going, and that's the end of it.'

Lisa flounced out to find Nellie's comforting, well-padded shoulder to cry on as she tearfully regaled the whole sad, I'm-being-sent-away, scenario.

After much persuasion, her mother eventually let Lisa see the prospectus, and she had been reading about its history. The austere building, originally constructed as a manor house in the 14th century, was extended over the years including the magnificent erection of a turreted tower in the 18th century. Lisa filled in the gaps in its history with the help of Arthur's impressive library of reference books. In a nearby field, bloody battles had been fought, a snippet firmly entrenched in her mind. She was far from impressed, the school had been refurbished after being used as a billet during World War II, but it looked cold and damp. The only sign of any new buildings were the classrooms, which had been converted from what used to be the stable block.

When the fateful day arrived, it was Jim and Nellie who took Lisa to Coln Castle to start her first term at boarding school. Her mother had rung a few days before and said, 'I've got an impossibly busy schedule in London this week, so Jim and Nellie will be taking you to your new school.' Lisa, although terrified of the thought of going away, had felt relieved.

Lisa shuddered as Jim drove up the impressive driveway to Coln Castle. 'It looks like the Sheriff of Nottingham's castle in *Robin Hood*,' she mumbled from the back of the car. As Jim got her trunk out, Lisa watched the other girls hugging and tearfully saying goodbye to both their parents.

'Well, goodbye, love,' Jim said, putting his hands on her shoulders. 'But we'll write to you regularly, I promise.' Lisa, who was trying very hard not to cry, hugged him tightly. He always smelt of the cleaning agent used in the milking parlour. How she would miss that smell. She looked up at Nellie, who was busily blowing her nose, her iridescent grey eyes brimming with tears.

'We're going to miss you so much, aren't we Jim?' Jim was at a loss for words.

'And I'm going to miss you too! So much.' Lisa flung her arms around her waist. 'I love you, Nellie!'

'And I love you too, my darlin'. And don't you ever forget that!'

She had never felt so alone. Struggling to control her sobs, she watched Jim and Nellie drive away. How was she going to cope without them?

'Lisa Grrrrraaaaannttttt?' Hearing her name called out made her spin around, her buckled Start-Rite shoes crunching on the gravel. A small, rotund woman in her sixties waddled across the driveway towards her. Her body rocked from side to side with each step, her ill-fitting wartime Mary Jane court shoes, causing more than just a slight degree of pain. A tired and ill-fitting ankle-length tweed skirt clung to her hips with a cream silk blouse tucked in at the waist. Her long, grey hair was wound into a chignon, but a few bobby pins had slid out under its weight. It would never stay upright for the rest of the day.

'Yes…' Lisa managed.

'Come ziz vay, pleeeze. I am Mademoiselle Petit your 'ousemistrezz. Vas zat your mozur and fazur?' She asked, pointing in the general direction of the drive.

'No, Mademoiselle Petit, my father lives in Portugal, and my mother is busy in London.' She said quietly, her eyes rooted to the floor.

'Ahh yes, I zink I know zomesink aboot your fazur… Now come viz me, please.'

The palms of her hands felt cold and clammy as she followed Mademoiselle Petit into the forbidding building, wondering how many other people knew zomesink aboot her fazur.

Boarding school was everything Lisa had imagined it would be, a bloody nightmare, into which she found it difficult to adapt. She was sharing a large dormitory with seven other first years. As the weeks passed, they built up a strong camaraderie struggling to survive without any of the home comforts they had taken for granted over the last ten years. The ceiling in the dormitory was at least twenty feet high, with a huge sash window overlooking the substantial lawns and the tennis courts beyond. Both sash cords were broken, so the window couldn't be closed. It was stuck four inches above the bottom of the frame, which provided excellent ventilation during the summer months but, in the winter, Siberian winds gushed through, escaping through the gap under the door. In September, the temperature during the night was just about bearable. By October, eight sets of teeth chattered under the covers, and there was a very high chance that any dewdrops on noses would have turned to ice by morning.

Lisa's bed was next to a girl called Adele Wilde, one of the nicer girls in her class who was always friendly and seemed to be adapting to boarding school life well. It hadn't escaped Lisa's notice that Adele received letters regularly from her parents, as well as from her older brother, Jack. A slightly plump girl, Constance Cookson, occupied the bed on the other side. Her parents sent her letters and parcels on an almost daily basis, but she still spent most of her first term in tears. At night she would cry herself to sleep, muttering, 'I hate this place. I want to go home. Mater and Pater don't understand.' One of the 'essential items' the girls were asked to bring in their trunks, was a torch. On their first night, after they'd changed into their pyjamas and were wondering what to do next, a prefect came into their dormitory.

'Good evening girls, and a warm welcome to you all. I'm Fenella Bagworth and, as you can see...' she tapped at her red shield badge pinned to her cardigan and adorned with gold letters... 'I'm one of our seven prefects for this year. So! As it's your very first night at Coln Castle, I've just popped in to remind you that, if any of you need to pee during the night, you will need to take your torch. As I'm sure you've already noticed, the first-year dormitories are a considerable hike from the bathrooms so, you should be aware that Matron turns all the landing lights out from a central switch at 10.00p.m. sharp, every night. We've all had to do it, wee-wee during the night that is, even me! Five years ago, I had my first night in this very dorm.' Fenella sighed. 'It all seems such a long time ago now, it's hard to believe I'll be all done and dusted by the end of next year, and on the hunt for Mr Right. Anyway, back to finding the loos after all the lights go out. Unfortunately, your route takes you past the dreaded Red Landing where, the Grey Lady prowls at night.' There were a few gasps and a whimper from Connie. 'Yes, she wanders silently; up and down, and up and down.' Fenella's voice trilled on the ups and lowered on the downs. 'She won't hurt you, but she's not very pretty to look at, so, never forget to take your torch, if you need to wee-wee after 10 o'clock and, if you are unfortunate enough to see the Grey Lady's eerie presence, just point your torch at her and she will float away. Sleep well, girls. Brekkie is served at 7.30 a.m. and assembly starts at 9.00 a.m. sharp when the Head and all the other teachers come in, so you need to settle yourselves in there around 8.45. Have a good night!'

'Grey Lady?' scoffed Adele.

'I hate the dark and don't like the sound of the Grey Lady.' Connie snivelled. 'Is she a g,g,ghost, Adele?'

'No, of course not! My cousin came to this school and she warned me that the older girls always tease the first years about the Grey Lady.'

'So, she's not real?'

'No!'

'Do you know where your torch is, Connie?' asked Lisa.

'Yes.'

'Well, just in case you need to go to the loo during the night. Don't be frightened. Wake me up, I'll come with you.'

'I don't normally but, thank you. My sense of direction is a bit of a problem. I'm not very good at finding my way around.'

The food was abysmal - green mush masquerading as curry, with boiled to death rice. Brown slush, served up as casserole, served with large clumps of glutinous mashed potato. Old broilers served with tough, flannel-like cabbage and disintegrating potatoes. The best meal of the week was served for supper on Saturday's - a slice of cold ham, a tomato, and a baked potato.

Lisa had to wait until the weekend of her eleventh birthday before her first exeat. She was waiting for Jim outside as he drew up to the front door and threw herself into the car.

'I cannot tell you how pleased I am to see you! And I'm *so* hungry! I have been fantasising about Nellie's cooked brekkies since I've been here!'

'Ah, Nellie thought you might be hungry, so she sent you one of her chocolate muffins for the drive home.' Once home, Lisa bounded through the front door into the arms of the waiting Nellie.

'Lisa, lovie!' Nellie looked worried as she held her gently at arm's length, squeezing her shoulders. 'Don't they ever feed you in that place? I sent away a healthy, well-fed child with flesh on her bones and now look at you, you're a skinny little Lizzie! Auntie Nellie needs to feed you up.'

The following day was Lisa's birthday, and she started it by gorging on one of Nellie's full English breakfasts.

'Here's your mum's present.' Lisa watched Nellie move her well-scraped breakfast plate from in front of her and replace it with the small parcel inside a Harrods carrier bag. She sighed. Her mother had never been at home for any of her birthdays. She had no relationship with Elizabeth and saw her as an irritating troublemaker who dipped in and out of her life when it suited her. She was still very hurt and angry about her father's disappearance, but a constant niggling kept telling her not to give up on him. She looked down at the Harrods bag thinking about all the child-chic birthday presents her mother had given her since the frilly blue dress and black patent leather accessories. What treat did her mother have in store for her this time? She ripped the package apart and a lacy suspender belt, together with four pairs of silk stockings, flew out. Lisa dangled the Berlei gypsy garter belt by one suspender and waggled it.

'That's going to be useful, isn't it?' She giggled, and Nellie joined her with uncontrolled belly laughter. 'I wonder if my mother has any idea how *cold* it is during the day, and especially during the night at Coln Castle?'

With a sympathetic sigh, Nellie left the room. When she returned, her outstretched arms were loaded with beautifully wrapped parcels. 'Happy birthday, my darling!' she panted, as she slid the heavy pile onto the table.

Lisa ripped them open with delight. There were several pairs of thick tights, half a dozen pairs of thermal knickers and a selection of forty-fives: The Kinks, T. Rex, The Jackson 5, and the icing on her eleventh birthday cake: a portable record player.

'Thank you, Jim and Nellie, that's fantastic!'

'Happy Birthday, Lisa!' Arthur wheeled himself through the kitchen door, balancing a wooden box on his knee. It was painted yellow, with her name printed in bright red at the centre. 'I thought the contents might come in useful. They'll keep you going until half-term anyway.'

The box was stashed with sweets and biscuits—the ultimate tuck box. There was also a selection of paperbacks, including Gerald Durrell's *Birds, Beasts and Relatives*, and at the bottom of the box, another surprise, a bicycle pump. She pulled it out and looked at Arthur, who laughed.

'You'll find what it needs to be attached to parked outside the front door!' She threw her arms around his neck.

'Thank you, Arthur. Thank you so much! And you too, Jim and Nellie! You always give the best presents.' They all continued to spoil her for the rest of the day until Jim took her back to Coln Castle later that evening. He helped her carry her birthday booty inside, including the bike, together with an enormous chocolate cake Nellie had baked for all her friends.

She didn't feel too sad about going back, Adele and a cluster of other friends were waiting for her. 'Happy Birthday, Lisa!' Adele said, giving her a hug. 'I'm so pleased to see you, and your cake!'

Waving goodbye to Jim, she realised just how much she cared about him, and she wouldn't know what to do without Nellie, Arthur too. She was a better, stronger person for having them all in her life, but she needed to become much tougher if she was going to survive the rest of her first term.

The Truth is Out

Still unaware of the real reason her father had left home, Lisa wouldn't have to wait much longer to find out the truth. Some pubescent girls can switch on bitchiness as easily as flicking a light switch; others are born bitches.

Lisa enjoyed sport and liked her PE teacher, so she would often stay behind to help put the equipment away, which meant that she would be last in her year to leave the changing rooms. Tucked away in the bowels of Coln Castle, the changing rooms were the ideal place for premeditated attacks.

'Look at those chubby little thighs over there!' Lady Caroline Armitage squealed with delight when she saw Lisa slipping her tracksuit bottoms off as she walked in, flanked by her entourage of pretentious little friends. Caroline was two years above Lisa and had a reputation for tormenting the new girls. Lisa did her best to ignore them and carried on getting changed.

'Well, well, well, look who we have here. Did you know, girls, that my father says that Lisa Grant's father is a poof?' She exhaled as she said the word poof for a more dramatic effect. Spurred on by her sniggering friends, she enunciated her carefully chosen words very slowly. They walked slowly towards Lisa, taking exaggerated steps until they were standing over her.

'A willie woofter, a fairy, a... faggot.' Lowering her head, she whispered in Lisa's ear, 'homosexual.' She said the word very slowly and very precisely, before spelling it out.

'H-O-M-O-S-E-X-U-A-L. You know, men who prefer to snog men rather than women.' Caroline started making kissing noises with her lips, and the girlie giggles turned into loud guffaws.

Lisa swallowed. It felt uncomfortable, painful, like a stone was lodged in her epiglottis. She tried to focus on tying her shoelaces, wishing the ground would open and swallow her as Caroline's tirade continued.

'He went off with the polo player Thomas Cahoon, you know. My father plays polo with both Thomas Cahoon and Lisa 'chubby-thighs' Grant's father, Willopoofto. The Poofy Boys, as my father calls them, or I should say, he used to. It was all such a dreadful scandal for dear old Gloucestershire at the time. Poor Mrs Grant had to pack the poofy pair off to Portugal.' Her lips cracked open into a smug, irreverent smile. Her haranguing was going well, her victim was rendered speechless and her entourage, in hysterics.

Lisa took a deep breath, trying to digest what was being said when, for the second time in her life, since decapitating her mother's prized autumnals, she felt anger rising inside her. She sprang to her feet and gave Caroline a glare that gave away her bubbling rage.

Unnerved, Caroline, took a step backwards. Her henchmen gasped. Their victim was refusing to be reduced to a snivelling, whimpering wreck. She was going to fight back.

With no clear idea what she was going to do or say, Lisa's stifled anger was about to spew all over a visibly retreating Caroline Armitage. Drawing herself up to her full five foot two, she leaned in towards her tormenter. 'Caroline Armitage!' she hissed, pleased that she sounded in control, as well as assertive and menacing. 'If my father is a poof, how come I'm here?' Caroline looked vacant. 'You hadn't thought about that, had you?' Lisa prodded Caroline's shoulder with her forefinger, just hard enough to make her flinch. 'Or do you think I am the result of Immaculate Conception?' Thank goodness that, for a few minutes at least, she had paid attention during last week's eternally boring scripture class. Caroline seemed at a loss for words. 'I take it you know what Immaculate Conception is. You're two years above me, so you bloody well should. I daresay my mother would have something to say about it too. She told me that giving birth to me was such a painful process, she would never do it again. You are a venomous bitch, Caroline. Everybody says so!'

'You can't talk to me like that! One comes from a highly respected and extremely powerful family!'

Fists clenched and determined to be just as bitchy, Lisa edged closer to Caroline, who backed into a stray hockey stick, lost her footing, and fell arse-first onto the chilly linoleum floor. With a menacing laugh that even Count Dracula would be in awe of, Lisa bent over her cowering prey. 'Ha! Not so high and mighty now are you, *Lady* Caroline Armitage? How does it feel to be grovelling on the floor? That's about as low as anyone can get.'

'You simply cannot talk to me like that! One's father is the queen's cousin, six times removed!'

'I don't care who your father is related to, and I will talk to you how I bloody well like as you insist on being so poisonous about mine. You and your father should get your facts straight before you start casting nasturtiums.'

'Nasturtiums?'

'Yes, nasturtiums… aspersions, whatever you want to call it, just make sure you know what you are talking about in future before you open that grande bouche of yours.' Caroline's enormous mouth was hanging open as she looked up nervously. Lisa bent down to pick up the hockey stick, and Caroline gave a little yelp, covering her face with her arms.

'Oh diddums! I'm not going to hit you with it; I want you to put it in the chest on your way out. That would be most kind. Thank you. And one other thing, Caroline. In future, if you can't say anything nice about people, don't bloody well say anything at all. Didn't your mother ever tell you that? Shame on her!' And to end her Oscar-winning performance, Lisa flung the hockey stick against a wall. It bounced off, falling to the floor and clattering, precariously close to Caroline's head.

Looking disappointed with Caroline's dismal performance, her clique of friends shuffled towards the exit. 'Girls! Where are you going? Come back here and help me up.' Voice still quivering, she looked up at Lisa. 'One will have to report this to the headmistress, Lisa Grant!'

'Report what?' Lisa stood over her with her arms folded. 'That you're a bully, and you've been taunting a junior. Telling tales about her father being a homosexual? Report me to who you bloody well like, Caroline, including your father's six times removed cousin. But don't monarchs cut off heads for lies and treason? Good luck with that!'

Lisa held out both arms towards Caroline. 'Come on, up you get.'

'Please don't hurt me!' she squeaked, grabbing hold of Lisa's hands, who pulled her up.

'Oh, for goodness sake, Caroline. What do you think I am going to do to you? I can see it in the *Coln Castle Chronicle* now, *Insignificant Eleven-Year-Old Third Former, Lisa Grant, Beats Up Upper Fourth Captain, Lady Caroline Armitage in Changing Rooms after Armitage, Tells Grant Her Father's a Poof.* Grow up, Caroline!'

'I haven't finished with you yet, Lisa Grant!'

'Really? Well, I haven't finished with you yet either. So put that in your pompous little pipe and smoke it.' With that final warning, Lisa stormed out of the changing rooms with her head held high. At last, she knew the truth about her father, but she wasn't sure how to deal with it. Homosexual wasn't a word she was familiar with. She headed to the school library to do a little additional research.

Sexually attracted to people of one's own sex. Lisa read the quote and slammed the weighty volume shut before heaving the Oxford English Dictionary back on the shelf. So what? And why hadn't her mother ever told her the truth? Telling the truth was so important. If you tell a lie, somebody will always find out, eventually. Elizabeth should have told her, not some bitchy teenage relative of the Queen, umpteen times removed.

Will was her father, and she had loved him with all her heart. And even though she hadn't seen him for five years, she refused to let Caroline Armitage or anybody else belittle or bad-mouth him. She closed her eyes and imagined her father softly saying the words, *if there ever comes a day when we can't be together, keep me in your heart. I'll stay there forever*, before kissing her goodnight. She must still love him because he was in her heart.

It was the end of lessons for the day so, on leaving the library, she ran out to the mighty oak tree in the middle of the lawn and sat leaning against its trunk. Tipping her head back, she looked up through its majestic branches. She was proud of her tirade, which had shut the poisonous Caroline up and she was right: if her father did prefer men to women, how come she was here?

'Lisa…' It was Adele. 'I overheard that hoo-ha with Arsey Armitage just now. I went back for my jumper and heard her having a go at you. She is such a bitch. The way she and her little friends bully new girls is just pathetic, but you did such a brilliant job! You're a bit of a female swashbuckling Robin Hood really, aren't you?'

'Huh?'

'Escorting scaredy cat Connie to the loos during the night and leaving hockey sticks lying around to trip up Arsey and leaving her speechless on the floor! And that laugh! You scared the living daylights out of her. Just brilliant. Well done. I don't think she will be bothering you again.'

'Hope not. Did you know?'

'About your father? Well, er, yes. Arsey's big mouth is prone to spreading mucky gossip, but is it true?'

'The truth is that I don't know. I know my father went to live in Portugal, just before my sixth birthday. My mother said they had *irreconcilable differences*, whatever they are. I wondered if he might have a girlfriend, but I never thought about a man. And I do remember him, Thomas. He always seemed to be at home when my mother was in London, and he was always very nice to me.' Lisa stifled a snivel and wiped her nose with the back of her hand. 'My dad's forgotten about me anyway. He's never been in touch with me since he left, not once.'

Adele sat down beside her, resting her head on Lisa's shoulder.

'I'm sure he hasn't forgotten you. What does your mum say?'

'My mum? I don't see much of her these days either. She spends most of her time in London, and to be honest, I'm much happier when she's there.'

'Perhaps you could come and spend a weekend with my family sometime? I've told my Mum and Dad all about you and they can't wait to meet you.'

'Oh yes. I would like that very much.'

The dinner bell rang, and Adele jumped up, holding out her hands to pull Lisa up. 'You can come home with me on one condition, Lisa Grant…'

'What's that?'

'You promise to be my best friend.' She held out her little finger and linked it with Lisa's.

'Pinky promise! Best friends forever!'

'I'll hold you to that, Lisa Grant. Forever means forever. I'll race you to the dining room! I'm starving!'

Mother v Daughter: Round Two

Seven years, 14 A grade O-levels, and 3 A* A-levels later, Lisa came home from Coln Castle for the last time with dreams of pursuing a career as a journalist. But Elizabeth had other ideas. She still planned to send Lisa to the Debutantes' House in London for a year, the platform from where her only daughter would be launched into high society and find a wealthy husband. A plan that was about to spectacularly backfire, as the nucleus of Lisa's rant was about to burst and expel large quantities of bottled-up putrefied emotional shrapnel all over her mother.

'Not only was I bullied during my first term, but that's when I found out the truth about my father!'

Elizabeth sucked in an audible gulp of air.

'Yes, Mother, I know the real reason why my father left. You kicked him out!'

'Now, Lisa, that's not entirely true! You obviously don't know the whole story; I didn't kick him out, exactly…'

'Of course, you did! *Irreconcilable differences*, that was the crap you fed me when I was six. How was I supposed to know what that meant? Just how did you expect a six-year-old to get her head around *irreconcilable differences?* At no time since then have you tried to explain to me why he left. Thanks for that! I had to hear the truth from a vile, thirteen-year-old cow at school, Lady Caroline Armitage. That would impress you, Mother, a title! And what a little bitch she was, and still is. She took great pleasure in not only telling me my father left you for Thomas Cahoon, but do you know what the worst thing was, Mother? The whole bloody school knew. Everybody knew! The teachers, the girls, everybody, I was a laughing-stock! I couldn't go anywhere without gaggles of pubescent schoolgirls pointing at me. Can you imagine how that felt at eleven, Mother? Have you *any* idea?'

'You have no idea how awful the whole business was for me!'

'Ahh! But that's just it, Mother, isn't it? It's always been about you. Even my prospective boyfriends. They will always have to look at you first. Did you at any stage wonder how I might have felt? I was a child for God's sake! I was heartbroken by the way. In the six years my father was around, he made me feel loved, and I honestly think you are incapable of loving anybody!' Her heart was racing as she looked directly at her mother, who averted her gaze but, for a split second, Lisa, thought she saw a glimmer of remorse flash across her mother's face.

'Anyway, I know the truth. My father is gay, he went off with Thomas Cahoon. The biggest scandal Gloucestershire had seen in years, so I was told. So bloody what? He has no interest in me anyway. I have blotted him out of my life, and you don't have to worry about me, or my feelings anymore, well, you never have anyway.' She looked at her mother again expecting a response, but there was nothing. 'Getting back to me, Mother, Mr Barraclough, my English teacher, encouraged me to write articles and stories when I was fourteen, and he's helped me get them published in magazines and newspapers. So, nothing is going to stop me getting a job as a journalist now. Nothing! And that includes you and your ridiculous idea about sending me to finishing school. We are talking about my life, not yours, and I have no intention of finding myself a husband now, or at any other time!'

'Oh, God, Lisa! You're not, are you?' Her mother's nose wrinkled in disgust. 'Life is complicated enough, without being a lesbian! Something else you've inherited from your father, I expect, along with his temper.' Elizabeth spat out the words with such venom Lisa could see her spit flying in a shaft of sunlight.

'Honestly, just how much more ridiculous can you get? You think I'm a lesbian because my father is gay, and I share his genes? I imagine, academically, you must have been a complete waste of space. You know absolutely nothing about me, Mother. So, please, let's keep it that way. There is no need for you to start taking an interest in my life now. You are seventeen years too fucking late!'

'How rude and unkind you are to your mother, and your language is appalling. I didn't send you to an establishment for young ladies for you to become so foulmouthed! I'll be writing a letter of complaint to the headmistress.'

'You do that! She presented me with the Principle's Exceptional Student Award when I left, so I am sure she would be delighted to hear from you, considering she never had the opportunity to meet you. I have read *The Female Eunuch,* and *I Know Why the Caged Bird Sings,* and I also know what I want to do with my life, and, unlike you, it doesn't involve spending a year at finishing school learning how to pour a cup of tea. For God's sake, Mother, why do you always have to talk such bloody rubbish? You never took any interest in me as a child, so why would you want to start now? We are done here, and we are never going to have this ridiculous conversation about me going to finishing school again. I *will* be getting a job, whether you like it or not. You can stuff your idea about marrying me off to little Lord Fauntleroy any time soon and, I don't have to dress up like a bloody tart to attract a man. I want somebody to love me for who *I* am and not what *you* look like! No society wedding for me! It'll be barefoot on the beach if I ever do decide to get hitched and, guess what? You won't be getting an invitation.'

Elizabeth's eyes were stretched wide, and her bottom jaw hung open, revealing her lower set of pearly white Harley Street enhanced teeth. 'I beg your pardon?'

'You heard what I said, and I don't have time to go clothes shopping and, please, close the door on your way out.' But Elizabeth wasn't quite ready to leave.

Moving towards Lisa, their noses just inches apart, Elizabeth slowly raised her chin at her defiant daughter. 'I'll be outside in my car at 2 p.m. and we *will* go shopping together.' Sweeping out of the room, she slammed the door behind her with such a force the poster of the smiling Peter Frampton sellotaped to the portal, slid to the floor.

'You just can't bear it, can you, Mother? You always have to have the last bloody word!'

Eighteen

Three weeks before her birthday, Lisa was offered a job as a junior reporter with the local glossy *Inside Gloucestershire.* She had her foot on the first rung of her chosen career ladder; the best eighteenth birthday present she could have hoped for. She felt she had broken free of the shackles of her childhood, having stood her ground, and triumphed over her mother's pig-headedness and out-dated philosophy.

Jim taught her to drive in her father's old Land Rover, which had been redundant since he left, and she passed her test first time. With her own set of wheels and a second-hand Praktica camera she had bought with the proceeds of her freelance contributions, the intrepid reporter set off in search of stories. She interviewed local choirs, fire brigades, and members of the Women's Institute, as well as running around the woods near Stroud searching for wild boar. Her world was about as good as it had ever been.

Lisa and Adele had become like sisters. They were physically alike, the same height and weight, distinguishable from a distance only by the colour of their hair.

Adele's hair was straight and jet-black, which set off her vivid blue eyes. 'I am a clone of my mum, and Jack is the spit of my dad. He got Dad's curly hair and dark brown eyes. Funny old things, genes.'

'According to my mother, I look like my dad. So, hopefully, all I've inherited from my mother is the colour of her hair.' She looked down at her birthday present from her mother, a small parcel wrapped in green and gold tissue paper. 'What sexy little number do you think she's bought me this year?'

Adele picked it up, holding it between her thumb and forefinger, viewing it with suspicion. 'It's very light. Another naughty negligee, perhaps?

'Whatever it is, it won't be something I would choose to open in a public place.' Lisa pulled at the tissue paper, and the ultimate in seductive underwear floated out onto the table. Four flesh-coloured, see-through bras, and matching diaphanous pants.

'What does she want you to do? Set up Silkwoods as a knocking shop?'

'I could advertise in the *Standard. Enjoy sex just like they did in the 16th century at Sultry Silkwoods, Gloucestershire's finest bordello. Learn everything you need to know from Madame Elizabeth, who has the whip hand over her sex slave, Jeremy.* Help yourself, Adele, take a pair of the slinky skimpies and we can set ourselves up!'

'And why is the birthday girl hiding in here?' Arthur wheeled himself through the door as the girls hastily covered up the saucy strips of material.'

'Opening my mother's present.'

'Well, whatever it is has triggered much amusement.'

'Let's just say it's pants, Arthur.'

Enter Henry Stage Left

Leading up to Christmas, Lisa was asked to interview the local branch of the Young Farmers' Club, about their forthcoming production of *Cinderella Rockefeller*.

'Really? Can I come?' Adele rang to ask.

'No, you can't! You'd put me off, but why would you want to come anyway?'

'Honestly, Li, for someone who got A*'s in absolutely everything, you can be a bit slow sometimes. The Young Farmers' Club is the ideal place to find a boyfriend.'

Before setting out to interview potential boyfriend material, Lisa had a bath and washed her hair. Standing in front of a full-length mirror, she cautiously let her bath towel drop. She had never scrutinised herself naked before. She had seen the film *Emmanuelle* and wondered if her own body was destined to create as much excitement as Sylvia Kristel's.

She was lean, not skinny, a similar figure to her mother although her legs were a little shorter and her thighs slightly plumper, with a flat stomach and slim hips. Unlike her mother, her breasts were small, so she didn't bother wearing a bra, partly in solidarity with the American feminists, and because there seemed little point.

'Pert!' she thought. 'Pert is good!' She was happy with the way she looked naked and made a mental note never to let her body shape deteriorate. She slipped on a rugby-style shirt over her braless chest, before easing herself into her new kick-flare jeans, then sat down at her dressing table to blow-dry her hair.

She was blonde, like her mother, but her hair was dead straight. Her mother was right. She did have her father's facial features, including his large green eyes, to which she applied a smidgen of eyeliner and a little mascara. Quite unlike her mother, who never went anywhere without using a theatrical amount of makeup.

'Lisa! You're looking particularly gorgeous tonight, my darlin'. Lucky young farmers, eh, Jim?' Nellie winked at her husband, who nodded in agreement. Lisa's cheeks flushed a little as she lowered her head to kiss Nellie on the cheek, before hopping into her Land Rover and chugging her way to Appleton Village Hall.

Walking through the door, several young farmers were sitting on the edge of the stage swigging beer out of tins. They all whooped and cheered when they saw Lisa.

'Gentlemen, our prayers have just been answered, enter Cinderella stage left.' A tall, skinny guy, with long black hair and a red bandana tied around his head was looking straight at her.

'Er, I'm looking for Roddy Jenkins.'

'And I am indeed the Roddy that you seek, mademoiselle,' the red bandana responded. 'AKA writer, producer and director of our forthcoming, highly regarded theatrical extravaganza, *Cinderella Rockefella*. Are you here to audition for the part of Cinderella? Please tell me you are. No, wait, there is absolutely no need for you to audition; the part is yours. You are perfect, and a million times more beautiful than this blond idiot here, otherwise known as Henry, who seems intent on playing the part. His feet are so big we can't find a glass slipper in Heffalump size, and he can never remember his lines at the best of times and all he does is laugh about it!'

Lisa looked at Henry who was laughing so hard, his long, golden curls bounced against his bronzed neck. His blond ringlets were entirely his own, and not a wig for the part of Cinderella. Roddy must be blind; Henry was the most beautiful man she had ever seen. She remembered an old saying 'a picture paints a thousand words' then suddenly David Gates was singing inside her head.

Henry was mind-bogglingly beautiful. He had the face of an angel, so an obvious choice to play the part of Cinderella in the pantomime, as precious few girls were going to Agricultural College in 1977. Managing to snap herself out of her David Gates' reverie, she turned her attention back to Roddy.

'I'm Lisa from *Inside Gloucestershire*. I rang you last night about coming to interview you all about your pantomime.'

'Ah, yes, of course, I remember,' Roddy said, sliding off the stage and holding out his hand. Lisa, assumed he was going to shake hands, caught hold of his, as he pulled her towards him, scrutinised her face for a moment, then dipped his head to kiss the back of her hand which incited a wolf whistle and a chorus of, 'who do you think you are? Rudolph bloody Valentino?'

'Quiet, you motley crew!' he snapped. 'Clearly, none of you unromantic rapscallions have any idea how to treat a lady!' Once more, he looked at Lisa's face, this time pleadingly.

101

'I don't suppose you could find it in your heart and jiggle your busy schedule to play the part of my Cinderella, could you? By treading our humble boards and without even opening your mouth, you would enhance the quality of the production by one hundred percent.'

'I am flattered, kind sir, but I have deadlines to meet, and my acting days came to an end when I fell over Mercutio in our O-level production of Romeo and Juliet.'

'A girl after my own heart,' giggled Henry, and Lisa flashed him her best Colgate 'ring of confidence' smile.

'I thought I would do the interviews now and come back and take some photos during the dress rehearsal.'

'That sounds good to me!' enthused Roddy, before sighing heavily and adding, 'So, unless there is anything else we can do to woo you into playing the part of our fair Cinders, I will leave you with a heavy heart and this git with the big feet who is intent on being the star of our show, despite being incapable of remembering his lines. I despair! I need to get on with whatever it is writers, producers, and directors are supposed to do. Why don't you go into the Green Room, or the kitchen, as it's more generally known round here, while I try to whip this motley crew into shape? Now let's start with you two ugliest of ugly sisters and your rendition of *Big Spender*, from the top, please!'

Lisa and Henry sat facing each other across the kitchen table's distressed-to-perfection surface. A place where thousands of jam sandwiches had been prepared for too many rained-off outdoor fetes, as Lisa kicked off the interview.

'What made you want to go into farming?'

'I hate wearing a suit. No, not really, my father's family has always farmed, so it was not a case of wanting to but having to. My older brother is training to be a doctor, so he chose surgery over silage, which left me to run the farm. My father left home when I was eight, and my mother has been running it with the help of my grandfather, but he's a bit passed it now. So, my mind was made up for me. By the way, I would rather you left that bit out about my father leaving home, because it's not a happy memory for my mother.

'Of course! I understand.' Nobody could understand more than Lisa. 'Did you ever do any acting at school?

'Not really, we did the *Taming of the Shrew* in our O-Level year. How ridiculous is that in an all-boy's school?'

'About as ridiculous as staging a production of Romeo and Juliet in an all-girl's school!' They both found Lisa's comment ridiculously funny.

'I played the part of Katherine, and I couldn't remember my lines then, either. But, having already played a female role, I didn't mind auditioning for the part of Cinderella. Actually, just between you and me, I had no competition. Don't suppose you've got any girlfriends with size twelve feet, have you? I am struggling to find anything that resembles a glass slipper in my size.'

'I don't think so, but you could try one of the charity shops?'

'That's a brilliant idea! Would you like a beer?'

'I would, but I best not, thanks. I imagine drinking on the job is a sackable offence, and I've only been doing it for three months. Perhaps you could ask me that question another time?'

'I would like that. Please, could I have your number?'

Her interview continued apace during which they laughed a great deal, and she felt a bit miffed when Roddy came into the room.

'Okay, Lisa! Time to interview the boss! You, Goldilocks, go and rehearse with your Prince Charming.'

'My favourite part!' Henry flashed Lisa a smiled, flicking his blond curls over his shoulder. 'I'll ring you, okay?' Lisa nodded as Henry sauntered off singing *Cinderella Rockefella*, in the wrong key.

Her interview with Roddy was far more straightforward. He gave her all the information she needed, including a copy of the cast list.

'Thank you, Lisa. I look forward to seeing you on Friday evening for the dress rehearsal.'

She scampered back across the potholed car park while looking at the cast list: *Cinderella: Henry Cahoon*. She tripped, narrowly avoiding falling flat on her face. No, surely not, he couldn't possibly be. Could he? But his father left home when he was eight. It was too much of a coincidence, he had to be Thomas Cahoon's son. This blond bronzed Adonis who had made her heart stop for a few moments and something unfamiliar twitch inside her, was his son. How could it be? How could fate be so unkind? How could she possibly go back, look him in the eye and tell him how adorable he looked in his pantomime regalia? She got into her Land Rover and drove rather unsteadily home to ring Adele.

'Hi, Li! How were the young farmers?'

'Well, I met someone.'

'I *told you* the Young Farmers' Club was a good place to find a boyfriend. Are you going to see him again? Has he got a good-looking friend?'

'Well, no, but yes. He asked for my number.'

'Excellent.'

'But, um, you're not going to believe this.'

'Try me…'

'He's Thomas Cahoon's son. He's completely, gorgeous. Long, curly, blond hair. Sort of cherub-like, I mean Greek God-like, but he's Thomas Cahoon's son.'

Nothing ever fazed Adele. '*The* Thomas Cahoon? The one who went away with your dad? So?'

'So? Is that all you can say? Getting to know each other is going to be awkward, isn't it? Discussing what our fathers have been doing for the last twelve years!'

'Personally, I don't see what the problem is. It's one way of breaking the ice. Does he know who you are?'

'No, but it's not going to take him very long to work it out, is it? I suppose, deep down, I want to know how my dad's getting on. Not that I'll ever forgive him for abandoning me for the last twelve years.'

'Well, if it were me, and he asked me out, I would go. It's not *his* fault he's Thomas' son, is it? If he's as gorgeous as you say he is, you should go out with him. Seriously, what have you got to lose? I'm sorry Li, but I've got to go. Jack's at home, only briefly though, just for tonight. You know he's been working for a publisher in Oxford since he left University? Well, he has finished there now, and he's been offered a job in London starting next June. So, as he never took a break after school and university, he's decided to go travelling for a few months before he starts work. He's leaving at the crack of sparrows tomorrow, so he's planning on getting an early night. He popped in to see you earlier, apparently. Nellie told him you were working. Anyway, he sends his love.'

'Aw, that was nice. I'm sorry I wasn't here. I would have loved to have seen him. Send him my love and tell him I hope he has a wonderful trip.'

'Will do, and don't rule this Henry out as a possible boyfriend just yet. I'll ring you tomorrow, okay?'

Lisa put the phone down with a sigh. Jack had come to say goodbye to her, and she hadn't been there. The last time Lisa had seen him was at the Mad Hatter cafe, just before her birthday. She had always felt close to Jack, in a sisterly sort of way, but that evening she saw him in a different light.

He had bought her flowers. A bouquet of long-stemmed pink roses. Nobody had ever given her flowers before and they smelt wonderful. He smelt pretty good too, probably, Brut. He'd kissed her on both cheeks and given her a hug, his thick black curls brushing against her ear, which made her feel tingly. He wore a black leather jacket, black T-shirt and black jeans, his lean athletic body, even covered up, was very appealing. She thought about him since then but, after she threw herself into work mode, she found little time for anything else. The phone rang, breaking her Jack reverie.

'Okay, Della. Which part of your pep talk did you forget?'

'Oh, hello. It's Henry here.'

'Um, Henry?'

'Yes, we met earlier this evening. I'm playing the title role in the Young Farmers' production of *Cinderella Rockefeller*, and you're kindly writing a review about our extravaganza before we take it to the West End.' He laughed awkwardly, and she imagined his blond curls bobbing against his bronzed neck.

'Henry, yes, of course!'

'I wondered if you would like to come out for a drink and a bite to eat, perhaps tomorrow evening, or any other evening come to that, except for Friday, as its the dress rehearsal, by which time I really will have forgotten all my lines. The bar meals at the Hare and Hounds are pretty good; we could go there.'

'I'd love to. Tomorrow would be great.' The words tumbled out of her mouth faster than she would have liked and she bit her bottom lip, regretting appearing too hasty, too keen.

'Great, I'll pick you up at 7 p.m.'

'I live between Cirencester and Colesbourne by the way, it's a farm called Silkwoods which is just…'

'I know where it is,' interrupted Henry, 'and, I thought so. You're just the other side of the woods from me, and we have something, or rather someone, in common. My surname is…'

'Cahoon. Yes, I know, and, yes, we do.'

Henry arrived at Silkwoods driving a small tractor with a buddy seat, but no cab. He was planning to take the route known locally as the ABC. The 'anti-breathalyser course,' which followed B roads and farm tracks, avoiding main roads and any danger of being breathalysed. It was a chilly January evening, there was no snow, but it was threatening. Lisa was pleased she'd worn an army surplus overcoat she'd found in the attic, despite it being several sizes too big. A stout pair of Doc Martens covered her feet and ankles completing the look. An image that would make her mother cringe.

Henry smelt good. Brut again, and nothing beat the great smell of Brut. She felt excited, not only because she found Henry physically attractive, but she was about to discover what her reprobate father had been doing for the last twelve years.

They sat at a small table by an enormous fireplace, the unseasoned logs aggressively spitting wet sap, while they ate steak and chips, washing it down with pints of lager.

'They are very happy, you know.' Henry was referring to their fathers who, much to Lisa's irritation, he had seen a great deal of since they left the UK.

'Will is devastated that you've never been in touch with him.' Henry's white-blond eyebrow arched as he delivered the words.

Lisa stopped eating and took a swig of lager. '*He* is devastated? I was six when he left home, and he has never, ever been in touch with me. Not once! It was my birthday just after he left, and he didn't even manage to send me a card. I've heard absolutely nothing from him since he left. Zilch, zero, nada, so forgive me if I find it completely outrageous that *he* feels devastated! I had no idea why he left either, my stupid mother told me that she and my Father had irreconcilable difficulties. I found out the truth from a bitch of a girl at Coln Castle, when I was eleven.'

Henry was staring at her and frowning.

'What?' She forced a nervous laugh.

'That's not what he told me,' he said, tilting his head to one side, his golden curls following, slowly, one freeze-frame at a time.

'Okay. What's *he* been saying, then?'

'Well, he told me that he's written to you regularly since he left, and he still writes to you hoping you might respond one day. He's never given up hope on you contacting him, Lisa. He thought that maybe when you got older, and were more able to understand, you might find it in your heart to forgive him. Honestly, hand on heart, he says that he has always sent you cards, and presents, at Christmas and on your birthday.'

She felt like Henry had just thrown a bucket of ice-cold water in her face. Her heart was banging against her ribcage. She tried taking a few deep breaths to calm herself, as her tough rookie-reporter façade started to crumble.

'Lisa?'

'But I've never had *anything* from him!' Her voice cracked, and her bottom lip started to quiver. Henry instinctively moved closer, putting both arms around her and, overcome by such a public show of affection, Lisa burst into tears. She felt ridiculous; she never cried, well, never in public, and never in the arms of a complete stranger. 'I had no idea!' she croaked. 'Honestly, I've never received anything from him.'

'Oi! Is she drunk?' The landlady slapped both hands down on the bar.

'No, of course, she isn't! She's just upset,' Henry snapped, before whispering in Lisa's ear. 'Just ignore the old bag. She's not a fan of students, agricultural or otherwise, and/or young people in general.'

'I can see she's upset, Goldilocks. But I don't want 'er upset for long. I don't like drunks or snivellers in my pub! One usually goes with the other anyway.'

Henry ignored her, continuing to whisper into Lisa's ear. 'Maybe your mother's hidden everything from you? I've heard she's a bit of an old harr… oops, I'm sorry, I mean, a bit of a tough cookie. Come on, Lisa. I'll take you home,' he said, pulling a crumpled, red cotton handkerchief spattered with a few oil stains out of his pocket and handed it to Lisa, who blew her nose loudly. Rising to his feet, he held out his hand, which she obediently took, and they left the pub under the intense scrutiny of the landlady's stare.

The Ultimate Betrayal

Lisa slammed the heavy oak front door behind her and stood with her back against it for a few seconds, trying to calm her laboured breathing. She felt cold. Her body temperature had plummeted, instinctively tugging at the lapels of her army surplus overcoat, pulling it around her neck. Her heart pummelled against her ribcage, and she was shaking. Her emotions vacillating from the urge to burst into tears, to screaming with rage.

'How could she do this to me?'

Grabbing a torch from the kitchen, she ran up the oak staircase two steps at a time. The clumping sound of her Doc Martens impacting with the ancient wooden steps created a ripple effect in the cavernous hallway, which reverberated around the house. Her mother was in London, so she could carry out her search for the cache of the letters, cards and presents that her father had been sending her for the last twelve years, without any interruption, but where to look?

'I will kill her if she's destroyed everything,' she muttered under her breath, as she climbed the steep winding stairs to the attic. Crashing around in the eaves, she investigated the old priest hole thoroughly, before tearing apart boxes and suitcases, including the old trunk containing an assortment of papers. She opened a tin concealing the fading black-and-white photographs, vaguely remembering having seen them before. There was an envelope tucked underneath with the words *Lizzie's birth certificate*, scrawled across the front. In her highly charged emotional state, Lisa opened it without thinking, and frowned. The mother's name, Gertrude Clemmens, meant nothing to her, so why was the birth certificate for her daughter, Elizabeth, in the attic at Silkwoods? The date of birth jumped out at her. It was the same as her mothers.

'Lisa?' It was Nellie. 'I hope it's you up there. Jim was about to get his twelve-bore out because he thought we had burglars. What on Earth are you doing up there at this time of night?'

Lisa stuffed everything back into the tin and slammed the lid of the trunk shut. In her urgency to regale to Nellie what Henry had told her, she took the steep stairs too quickly. The heel of her boot caught in the hem of her overcoat, and her legs shot out from under her. Falling on to her bottom, she slid down the stairs before collapsing at Nellie's feet where she burst into tears.

'Darlin' girl, whatever is the matter? What's that Henry Cahoon done to you? Jim will use his twelve-bore on him if he's laid a...'

'No, Nellie, it's not anything that Henry's *done!* It's what he's *told* me. He says my dad has been writing to me regularly since he left, which can only mean that my mother must have hidden everything. I can't find anything in the attic, though.' Nothing from her father anyway.

Nellie was outraged. 'Well, I never thought that even she would sink so low!'

'Can you think of anywhere else in the house my mother could have hidden everything?'

'I check all the cupboards for damp regularly, and if she'd hidden anything outside, then Jim would have found it for sure. Hang on a minute! There is one place where nobody, but your mother goes, but she keeps it locked mind. There's a cupboard at the back of her walk-in wardrobe. So, that might be worth a try?'

Lisa headed to her mother's bedroom, somewhere she had rarely ventured since the day she was born. Displayed on every available surface was a spectacular self-portraiture collection. Photographs of Elizabeth, leading up to becoming debutante of the year, as well as outside Westminster Registry Office, smiling like a triumphant trophy killer, in both 1959 and 1967, but she'd cut her father and Arthur out of the pictures. Lisa picked up the only photograph that included her, at her christening. Elizabeth was holding her under her arms, dangling her over the font with a concerned-looking vicar, possibly wondering if he might have to dive in and fish her out.

'There's one problem, Lisa, lovie.'

'What's that?' she asked, putting the photo down with an irritated thud.

'It's kept locked, and I have no idea where she keeps the key.' Lisa peered into the walk-in wardrobe, which was stashed full of designer clothes on both sides. She could see the cupboard at the far end, which had a rail fixed to the front of it where designer scarves neatly hung. Lifting the curtain of chiffon and silk, a chunky medieval-looking padlock hung from a flimsy looking bolt.

'Who needs a key, Nellie?' She ran downstairs and came back with a hammer and a screwdriver. After a few vicious blows with the hammer to the butt end of the screwdriver, the padlock fell to the floor. The door flew open under the weight of twelve years' worth of letters and parcels, all addressed to Lisa in her father's handwriting, and all redirected to Elizabeth care of a post office box in Cirencester.

Nellie started to cry. 'Oh, Lisa, lovie, I can't believe she's done this to you.' She helped Lisa carry the stash to her bedroom. 'Are you going to be all right, my dove?'

'Oh, I'll be fine,' she responded, throwing her arms around Nellie's neck, snuffling into her shoulder. 'And thank you for your help. I would never have thought about looking in there.'

'Well, goodnight, my darlin'. I'll leave you to catch up with your dad.'

Lisa meticulously put everything in date-stamp order, before standing back and staring at the pile of presents, letters, and cards. She felt ashamed of the times she allowed herself to believe he had forgotten her. She picked up her camera and took a few photographs of the evidence, before opening the first letter with trembling fingers, which Will had posted on the day he left.

24th July 1965

My darling Lisa,

Daddy is not someone who breaks his promises, and I promised I'd catch you a trout for your supper, but I'm not going to have time to catch one.

I have to go away, and I'm going to live in Portugal, but you can

114

come and see me any time you like and stay with me for as long as you want to. Forever, if you want to. I'm counting the days until I see you again. You will have to fly on an aeroplane, and I know you'll find that exciting and I will be there to meet you.

I know you will find it difficult to understand now, but I will explain everything to you when you get a bit older, but I want you to know that even though I am not with you, my gorgeous girl, you will always be in my heart.

So, please, never, ever forget what we always say together, if we ever need to part, I'll take you with me in my heart, so when I close my eyes at night, I'll think of you and feel alright.

All my love, always and forever, Daddy xxxx

Her father had finished his epistle with a rough sketch of Pooh and Piglet holding hands. Some of the inked words spattered with her father's tears. Stains long since dried but soaked again by her own that had dribbled down her cheeks onto the page. She wiped her nose and cheeks with the palm of her hand.

'Elizabeth Goldsworthy-Grant can seriously damage your health!' she muttered under her breath. It was impossible to believe that they were related. An umbilical cord had once bound them together. Beyond the womb, an invisible tie should always keep them together for the rest of their lives, not make them enemies. She closed her eyes. She never wanted to see her mother again. It was time to cut the cord.

Getting Back in Touch

Lisa stood with her forearms resting on the handrail of the wooden bridge her father always affectionately referred to as Pooh Sticks Bridge. Should she ring him or write to him? What was she going to say? She was still struggling to tell the wonderfully comforting Nellie how she felt, so she decided to write. It was the one thing she was confident she did well. All too often, when she opened her mouth, the words came out wrong, especially when emotionally charged.

She had a few false starts, *Dearest Pooh, Darling Daddy, Dear Will*. It was tricky deciding how to refer to her father, given that she hadn't seen him for twelve years. Once she decided on *Hello Dad,* the words flowed. She told him how bereft she had felt after he left. *'It was like the world had fallen out of my orbit.'* And how she had tortured herself about why he'd never been in touch. Although she had never lost the underlying belief that he would never abandon her, and he hadn't. She told him she had methodically put all his cards and presents in date-stamp order, opening each one with a full heart and a childish delight. They were the perfect presents for that stage of her life, as were the sentiments he lavished in each card or letter, some of which he had addressed to Piglet and signed Pooh. For the last twelve years, her father had poured his heartfelt emotion onto paper, desperate to hear from his daughter. During the same time frame, her mother had allowed Lisa to believe that he had deserted her.

My mother has never attempted to make our relationship a loving one. She has never shown any affection towards me, dried my tears or hugged me. Nellie is the best hugger in the world! My mother has always treated me a bit like she treats Silkwoods, better out of sight and out of mind, something to revisit when it suits her. Her London life is the only thing she cares about and her boyfriend, Jeremy Jermayne. I assume you knew about him and that she got married again?

Poor Arthur Goldsworthy fell into her Venus flytrap, twenty-five years her senior, and not a well man. If the world were in any doubt, which seems unlikely, she married him for the size of his Coutts' bank account, and like me, she shuts the door on him when she leaves Silkwoods. He never sees anybody these days, apart from me, Jim, Nellie, and his carer. He found travelling to and from London too much some time ago. He has been a brilliant stepfather in many ways. He's bright, funny, and was unfaltering in his determination to make sure I did well at school, so I could find the job that I wanted. Of course, my mother wanted me to go to farcical finishing school but, I put my foot down! I got fourteen O-levels, by the way, and straight A's for my A-levels. So, I inherited your brains. Thank goodness! So, I was damned if I was going to waste all that hard work on pouring a cup of tea.

I love Silkwoods, Dad, just as much as you did. I cannot imagine how awful it was for you to leave it. It's in good hands, though, with Jim and Nellie, and Arthur, of course, as well as a little input from me these days.

I know you went away with Thomas Cahoon, and I don't care who you went away with, so long as you are well and happy, that's all I care about. My mother never told me why you left. I found out from a thirteen-year-old cow during my first year at Coln Castle. The Earl of Barford's daughter. You and Thomas used to play polo with him. Anyway, I want to get to know you again and be a part of your life, and Thomas's too. I really, really want to see you. Lisa finished her letter by saying that words could not describe how upset she felt about her mother's betrayal. Although she was not entirely surprised, given her mother's total lack of empathy.

I'm not sure if I can come back from this, the ultimate betrayal. I have always felt ambivalence towards the woman who gave birth to me but was incapable of raising me. I honestly don't think I can continue being a part of our bogus relationship.

It was a twenty-page missive, typed on A4 paper, embodying twelve years of pent-up emotion. There were a few handwritten additions here and there, including a *P.S.: I'm so happy I met Henry, Dad! Thank goodness I was asked to review Cinderella Rockefeller! It's such a shame you and Thomas couldn't have seen the performance. Henry looked adorable in his Cinderella costume, with all his blond curls!*

*

The day Lisa's letter arrived, Will was walking back to the house from the renovated outbuildings they had converted into guest accommodation and offices. During the twelve years of their enforced exile, Will and Thomas transformed a run-down vineyard into a thriving, well-respected winemaking estate. The once-neglected farmhouse was now the elegant-looking *Casa Monte das Uvas,* draped with the original bougainvillaea plants that once covered its cracks. He slowed his stride as he heard the carteiro's motorcycle spluttering up the hill. He was in an excellent mood. It would be an early harvest, which meant that the grapes would be good.

'Bom dia, Carlos!' After twelve years, Will's Portuguese was excellent, which he attributed to years of bartering in the local markets.

'Bom dia, Will. There is a letter, from Inglaterra for you.'

'A letter? For me? From England?'

'Sim. Te vejo amanhã,'

'Yes, Carlos. See you tomorrow.'

He looked at the A4 envelope, and the postmark jumped out at him. Cirencester. He turned it over. *Sender: Lisa Grant.* His heart lurched inside his chest as he half-walked, half-ran to the veranda where he slumped into his high-backed wicker armchair, ripping open the envelope with trembling fingers.

'Hello Dad, I don't really know where to start other than to say I have thought about you every single day since you left...'

After reading Lisa's emotionally charged missive, Will pulled a handkerchief from his trouser pocket and blew his nose. It had been painful leaving Silkwoods and the UK, but it was nothing like the excruciating, heart-wrenching pain of leaving his six-year-old daughter behind. As soon as he composed himself, he rang Lisa, and

119

they chatted for almost two hours, trying to cram in twelve years' worth of their lives spent apart. Lisa's pent-up emotions quickly dissolved into floods of tears, which convulsed down the phone. But Will promptly turned the conversation around, and they were soon laughing about the trout he had promised to catch her on the day he left. He was so easy to talk to, so different from her mother. They picked up where they had left off.

'I can't wait to see you! When can you come and stay? You can come any time you like, and you can stay as long as you like. Just let me know when and I will book your flights. Why don't you come out with Henry? We are both so pleased to hear that your paths crossed. I cannot believe that Elizabeth did this to you, darling. I'm so sorry.' Will was gabbling with excitement. 'When do you think you will get time off work? Your job sounds very exciting. I can't wait to hear more about it.'

New Beginnings

Will didn't have to wait very long to see Lisa as she took two weeks off around the Easter break to fly out to Portugal with Henry. As they made their way through Passport Control, the smell of Português Suave cigarettes hung heavy in the air. The stickiness of their olfactory pungency seeped into Lisa's memory banks and always served as a constant reminder of being reunited with her father. Handing her passport to the immigration officer, she realised she was shaking. The last time Will saw her, she was under four foot in height, with white-blonde hair and wearing a brown school uniform. Now two foot taller, with honey-blonde hair, wearing bell-bottomed trousers and a skimpy T-shirt, she wondered if he would be able to recognise her. She put her passport back in her bag then stood, stock still, as she took a few deep breaths.

'Are you okay?' Henry looked concerned, taking her hand in his.

'What if he doesn't like me, Henry?'

'Li, I have no doubt that Will is the other side of that door, pacing up and down, trying to curb his impatience to see you. So, come on, let's go and put him out of his misery.' Leading her out into the arrivals hall, he started waving at two tall slim and very bronzed, smiling men with bleached blond hair striding across the concourse towards them.

'Here she is!' Henry shouted.

Lisa's heart pounded underneath her ribcage, as Will broke into a run, looking excited to see her. A panicked thought crossed her mind

'Should I hug him, or kiss him on the cheek?

'Piglet!' he yelled, almost stumbling over someone's suitcase.

'Pooh!' she squealed, taut with emotion, her voice an octave higher than usual. Dropping her cabin bag, she launched herself at him, throwing her arms around his neck.

He picked her up and swung her around before putting her down gently, placing his hands on her lean shoulders.

He choked out the words, 'Oh, Lisa! I've missed you so much. I can't believe the six-year-old girl I left behind has grown into such a beautiful young woman.' He wrapped his muscular, tanned arms around her once more. 'I love you so much, Piglet.'

Overcome with emotion, Lisa burst into tears.

Later that evening, they shared several bottles of *Monte das Uvas,* and Will cooked fish on the barbecue. 'It's not trout, Lisa, it's red snapper, but I think you'll enjoy it.'

'I was so cross with you about forgetting to catch my trout!'

'I knew you would be. You were a tiny little thing, but you always knew what you wanted, and you loved your food!'

'I still do!'

After Lisa went to bed, Will entered her room to say goodnight. 'Last time I said goodnight to you, I read you a story about the *Hundred Acre Wood*, do you remember?'

'Of course, I do, and a little A.A. Milne philosophy goes a very long way, but what's kept me going over the last twelve years are the words we used to say together before you kissed me goodnight.' Will sat down on the side of her bed and reached for his daughter's hands and together they recited the words, *if we ever need to part, I'll take you with me in my heart, so when I close my eyes at night, I'll think of you and feel alright.*

'I've been dreaming of this day for a very long time, Lisa. I cannot express how happy I am to be with you again. Goodnight, my gorgeous girl.'

The following morning Will took Lisa for the short drive to the coast. He turned off the main road and headed for the beach at Praia do Trafal. They wound their way along a pot-holed track, past decaying sandstone buildings daubed with anti-establishment slogans, a legacy of the 1974 Carnation Revolution. Will's four-wheel-drive vehicle bounced along the dirt track spewing up a vast dust cloud behind them. He parked beneath a canopy of umbrella pines, a fresh pungent, fragrance filling their lungs.

They kicked off their shoes and ran across the ochre-coloured sands kissed by the waves of the Atlantic Ocean. They walked, paddled, and swam towards the soon-to-be flourishing resort of Vale do Lobo, which had just been taken over by the Dutch entrepreneur Sander van Gelder, where they drank fresh orange juice and coffee in the Praça, before moving on to Praia do Garrão, stopping for a very long lunch at Antonio's before walking back to Praia do Trafal.

It was strange getting to know her father again. He was so very different from her mother. He oozed warmth, bowled along by a great sense of humour, and a unique ability to make her believe she was the only person in the world who really mattered. All these things she remembered about him, but something was different. His complexion, of course, was different. His sun-kissed, well-toned body made him look much younger than thirty-eight, but his overall demeanour had changed to that of a very relaxed and happy man. It was heartwarming to see how much Will and Thomas cared about each other. Their relationship, considered unconventional during the seventies, had stretched their lives to breaking point but together they had survived.

It was an emotionally exhausting day for them both, cramming in twelve years of repressed feelings, much laughter, and a tear or two of joy. All either of them had wanted was to have each other back in their lives. Now they had it, the final piece of their emotional jigsaw slotted into place, their lives complete, once more.

Every evening they enjoyed a few glasses of *Monte das Uvas,* Vermelho, Branco, and Rosa, exchanging memories and getting to know each other again, in the warmth of the Portuguese night, with crickets scissoring their legs under a canopy of stars. For the first time in her life, Lisa Grant felt truly at home in the bosom of her family and throughout her visit and the months of phone calls that followed, she began to piece together the sequence of events that her six-year-old self had not been aware of.

Into Exile

During the summer of 1965, Elizabeth cultivated an unlikely friendship with Thomas' wife, Anna, who she had studiously ignored for six years after Anna offered her support before Lisa's birth, referring to her as *all brawn and no* brain behind her back. Anna loved everything about country life, especially living on a working farm, and her reputation as a horsewoman was legendary. She could back a green Argentinian polo pony as well, if not better, than any man. She was also well-known for mucking in on the farm and was an invaluable asset during the calving season. Elizabeth was horrified. How could anybody, especially a woman, be so totally unfazed when sticking an arm up a cow's vagina? They had nothing in common, apart from their husbands, and they were the reason Elizabeth had reached out a hand of bogus friendship.

Elizabeth found out that Thomas had been expelled from school for being caught in flagrante delicto with another boy, which fuelled her suspicion that Will and Thomas' relationship was more than being drinking buddies in the clubhouse bar after a polo match.

Elizabeth plied Anna with gin and tonic during their meetings, filling her head with unsubstantiated rumours about their husbands. 'They're always out riding together or travelling to and from polo matches, which sometimes necessitates spending nights away, and, let's face it, Anna, horseboxes have a reputation for being used for secret assignations. It must be something to do with all that bouncing around in the saddle all day. Archie Fernsby said he was hacking past that old barn, just off the White Way, and saw their horses tied up outside, and there was groaning coming from inside.'

'One of our mares escaped from the field and foaled in there, Elizabeth!' Anna exploded.

'Well, possibly, but there have been plenty of sightings of them wrapped in each other's arms in the woods and swimming together, naked, in the lake, here at Silkwoods.' Elizabeth lightly patted a distraught Anna on the back.

'I don't believe you!' Anna sobbed.

'Leave it to me, Anna, darling. I'll find out exactly what they've been getting up to behind our backs.'

Elizabeth wanted out of the marriage and had been planning to set a trap for Will and Thomas for some time, but they played straight into her hands. She had been irritated after Jeremy told her that he and his wife, Penelope, were going away for the weekend to a society wedding up north, so Elizabeth decided to spend hers at Silkwoods. Under normal circumstances, she would forewarn Will that she would be staying for a few days, but, on a whim, she had taken the last train out of Paddington to Kemble Station and arranged for a taxi to meet her there. Elizabeth arrived at Silkwoods at around 10.00 p.m. The front door, as always, was unlocked, so she let herself in noiselessly; the last thing she would have wanted to do was wake the child.

The first thing she heard was the soulful voice of Otis Redding singing, *That's How Strong My Love Is* coming from the sitting room. The Pye Princess record player was turned up to full volume, muffling the sound of voices coming from inside and logs being thrown on to the fire, which made it crackle and spit, which Elizabeth thought was odd. Why would the robust Will feel the need to light a fire in July? Taking off her shoes, she walked in her stockinged feet across the cool limestone flags. The sitting room door was ajar, and she peered around it. The only light in the room was from the flames of the fire and candles on the mantelpiece. Her heartbeat accelerated, aroused by the sight of Will and Thomas' naked bodies, clearly visible in front of the fire. Two young men in peak physical condition, their bodies taut and muscular, so unlike Jeremy's lean physique. Will popped a cork from a champagne bottle and filled two glasses, handing one to Thomas.

'Here's to us…'

'To us…' Thomas repeated, chinking his glass with Will's. They took a sip, placed their glasses on the mantelpiece, then fell into each other's arms. 'Close your eyes and think of me.' Will whispered into Thomas's ear. Unaware Elizabeth had slipped into the room, his lips and hands wandered slowly across his lover's body. Transfixed, and scolding herself for enjoying the spectacle too much, she flicked on the light. The two men flew apart. Watching them flounder around, searching for the clothes they had so recently discarded, a satisfied smile slid across Elizabeth's face as she watched their humiliation.

'Good God, Will, is this what you get up to when your wife is away? With a child in the house as well, you disgust me, the pair of you. I will be speaking to my solicitor in the morning. And you, Will, I want you out of the house as soon as possible, or I will have no option other than to advise the police about your filthy habits.'

Elizabeth had fantasised about the divorce settlement she would screw him for, and now it would happen sooner rather than later. She launched herself into the role of scorned-wife vigilante, single-handedly building up the biggest brouhaha Gloucestershire had ever seen and made sure the scandal was passed around London's social circuit. Honing her world-renowned skills for troublemaking and gossip-mongering, the Elizabeth-driven bush telegraph was rife, beating out disturbing accounts of Will hosting drunken gay orgies at Silkwoods with Thomas, as well as malicious accusations of wife neglect and abuse. The news of the poor, young, society wife catching her husband in flagrante with another man in rural Gloucestershire spread like wildfire. It would be another couple of years before homosexuality became legal in the UK, but, given the attitude of the echelons of society Will and Thomas had been born into, acceptance would take a great deal longer. Thomas's father had disinherited him, leaving everything to his two grandsons, and Elizabeth, true to her word, screwed Will for everything he had.

*

The weight of living a lie had become too much of a psychological burden for Will and Thomas to bear. Keeping up the daily charade of living a happy family life, for the sake of their children, had been impossible to sustain; their love for each other was too strong. Elizabeth made sure they became outcasts amongst their friends and banished from their homes, making it impossible for them to stay in the UK. Battling with unforgiving wives and leaving behind the children they adored took its toll, not only on their emotions but their self-esteem as well.

Will left Gloucestershire shortly after dropping Lisa off at school. He had tried to tell her he was going away during the fifteen-minute drive, but his aching heart made it impossible for him to find the words. How do you explain to a six-year-old that you're leaving home and never coming back? How do you explain infidelity to a child? After he'd said goodbye to her, he watched her run through the school gates, happy and carefree. Her soft, blonde baby hair glistening in the summer sunshine. The very last memory of his much-loved daughter.

During the short drive home, his gut felt like it was tying itself in knots. A sharp, stabbing pain that showed no signs of subsiding, his mind flooded with thoughts of his daughter. Arriving at Silkwoods, he went straight to his study. He moved the divorce papers served by Elizabeth to one side of his desk and sat down. He filled his pen with ink and feeling like a condemned man, his eyes brimming with tears, he tried to explain to Lisa why he was going away.

Will and Thomas agreed that they needed a project, something they could immerse themselves in, as they tried to blot out the very raw trauma of their last few weeks in the UK. Will had heard about a remote, ailing vineyard inland from Guia in the Algarve, which needed a *'little renovation.'* So, they opted for the vineyard venture - the sale of a few personal possessions funding their new life in Portugal.

The first time they set foot on the parched earth of their new home and future income source was a shock. Dropped by taxi during the late afternoon, they stood like a pair of refugees, surrounded by their modest collection of baggage. They were both still under thirty, blond and outrageously good looking. Two young men that you would expect to find on the front cover of *Vogue* magazine, not embarking on a seriously get-your-hands-dirty project.

Tired and emotionally drained, they stared out across the barren earth baking under the glorious Algarve sunshine. The heavy red clay soil had set like concrete due to years of neglect. Making the overcooked earth fertile again would be a monumental task. They were aware that the property had been on the market for some time, but as a working vineyard, it was clear that the last drop of wine was corked a very long time ago.

The house, too, had seen better days. There was nothing white about Casa Branca anymore. Large cracks streaked across the fading façade of what once was a fine-looking building. Long since used farm equipment lay scattered around the outbuildings, abandoned, and left to rust several years before. Unspoken angst rushed through Will's mind, weighing up what they both had so recently lost against what lay before them. What had seemed like a good idea at the time now looked more like a terrible mistake.

Thomas stabbed the heel of his Chukka boot into the concrete-like soil. 'Bloody hell, Will. What *have* we let ourselves in for? I can't imagine anything growing in this!'

Will approached Tommy and held him close. 'Hey, come on. Our future is here, there's no going back for us, not now. This is our new life - yours and mine. We were under no illusion when we came out here. We knew it wasn't going to be easy. Look, if anybody can do this it is you and me. Together, we can rebuild this place and restore it to its former glory. Not just for us but for our children as well. We will make it somewhere they can come and stay whenever they want, and for as long as they want.'

Bolstered by Will's reassuring words of encouragement, Thomas' enthusiasm returned. 'You're absolutely right! We've come this far, so falling at the first hurdle is not going to happen. Come on, let's go and explore minha casa e sua casa.'

Will gave Tommy an admiring look. 'I'm very impressed with your Portuguese, given that you only looked at the phrasebook for about ten minutes on the aircraft.'

'Well, one should always be prepared on the basics.'

They picked up their bags and went inside the house, shut the door behind them and walked towards the heart of their new home. There was a resounding crash as the rusting hinges of the massive pine door came away from the wall. As it smashed onto the debris encrusted tiled floor, they didn't flinch or turn around. As if they had been expecting it to collapse, they just carried on walking.

Instinctively they were drawn to the veranda where they stood for some time, mesmerised by the view. It stretched beyond a small orange grove, across the vineyard, sloping gently down towards the

Atlantic Ocean. In the pastel shades of evening sunshine, the view was stunning.

The smell of dry, dusty earth was replaced by the fresh, pungent scent of tangy pine emanating from the abundance of umbrella pine trees mingling with the sweet scent of lavender growing rampant and spilling over what used to be flowerbeds. The bougainvillea, too, ran wild and unrestrained. Draping itself around the house, as if trying to cover the cracks, in a fusion of pinks, purples, and reds.

Will and Thomas began to feel tension in their bodies trickling away as they breathed in the soft, aromatic air. The sun had started its descent into the Atlantic Ocean, and its orange glow fanned across the horizon for as far as the eye could see. Crickets began scissoring their legs, and the calming resonance soothed their minds.

'There may be a lot for us to do, Tommy, but just look at that! Nobody told us we had a view. I don't know about you, but I can see us sitting here in the evenings and sampling our latest vintage for many years to come.' Thomas nodded agreement as Will opened a bottle of wine; one of several he'd bought at the airport. 'I should have picked up a couple of glasses as well, but never mind. Here's to us!' he said, as he raised the bottle in the air, took a swig, then passed it to Thomas.

With no chairs to relax on, Will sat beside Tommy, dangling his legs over the low, azulejo-tiled wall that encompassed the veranda, captivated by the sunset. 'The first of many sundowners we will share on this terrace with its spectacular view. Then one day, we will celebrate having successfully breathed new life into this desiccated earth and start drinking our own. How about *The Mount of the Grapes* as a name for our new vineyard?'

Thomas looked thoughtful. 'That would be, er, *Monte das Uvas,* in Portuguese I believe. It sounds much better, don't you think?'

Will's heart went out to Tommy. Whatever obstacles lay before them, he could think of no better man to share his new life with. 'It certainly does. I'll drink to that. Here's to *Monte das Uvas,* and here's to us.'

They carried out the initial clean-up operation themselves, turning their hands to fixing, building, and getting everything as ship-shape as possible given their meagre resources.

By the end of the first summer, the sun had bronzed their lean bodies and bleached their hair white. For the first time in their lives, both were truly alive just being together and being themselves.

Thomas soon began receiving letters from his boys. Although he was never one to display his emotions, his face betrayed his heartbreak when nothing ever arrived from Lisa for Will. 'Don't fret, old thing. It wouldn't surprise me if your evil ex-wife is filling your gorgeous girl's head with poisonous lies about you. Lisa *will* answer your letters, I'm sure. Just give her time.'

During the first two years, they laboured tirelessly in the twenty acres of sad, withering vineyard, replanting, and reviving. They each acquired a horse, as it seemed a sensible way of getting around and, over time, their animal family grew with the arrival of several hungry, itinerant dogs and cats who no longer had the need to stray.

Three years later, they took on extra help, including a young Rui Santos, as the resident winemaker. Rui had grown up on a vineyard run by his father, and at the tender age of twenty, knew more about winemaking than either Will or Thomas.

After twelve years, *Monte das Uvas* had become one of the finest vineyards in the region. Will and Thomas successfully used their combined business and marketing skills, together with their passion for wine, to lovingly restore the vineyard. Their reputation for being the perfect hosts at many wine tastings was well-known within the winemaking fraternity.

The Truth About Henry

'I have to say, Lisa, lovie, being so tanned suits you. It makes you look even more gorgeous. We've missed you, though. Haven't we, Jim? This big, old house is very quiet without you.'

'I've missed you both too, Nellie. Portugal was fantastic, and the weather for April was amazing. Dad said he would love you to both go and stay with him, anytime.'

Jim looked anxious. 'That's very kind of him, and we would love to see him again for sure, but I don't know if I would choose to fly. If God had meant us to fly, he would have given us wings, eh Nellie?'

'Take no notice of him, Lisa, lovie. He's turning into a real old codger. Getting him to go to Cheltenham these days is an effort. You tell your dad we would love to go and stay with him.'

'That Henry Cahoon's a lucky blighter!' Jim chipped in, winking at Nellie.

Lisa felt the heat rise in her bronzed cheeks. 'He's a good friend, but that's all…' The tone of her voice was unconvincing as the image of Henry bouncing around on the beach playing Frisbee popped into her head. His skimpy Jantzen swim shorts showcasing the rippling muscles of his solid six-pack and his rugby-playing thighs, with his golden-blond curls flying wildly in the breeze. Clearing her throat, she tucked into her breakfast.

'That's right, Lisa, lovie,' interjected Nellie, 'he's a man, well, just a boy really. It will take him a bit of time to work things out.' She gave Jim a secret smile. 'It took this dozy old bugger a whole year before he even kissed me!'

'Did my mother put in a guest appearance while I was away?' Lisa asked, changing the subject.

'She did, just to check up on dear old Arthur, then she packed her bags and said she was going back to London indefinitely.'

'Did she have anything of any consequence to say?'

'Not really, there was a lot I wanted to say to 'er mind, but I value my job here. Jim and I both love Silkwoods. It's our home. Like you, Jim was born here, well in the Old Lodge.'

'I know, Nellie. And you will never have to worry about living anywhere else. Not while Arthur and I are around. You and Jim are my family, so I wouldn't let you live anywhere else. Did she have anything to say at all… about me? Did she ask where I was?'

'She did ask where you were, and I told her you had gone away with Adele for a bit, like you said. I don't know if she believed me or not. I suppose she must realise what damage she's done.'

Lisa rolled her eyes and laughed. 'This is my mother we are talking about! Anyway, she has gone back to London, hopefully with her tail between her legs and let us hope for all our sakes that she stays there.'

Lisa had written to her mother before she went to Portugal and posted it, together with the photograph of the cache of letters and presents from her father.

How could you be so incredibly cruel? How could you allow me to believe that my father had no interest in me? For twelve years, you've kept up this cruel charade, but you've finally exposed yourself for the deceitful woman you are. I am so upset, so angry. Betrayed by my own mother! Bloody hell! Things don't get much shittier than that. You might as well have stabbed me in the heart. I'm not sure if I can ever come back from this, Mother, so please DO NOT contact me... I have nothing to say to you.

*

'Would you like some?' Adele was munching her way through a large bag of popcorn, waiting for a screening of *Star Wars* in Cheltenham.

Lisa plunged a hand into the bag. 'I never thought you would ask. Thanks.'

'Where's Henry tonight? I would have thought a little intergalactic action would be right up his street.'

'I tried calling him a couple of times today, but he hasn't been around. You know what farming is like. There is always something to do, and now, he's out with the lads, I expect. I really like him, Adele.'

'I had noticed, and I'm happy for you. Henry is a lucky guy. I hope he realises it. If he doesn't, he has me to answer to, and Jack.'

'Jack?'

'Yes, on the rare occasions Jack calls from some far-flung place on his travels, I ask him how his trip is going, but he seems to be more interested in how your romance is progressing.'

Lisa's thoughts flitted to Jack, imagining him tanned on a desert island in the Indian Ocean, wondering if he had a six-pack.

Adele continued. 'What's he like in bed then?'

'Who?'

'Who are we talking about? Henry, of course!'

Lisa's hand dived into the air-popped corn again. She paused holding a kernel close to her lips. 'Well, actually, we've never been to bed together, and we've never kissed properly, either. Henry's a great hugger, and he kisses me on the cheek, occasionally.'

'Oh, I see. Well, sometimes, with boys, you have to take the lead,' Adele confidentially offered sagely nineteen-year-old advice on the male of the species, even though, like her best friend, she was yet to have a boyfriend.

*

Lisa's carefree teenage years were about to end, and she had started to find that her job wasn't challenging enough. 'I want to interview famous people and write gritty pieces about their lives, their successes, and failures, and the inherent good they do for others. Oh, and I would love to review West End productions! But I can't do while I'm based at Silkwoods.' She knew Adele had decided to find work in London and would be looking for a flatmate.

'You are the obvious choice, Li, but there's not much point in asking you to come with me while Mr Greek-God-look-alike-with-a-six-pack is around.'

Henry was the only distraction holding Lisa back from furthering her career and moving to the City. He was fun, kind, and made her feel loved, in a brotherly sort of way, but she wanted more from their relationship than just holding hands. Even her saintly mother had lost her virginity at eighteen. Adele was her only friend who still had her hymen intact - despite her apparent in-depth knowledge of sex and the workings of the male mind. Nellie said it would take time, and Adele had told her that sometimes you had to take the lead with boys. So, it looked like initiating any action was going to be down to her.

One August evening, the air smelt dry and dusty. Bales of hay lay strewn around most of the fields in the county after the harvest. Earlier that day, Lisa had taken Henry's lunch to the fields, artistically arranging a selection of sandwiches and fruit on a travel rug she had unearthed in the boot room. After they had eaten, they lay on the rug as Lisa twirled his long, blond curls around her fingers. He giggled, chewing on a piece of straw, his perfect white teeth glowing in the sunshine. Henry smelt sweet, even mingled with the sweat from a morning's work in the heat, and Lisa found his muskiness intoxicating. Propping himself up on one elbow, he leaned over Lisa. She looked at him expectantly, parting her lips and licking them seductively as Henry's face moved closer to hers. Finally, it was going to happen, their first kiss. He smiled, and she gave a little gasp of anticipation, before closing her eyes. Feeling his lips deliver a fleeting peck on her forehead was a crushing disappointment. Opening her eyes, she watched him leap to his feet, stride back to his tractor, and jump on.

'That was delicious, Li, thank you,' he shouted over the tractor's engine noise. 'I could get used to this!' He pushed the throttle lever forward and drove away, leaving behind only a cloud of black smoke.

She propped herself up on her elbows, her lips tightly pursed. 'Why isn't he interested? Am I doing something wrong?' she thought. 'What has Sylvia Kristel got that I haven't?'

The heat was getting to her, and it wasn't just because the UK was, unusually, enjoying Mediterranean weather. The heat was welling up inside her, and all she could think about for the rest of the day was every inch of Henry, naked. Her passionate urges could wait no longer. It was time to lose her virginity.

That evening, she planned to take Henry by surprise after the long hours he'd spent bouncing up and down on the tractor. Before arriving at Henry's cottage, she made two planned pitstops. At the supermarket, she bought a chilled bottle of Cava and two punnets of strawberries, and at the chemist she purchased, condoms.

From previous visits to the chemist, she had spotted condoms stacked on the shelves behind the counter. Bursting through the door of the tiny pharmacy, she froze. She was overwhelmed with an urge to make her excuses and run out of the shop as Mrs Shrubsole, who she had known since she was a child, was standing between the counter and the condoms.

'Hello, Lisa... what can I help you with today?'

'Er... hello. I'm, er, looking for, er, condoms...' There, she had said it, hastily adding, but without much conviction, 'for a friend...'

Mrs Shrubshole's eyebrows arched, and her eyes widened, as Lisa looked down her nose, wondering if it had grown.

'Goodness, Lisa, what a kind friend you are. Do you know what *type* your friend normally uses?'

Lisa's face burned the colour of her strawberries, her eyes betraying her ignorance on the subject of rubber johnnies. So, the affable, Mrs Shrubsole, had decided to help her out.

'Climax control, extra strength... flavoured?'

'Ah yes, extra strength, those are the ones.' Relieved, she watched Mrs Shubshole pack them away in a good-sized bag.

It was a liberating experience, taking the initiative to organise what would be a momentous occasion in her life. She was almost panting by the time she strode up the garden path to Henry's cottage. The door was never locked, and she let herself in.

Once inside, the excitement of losing her virginity to the beautiful Henry was so overwhelming, she imagined she could hear the breathy sound of heated passion. Then, standing stock-still for a few moments, she realised the heavy breathing was not her imagination. Perhaps Henry was in the process of relieving himself? She was irritated; he could have waited for her. Then she realised she could hear two people panting.

A cold sweat began to dribble down her spine, which would be the cue for most people to slip away silently, but not Lisa, not with her insatiable curiosity. Henry's bedroom door was tantalisingly ajar, so she gently nudged it with the bottle of Cava, and it creaked open. Her jaw dropped, as did one of the punnets of strawberries. Henry, naked, grinning from ear to ear, on all fours on the bed, looked up, his face flushed down to the tops of his muscular shoulders.

'Li! What a surprise!' His voice wobbled with mortification, grabbing a stray pillow to cover his nether regions, as the scene began playing out in slow motion, with Henry's voice becoming a low growl.

'This is my old friend, Ralphie Ferris. We were at school together.' Ralphie snatched his hands away from Henry's taut buttocks, shot off the bed and covered himself with a towel. Sweat trickled down the finely chiselled features of his very red face, which was almost as flushed as Lisa's. 'Ralphie, this is my stepsister, Lisa!'

'Hi, Lisa! How are you doing?' Ralphie puffed. 'Hen has told me so much about you.'

'*Hen? Stepsister?*' Lisa was doing very badly, wishing the ground would swallow her whole. How could she have been so naïve? No! How could she have been so stupid? She felt such a fool. She couldn't speak. She tried something along the lines that she was sorry to interrupt, but her tongue felt like it had quadrupled in size as it was wedged inside her mouth. She slowly backed out of the room and ran out of the cottage, still clutching the bottle of Cava and the surviving punnet of strawberries. Jumping into her old Land Rover, she drove home chastising herself.

As soon as she arrived home, she ran upstairs to her room and put her new Dr Hook album on the turntable, which belted out *Better Love Next Time*. She rang Adele, having popped the Cava cork to drown her sorrows, intermittently popping the odd strawberry in her mouth.

'I cannot believe I have been so stupid.'

'Well, it wasn't obvious, beautiful he may be, but camp? No, not exactly!'

'What do you mean, not exactly!' she snapped. 'You wouldn't know to look at my father that he bats for the other side either, but I should have read the signs, Adele. *We* should have read the signs! All the cosy nights in, Henry painting our toenails.'

'Well, there you go. You can't always judge a book by its cover, you of all people, should know that. Listen, I'm going to pop round and help you finish that bottle of Cava, okay?'

So, if Henry had been holding her back from going to London with Adele, she now had no excuse. It was time to forge ahead with her career.

Luck be an Iron Lady

On the 4th of May 1979, Margaret Thatcher became the first female British Prime Minister and embarked on a countrywide campaign to stir up public support.

'A penny for them?' Arthur's gravelly voice broke the silence. Lisa had been reading snippets from *The Telegraph* to him, but her thoughts had drifted. She was staring out of the mullioned window watching a pair of swans gliding serenely across the lake.

Arthur's question jolted her back to reality. 'Oh, I was just thinking... a majority of forty-three is not exactly a landslide victory, is it? I'm excited that we have a female Prime Minister, but it's sad that Emmeline Pankhurst and her supporters aren't around to witness it. After all the pain and suffering those women went through, sixty-six years after Emily Davidson threw herself under the King's horse for the right to vote, we finally have the first, of hopefully many, female Prime Ministers.'

'I would have thought *you* would want Callaghan back in power?' Arthur teased.

Despite being born into an upper-middle-class family, Lisa's political views had always veered left of centre. 'Okay, I probably did, but I'd still rather see a woman at the helm. No offence, Arthur.'

'None taken! You know I'm a staunch supporter of equality for women. I never thought Maggie would do it, but good on her.' He coughed, a wheezy rattling coming from inside his chest.

'Are you okay?'

'I'm fine, Lisa, there's plenty of life left in this old dog yet. It's you I am worried about.'

'Me? You don't have to worry about me, Arthur. I'm absolutely fine!'

He shook his head. 'Lisa, the amount of time you and I have spent together over the last few years, I *know* when you are *not* fine, and you are *not* fine now!'

There was a degree of frustration in his response, which made her look up from the newspaper. Henry was a regular visitor to Silkwoods. But he'd not been around for some time, and that hadn't escaped Arthur's attention. Did he sense she was trying to block out another disappointment? 'No, really. I'm fine, thanks.'

He cleared his throat, a smile rippling across his face. 'Maybe it's time for you to spread your wings and leave the nest? I think in your heart you know that you need to do this. *Inside Gloucestershire,* have been very lucky to have you. But, like all young people, you need to experience the city. There will be many more opportunities for you to develop your writing in London than around here.'

She knew he was right. 'But living in London will mean spending my life dodging my mother, so I'm not sure.' She intended the remark to be a joke, but Arthur looked serious.

'Your mother, my wife, has a great deal to answer for. You're always trying to avoid her when she comes here! I know what she did to you as a child, Lisa. Telling you your father never tried to contact you was unforgivable. If I was missing any of the details, Nellie didn't hold back. I know you haven't seen or spoken to your mother since hooking up with your father again, and I don't blame you. She will never admit that she is wrong or try to see things from someone else's point of view; it's ingrained in her persona. Freud would have had a field day with her, I think. She lacks the emotional gene that instinctively tells you how other people are feeling. Maybe it's something to do with how she was brought up.'

'She never talks about her childhood; it's like she's blotted it out. I know she was brought up by a battle-axe of an aunt, but I know nothing about my maternal grandparents. I asked her about them once, and it obviously touched a nerve, as it brought on one of her tirades.'

Arthur gave her a sympathetic look. 'I also knew about the aunt. Both your mother's parents died at the same time when she was very young, so I assumed it was during an influenza outbreak. But it is a subject that I too learned very early on is best to avoid.'

'I have found out something though, which I've never told anybody about, and I would rather just keep it between you and I just in case I've got it wrong. I discovered some old photos and papers in a trunk in the attic, including a birth certificate for someone called Elizabeth Clemmens, who I've never heard of, but curiously, she was born on the same day as my mother. The father's name is not on the birth certificate, but do you think Elizabeth Clemmens could possibly be my mother?'

'Well, well, Elizabeth of all people, with all her airs and graces and highfalutin ideas.' Arthur slapped the arm of his wheelchair. 'No wonder she's reluctant to talk about her family. Growing up, parentless, with the stigma of illegitimacy hanging over her? So, is she really Viscount Rutherford's granddaughter?'

Lisa shrugged, 'I don't know, but she's always said he gave her that diamond and sapphire necklace to wear at Queen Charlotte's Ball.'

'Growing up without either of her parents might explain her total lack of empathy, though.'

Lisa gave him a thoughtful nod. 'Yes, you could be right.'

'Elizabeth's heritage aside, your mother is both a selfish and self-absorbed woman, but I have a theory that adverse childhood experiences can be carried through to adulthood, so it may well be the reason for her total lack of compassion.'

'Why did you marry her, Arthur? She never spends any time with you.'

'Well, they say there is no fool like an old fool. I fell for her charms. The poor, bereft divorcee, struggling to bring a child up on her own.'

'Ha! That's a joke!'

'Yes, as I soon found out. Elizabeth was never equipped to be a wife, let alone a mother.' His steely eyes twinkled. 'An actress maybe... But, Nellie, and Eileen before her, have moulded you into a fine young woman.'

Lisa rose to her feet and planted a kiss on his forehead. 'My mother got one thing right, at least.'

'And what would that be?'

'You! You're a wonderful stepfather. I've never told you that before Arthur, and it's important you should know. You don't have to *look* like someone to love them, you know.' She perched on the arm of the sofa beside Arthur's wheelchair and hugged him. 'You won't leave me, now I've told you I love you, will you?'

He smiled, his crusty old face threatening to crack. 'I'm not going anywhere, and I love you too. I am very blessed to have you as a stepdaughter, Lisa. At a time when I thought I would never have children, you came into my life. A seven-year-old ray of sunshine who became the light of my life.'

She gave him another hug. 'Stop it! You're going to make me cry in a minute!'

'There's something else you should know. When Elizabeth and I married, I gave her the equivalent in cash to what the farm and the land at Silkwoods were worth at the time. Your father had the wisdom to put the house in your name when you were born. And I will continue to look after it, and the farm, to the best of my ability. It makes me happy; you make me happy! But you need to think more about yourself. I hear Adele is going to London. Why don't you go with her? Silkwoods is your home. You can come back at any time and always be welcomed with open arms. No one will miss you more than I will, but go to the city with Adele, Lisa. Have some fun and be who you want to be. Interview the great and the good, then write about them. Write a novel! I bet there's at least one book inside you bursting to get out. Whaddaya say? Go spread your wings.'

Arthur had sown the seed in Lisa's brain. One day, she would catch a train at Kemble Station and head for London.

*

A few weeks later, Arthur was sitting in front of a crackling log fire in the drawing room when Lisa burst through the door.

'Arthur! Margaret Thatcher is speaking at the Conservative Party conference on the 12th of October in Blackpool, and I would really like to go.'

'I had heard! And you *must* go - you never know, you might get the opportunity to meet her.'

'Well, the opportunity to hear her speak is good enough for me, so I'll definitely go. Did I ever tell you she became a member of Parliament for the first time, representing Finchley, on the day I was born? She was only thirty-four. I hope I can achieve something of note by the time I'm that age.'

'I knew she represented Finchley, but I didn't know the exact date she was elected. That is indeed an uncanny coincidence. So maybe fate is hatching a plan for you both to meet? I am certain about two things, though. The first thing is that you *will* achieve. You *know* what you want to do, and you are passionate about your writing. And the second thing is that when you are passionate about doing something, fate, together with a little determination, often plays a part in helping you achieve it.' A whoosh of cold air blew down the chimney, causing smoke to billow into the room. 'Now, we must do something about that downdraught before winter is upon us.'

On the 11th of October 1979, Lisa jumped into her Land Rover and headed for Blackpool to hear Margaret Thatcher speak. When she arrived, she hurried to park and find somewhere to stay near the Winter Gardens, as she suspected most B and B's would be booked for the conference. After successfully reversing into a roadside parking space, she checked her wing mirror. The road was clear, so she flung the door open, and fate intervened. There was a thud, then a shout.

'Christ Almighty!'

Lisa jumped out of her Land Rover to find herself straddling a man lying flat on his back. He was wearing a black suit, black tie, and white shirt. She thought he looked like an undertaker, not that she had ever met one. 'Oh, my God! I'm so, so sorry, but I didn't see you. Are you hurt?' Concerned, she extended her hands to pull him up.

'No, I'm okay, thank you. Just look where you are going in future.' He motioned to a black Daimler parked in front of Lisa's vehicle. 'If we hadn't got a damned puncture, this wouldn't have happened. Never mind, I've called a garage. They'll be here soon to fix it.'

'I can change a tyre. I live on a farm.'

His eyes scanned the Land Rover. 'I thought you might, and believe it or not, so can I, but it's probably best if a professional does it. So no, really, it's fine, but thank you for the offer.'

A rear door of the limousine opened. 'Michael? What on Earth is going on? I need to get to the hotel now! What's happened to the back-up vehicle anyway? I can't sit here all day, and it's getting dark. I have people to see, there is so much to do, and I can't do it all from the back seat of a car!'

Lisa was sure she knew that forthright, well-spoken tone, thankfully not her mother's. Then she twigged. It was a voice she had heard so many times before. On TV and on the radio, but not in Blackpool at 6 p.m. in the evening.

'That's,' Lisa whispered, her voice quivering, as she stared at Michael's, my-lips-are-sealed-I-don't-know-what-you-are-talking-about expression. 'Oh, my God! It is, isn't it? It's her, it's *Margaret Thatcher!*' Her eyes lit up like the Blackpool illuminations. She was so excited, she reached out to hug the nodding stranger in front of her, then thought better of it. In barely more than a whisper, and at a hundred miles an hour, Lisa continued, 'I'm Lisa Grant. I'm a reporter for *Inside Gloucestershire*, and I'm a great admirer of Mrs Thatcher's. She is the *only* reason I am here now... to listen to her speak tomorrow.' She sunk her hand into her pocket and pulled out her Press Card. 'Look, I'm official. Are you her... er... driver?'

'I am. But if you want to interview her, you must make an appointment. The PM is very busy, you know.'

She took a deep breath to calm down. 'I don't suppose I could speak to her *now*, could I? I mean, it's not like she is going anywhere until the tyre gets fixed.' She gave him one of her best pleading smiles. 'Just for a minute? I've driven all the way from Gloucestershire.'

With just a glimmer of a grin, Michael repositioned his black-framed glasses on his nose and turned towards the limousine. 'Everything is under control, Prime Minister. The garage man said he would be here in about twenty minutes. I was just talking to this nice young lady from the Land Rover parked behind us. Her name is Lisa Grant, and she's a reporter for *Inside Gloucestershire*. She's driven up from Gloucestershire to hear you speak tomorrow.'

Lisa could hardly breathe; her head was buzzing. Her name had just been mentioned to the British Prime Minister. Open mouthed, she spun round as an unmistakable voice boomed out behind her.

'*Inside Gloucestershire?* Doesn't she realise she is *inside* Lancashire? I must speak to Kenneth Baker about raising the standard for teaching geography in this country.'

Luminous in her magnificence, standing on the pavement almost within touching distance, was the 48th British Prime Minister, Margaret Thatcher. Dressed in a true-blue suit, with cream piping at the ends of the sleeves and around the collar, she was immaculate in every respect, even her hair, despite the biting wind.

'I got 14 A grade O-levels, and one of them was Geography, and got 3 A-levels.' The words tumbled out of Lisa's mouth.

'And what did you get for your A-levels?'

A burly looking man climbed out of a front passenger seat, his eyes darting around. 'Please get back in the vehicle, Madam.'

'Stop fussing, Larry… let her speak.'

'A*'s, Madam, erm, Prime Minister, English Language, English Literature and Philosophy.'

'Not a scientist then, but reasonably bright.'

'I'm a junior reporter for *Inside Gloucestershire*. I've always wanted to write. I am so, so sorry, but I opened my car door and...' She gesticulated towards Michael.

'Yes, yes and he, no doubt, walked straight into it. Now, go on, Michael, find out what's happened to the back-up vehicle and chase this garage chap.' She turned to Lisa smiling. 'If you work for *Inside Gloucestershire*, shouldn't you be reporting on events *inside* Gloucestershire?'

Lisa's heart cartwheeled. 'Yes, Prime Minister, and normally I do, but I want to spread my wings and write about inspiring people, like you...' She bit her bottom lip, instantly regretting the corn-fed words.

'Well, Lisa Grant, you can call me Mrs Thatcher.' She turned to her bodyguard. 'This young lady and I have things to discuss.'

'But, madam,' protested Larry.

Mrs Thatcher gave him a superior glare. 'Does Lisa Grant really look like a terrorist or a red-hot Labourite to you? Now, will you open the door for us to get in, or must I do it myself?'

Lisa managed a weak smile, imagining her chameleon gene turning her true-blue from head to toe. She was about to get her first big break, so it was of paramount importance that she kept her political views to herself and her nerves under control. Grabbing a notebook from her Land Rover, she took a deep breath and slid into the limousine beside Mrs Thatcher. Never in her wildest dreams had she thought she would conduct a one-to-one interview with the Iron Lady. She couldn't wait to tell Arthur. His words, *you might get the opportunity to meet her,* had been spectacularly uncanny. She had nothing prepared, but after being momentarily fazed by the Right Honourable Lady's expectant, piercing blue eyes, she went into overdrive. Fate had presented her with the most significant opportunity of her life to date, and she had no intention of blowing it.

'Mrs Thatcher, you are, unequivocally, an inspiration and role model to myself and all young women of my generation. After your chemistry degree, you worked as a food scientist, which led to creating my favourite ice cream, Mr Whippy. Then you brought up two children before becoming Prime Minister of the United Kingdom. You are living proof that women can do every bit as well as men, if not better. What is the secret of your success in a male-dominated world?'

By the time the back-up vehicle arrived to whisk the Right Honourable Lady away, Lisa had enough material to produce an article about the real Margaret Thatcher, which would make Lisa's editor extremely happy and the sales of true-blue *Inside Gloucestershire* soar.

The following day, she arrived early at the Winter Gardens and was surprised to find Michael waiting for her. He ushered her to a seat overlooking the stage from where she took the best photographs she had ever taken, as she listened to the first of many Iron Lady speeches she would witness over the years.

'Let us work together in hope and above all in friendship. On

behalf of the Government to which you have given the task of leading this country out of the shadows, let me close with these words: You gave us your trust. Be patient. We shall not betray that trust.'

This is the conclusion of Margaret Thatcher's speech at the Conservative Party Conference, Winter Gardens, Blackpool on Friday, October 12th, 1979.'

Escape to London

Adele and Lisa took out a lease on a small, recently refurbished three-bedroomed flat in Notting Hill with their old school friend, Connie. The landlord had painted the whole stucco-fronted pillar-porched house bright yellow, which added to the buzzy, vibrant feel of this multicultural area of central London. Adele had already found a job working for an estate agent and, having failed an audition for RADA, a disgruntled Connie was at a secretarial college.

Lisa was eking out a living writing freelance contributions while trying to find a permanent job. Arthur had offered to pay her a monthly allowance, and she was touched by his generous offer but had refused it saying, 'I'd be breaking my own rules, Arthur! I could never call myself a strong, independent woman if I couldn't fend for myself.'

She had cut off all communication with Elizabeth, who enjoyed free rein with what was left of her divorce settlement, as well as plundering the Goldsworthy bank accounts. Whatever life had in store for Lisa, she would never become a kept woman like her mother, nor could she ever forgive Elizabeth for her ultimate betrayal,

With time to spare between freelance assignments, Lisa began writing the novel that Arthur had suggested. 'I'm calling it *They Always Look at the Mother First*. Loosely, it's a work of fiction,' she told Adele.

'Ah!' Adele responded. 'What's that they say about truth being stranger than fiction? That would be your mother.'

It didn't take long for Lisa's Maggie Thatcher interview to reel in a potential employer; *Stellar* magazine called, inviting her to an interview.

Stellar's plush London offices were on the third floor of a recently converted Victorian building in Farringdon Street. The enormous open-plan office looked more like a sitting room, with an abundance of sofas, lounged upon by scantily dressed young women having their make-up done while waiting to be photographed.

A woman wearing a pixie hat and clad from head to toe in a brightly coloured smorgasbord of stripes and checks, appeared from nowhere. 'Good morning, and who are you, my darling?' she said, running her finger down a list of names on a clipboard.

'I'm Lisa Grant. I'm here for an interview with Penny Lindsay.'

'Ah, yes. Ms Lindsay is expecting you. I'm Miranda, Penny's personal assistant, delighted to meet you. Take a seat, and I will tell her you are here. Can I get you a coffee?'

Lisa's hands were already shaking with nervous anticipation. 'No. I'm fine, thanks.' She couldn't risk tipping the contents of a cup of coffee all over her pale pink interview suit.

'Well make yourself comfortable, I'm sure Penny won't be too long. By the way, I loved your Maggie piece! Especially the bit about her involvement in creating Mr Whippy ice cream. I had no idea.'

Twenty minutes later, a door opened, and a tall woman teetered out wearing four-inch bright-red heels. Swaying slightly, she hung onto the door handle for support. Her eye makeup was suspect, black eyeliner smeared beneath both eyes, and her bleached-blonde beehive hairdo was beginning to slump. Her eyes landed on Lisa. 'Lisa Grant? Penny Lindsay… editor. Come in.'

Lisa sprang to her feet and held out her hand. 'Pleased to meet you, Penny,' she said, expecting a handshake.

Penny turned away and tottered back into her office, and collapsing onto a swivel chair, its wheels propelled her backwards and crashed into the wall behind her. Using both her arms and legs, she heaved herself back under her kneehole desk. Disorderly piles of paper littered the floor, and long-since cooled, half-drunk cups of coffee cluttered most surfaces.

Settled at last, Penny studied Lisa's application letter, then motioned for her to sit. 'I see you were working for *Inside Gloucestershire*. I sincerely hope you are not related to that ghastly Elizabeth Grant woman, are you? Goldsworthy-Grant, I think she calls herself these days.'

Lisa froze. This was not a question she had prepped herself for. Her mother's reputation was everywhere it seemed, and now it threatened to ruin her interview. She panicked. How should she respond? Desperate not to lose this job opportunity, she crossed her fingers and lied, 'Well, I've heard of her… *I think*.' A burning sensation of guilt streaked across both cheeks, 'How do you know her?' she asked, with a sense of dread.

'How do I know her?' Penny scoffed. 'Unfortunately, I was at the Debutantes' House with the wretched woman, '57-'58.'

'*Oh, shit!*' Lisa thought, clamping her arms to her torso as she felt sweat bubbling in her armpits under her pale pink jacket.

'We were an interesting bunch that year,' said Penny, now in full flow. 'One went on to be an IRA freedom fighter. One married a pop star, and one became an international Marxist. Then there was Elizabeth, who ended up as debutante of the year. God knows how she managed it. I'm sure the young queen would not have approved. Elizabeth was so desperate to find herself a wealthy husband, she shagged everybody she met who was listed in Burke's Peerage. She finally pounced on a wealthy poof from Gloucestershire, poor sod.' He was a very handsome young man. I fancied him myself, but everybody knew he was gay. Elizabeth was after his money, of course, but he wasn't her first choice. She was after Bobby Grandborough, the queen's first cousin. Anyway, Will made her pregnant, apparently, which I doubt was part of her cunning little plan. And, of course, she was shagging my husband as well, and still is.'

A lump rose in Lisa's throat, and her brain worked overtime. '*Oh, bloody, Hell!*' Her mother's long-time boyfriend, Jeremy, had married a Lady Penelope Lindsay, who was at finishing school with her mother. '*Oh, no!*'

 Penny sighed, plumping up her beehive with both hands. 'Their sordid little relationship started while we were still at the Debutantes' House. No scruples, that one. She's married to an elderly wealthy American now. No doubt waiting for him to pop his clogs while she enjoys a bit on the side... *my husband*, Jeremy Jermayne! I use my maiden name for professional purposes.'

Lisa began to feel light-headed. This was her job interview, but she felt more like an agony aunt as Penny seemed intent on getting things off her chest. 'I'm so sorry,' she muttered, wondering why she felt the need to be sympathetic, but needing to change the subject, 'Maybe you should divorce him?'

'Divorce him? Why would I want to divorce him? I love the silly little shit, or I used to. Perhaps you're right. Perhaps I should. He thinks I don't know about their sordid little affair, but I'm a journalist, for God's sake. I research and investigate. How could he be so naïve to think I would never find out?'

Lisa sat transfixed. She was just about to change the subject and talk about her abilities as a journalist, when Penny took a hip flask from a drawer, poured most of its contents into a cold cup of coffee, and drained the contents.

'Anyway, I really liked your piece about Mrs T, so there's a job for you here if you want it. I don't know how you did it, but if you can wangle an audience with the sodding P.M., interviewing pop stars wearing ball-crusher trousers won't be a problem. Oh, and I need someone to cover the theatre, cinema, and music events as well. Impossible hours I'm afraid, but somebody's got to do it, and I'd like you to start tomorrow.'

Stellar

Lisa's desk at *Stellar* was in a recess on the landing at the top of the third floor stairs. A niche, in its Victorian heyday, that might have housed a mahogany linen chest. Close to the door of the unisex lavatories, the smell of hydrochloric acid constantly hung in an invisible cloud around her workspace.

An Apple II computer took up most of her desk, and a wheeled trolley next to it supported a printer the size of a tank. Everyone who arrived at *Stellar*, had to pass her, which tested her powers of concentration, and unless they were one of the Twiggy-esque models, they had difficulty squeezing past, to get to the lavatory. After only a few weeks in the job, she knew precisely how long each staff member took to perform their ablutions. Those with a book, or a newspaper concealed under an arm took only a few minutes, while others who exited in a cloud of pungent marijuana smoke took much longer.

Lisa enjoyed the job and was out of the office most of the time, although the inevitability of coming face to face with Jeremy Jermayne was always at the back of her mind. How would Penny react when she found out that she'd lied about who she really was?

She had just returned from interviewing Sigourney Weaver, who was in London promoting her new movie *Aliens,* and was rocking back and forth in her chair contemplating how to start the piece, when from the stairs a poorly rendered imitation of Rod Stewart singing '*if you want my body, and you think I'm sexy,*' grew louder until a tall, skinny man in a pinstriped suit appeared and plonked his backside on the edge of her desk. She looked up at him, scowling, as he flashed her a cheesy grin.

'Excuse me! I am trying to work here!'

'Well, it's good to know somebody actually works in this place,' he said, laughing, which to some extent camouflaged the whiny tone of his voice.

'Look… if you don't mind, I've got a deadline to make.'

'Oh, I am sure you have, Sweet Pea.'

'My name is Lisa!' she snapped.

'Ah, sweet and feisty! I know your name is Lisa, and I've no doubt you'll make your deadline. My wife is constantly singing your praises!'

'Your wife?'

'Yes, my wife, the adorable Penelope Lindsay, and your boss. I'm Jeremy Jermayne, how very lovely to meet you at last, Lisa Grant. I'll see you on the way out, Sweet Pea, and keep up the excellent work!' He slid off her desk and crossed the open-plan area to Penny's office, letting himself in without knocking, which brought on a loud tirade of expletives from his wife that everyone could hear until he hastily shut the door behind him.

'And don't you dare call me Sweet Pea again, you… patronising twat!' she hissed to herself. Then, switching to autopilot, she rattled off her piece on Sigourney Weaver within the hour. Jeremy was still in Penny's office. What on Earth could he be doing in there for so long? Penny was always so edgy, wanting to get on with things when she hadn't got something to get off her chest, so any meetings with her never lasted more than five minutes. It was almost 6 p.m., and she had every intention of being out of there before Jeremy repeated the palaver of perching on her desk again.

When raised and angry vocal exchanges were heard coming from Penny's office, Miranda scurried past her desk. 'Sounds like a row from hell, my darling. I would skedaddle if I were you!'

Lisa made a grab for her haversack and snatched her Sigourney Weaver piece off the printer, just as Penny and Jeremy stormed out of the office.

'One minute, young lady, where do you think you are going?'

'I've finished my copy, Penny, and I'm…'

'Oh, no. You're not going anywhere! You're Elizabeth Grant's sprog, aren't you? You lied to me!'

'I…'

'Answer me?'

'Well, no…, well, technically, yes, but I really wanted the job, Penny. I'm not in contact with her. I don't want anything to do with her!' She glanced at Jeremy who was leaning against the wall with a slimy grin on his face.

'Elizabeth was always a consummate liar, so it obviously runs in the family. Like mother, like daughter!'

'One thing I do not do, is lie!' Lisa protested. 'Lying is my mother's prerogative, and I am absolutely *nothing* like her! She told me my father had abandoned me and kept that little charade going for twelve years. I might have told you a little white lie, but it was only because I really wanted this job. Please do not put me in the same category as my mother. You don't know me well enough to judge.'

'Clearly! And by the way, you are fired!'

'Why? What have I done?'

'It's not what you've done! It's who you are! You can tell me as many porky pies as you like, but I draw the line at employing the spawn of the Goldsworthy-Grant trollop, and now my husband tells me he thinks he's your father!'

'What? There is no way I could be his daughter!' Lisa felt like Penny had just slapped her across the face. Anger rising, she stood motionless in disbelief, her eyes vacillating from Penny to Jeremy. Someone flushing the lavatory spurred her into action. Before she did something she might regret, she flew down the stairs two steps at a time. From the last flight before bursting out of the main entrance door, she heard Penny yell after her, 'And don't come back, Lisa Grant!' Then to Jeremy, 'And, as for you, you bastard, enough is enough, I am calling my solicitor.'

Agony Aunt

She ran as fast as she could, away from the offices at *Stellar* and the ghastly Jeremy. As she dodged people on the crowded pavement, there was only one thing she could think about. Had her mother been lying to her, for twenty years, about who her father really was? Lying to her about Will not getting in touch was unforgivable but lying to her about her paternity would be deceit on a totally different level. Just how low could her mother stoop?

She only stopped running when she came to a coffee shop. Crashing through the door, she threw herself onto a stool at the bar, trying to control her breathing.

'A penny for them, my little whirlwind?' A soft, reassuring voice penetrated her chaotic thoughts, and she looked up into the kindly smile of an older woman; her face creased with laughter lines, and a pair of wire-rimmed spectacles perched on the bridge of her nose, framing, and magnifying her dark brown eyes.

'You look like you have all the troubles of the world on your young shoulders.' The woman took Lisa's arm and guided her to an alcove table. 'Come, let us sit here and chat for a while. But first, what is your poison, bubala?'

'A white coffee would be great, thank you.' The woman looked familiar, or was it that she reminded her of someone?

'I'll bring them over,' the girl behind the bar shouted, as she started laying a tray.

'Thank you, that would be kind,' the woman replied, then turned

165

her attention to Lisa. 'My name is Mira. What is yours?'

'It's Lisa Grant, and I'm pleased to meet you.' While gathering her scattered thoughts and putting them into some semblance of order, she kept looking at this kind Samaritan's short dark hair and wire-rimmed glasses, she felt she should recognise them, but from where? Then as the waitress placed a tray on the table, it hit her. 'You're Mira Madre, *Focal Point's* Agony Aunt.'

Mira smiled reticently. 'Ah, my cover is blown! I would like to think that after all these years of straight-talking, or simply speaking common sense, which is what I like to call it, that, yes, I have helped some weary travellers along the road. Now I would like to help you. What could it be that troubles such a young soul with the path of life stretched out before her?'

Lisa didn't need much coaxing. The life and times of Lisa Grant came flooding out like a breached dam.

Several coffees later, Mira had homed in on the real problem. 'So, what are the overriding feelings you have for your mother?'

'Indifference, hurt and betrayal. She is my mother; nothing can change that. It's just that I can't feel it in my heart to *love* her. Does that make me a bad person?'

Mira reached across the table and took Lisa's hands in her own, 'No, it doesn't. It sounds like she has never given you affection, my little bubala, so I'm not surprised you cannot find it in your heart to love your mother. That must have hurt you so badly.'

'Yes, I was hurt. But most of all, I felt betrayed.'

'Ah, yes, the B-word crops up yet again.'

'Ever since then, I've tried to forget what she did and block her out of my life.'

'And have you succeeded?'

'No. My mother is always there, constantly niggling, irritating, intruding, not to mention demeaning.'

'Well, my sons may think the first three apply to me, but mothers should always have their child's best interests at heart. I cannot understand the mentality behind someone who demeans her daughter. A mother should love her children unconditionally.'

'She has never credited me for anything. According to her getting straight As in my O and A*s in my A-levels was a *stroke of luck.* She even came up with the bizarre idea that any boyfriend I might have will look at her first. The rationale behind her theory is that they will always look at her first to see if she is ageing well, which of course she is, and she never goes out of the house until she looks like the queen. I honestly feel that sometimes she thinks she *is* the queen with all her airs and graces. And now she's lost me my bloody job!'

'I think maybe she is a narcissist. It would seem she has a grandiose sense of self-importance. She lacks empathy and shows arrogant, haughty behaviours and attitudes. She sounds like a very mixed-up lady.'

Lisa shrugged. 'I've only just found my dad again, and now I'm worried that my mother's long-term lover might be my father. Surely she couldn't be so evil and have lied to me about that as well?'

'Let us hope not...'

'But whatever she does to grind me down, I don't hate her. I can't *hate* her, even when she continues to behave so outrageously.'

'Poor, Lisa Grant, it is so difficult for children with narcissist mothers, but you are beautiful, and you are strong. You will *not* let your mother grind you down. Maybe you should think about why your mother is like she is? Sometimes children who grow up without parents have low self-esteem, and you tell me that her parents died when she was young.'

'I've always believed that something in her past must have made her like she is.'

'Perhaps, so. But it doesn't excuse the way she has behaved. Growing up without your mother's love would not have been easy for you and, without your father's love too, for many years.'

'True, although I did, and still do, have people around me who care.'

'But still, your early years were not the easiest, my little bubala. Now, what is this you seem so intent on not letting go of?'

The printout of her interview with Sigourney Weaver lay on the table, a ring of spilt coffee in the middle of the page. 'Oh, I interviewed Sigourney this morning.'

'Ah, yes, I heard she was in town. So, what are you going to do with the piece now?'

Lisa thought for a moment. 'Penny only wanted a thousand words, and I took my own photos. Maybe if I beefed it up a bit, I could sell it. I freelanced before I worked for *Stellar*.

'I think Anna might be interested.'

'Anna Lockwood? Your editor?'

'Yes, I am sure she would be very interested. Due to sickness and maternity leave, we had no one to cover the story this morning. Finish your piece and let me have it as soon as you can. Oh, and please give me your telephone number, and I will pass it on to Anna. Listen, my little bubala, if you would like to talk more about Mummy Dearest, here is my number. Call me at any time. I make a good ear. Now, I'd better get back to the office and try to earn an honest living. It was very nice meeting you, Lisa Grant.'

'It's been wonderful meeting you, Mira.'

The Spark of a Flame

Just as Lisa was beginning to enjoy her adult life, the incident at *Stellar* rocked her to the core and triggered nightmares about her paternity. She needed to know the truth, but it was a conversation she was loathed to have with her mother and broaching the subject with her father would be awkward.

'Oh, by the way, Dad, was it really your sperm that headbutted my mother's egg?'

To take her mind off things, Adele suggested they stay with her parents for the weekend, leaving Connie in charge of the flat. 'A weekend in the country will do us both good, and what's the worst that can happen? Connie consumes a bottle of wine and shags her new boyfriend?'

Lisa feigned shock, but it made her think. After her first misguided lust for Henry, she'd thrown herself into work and hadn't allowed her mind to dwell on sex. Maybe it was time to reconsider?

As Always, Adele's family welcomed her with open arms, saying all the right things as she regaled the whole sad getting fired story. Jack was there too. She hadn't seen him since before he took off on his backpacking trip around the world. He'd left a gangly, overgrown schoolboy with a passion for beer and skateboards, and returned as a mature, conscientious, career-focused young man, eager to make his way to the top of his chosen profession. He'd graduated from university with an honours degree in History and English and recently joined an established London-based publishing firm not far from the flat he rented which was only a ten-minute walk from Lisa and Adele's.

Jack was listening intently as Lisa poured her heart out, and responded sympathetically when, after one too many glasses of wine, she burst into tears.

'Oh, Li... come here.' He wrapped both arms around Lisa, clasping her to his chest. 'Hey, come on now. It can't be that bad, can it?'

If it had not been for the wine, Lisa wouldn't have sobbed into his chest, but relaxing into his arms, she felt a sense of security flood through her whole being.

After Jack and Adele's parents went to bed, Jack put an LP on the turntable and opened another bottle of wine.

'I shouldn't have any more.' Lisa made a feeble attempt to cover her glass with her hand. 'Especially as I have just disgraced myself in front of your parents.'

'You've done nothing of the sort, you have every right to be upset,' Jack interjected, plonking himself on the sofa next to her.

Adele remarked, 'Jack's right, Li. Quite honestly, Lady Penelope, sounds like a really evil cow, and there is no way the supercilious Jeremy could possibly be your father. Just one more glass and, if you pass out, Jack will carry you up to bed.' It was just a joke, but by the time the record got to track five, Lisa was fast asleep.

'She's not been sleeping at all well since that business at *Stellar*, Jack,' Adele whispered.

'I'm not surprised! I'll take her up.' Jack got to his feet and cradled

Lisa gently in his arms. 'She's lost weight too.'

Adele noticed the intent, caring look in her brother's eyes, a look she had never seen before. 'I wonder?' She thought. 'Can sparks fly at unexpected times? I suppose both people need to be conscious at the same time, though.' She scolded herself for getting carried away, but she liked the idea of having Lisa as a sister-in-law.

Jack carried Lisa into his sister's room and lowered her gently onto the spare bed she had slept in when visiting since she was a child. Kneeling by the bed, he studied her face. His quickening heartbeat took him by surprise. She looked so vulnerable that he was consumed with an overwhelming urge to lie down next to her and hold her in his arms. For the first time since knowing Lisa, he appreciated her beauty. He'd always been fond of her, but at that moment, he realised he was feeling something much more profound. A warm, fuzzy sensation surged through his body, which his academic brain was struggling to process. He gently took her hand and held it against his cheek. He inhaled slowly, as his mind drifted back to the day Lisa had bought her first bottle of Paco Rabanne while on holiday with his family in France. She blew half her spending money on it.

'Sod the price, I smell wonderfully French!' she had said, dabbing her perfumed-soaked fingers against her neck.

'Paco Rabanne is Spanish!' Adele quipped.

'French, Spanish, who cares, I smell exotically European!'

He remembered bending his head towards Lisa's neck to inhale the perfume and saying, 'It really suits you…' Five years on and watching her sleep, he felt if he lost her, the bottom would fall out of his world. How blind he had been. He was about to kiss her lips when his sister walked into the room.

'It makes you wonder what life will throw at her next,' she whispered, putting her hands on her brother's shoulders. 'She's been so happy since she got the job at *Stellar,* and now this. Her bloody mother has a lot to answer for.'

Jack looked up at his sister and smiled. 'I'm happy that she has us.' Rising to his feet, he gave his sister a hug before quietly slipping out of the room.

Fisticuffs at Fanny's

Because it would be inconvenient and expensive for Lisa's friends to travel to Portugal for her twenty-first birthday, Will and Thomas made a rare trip to London to organise a party at Lisa's favourite restaurant in Soho, Fanny's Bistro.

Fanny was the most welcoming of hosts, a colourful character who stood out in the heart of London's West End. Her roots were embedded in the East End, but her parents originated from India and Thailand. Fanny's was well-known as a popular multi-cultural hub for young people, as she provided a DJ or live music most nights.

Working from home, churning out freelance contributions, Lisa had become a consummate workaholic, often skipping meals, her body running on adrenalin alone during the day. She was at her skinniest, her svelte physique showing off the outfit she had bought for the evening to perfection. It was a short, bandeau-style vintage velvet black dress made from a minimal amount of fabric that hugged her body, accentuating her tiny waist, hips, and thighs, the hem coming to an abrupt halt four inches above her knees. It was also the ideal outfit to showcase her bronzed shoulders and legs after two weeks in the Portuguese sunshine. The look was complemented by the 21st birthday present from her father and Thomas, a three-coloured gold necklace with matching bracelet and earrings. Even her mother would be impressed!

She loved Will with all her heart, but the possibility of him not being her biological father still hung over her like a black cloud. After meeting Jeremy for the first time, she knew he was the last person on Earth she would ever want to call Dad. It was bad enough with a mother like Elizabeth but having Jeremy as a father would be the ultimate genetic disaster. The only person who knew for sure was her impossible mother, but she had cut all ties with her, so it would be a conversation they were unlikely to have.

When the doorbell rang, Adele pushed her boyfriend towards the hallway 'That will be Jack! Let him in, Mike, then open another bottle of Cava, and I'll go and see if Li's ready, because we'll have to head for the Tube soon.' Just as she was about to tap on Lisa's bedroom door, it opened. 'Oh, wow! You look fab. Connie's boyfriend, Danny, is here and Jack's just arrived, we ought to think about making a move in about twenty minutes!'

Lisa did a dramatic pirouette holding her arms out to the side. 'Honestly, what do you think?'

'Well, I know you've been keeping me in the dark about what you were wearing, but you look fabulous.'

'Oh, good. I'm glad you like it. I got it in Kensington Market. It's my new favourite shop.' She fingered the expensive looking three-gold necklace. 'This is one of my presents from my father.' She held up her wrist. 'I say one, as he bought me this matching bracelet and the earrings, too.'

When Lisa entered the sitting room, Jack's jaw dropped.

'What?' She giggled, pushing him playfully in the shoulder. 'Is it that much of a shock I'm not wearing dungarees and Doc Martens?'

'Happy Birthday, Li. Not a shock, exactly, no. Just confirmation of what I already thought. You are drop dead gorgeous and I would be very proud to escort you to your birthday party. I guarantee that when we walk into Fanny's, heads will turn. You look stunning.'

After catching a tube to Oxford Circus, they all walked the short distance to Fanny's Bistro, where Lisa's father and Thomas were waiting.

Will kissed her cheek then held her at arm's length. 'You look terrific, my darling! I cannot believe that my beautiful girl is twenty-one.'

She wrapped her arms around him. 'I am so pleased you are here. Thank you so much for my beautiful present, and for organising the party.'

'It's an absolute pleasure, and Fanny is one in a million. What a character! It has been quite an experience working with her!'

'Oh, my, God!'

'What's the matter?'

'My mother...'

'What about her?'

'She's just walking through the door with Jeremy bloody Jermayne!'

'I didn't think you asked her'

'I hadn't!'

'Well, I'm the last person she would want to see.' Will turned to Thomas with an apologetic look. 'Apart from you that is. Why don't you check out the kitchen? If there's to be a scene, I'd rather handle it on my own, sorry.'

Lisa gripped her father's hand and watched her mother sweep into Fanny's like royalty, dripping jewels, and looking down her nasal bridge, as if half expecting to step into something unsavoury. A stampede of waiters jockeyed for position to take her coat. It was doubtful that the successful waiter had reached the ripe old age of twenty-one, but Elizabeth wouldn't think twice. She smouldered towards him, holding his stare, and pouting seductively. Rolling her shoulders, she extended both arms, and her ostentatious full-length mink coat slid into the young waiter's hands, revealing a full-length Vivienne Westwood designed silk taffeta off the shoulder ball gown.

'Lisa, dear,' she boomed in her best Foghorn-Leghorn-I'm-extremely-posh voice. 'I didn't want to disappoint you by not showing up to your twenty-first birthday party. I think your invitation must have got lost in the post.'

Lisa gave her father's hand a last squeeze then let go and whispered, 'Stay calm, Dad. I'll handle this. She's not going to ruin my birthday.'

Her mother glided over to Lisa, grazing her cheek with her own on both sides while simulating kissing noises.

'Happy birthday.' She pressed an envelope into Lisa's hand. 'It's a voucher for us both to be pampered from head to toe at *Harrods*. I thought it would be wonderful for you and me to spend some girly time together.'

Adele and Jack moved in grimly, like a pair of mafia bodyguards, and stood alongside Lisa and her father.

Elizabeth eyes scanned Lisa from head to toe. 'You look positively feminine, for once, Lisa, dear. Things are looking up.' Then peering closer at her daughter's knees, she added, 'although your choice of dress doesn't leave very much to the imagination. I understand you've already met Jeremy. You do know he's your...'

Jeremy clicked his patent leather heels together, looking at Lisa like an expectant puppy waiting to be thrown a bone.

Lisa held her breath, repeating the word *no* in her head several times. Surely Elizabeth wasn't going to bring up the subject of her paternity at her 21st birthday party in front of her father and all her friends.

Elizabeth smugly studied Lisa's face, searching for a reaction, before finishing her sentence, '... editor's husband, I understand.'

Lisa exhaled, but she knew her mother would find another opportunity to belittle or embarrass her. 'My ex-editor's husband, actually. I'm amazed Jeremy didn't tell you she fired me while he was standing there. And, from what I overheard, Jeremy should be my ex-editor's ex-husband by now. Am I right?' The room went silent as all eyes flitted from Lisa to her mother.

Sensing an impending conflict, Fanny arrived with a loaded tray of drinks and stood between Elizabeth and Lisa. 'A glass of w*h*ine for Lisah Granties mummy?'

Elizabeth's eyes scanned Fanny's face before giving the tray of wine a disdainful look. 'Not if it is that awful Monte das Uvas. No, I would prefer a gin and tonic.'

Fanny beckoned a waiter. 'That would be a Bombay Sapphire and tonic for Lisah's Granties mummy, Alfonso, thank you.'

'Oh, good heavens, *no*.' Elizabeth glowered at Fanny. 'I certainly don't want anything that's been brewed in Bombay! I only drink Gordons. I assume you stock fine English gin in this establishment?'

'Yes, that would be Bombay Sapphire, made in Hampshire. Gordons is made in Scotland, but our customers must always have what they want, but you must be the only person in the world who doesn't like Monte das Uvas, Lisah's mummy. Did you know it received the Wine of the World Award this year? You're missing out, you know.' Fanny tossed her flowing black hair over her shoulders and moved away. She paused as she walked past Will and whispered, 'Lisah Grantie is just like her dhaddy.'

Will laughed and stepped towards his ex-wife. 'How *lovely* to see you, Elizabeth, and Jeremy, too, *such* a surprise.' He glanced at Lisa. 'More of your friends are arriving, why don't you go and greet them? I'll join you in a minute.' He put a hand on Jeremy's shoulder. 'Go and grab yourself a drink, old boy. Our host with the most, Fanny, over there will sort you out.' Jeremy flinched at being touched by a gay man and beat a hasty retreat. 'It's been a long time, Elizabeth.' Will continued. 'Fourteen years, if you've been counting. My... how time flies. But today is a special occasion for our beautiful daughter. Tonight, is *Lisa's* night, and nobody is going to spoil it for her.' He dipped his head and whispered into Elizabeth's ear. 'And that includes *you*, my dear. Now, why don't you join your old friend Jerry for a drink, eh? Your gin and tonic should be ready by now.' He planted an emotionless kiss on her cheek, which she wiped away with the tips of her fingers.

When Lisa's father joined her at the entrance, she smiled as he pecked the cheek of one of her old schoolfriends. 'I'm so proud of you, you're such a charming host.'

'I try to be, Lisa. But I saw red when your mother made her entrée royale. I've had a word with her. Let's hope she takes the hint.'

'Knowing her I doubt it, Dad.' Then she realised that her mother and Jeremy were greeting people a short distance away.

'Oh, my goodness, Julia, *what* a lot of weight you've put on. Mind you, your mother always was a big lady, so it was inevitable, I suppose. It's in your genes, I'm afraid.'

Lisa gave her father a resigned look. 'Well, we can't throw her out, so I'm just going to ignore her. After all the trouble you've gone to, I'm determined not to let her spoil the party.'

Will and Thomas had arranged a superb sit-down dinner inspired by Lisa's favourite Thai dishes. Chicken satay, Thai-style poached salmon and mango sticky rice.

Lisa had chosen her table very carefully. Jack, Adele, and Mike. Henry and his latest flame Charles, Connie and her boyfriend, Danny, with Charlotte, Julia, and their partners. She felt sorry for her father and Thomas, who hastily reorganised their table to include her mother and Jeremy.

Before the tables were cleared to create a dance floor, her father tapped a glass with a knife indicating he wanted quiet in the room. 'Ladies and gentlemen, please could I have your attention? The sooner I have it, the sooner I will say what I need to, and you can all carry on and party. Firstly, I want to thank Fanny and her fantastic team for allowing us to take over her fine restaurant. I now understand why Fanny's is Lisa's favourite restaurant. Thank you *all* for coming here tonight to celebrate Lisa's twenty-first birthday.

'Being twenty-one is a milestone in a young life. Mine seems like a very long time ago, but I remember it very well. I was up all night and finally went to bed at around four o'clock in the morning. No, I hadn't been painting the town red.' Eyes glistening, as he paused. 'I was looking after my beautiful baby daughter, who had a very nasty bout of colic. I am so very proud of Lisa. She has been through a great deal in her young life. As some of you will know, her mother and I divorced when Lisa was six. It was a painful time for us all but particularly for Lisa, who was too young to understand. 'So many people have helped mould Lisa into the fine young woman she is today. Eileen Fisher, Jim and Nellie Liddington, the Wilde Family, who I'm delighted to say are all with us tonight. You have all been such a tremendous influence in Lisa's life, nurturing her from a beautiful, caring child into a beautiful, caring adult.' Thomas shouted, *Hear, Hear*, and Will paused again as Nellie pulled out a hankie and blew her nose.

An irritated Elizabeth mumbled something to Jeremy, who hissed, 'What about Elizabeth? You haven't mentioned her. She has been a *tremendous* influence on Lisa's life!'

Will looked at Lisa sheepishly, and mouthed, *sorry* 'Ah, yes, and Elizabeth, of course.' For those of you who don't know, this is Elizabeth, Lisa's fond mama and my ex-wife.' Elizabeth managed a royal wave. 'Elizabeth has been a *tremendous* influence on Lisa, in terms of *trying* to mould and shape her path in life.' The comment was met with jeers from Lisa's friends but, Elizabeth, enjoying her limelight moment, seemed not to notice.

Will continued. 'But those of you who know Lisa well will know that she has a mind of her own and has carved her own path in life!'

'Oh, for goodness sake!' Elizabeth growled.

Will ignored the interruption. 'And we mustn't forget Lisa's stepfather, Arthur Goldsworthy. Unfortunately, as Arthur finds the London commute too difficult these days, sadly he is not with us tonight. But Arthur is someone for whom Lisa has an enormous amount of love and respect. He deserves much credit for moulding my daughter into the intuitive young woman she is today. Arthur was always there to help and encourage Lisa, especially during her academic years. He nurtured her love for the arts, her passion for writing and supported her ambition to pursue a career in journalism. On a personal note, I am indebted to him for doing the job I would have relished had the circumstances been different. I have very much enjoyed being with you all this evening. My daughter has some wonderful friends. The night is still young and, as you will have already noticed, the disco is set up in the corner. So, I'm expecting everybody under the age of thirty to dance until the wee small hours or until Fanny kick's you all out, which will be long after us older folk have gone home to our dressing gowns and slippers.' He flashed Elizabeth a wry smile as waiters rushed around filling champagne glasses with pink fizz. The waiter who had removed Elizabeth's mink took his time filling her glass and gazing into her eyes, which, much to Jeremy's irritation, caused excessive fluttering of her false eyelashes.

'I think you will all agree that my daughter looks stunning tonight.' With whoops and cheers from the gathering, 'I can't believe that you are twenty-one, my darling. Where has the time gone?' He grinned at Jeremy stifling a yawn. 'Don't worry, Jerry, I'm just about to wind things up…'

'Thank God for that!' Elizabeth hissed.

I just wanted to say how proud of you I am, Lisa. I told you when you were six that you were my world, my universe, my moon, and stars. You still are, and you always will be. You are kind, loving, and one of the most tenacious people I have ever met. A chip off the old block, really! So, ladies and gentlemen, in honour of my beautiful daughter on her twenty-first birthday, Thomas and I have launched our new baby… *Monte das Uvas Champanhe Lisa…* our vineyard's first-ever champagne. Now, let us all raise our glasses to Lisa! Happy birthday, darling!'

By the time she had drained her second glass of champagne, Lisa's head was buzzing. She said goodnight to her father and Thomas, who were sharing a cab with Adele's parents, then headed for the dancefloor. She'd only taken a few steps when Elizabeth and Jeremy blocked her path. 'Ah, Mother! Are you both on your way out? I do hope so. Thanks so much for the girly gift and see you sometime… never!'

Jeremy took a step closer. 'Don't you dare speak to your mother like that!'

Lisa's mouth snapped open, her alcohol-fuelled brain scrambling into some sort of sobriety. 'And just who the hell are you to tell me what to do, Jeremy Jermayne? Just because you've been shagging my mother since before I was born, it doesn't give you the right to tell me what to do. Get it?'

For the second time that evening, complete silence fell at Fanny's as the needle on the arm of the record player scratched Abba's *Waterloo* to a halt.

'Lisa! How dare you! I cannot believe I gave birth to such a rude daughter!'

'And I cannot believe you gave birth to me at all! You're a consummate liar, incredibly selfish and someone who doesn't give a shit about anyone else but yourself! Maybe that's why you and Jeremy have stuck together for so long! Two peas in the proverbial pod and all that.'

Elizabeth flushed with anger, or maybe it was too much gin. 'Lisa,

I won't let you talk to me like this!'

'Great! Then stay out of my life, and I won't need to talk to you at all!'

'Fine, if you feel like that, then so be it. But before we go, there is something I do need to tell you! It's more than just a possibility that Jeremy is your biological father! I realise I should have told you before, but…'

There were more gasps from around the restaurant, and somebody dropped a glass.

'So you thought you'd hang on to that little gem for twenty-one years, did you, Mother? For twelve years you lied to me about my father not wanting to see me, and now this. How low can you get?'

Jeremy chimed in, 'So, as there is more than just a possibility that you are lucky to have me as a father, I would like to have more input in your life!'

'Shut up, Jeremy!' Lisa pushed him out of the way and eyeballed her mother. 'You know what? I don't believe one single word that comes out of your mouth anymore. In fact, I never have, and as for you, Jeremy, I am delighted that Penny finally kicked you out. The pair of you! Dipping in and out of your families' lives when it suits you. But, if you think you can ever play happy families with me, either of you, you can go to hell! And talking of families, Mother, why do you keep yours locked in a trunk? Were you ever going to tell me about *your* mother, Gertrude Clemmens?'

Elizabeth's expression changed instantly from smug to shocked.

'How do *you* know about her?'

'I found your birth certificate in a trunk in the attic. I was trying to find where you might have hidden all the letters and presents from my father that you kept hidden from me for twelve years.'

Jeremy's eyes widened. 'You told me you were Viscount Rutherford's granddaughter, Elizabeth.'

'Take no notice of her, Jeremy! I *am* Viscount Rutherford's granddaughter. Lisa has always been delusional, and now she is also disgracefully drunk. I have no idea what she's talking about.'

'As far as I'm concerned, I never want to see either of you again!' Lisa pointed a shaking finger at Jeremy. 'And there is about as much chance of him being my father as there is of you ever turning into a truthful human being, Mother!'

Lisa's outburst hit a nerve. She watched her mother's eyes narrow and her lips tighten, as she lifted her arm and swung it, slapping the palm of her hand against Lisa's cheek, which made her stagger backwards.

Jack moved in and snatched Lisa out of the way. 'Elizabeth… you really are a very nasty piece of work.'

'That's enough!' All five foot of Fanny waded in between Lisa and her mother. 'Time to go home, Lisah's mummy! Out of mah restaurant. Go and find your dressing gown and slippers, there's a good girl. Why you wud wan to sabotage your daughter's birthday party, let alone hit her, is beyond me. Granddaughter of a bloody viscount or not, I do not allow thugs in mah restaurant. Now get out!'

'You heard what she said.' Jack left Lisa's side and steered Elizabeth and Jeremy towards the door.

'But *I* haven't finished talking to *my* daughter yet. Jeremy said, spinning around as Lisa took a step towards him.

'I am *not* your daughter, and you are *not* my father, and you *never* will be! I never want to see either of you again!'

'Are you deaf, Mr Jermayne?' Jack asked. 'I could have sworn that I heard Lisa say she never wanted to see either of you again!'

When Jeremy pushed past to get to Lisa, Jack tapped him on the shoulder, and when he spun around, Jack punched him in the face, knocking him to the floor.

Lisa, who had been struggling to hold back the tears, puffed out her cheeks and burst out laughing. 'Good shot, Rocky! Great right hook.'

Jeremy looked up at Jack with a dazed expression and blood dribbling from his nose onto his pristine white dress shirt. From his top pocket, he unfolded a white, monogrammed handkerchief and dabbed at his face. 'Please don't hit me again!' he whimpered.

'Oh, get up, Jeremy!' Elizabeth snapped. 'One does not wish to stay where one is not wanted.'

A waiter pulled Jeremy to his feet as Fanny held Elizabeth's fur coat at arm's length. 'I'm not going to tell you again, Lisah's mummy! Out of mah restaurant!'

Followed by a snivelling Jeremy, Elizabeth draped her mink coat over one shoulder and swept out the door.

'Okay, who told my bloody mother about the party tonight?' There was a short silence.

'It was me!' Henry elbowed his way through the other guests standing motionless on the dance floor. 'I'm really sorry, Li, but she called me to ask if you had any plans for your birthday and...'

'And you bloody told her! Henry Cahoon, whatever were you thinking?'

'I had no choice! You know how impossibly demanding the woman is. She threatened to come round and see me if I didn't tell her.'

'You're such a wuss, Henry...' Lisa snivelled.

Fanny shook her head and waved a finger at Henry. 'Yes, how could you, 'enry? You're a bleedin' dolt.'

'I can't believe you've been quite so stupid.' Lisa took a step towards Henry, intending to playfully pummel her fists against his chest, but before she got close enough, Jack stepped in and, with another perfectly aimed right hook, knocked him out cold.

Charles rushed to Henry and knelt by his side, wafting his hands in front of his face in an effort to revive him.

'Ere, Lisah! What' ave you got up your sleeve for later, a bloody brawl? You got slapped, two blokes were thumped, and one's out cold! Fanny's is not a bleedin' boxing ring, you know!' Fanny stood over the unconscious Henry with her hands on her hips. 'This is the first time we have ever had fisticuffs at Fanny's! It's a good job we're not open to the public tonight! Mah reputation would be going down the bloody pan.'

'I promise you, Fanny, there will be no more brawling tonight.' Lisa pleaded.

'I hope not, any more trouble an' you are all outa here. Alphonso, please fetch a bucket of ice and two tea towels, one for his head and one for Rocky's fists.'

Lisa took Jack's bruised and swollen right hand in both of hers, brushing his knuckles with her lips.

Despite the lightness of her touch, Jack winced. 'Ouch! I had no idea that this fist could actually knock anybody out.'

'Never underestimate the strength of *Monte das Uvas,* Jack; it always packs a punch, especially *Champanhe Lisa*,' she teased, before yelling at the top of her voice, 'what's happened to the DJ? Or have you knocked him out as well, Rocky Wilde?'

Katzenjammer

The sun streamed through the sash window of Lisa's bedroom. She blinked her eyelids open, then batted them shut again, overwhelmed by the brilliance of the sun's rays, having forgotten to close the curtains before falling into bed. Outside, a pigeon flapped its wings before bursting in an ear-splitting, *coo roo-c'too-coo*. She clamped her pillow over her ears, trying to blot out the din. Moving her head from side to side, she attempted to alleviate the pressure from what felt like a one-ton weight perched on top of her head. It didn't work. Her tongue cautiously ventured out between her lips, then snapped back again, viper-like, into her mouth. It tasted like the bottom of a budgie's cage, long overdue a clean. Despite the fuzziness in her head she squeezed out just one thought; *Never, ever again.*

She checked to make sure she was still wearing the necklace, bracelet, and earrings her father and Thomas had given her and was relieved to find that she was. Running her hands down her hot, clammy, naked body, she rested her palms on her stomach. A cacophony of gastric rumblings from the fermenting brew inside her was competing with the sound of shallow breathing. She held her breath for a moment, but the breathing continued. She was not alone.

The rumblings in her stomach became louder, and an acidic fountain started bubbling up her oesophagus into her throat. Clasping a hand to her mouth, she leapt out of bed and rushed to the bathroom, only to find the door locked and the sounds of strangled retching coming from inside.

Instinct triggered Plan B. With no time to return to her bedroom for a dressing gown she made a wild dash for the kitchen, arriving just in time to throw up in the sink. Hanging on with both hands, eyeballing the plughole, she watched what smelt like neat alcohol dribbling down the plughole before her diaphragm started to heave again in preparation for the next retch.

'Nice arse!' a voice behind her sniggered.

Her head jolted out of the sink and she spun around. Connie's boyfriend, Danny, sat at the kitchen table with a broad smile on his face and what looked like a full English breakfast in front of him. His wide-open eyes scanned her breasts. 'Nice tits too,' he said, slowly lowering his gaze.

Lisa swivelled around again, grabbing a tea towel to cover her *nice arse*. The smell of Danny's food was too much. Craning her neck over the sink, she was violently sick one more time before sidling out of the room.

'Don't worry!' Danny called after her. 'I will clear up your mess! I've been doing the same for Connie since midday. It's four o'clock now… just in case you had plans.'

Vulnerable in her nakedness, she scampered back across the sitting room to the sanctuary of her bedroom. She couldn't quite remember who had come back with them from Fanny's. She caught a glimpse of Henry and Charles, wrapped around each other on the sofa, fully clothed. Henry had a nasty bruise on his left cheek, which quivered every time he exhaled. Connie's Spandex trousers with their ripped back seam were dangling from the chandelier, prompting the memory of playing Twister after they got back.

Making it back to the safety of her bedroom, she shut the door firmly behind her. Leaning against it with her hands flat on the smooth wood, she breathed a sigh of relief while mumbling, '*Nice arse, bloody Danny!*' But her attention shifted as somebody exhaled deeply in her bed, the sheet pulled up over their face. Her brain went into overdrive. She scanned the room. Pages of her manuscript, *They Always Look at the Mother First,* were strewn all over the floor like giant confetti. What on Earth had possessed her to throw her hard work all over the place? Her expensive velvet dress was screwed up in a ball on top of her typewriter. Her strapless bra *and* bikini briefs, strewn at opposite ends of the room. But there were no other tell-tale items of discarded clothing that might jog her memory of who she had just spent the night with.

Who came back to the flat after Fanny's? Managing to squeeze out a small amount of functioning cognitive recall, she remembered six of them left the flat to go to Fanny's, and eight had returned. Adele and Mike would be tucked up together. Connie was throwing up in the bathroom, and Danny was playing voyeur in the kitchen. The two blond bombshells were curled up on the sofa, which just left herself and...?

There was a rustling sound and movement from under the sheets as two hands made a grab at the bedclothes. The knuckles of one hand were bruised... from having punched both Jeremy *and* Henry.

A mass of black curls slowly emerged, followed by two enormous, Bambi-esque eyes, a totally shameless smile framed with a little soft-looking stubble. Instinctively, Lisa grabbed a couple of her manuscript pages to cover up her nether regions and her breasts, as he laughed and said, 'Shit, Lisa! That was one hell of a party!'

The Feeling Never Dies

Despite an alcoholic fug inside Jack's head, he remembered every single second of the night before. At around 5 a.m., Lisa had performed her undressing routine while singing *Honey Bun* from South Pacific, modifying the lyrics as she bounced around the room.

His hair is black and curly——the bit where Lisa planted both hands on his head, while his eyes were riveted to her perfectly formed breasts, bobbing up and down to the rhythm of the synchronised beat.

His curls are hurly-whirly——the bit where she ruffled the curls of his jet-black hair as he studied her face. She was trying to sing while laughing. He had always loved the way she laughed, a soft unstoppable and very infectious giggle.

His lips are mwah—the bit where she brushed his lips with hers.

I call his hips wildey and wildey—the bit where she grabbed his naked buttocks, and they danced around the room.

For a finale, Lisa had thrown herself face down on the bed, and Jack followed, the mattress springs protesting before giving way.

'Oh shit! I need a new bloody mattress anyway.'

They laughed until they cried as if cavorting naked had been something they had been doing together for years. But the show wasn't quite over. Lisa, sitting naked and cross-legged on the bed, began to read from her manuscript, *They Always Look at the Mother First,* in her best Foghorn-Leghorn-upper-crust but pissed voice. 'Ith's a story about a mother and daughter, Jack,' she slurred. 'And ith's loosely disguised as fiction. Here we go…'

Jack thought it was the funniest thing he had ever heard and had laughed until his ribs ached. 'Shame mine is a historical press. If it were a hysterical press, I could get that published tomorrow. I've really felt for you over the years... being stuck with a mother like Elizabeth.'

'Tell mees about it, and sheeez only forty now! I will be schtuck with her for eeeyons! But don't feel shorry for me, Jack. I adopted your mother years ago.'

When her eyelids started to close, she threw the rest of the pages over her head and slumped back against the pillows. Jack lay down next to her, pulling the covers over them both.

'I've wanted to be this close to you for a very long time,' he whispered, but she didn't hear the words he had been longing to say as she melted into his arms and passed out with a little snore. He smiled, brushing her lips with his, a light, lingering kiss, savouring the moment before pressing her sleeping body to his.

The sensation of her breasts rising and falling against his chest, combined with her soft breath against his neck, took him by surprise. His heart raced, and his whole body became overwhelmed by a surge of emotion; a powerful feeling, so much more than sexual. Lisa had claimed his heart, without him realising it. Had she somehow found her way into his soul, too?

For as long as he could remember, he had kept his feelings for Lisa tucked away inside his heart. They had been too drunk when they fell into bed that night, and each suffered from inevitable hangovers when they woke up together the following morning, so nothing had happened. But, after spending a night in her bed, drunk or not, he couldn't get her out of his head.

*

It took three days for Lisa's hangover to wear off, and, as the reality of leaving *Stellar* sunk in, she threw herself into churning out freelance articles. Her interview with Sigourney Weaver appeared in *Focal Point,* which was a big boost for her career.

Mike and Danny had both permanently moved into the flat, and Jack called in most evenings. So, they would all either watch TV together or go out as a group.

One evening, it was Lisa's turn to cook. 'Vesta chicken curry okay for everyone?' she asked but was answered only by silence followed by groans.

'Erm, to be honest, Li, I fancy a proper curry. I'm pretty hungry tonight. Why don't I pop out and get us all a takeaway?' Adele volunteered.

'I'll come with you.' Jack offered, getting to his feet.

Once outside the flat, Adele laced her fingers with her big brother's. 'Li's never been interested in cooking, and eating isn't at the top of her list these days, either. Anyway, how's your not-so-new job going?'

'Yeah, it's good, thanks. I'm enjoying it,' Jack said, tugging on his sister's hand.

'You've been with them for a while now. Have you had a pay rise yet?'

'I have, actually, and I've been offered a different role within the company which not only pays a better salary, but has an apartment to go with it.'

'An apartment! That sounds very American.'

'*Very* American, actually. The job is in their New York office.'

'That's brilliant, Jack! Congratulations! Mum and Dad will be so pleased for you. I love having you just down the road, but New York? You must be over the moon?'

Jack stopped walking. It had started to drizzle, and clusters of tiny puddles began to appear on the pavement, flickering in the glare of the streetlights. He ran his fingers through his unruly black curls and pulled the collar on his jacket up around his ears, and said, 'I've told them I don't want it.'

'What?'

'I've told them I am not ready for it.'

'Not ready for it? For God's sake, Jack, what were you thinking? It is a fantastic opportunity for a twenty-three-year-old. You *must* be mad. I can't think of *anything* that could stop you from going.'

'Can't you?' He rolled his big, dark-brown eyes. 'Or *anyone*? I thought it was so bloody obvious why I keep coming round to your place *all* the time. Well, if *you* haven't realised, it is not too surprising that *she* hasn't either!'

'*She?* Oh my God, Jack. You mean, Lisa, don't you? I'm sure she has no idea. I mean, I know you both woke up together the morning after her 21st, but Li said nothing happened because she passed out.'

'Which is true. Nothing did happen.'

'You've got to tell her how you feel, but… you need to know that, although she's confident and bloody brilliant at her job, she's very fragile emotionally. She'd never admit to it, but she's wary, if not terrified, about getting into a relationship. She might joke about turning into Elizabeth one day and not wanting to inflict that on anyone, but there's something else. A deep-seated childhood insecurity that's holding her back. Brought on, I think, by the people she loved as a child leaving her, first Eileen, then her dad, obviously. Whatever it is, it's scarred her emotionally. I care about you both very much, and I don't want either of you to get hurt. But I can't think of anything better than Lisa finally becoming an official member of the Wilde family…'

'Hang on a second, Adele, I'm not about to propose…'

'I know. I'm sorry. I'm getting carried away, but my best friend and my brother? Sounds like a match made in heaven to me. Anyway, the best advice I can give you is to ask her out. I can't understand why you haven't already. But take your time before telling her how you really feel, you don't want to frighten her off.'

With a bit of input from his sister, Jack gave a great deal of thought to what they should do on their first proper date, and between them they got it right. He rang Lisa one afternoon to say he had tickets for *Evita* at the Prince Edward Theatre, with Elaine Page in the title role.

Jack picked her up at 6 p.m. to take her for an early meal at Fanny's before the performance.

'Always good to see you, Lisa Grantie, but I do hope Rocky here won't be knocking any of mah customers out tonight! No more brawls at Fanny's, okay? Won't do mah reputation naa good! Come with me, my darlings. Our best table for two, nice and quiet.' Fanny ushered them to a dimly lit table in an alcove. A bottle of *Monte das Uvas,* was chilling in an ice bucket on their table. 'On the 'ouse, my darlings. I've started getting it direct from this very nice man in Portugal. I can't get my hands on enough of it. It's sellin' like otcakes.' Then, tapping Jack on the shoulder, she said, 'You promise me, mate… no fisticuffs tonight.'

'I promise you, Fanny. No more fisticuffs, ever. I've never hit anybody before, and I have no intention of ever hitting anybody again. I really don't know what came over me that night.' He flashed her a smile, highlighting his perfectly straight, white teeth, his dark eyes twinkling in the candlelight.

'I know what came over you, mate, you were defending the honour of this beautiful young lady, and if I were a bloke, I'd have done the same. Enjoy your dinner, my lovelies. It's all good tonight, whatever you choose.'

*

Things started to move quickly over the weeks that followed. Lisa's self-imposed emotional barricade began to slide as she let Jack into her heart. It reminded her of those heady, carefree Henry days when hopes were high but never came to anything. But this was different. This was turning into a proper, grown-up relationship.

The first time Jack took her to his flat, they made love. After too many years in the boyfriend-less wilderness, sex had been a long time coming, and she totally abandoned herself to his touch. Adele and other friends had told her that sex for the first time hadn't quite been the earth-quaking experience they were hoping for. In Lisa's case, she thought her first time was bloody brilliant, although it happened too quickly. Once they got their breath back, they did it again and again until they fell asleep exhausted in each other's arms.

After that, Lisa regularly spent nights at Jack's flat. At the weekends, they often spent whole days in bed, eating, sleeping, and making love. He treated her with kid gloves; he was kind, thoughtful and loving. Surprises were his speciality. Impromptu weekends staying in cosy B and Bs by the coast or spending time with Arthur at Silkwoods. 'I bet you have no regrets about going to London now?' Arthur would tease, and she had no reason to disagree.

'I thought we could go and explore Stratford-upon-Avon this weekend.' Jack said, during one hectic week. 'We need to escape the rat-race for a bit, what do you think?'

'That would be lovely, Jack. I haven't been there since Della and I were at Coln Castle.'

They arrived on a Saturday afternoon, and Jack produced a picnic basket from the back of his car, filled with champagne, smoked-salmon sandwiches, and strawberries. They devoured its contents on the banks of the River Avon before he took her to see *A Winter's Tale*.

The highlight of that summer was spending a blissful two-weeks with Jack at *Mont das Uvas*. Walking hand in hand along the sun-kissed beaches, lying next to each other in the shade of the sweet-smelling umbrella pines, and making love in the warmth of the night to the cicada chorus.

Shortly after Lisa and Jack returned to London, Adele asked Lisa and Connie to meet her during their lunch hour.

'Connie's always late, so I've ordered us both a BLT. I'm the only one in the office this afternoon, so I must be back at 2 o'clock sharp.'

'Oh, great, thanks!'

'I saw Jack on the way to work this morning. I've never seen him so happy. You are all he talks about. You won't break his heart, Li, will you?'

'Of course not! What on Earth made you say that? I know he cares about me, Del. How could I possibly *break his heart?* That's a ridiculous thing to say!'

'I know you wouldn't do it intentionally, but he really *loves* you, you know.'

'Yes, I know he does… and I…' Lisa wanted to say, *'and I really love him too,'* but the words caught in the back of her throat just as Connie burst through the door. Jack had told her countless times how much he loved her, and her response had always been, 'me too you,' but it wasn't quite the same. Why did she find it so hard to say the words *I love you?*

'Have you told her yet?' Connie asked Adele.

'No, I was waiting for you…'

Lisa was confused. 'Told me what?'

'Mike asked me to marry him and I accepted. I was going to keep it a secret until I chose a ring.'

Excitedly, Connie added, 'It's infectious, Li because Danny and I are engaged, too!'

'Engaged? I go away for two weeks, and you both get *engaged?*'

Connie sat down, throwing both arms in the air. 'I'm beyond excited! I've always wanted loads of children, and I have a funny feeling you'll be next, Li!'

'Oh, I don't think I will be. I'm very happy for both of you, but getting engaged is not at the top of my list. Not now, or at any other time. I'm allergic to marriage. I thought everybody knew that. It's something I've inherited from both my parents.' She attempted to laugh it off, but Adele wasn't amused.

'I can't believe you've just said that! What if Jack popped the question?'

Lisa felt a wave of anxiety flush through her. Getting engaged to Jack had never crossed her mind. 'It's just that I find the whole marriage thing a bit claustrophobic, that's all. Plus, my career has only just started, and I feel I've got so much more to give. Maybe, I'm just not the marrying kind.'

Adele frowned. 'Who on Earth *is* the marrying kind, for goodness sake? And what makes you so different from the rest of us? Surely, settling down to spend the rest of your life with the person you love is what everybody wants, isn't it? Whether it happens now or when you are in your forties.'

'I am sure it is!' Lisa replied, curtly. 'But the sad reality is that you can't guarantee that the person you love *will* spend the rest of their lives with you. It's just that the word marriage, for me anyway, stands for infidelity, absenteeism, and betrayal. So, why would I want to sign up for all that?'

Adele rose to her feet in a huff. 'Honestly Li, I sometimes think you live in cloud cuckoo land and, quite frankly, if somebody is misguided enough to ask you to marry them, you better think long and hard about what your answer is going to be because you run a very high risk of breaking his heart. I'm sorry, but I've got to go back to work now.'

'Della, I…'

'I'll see you later. I've got to go!' The shopkeeper's bell at the top of the door clattered as she went out.

'What did I say, Connie?

'Oh, Li, I think it's more about what you *didn't* say that's the problem.'

Despite her awkward exchange with Adele, Lisa still didn't see it coming. She hadn't fully grasped what Adele was saying, or shared the funny feeling Connie had.

*

For Lisa's twenty-second birthday, Jack took her to Paris. With the Eiffel Tower as a romantic backdrop, he dropped to one knee and asked for her hand in marriage. Why hadn't she seen this coming? Her brain froze, and she was rendered speechless.

Jack was looking up at her, making facial gestures, to encourage her to respond. 'Li, I'm getting cramp in my knee. How much longer must I stay down here?'

She panicked, her garbled response spontaneous, immature, and unintentionally cold, 'Oh, come on, Jack! Why on Earth would I want to *marry* you? Aren't we a bit too young to be thinking about such grown-up things? I'm allergic to marriage anyway. I thought you would have known that?' It was a flippant and hurtful remark. Even if she had intended it to be funny, Jack obviously didn't think so.

The expression on his face gave away his feelings. An image that would haunt Lisa's dreams for years, along with Adele's words, *you won't break his heart, will you?* She'd cut him to the quick. Obviously he'd been planning this for a long time, and as he got up, the look of failure on his face cut her to the quick.

'Jack?' She placed her hand on his cheek, but he pushed it away; his face contorted, like someone who'd been shot at close range with a twelve-bore. He said nothing, and his beautiful, sparkling, Bambi-esque eyes glazed over as he turned and walked away from her. 'Wait, come back... I didn't mean...' She could have run after him, but instead, she watched him walk away.

Moving On

'There, there, my duck. Things will get better… in time.' The soothing Gloucestershire cadence of Nellie's voice, normally guaranteed to calm and soothe, was struggling to make an impression. Lisa was sitting on her bed at Silkwoods, sobbing into Nellie's ample shoulder. She had decided to take time off and leave London for a while. She felt she needed time to reflect on where dumping Jack had left her, as well as the implications it had on her relationship with Adele and their parents.

'Oh, Nellie! I told Adele I wouldn't break Jack's heart, but I did just that. I was about as subtle as a bloody brick! How could I have been so unkind? If only I had engaged my brain and given some thought to what I was going to say, I wouldn't have hurt him so badly. But, oh, no, not me! Out it came! And it was such a stupid thing to say and, you should have seen his face. It was like I stabbed him in the heart. I cannot believe I've been so cruel, and now he's going to live in New York, and it is all my fault!'

'Affairs of the heart are never easy, Lisa, lovie. I was fortunate with my Jim. I knew from the day I met him that he was the one. But you were right. If you weren't sure, better to break his heart now rather than a few months after being wed.'

'But that's just it, Nellie! I think I was sure, but I couldn't say yes, and I couldn't tell him that I love him, and I do, I really do, but I just couldn't say it. Maybe if I had told him, I loved him, he might not have gone away, but I'm *scared* of saying it. It's stupid, I know, but every time I've told someone I love them, they went away and now, because I *couldn't* tell Jack I loved him, he's gone away as well. What is *wrong* with me?'

'Oh Lisa, lovie, there's nothing *wrong* with you! You were hurt very badly as a child, with your mum the way she was, and your dad leaving, and all. You'll be able to say those words when the time is right.'

After a restless night, Lisa got up at sunrise and went for a walk along the banks of the river Churn to the sound of the morning chorus. She was disappointed that the age-old adage that *things will seem better in the morning* hadn't lived up to expectations.

Walking through Clifferdine Woods only stirred up memories of her childhood. Her father taking her for walks on his shoulders, and the carefree days with Eileen. She stopped to lean on the handrail of Pooh Sticks Bridge, where both she and her father had come to reflect over the years. It was the most idyllic place on the estate, the soft, babbling heartbeat of the Churn, trickling towards the River Thames, helped to calm the turmoil inside her. The ethereal stillness disturbed only by the flapping wings of a passing pigeon or the odd croaking frog. The verdant splendour of the canopy of leaves from the branches of the trees towering above which, when teased by the wind, let in rays of sunlight for the ferns and flowers of the woodland floor to absorb.

She watched a moorhen preen itself with its bright red beak before swimming away, creating an arrow-shaped ripple in the water. How she wished she could go back in time to Paris and play out the scenario with Jack again. When he said, 'Lisa, I love you so much, I always have, and I cannot imagine my life without you in it. Please make me a happy man and marry me?' Instead of making that flippant and immature remark, what she *should* have said was, '*Jack, I love you, too.*' Then she could have reeled off the reasons why she felt she wasn't ready to get married. Too young, fear of commitment, terrified of going through the 'momopause' and turning into her mother. The recurring nightmare she'd been having about waking up one morning, rolling onto her side, and prodding Jack in the back saying, '*Good morning, Jack, dear, I want a divorce because we've irreconcilable differences.*' She wouldn't wish that on anybody, least of all, Jack.

She should have told him she was an emotional mess. He would have understood. He was the most sympathetic and understanding person she had ever met. She imagined him recoiling with apologies, holding her in his arms, and saying, '*Oh my God, Li... I should have realised, I do understand, of course, I do. I'm a bleedin' dolt. The last thing I ever want to do is to put pressure on you to do anything you don't want to do.*' Why did she find it so hard to say the words *I love you?*

Several cows mooed in the distance. Jim must have finished milking, and the girls were heading for the lush, green pasture, relieved that their milk-giving udders were drained of the extra weight. Suddenly aware that Nellie was calling her name, she headed back towards the house.

'Lisa, lovie! Where *have* you been? I have been calling you for ages.'

'I'm sorry, Nellie, I should have left you a note. I went for a walk along the river. It's such a lovely morning.'

'I've had this woman on the phone from London three times now, wanting to speak to you. Anna Lockwood from *Focal Point.*'

'Anna Lockwood? She's the *editor,* Nellie. Maybe she wants me to do some more freelance pieces for them?'

'I think she wants you to do a lot more than that, my duck; she wants to offer you a permanent job. Here's her number. Now go and give her a call, best not keep her waiting.'

Bloodletting

Lisa threw herself into her new role with *Focal Point*, always the first at her desk in the mornings, and the last to leave at night. A job she'd only dreamed about. Interviewing inspirational people, as well as taking on the role of *Focal Point's* Theatre Critic, she channelled everything she had into making it a success.

Another plus was that she got on with everybody she worked with, especially Finty Sharpe, *Focal Point's* resident film and literary critic. Sharing an office together, they found out they had the same taste in most things, especially the arts, but also in men. Working for *Focal Point,* they enjoyed a healthy social life. The opportunity to meet new people presented itself daily. Neither of them wanted to be in a long-term relationship, particularly Lisa, who tried not to allow herself to think about Jack, as it hurt too much, and vowed she would never let anybody else into her heart again.

Her relationship with Adele had been severely tested, but fortunately it was strong enough to survive the fallout from the Jack fiasco, much to her relief.

When Adele discovered she was pregnant with their first child, she and Mike moved back to Gloucestershire, and when the lease on the Notting Hill flat expired, Connie and Danny took out a mortgage on their own place. Lisa, unfazed by being on her own, moved into a one-bedroomed studio flat in falling-out-of-bed distance from the *Focal Point* offices, which fitted in well with her workaholic lifestyle.

Lisa had become an expert on blocking out emotional trauma, but pushing anxieties to the back of your mind doesn't free you from them because they have a nasty habit of coming back to haunt you. In Lisa's case, they started manifesting themselves in unsettling nightmares about her paternity.

Flotillas of sperm racing up her mother's vagina to her uterus, squeezing through her cervix and jockeying for position as they powered their way towards her fallopian tubes. As the majority started to slow down, there were two still wagging their tails. They were hypnotised by one enormous egg with Lana Turner eyelashes and red lips. An egg so much bigger and better than either of them had ever imagined. Squealing with delight, they swam like torpedoes towards the Lana Turner egg. The evil-looking sperm, wearing a pinstripe suit, shouted, *I'm coming in!* The other, with a face like Bacchus, clutching a bunch of grapes, calmly repeated the words, 'Here's to a new life! *Monte das Uvas Champahne Lisa.*'

Lisa would always wake up gasping for breath, before finding out which sperm transformed the albuminoidal bundle into the screwed-up persona that had become her. It was a worry. What would Freud have to say about a twenty-five-year-old woman dreaming about her mother's reproductive system?

For her own sanity, she needed to know the truth, and she had two options. To have the paternal sperm conversation with her mother, or to organise paternity tests. Luckily for Lisa, a third less stressful option presented itself.

All the *Focal Point* employees signed up to donate blood, and the

Red Cross moved into their offices for a day to collect a few pints for the bank. One of the nurses squeezed Lisa's blood collection bag and sighed, 'You're not too keen to part with yours, are you? Do you want to try for a bit longer, or do you want to call it a day?' After lying on a put-up bed for well over an hour, Lisa had only produced a dribble, so they agreed that it was time to stop. Finty, lying next to her, was complaining about feeling lightheaded.

'I'm not surprised,' said Lisa, glancing at Finty's bag. 'It looks like you've donated enough for the whole bloody office.'

While waiting for her blood donor card, Lisa asked the nurse if it was possible to tell who her parents might be from her blood group.

'Well, you can eliminate a few.'

'Is there any chance you can tell me who I can eliminate?'

'Leave it with me. I'll send something to you.'

True to her word, the nurse sent Lisa a list of parental blood-group combinations under the headings *Possible Children* and *Impossible Children*. At last, she had the information she needed to find out who her biological father really was.

She spoke to Will regularly, so finding out his blood group wasn't a problem. In fact, she managed to score twice in one telephone conversation.

'Hi. Dad?'

'What have you been up to this week?'

'Oh, busy, as usual, but I'm not complaining. I met and interviewed the Green Goddess this morning.'

'I don't think I've heard about her. What planet is she from?'

'She's a fitness guru called Diana Moran, and she's currently wearing out the viewers of a TV programme called *Breakfast Time*. She's almost twice my age and makes me feel like a real lazy moo. After the interview, she asked me if I worked out, and I said that because I worked such long hours, I didn't have the time. She told me it was a poor excuse because I don't need to go to a gym to work out as the best place to exercise is… wait for it… in my own home… in the nuddy, so I would feel totally free.'

'An interesting concept!'

'Indeed. Oh, yes, and we all gave blood at work the other day. Only my veins didn't want to part with much of mine. The nurse gave up on me after an hour when I'd only produced a trickle. At least I know what my blood group is. It's B.'

'Ah, well, us Grants like to keep it in the family. I'm a B too, and I just happen to know that your mother is Group A.'

She checked her list. A + B possible children = A or B or AB or O. Now she needed to broach the subject with Jeremy. She hadn't seen her mother since her twenty-first birthday, so the thought of having to suffer the indignity of ringing her was not appealing. But this was important; she had to find out.

'Hi, Jeremy, it's Lisa.'

'*What* a surprise, your mother and I didn't think we would ever hear from you again. She's not here,' A sense of relief washed through her. 'She's having a head-to-toe massage at Harrods. She could be gone for hours.'

'Actually, Jeremy, it's you I want to speak to. I really need to know if you are my father or not.'

'Do you want me to take a paternity test?'

'I'm hoping that won't be necessary if you know what blood group you are.'

'Funnily enough, I found out very recently. I had a blood test to check that my thyroid was okay, which of course it was, and I found out that my blood group is… O'

Lisa breathed a silent sigh of relief and quickly scanned her list *A + O - Impossible children: B and AB*. She covered the mouthpiece for a few seconds, hissing, *'Yes, yes, yes,'* at the ceiling, before calmly adding, 'It's great news that your thyroid is okay, but, Jeremy, I'm not your daughter because it's a biological impossibility. My mother is Group A, and A and O blood-group parents can't have a group B child.'

'I never thought you were, Sweet Pea. I've been firing blanks for years, apparently. I only found out after I married Penny. She wanted children, and we couldn't understand why she wasn't getting pregnant. Anyway, I went through all the tests, and it turned out that the problem was to do with my small, firm testicles.' While Lisa tried to blot out the picture of Jeremy's genitalia, he added, 'It was your mother, Lisa. She *told* me to tell you I was your father. I'm sorry.' A few seconds of silence followed while Lisa digested what he had just said. 'Lisa? Are you still there?'

'Yes, I'm still here. I think I've known for most of my life that my mother is a pathological liar, but the whole scenario is a bitter pill to swallow. Why can't she ever be honest? Why does she find it so hard, to tell the truth? What is *wrong* with her?'

'Don't be too hard on her, Sweet Pea. Your mother never gives much away, but I think she is haunted by things that happened to her in the past.'

'What things?'

'As I say, she doesn't give much away, but something must have happened to her before she came to London, which scarred her very deeply. It was upsetting her when I first knew her when she was still at the Debutantes' House. She refused to tell me what it was, then, and still refuses to tell me now. Whatever it is, she can't forget about it.'

'How did she meet my father?'

'I think she bumped into him, by accident, outside his office in the City. She met your father before meeting Lord Grandborough.'

'Lord who?'

'Grandborough. Bobby Grandborough. The blond, blue-eyed peer of the realm, with pots of money and a house the size of Sandringham, and an ego of similar proportions.'

'Oh, yes, his name does ring a bell. Penny dropped his name into conversation during my interview at *Stellar!*'

'Anyway, your mother set her sights on marrying him, but when he found out she was pregnant with you, he dumped her like a hot brick, the rotter. That was horribly upsetting for her.'

'I bet it was! So, she went crawling back to my dad. Anyway, Jeremy, I think both you and my mother have both got what you wanted in the end… each other!'

Double Disloyalty

The years flew past, and by the time 1989 arrived, Lisa had immersed herself in her work, she had no time for socialising.

One evening, knowing there was no food in the fridge in her flat, she headed for Giuseppe's, an Italian restaurant around the corner from *Focal Point*. She had been feeling out of sorts all day. Physically she felt okay, and there was nothing wrong with her appetite; she was starving. It was more of an inner niggling, which she found unsettling because she didn't know the cause.

Life was as good as it had ever been. Since establishing that Jeremy was not her father, she had slept much better. Her job made her very happy, even if she was working 24/7.

Five years previously, on the night of her twenty-fifth birthday, she had started a relationship with a paparazzi photographer. Rory Collins' job took him all over the world, which suited Lisa because there was no commitment. When he was around, he could be relied upon to provide great bed-rattling sex. When he was away, she kept reminding herself she was in lust, not love. She didn't want any ties. But recently, and much to her irritation, she began to miss him when he went away. Was this the reason she felt unsettled?

While waiting for her food to arrive, she pushed her Filofax personal organiser into the middle of the table. Closing her eyes, she rested her head against the padded banquette behind her, and Jack's image popped into her head. But when she tried to squeeze it out, a plummeting roller-coaster sensation washed through her stomach. She would never admit to anyone how much she missed Jack. Maybe he was *still* her problem? Was she using Rory and his bedroom gymnastics to mask her unrequited feelings for Jack?

When a waiter thumped a plate of carbonara onto the table, her eyes jolted open. Through steam rising from the pasta, she peered at the revolving entrance doors. Someone, oozing sophistication, and looking remarkably like her mother, stepped into the restaurant.

Lisa wanted to crawl under the table. She needed to be in the right frame of mind to deal with Elizabeth, and now was not the time. She wanted to eat her meal and go back to the office, to finish the piece she'd been working on after being granted an official interview with Margaret Thatcher who had completed ten years as Prime Minister.

Attempting to flip her sunglasses from the top of her head onto her nose, they missed and fell into the carbonara. 'Oh shit!' she mumbled, but she knew she'd need a better disguise than sunglasses to conceal herself from her mother. Elizabeth, with the eyesight of a hawk, had already spotted Lisa, her exaggerated, look-at-me catwalk stride broke into a canter as she loped towards Lisa's table glowering at the pile of pasta.

Caught! Carbonara-handed. Lisa looked up at her mother pleading, *'guilty as charged.'* While waiting for Elizabeth's anticipated jibe, she dipped her sunglasses into the wine bucket and dried them with a napkin.

'Why, Lisa, dear, I'm sure pasta in that...' Elizabeth paused, putting hands on hips, and craning her head forward, exhaling the words, '… *enormous* quantity would not be on the *Weight Shifters* diet. You obviously didn't ask the chef to weigh that mountain of carbohydrate before serving it to you. If you did, he must have weighed it in pounds, not grams. And so much for alcohol abstinence, I see!' Her mother lifted the half-empty bottle of *Frascati* disdainfully between two fingers before dropping it back into the ice bucket. 'I hope you're not turning into an old soak like your father?'

'Mother! What a surprise! Would you care to join me for a glass of wine and more of your delightful repartee?' Elizabeth moved towards a chair, and a swarm of waiters appeared from nowhere to tuck her in.

'I can't stay long Lisa, dear. I'm off to the theatre with Gloria Beckingham-Clarke, so I thought I would pop into your office and say hello. The little man at the desk where you work…'

'His name is Fred Styles, Mother.'

'Well, I wasn't to know. Anyway, the little chap said you'd be here, and I have heard through the grapevine that you've been seen dining alone here recently. Acquired a passion for pasta, have we? And garlic bread too? Oh, dear, Lisa, you need to be very careful! Before you know it, you'll be the size of a house.'

'Glass of wine, Mother?' Stifling a snarl, Lisa held up the recently rejected bottle.

Several waiters lunged, but Giuseppe grunted something in Italian and got in first. He snatched the bottle and hovered over Elizabeth. 'Bella Senora, allow me to pour you a glass of our finest wine.' Half an hour ago, he had dumped the bottle of their 'finest' aka 'house' wine on her table in an ice bucket and let her get on with it.

'Eating, and drinking alone these days, Lisa dear? That's a bit sad.'

'Sometimes, I need to be alone. Especially when I have a deadline to meet... Like tonight.'

'Well, don't mind me, dear. I'm only staying for one drink.' Elizabeth took a sip, wrinkling her nose in protest. 'How you drink this cheap house wine is beyond me. It's gut-rot stuff, goodness knows what it's doing to your liver.'

Lisa wished she'd popped out for a takeaway and gone back to the office. She made a mental note to tell Fred Styles never to reveal her whereabouts to her mother.

She was staring at the revolving doors planning an escape, when to her surprise Rory Collins appeared.

'Lisa! *There* you are! You're impossible to track down sometimes!' Rory hurried across to her table and helped himself to a piece of garlic bread. 'I need to show you the photos from last night's shoot.' His voracious eye vacillated from Lisa to her mother, where they crash-landed, transfixed on Elizabeth's coyly fluttering false eyelashes. 'Whoa! Lisa, are you going to introduce me to your gorgeous friend?'

'Of course, Rory... not a friend, actually. This is my mother, Elizabeth Goldsworthy-Grant. Mother, this is Rory Collins.'

'Hello, Rory,' responded Elizabeth, dipping her head and licking her lips like a vamp, reaching out her arm to shake hands with Rory.

Instead, he picked it up and kissed it. 'Enchanté, Elizabeth. Your *mother?* Lisa, you told me your mother was an absolute...' Lisa flashed him a look, which went completely unnoticed by her mother, who was too busy gazing at Rory. '... an absolute stunner and, indeed she is. You could both so easily be sisters.'

Lisa bit her bottom lip, trying to contain her irritation while thinking, *'you're a patronising twat, Rory Collins!'*

'Rory!' Elizabeth stroked his arm. 'Why don't you join us for a glass of wine.' With an enthusiastic grin, he drew up a chair and sat between mother and daughter.

Sickened by her mother's outrageous behaviour, and Rory's lapdog expression, Lisa turned her attention to her fast cooling carbonara.

'Well, this is nice,' her mother enthused, moving her hand down to pat Rory's thigh before gesticulating to the waiter to bring another bottle of wine. 'We'll have a bottle of the Fiorano this time, thank you. How Lisa can drink that filthy house stuff is beyond me.'

'I thought you were only staying for one glass, Mother?' Lisa snapped.

'I am, but I want to enjoy it, and I can't do that if it tastes like cider vinegar.'

The animated conversation between her mother and Rory continued at a pace as they consumed the bottle of Fiorano between them.

Rory was captivated. 'Do you know what, Elizabeth? When I arrived just now, I thought Lisa must be in the middle of one of her

Rich and Famous interviews.'

Lisa grimaced. *'Oh God, Rory, don't get her started.'*

'Such an easy mistake, I'm often stopped in the street as people think I'm Olivia Newton-John.'

'One of my favourite people.' Rory rested his arm on the back of Elizabeth's chair.

'Of all the gin joints in all the world, she walks into mine.'

A group of Japanese tourists on a nearby table applauded. 'Aww, Humpfwey Bogart! Vewy good.'

But Lisa was not impressed. Rory had no scruples. It was barely twelve hours since he left her bed, and he was now outrageously flirting with her mother. She tried to pour herself another glass of wine, the last dribble splashing noiselessly into her empty glass.

'Well, I hate to break up our little party, but it's time for me to make a move,' Elizabeth announced, giving Rory an encouraging look. 'The problem is, I can't remember the quickest way to Drury Lane from here.'

Rory sprang to his feet, 'Elizabeth, please, let me take you.'

'Sir Collins, my knight in shining armour,' her mother purred, taking his arm.

'I should warn you, Elizabeth, this knight's trusty steed is a Honda motorcycle with a shared seat, so bum space is pretty tight.'

'There's always a first for everything and, as I'm sure you will agree, I'm so much slimmer than Lisa, so I'll take my chances. Can I ride side-saddle?' Elizabeth rarely joked, but she giggled like a schoolgirl at this attempt at humour… and so did Rory. 'Well, I will see you anon, Lisa, dear. Don't work too hard at whatever it is that you do.'

'You don't even know what work is, Mother.'

Elizabeth ignored her comment and gave Lisa's empty plate a distasteful look. 'I can't believe you've managed to finish that huge mound of pasta, *and* most of the garlic bread. I sincerely hope you are not contemplating any biscotti for dessert. Now, Sir Collins, let us go and try this engine of yours out for size, shall we?'

Lisa watched as the revolving doors twirled the giggling pair out of the restaurant, squashed together into the same section. Rory's arms wrapped around her mother like a lecherous octopus, leaving Lisa with a deadline to meet and the bill for the Fiorano. She was piqued. Rory had been so preoccupied with her mother that he hadn't even bothered to say goodbye to her, let alone show her the bloody photographs. If she had been thinking about him becoming more of a fixture in her life, it was never going to happen now.

'Sod you, Rory Collins! You're not getting back into my bed again any time soon.'

And he didn't. A week after Lisa saw him leave the restaurant with her mother, she still hadn't heard from him.

Although she considered Finty to be one of her closest friends, she had never discussed her relationship with Rory with anyone. She had kept schtum about him because of what Finty had told her the night she first met him.

'I saw that look, Lisa Grant, the way you looked at Mr Paparazzo. A word of warning, though, he may look irresistible on the outside, with that great body and come-to-bed eyes, but I have good reason to believe he has slept with most of the women at *Focal Point,* as well as the women who work for the other publications he freelances for. So be careful. His charm offensive may be off the Richter Scale, but he's about as reliable as a chocolate fireguard. No, that's way too nice; he's a complete, and utter, shit.'

Lisa rarely ignored a close friend's advice or took someone home after meeting them for the first time and let them shag her senseless, but she had done that with Rory.

She was considering filing a missing person's report when Finty casually dropped into conversation, 'Did you hear that Mr Consistently Unreliable, aka Rory Collins complete and utter shit, was offered a gig in Australia?'

'Australia?'

'Apparently so…'

'How did you find out?'

'I just happened to be at reception when he popped in with the photos for your piece on *Candide,* and he said he was just on his way to the airport.'

'Did he say anything… about me… I mean… about how long he was going for…?'

'Indefinitely, apparently. I didn't give Rory any time to say anything! I was telling him what a complete and utter shit he is, given he'd spent the last three nights in my bed. The only thing he had to say about anything was that he was sick of the British climate.'

'Bloody hell, Finty! He'd spent the previous five nights curled up with me. You're right. He's a complete and utter bastard!'

Charred Remains

By 1997, Lisa had reached the pinnacle of her career. She had worked hard to reach the top of her tree, but her private life had suffered as a result. During the months after Rory dumped her, the affirmation from her teenage years, *I don't need a man to complete me,* started seeping into her brain. Maybe her career was fulfilling enough? Perhaps she didn't need a significant anybody in her life?

Lisa's popular *Rich and Famous* interviews included a host of celebrated achievers; Oprah Winfrey, Baroness Boothroyd, The Spice Girls, French and Saunders, Fascinating Aida, and Helen Fielding. Helen's heroine in *Bridget Jones's Diary* had reminded her, very much, of herself.

She was looking forward to her next assignment, interviewing one of her favourite actors, Harrison Cruise, at the Dorchester Hotel. He was in London promoting his new film, *As Bad As It Gets,* and Anna Lockwood had sent *Focal Point's* staff photographer, Zac, with her.

'You don't mind, do you, Li? I've got to justify his existence somehow.'

'Honestly, Anna, I really don't have a problem with Zac or anyone. Rory Collins is the only photographer I refuse to work with!'

'Hi, Harrison, I'm Lisa Grant from *Focal Point,* and this is Zac.'

'Ah, yes. *Focal Point.* My wife buys that one. She has it shipped to the US. She says it is a politically radical, beautifully designed, as well as intellectual women's magazine.'

'I'm delighted to hear your wife reads it. Our editor, Anna

225

Lockwood, will be too. It's a tremendous boost to us all when we receive positive feedback like that. What a pleasure it is to meet you, Harrison. Like thousands of others, I'm a huge *Louisiana Jones* fan. I loved all three Indy films, and *As Bad As It Gets* came up to all my expectations.'

They were sitting close to each other at a small circular mahogany table. Harrison smiled, his perfect incisors gleaming as he moved his head closer to her ear. He smelt wonderful. Dior Sauvage? In a half-whisper, he said, 'I'm so glad you enjoyed the *Louie* films. I'd love to do another. It's a rollicking good movie ride for the audience, and with Dickie Rosenberg as a director, what's not to like?'

Still glowing from the few seconds that she was in kissable distance of Harrison Cruise, her mobile phone vibrated in her pocket. She took it out, hit the red button, then put it back. 'Sorry about that.'

Harrison shrugged. 'No big deal, Lisa.'

'Damn it!' The phone buzzed again. She gave Harrison an awkward smile and fished around in her pocket in an attempt to turn it off.

'Why don't you just answer it?' Harrison suggested, flashing her one of his trademark smiles.

'Thank you, I will, and I'm so, so, sorry about this. It must be some sort of emergency. Most people just leave a message when I don't pick up.' She walked away from Harrison and Zac, and was incensed when she realised it was her mother calling. She had never given Elizabeth her mobile phone number for this very reason. She would have something to say to the person responsible for passing on such sensitive information. Although whoever it was would be forgiven because they would have crumbled under intense interrogation.

She hit the green button and put the phone to her ear. There was a strange crackling noise. She couldn't quite make out what it was because of the intensity of her mother's laboured breathing. 'Mother! I'm working! It's *not* a good time,' she snapped.

'I fear this may be the last time we ever speak, Lisa dear...' Her mother was panting out the words, 'Silkwoods is on fire. I am trapped inside, trying to rescue Arthur. As its looking like we are both about to be fried alive and I will never see you again. I need to know that I can rely on you to sort everything out. Now I must try to save poor dear, Arthur!'

'On fire! Silkwoods? Mother?' Lisa shouted, causing both Harrison and Zac's heads to turn. '*How* did it catch fire?' Then, with the sound of a wailing emergency vehicle siren, the line went dead. She tried to call her mother back several times, but there was no response. For a few moments, she just stared at the phone, then a tear trickled down her cheek. *Please God, let Arthur survive!* The thought of her mother being his only chance of survival, didn't bode well. Her heart was pounding, dimly aware of an exchange between Harrison and Zac behind her.

'Silkwoods?' hissed Harrison to Zac.

'Hmm... the family pile. Apparently, her father put the house in Lisa's name when she was born. I've never been there, but I've heard it's a big draughty old barn of a place that's been around since the Battle of Hastings.'

'You don't say? 1066 and all that.'

Conscious of the queue of waiting journalists in the next door room, Lisa pulled herself together and turned to face them. 'I'm so, so sorry for the interruption,' she sniffled. 'Very unprofessional of me, I know, but there's been a bit of a family crisis.'

'No need to apologise.' Harrison got to his feet and, much to her surprise, he hugged her. 'Look, I heard what you said to your mother, and Zac filled me in on your historic family home. Our families and homes are so important, Lisa. You go and put out the fire Louisiana Jones-style, while I give Zac here all the information you will need, and more.'

She flew down the M4 motorway with the soundtrack from *The Temple of Gloom* ringing in her ears. Visions of finding her mother's charred mobile phone amongst the ashes or, even worse, the charred remains of her mother and Arthur, at the forefront of her mind.

Roaring up the drive at Silkwoods, the wheels of her Honda 600 Coupe scattered the gravel before scrunching to a halt. She flung the car door open and ran towards the smouldering pyre that once was one of the best examples of a Cotswold stone manor house. 'Mother? Arthur?' Her voice was an emotional breathy whisper, like Melanie calling Ashley's name in *Gone with the Wind* as she ran towards the front door, only to be restrained by a burly fireman. 'No, no! You can't go in there, the roof's about to cave in.'

'But it can't! Don't let it! My mother and stepfather are in there!'

'Are you Lisa? Mrs Goldsworthy-Grant's daughter?'

'Yes, and Arthur Goldsworthy is my stepfather. Have they been taken to hospital?'

'Don't fret my lovely. When we arrived, your mother was sitting in her car. She's left for London now, but said you were on your way to take care of everything. Apparently, Jim and Nellie...'

'Nothing's happened to them, has it?' Lisa interjected.

'No, my lovely, they are safe. According to your mother, they had taken your stepfather to Cheltenham. She also told us that she was in the attic when the fire started but made it out before it took hold.'

'*In the attic? She never goes in the attic.*'

The sound of groaning ancient timbers prompted the fireman to scoop Lisa up in his arms and carry her away from the smouldering wreck. She felt helpless as the midsection of the roof collapsed with a thunderous crash, and billowing, smoky debris gushed everywhere. So, her unscathed mother's Oscar-winning telephone call was made from the comfort of her Triumph Stag while waiting for the emergency services to arrive. What was wrong with the woman? Why was she incapable of telling the truth? Lisa would still have dropped everything and driven there. So why lie about being trapped inside the inferno? Another lie: another mother-induced mess. But the worst was yet to come.

When Lisa finally caught up with her mother on the phone, itching to ask her what she had been doing in the attic, a life-shattering revelation hit her like a sledge-hammer blow.

'Now... and I don't want you to be cross, Lisa, dear, because these things do happen, but I'm afraid I forgot to pay the insurance premium.'

Lisa was speechless as her mother droned on about how devastated she was about the incineration of her Giorgio Armani suits, which she had meant to take to London. Her whinging monologue finally came to an end with the tragic conclusion that she had intended to wear the blue one at Ascot. By that time, the words *'Forgotten to pay the insurance premium'* had drilled their way into Lisa's scrambled brain, she considered her mother very fortunate. Had Elizabeth delivered the news face to face, Lisa would not have been accountable for her actions.

'But these things don't *just happen...*' Lisa screamed down the phone, but her mother had already hung up. 'Except when you are involved!' she added, miserably, listening to the dial tone.

*

After hanging up, Elizabeth calmly walked back to the sitting room of Arthur's Belgravia mansion.

'How did it go, my love?' Jeremy asked. 'What did she say about the insurance premium?

'Oh, it went very well, I think. I was expecting a tirade, but, for once, Lisa was at a loss for words. It was all such an unfortunate *accident*. I was looking for some papers, which I thought were in a trunk in the attic. Then there was a power cut and, as I couldn't find a torch, I had to light candles. Unfortunately, one of them fell into a pile of old newspapers. I did *try* to put the fire out myself, but I probably should have called the fire brigade sooner. It was a split-second decision, you understand, and one's number-one priority was to save oneself, but the real tragedy about it all is that I couldn't save my beautiful Giorgio Armani's. Thank God I got out alive, and I will never have to go there again. I've never liked the bloody place anyway, so good riddance is what I say. I'm very relieved Lisa is there to sort out the mess. There are some advantages in having a feisty daughter. She is very good at organising things, including arranging for Arthur to go into a nursing home, which suits me very well. So, we can relax now, so I'll have another gin and tonic.'

*

Lisa was devastated. Silkwoods was the one thing in her life, thanks to her father, that was undeniably hers. So much had been lost, including Arthur's magnificent library of books, burnt to a cinder, along with so many irreplaceable memories, including her mother's suitcase of ghosts in the attic. It was just as well she'd had the foresight to switch the originals with copies on a previous visit - just in case they were ever needed.

The once majestic Cotswold stone manor house had taken on the guise of a giant open-mouthed gargoyle shouting at the sky, now that the roof had gone. Generations of Grants had been born and raised there. It had received a mention in the Doomsday Book, going on to survive both the War of the Roses and Oliver Cromwell's rampaging armies. Hundreds of years of history, destroyed in a handful of hours by her mother's mind-blowing carelessness, which she had to own up to after the arson investigator's report was received.

Her mother had never worked a single day in her life, spending her days flitting from spa to spa. How on Earth could she forget something as simple as paying the insurance premium once a year? For the same reason she had been irresponsible enough not to err on the side of caution taking candles into the tinderbox that used to be the attic. It wasn't that much to ask. But Lisa was cross with herself also. She should have taken on paying the insurance premium herself years ago, but she had always been so embroiled in her work.

In a deluded state of mind, Lisa made an irrational decision to sacrifice her love for London and her much-loved job with *Focal Point*. Both her father and Arthur told her it would be a reckless thing to do, but she did it, anyway. She returned to Gloucestershire with the ridiculous notion she could rebuild Silkwoods to its former glory. She had built up a healthy savings account and had been frugal with her money throughout her working life.

Jim and Nellie moved back to the Old Lodge, which Arthur had recently refurbished, and Lisa rented a dismal cottage just down the road from Silkwoods, owned by a neighbour, Quentin Fernsby.

She took a temporary job in Cirencester with a copywriting agency, and threw herself into restoring the house. As the months passed, she did what she could, but her savings soon bled dry. Restoring Silkwoods had been little more than a pipedream.

Arthur offered Lisa the money to finish the work, but she was too stubborn to accept his generous offer. It just didn't seem right. He was now living in an expensive nursing home and still supporting her mother, who had refused to agree to a divorce. He was a very wealthy, very generous man, but allowing him to pour more money into a property he had never owned would be nothing short of extortion. Lisa cared about Arthur too much. Despite his persistence over the years, she had never taken money from him. She couldn't be like her mother, who constantly dipped into Arthur's bottomless money well.

Tessa Barrie

1999 - 2000

Lisa Dear

Rapsgate House was a fine example of Georgian architecture that had been converted into a nursing home some twenty years previously. Set in picturesque landscaped gardens, the sprawling lawn flowed down to Clifferdine Woods, where the manicured and the untamed met, separated by an incongruous, high, green, plastic fence. It had been erected to prevent the deer from feasting on the rhododendrons and azaleas, but nothing could stop the rabbits from destroying the tulips in the spring. Lisa visited Arthur as often as she could. His body was frail, but his mind was as sharp as ever and he was always so pleased to see her.

'Hello, Arthur.' Lisa burst into his room. He was sitting in his wheelchair in the near darkness, staring at his knees. She bent down and kissed his cheek.

'Lisa! My dear girl, how lovely to see you, as always.' I was just about to pour myself a glass of Highland Dew. Please join me.'

'I can't think of anything nicer. After a day writing the blurb for a proposed new block of state-of-the-art public lavatories, a glass of Scotch would be very welcome, thank you. It's very dark in here, would you like me to turn some lights on?'

'Of course! I'm afraid my eyesight is so poor now; I don't notice if the lights are on or off.'

Her heart lurched as she turned on the overhead light. It seemed to make little difference to the overall gloaming in the room that three years ago she had tried so hard to make Arthur feel at home in. It had felt like an impossible task, given that all their personal possessions had been destroyed in the fire, including Arthur's extensive collection of books, which had taken him a lifetime to collect.

She hated seeing him in such a soul-less environment. She had done her best, but in her heart, she felt she had failed him. His ground-floor room had stunning views and easy wheelchair access into the gardens to breathe in the fresh air and absorb the pastoral beauty of the surrounding countryside, but it could never be considered home.

Another constant irritation was the smell of stale cooking. Arthur's room was at the furthest end of the building from the kitchens, but the aroma of yesterday's food lingered everywhere. She had tried everything she could think of to mask it. Throwing the windows wide open during the summer, and secreting sweet-smelling sachets in various nooks and crannies during the winter, but the invasive smell seemed to have permeated its way into the very structure of the building.

Another uncharitable thought about her mother flashed through her mind as she unscrewed the top off the bottle and poured two glasses. Arthur wouldn't be here now if it hadn't been for her mother's utter stupidity, but common sense kept telling her he was in the right place to receive the level of care he needed.

'Slangevar, Lisa. Did you have a good birthday?'

'Cheers! Yes, I did, thank you,' she responded, chinking her glass with his. 'But I confess, I felt pretty seedy the following morning…'

'Naughty girl!' he teased. 'But Mae West believed that *good girls go to heaven, bad girls go everywhere.* So, don't you ever stop being naughty! Which reminds me…' He reached out his hand and felt around the tabletop next to him. 'Here's a belated Happy Birthday present for you.' He handed Lisa a neatly gift-wrapped parcel. 'Well, it's a token present really, as you will never accept my offer of a financial gift.'

She untied the ribbon, and the paper fell apart to reveal a book, *The Oxford Dictionary of Humorous Quotations.* 'Ahh, how wonderful, thank you so much.'

'I remembered how much you loved my old copy, which was destroyed in the fire. We had so many laughs going through it, didn't we? This is an updated version, of course.'

'And I am thrilled with it. I often dream about your wonderful library of books… they were far more precious than my mother's bloody designer clothes.'

'But we must console ourselves that nobody was hurt.' His eyes twinkled as he straightened himself in his chair. 'Now, you promised me on your last visit that you would start reading your book to me. Have you had any bites yet?'

'No, but the rejection letters have started rolling in and, believe me, if I do hear something positive, you would be the first person I would tell.'

'You need to be patient… Margaret Mitchell had umpteen rejection letters for *Gone with the Wind.'*

'Yes, but... *Gone with the Wind* is an epic story. Mine is a spoof about my life, but even if I don't find a publisher, it's been a trip down therapy lane for me. I badly needed to exorcise my childhood demons, and with my mother loosely disguised as the main protagonist, writing about my formative years with comedic slant has helped me face up to them. We can't change the past, I know that. What has gone has gone, it can't be changed, so you've just got to pick up the pieces and move on, which is exactly what I am doing... finally.'

'I hope you've brought the manuscript with you. You said you would.'

'Of course, I have. I promised.'

'Well then, read away.' Lisa took another sip of whisky, making herself comfortable in the armchair before starting to read.

Chapter One: Narcissistic Heaven

In Cynthia's mind, it was perfectly natural for Katie's boyfriends to look at her first. From an early age, she had warned Katie that her prospective boyfriends would always look at the mother first. She honestly believed that if young men saw that the mother was looking youthful, it was a good indicator that the daughter's looks would last well into middle age and beyond. Why Katie would always respond to her words of wisdom by saying, 'For God's sake, Mother! Why do you always have to talk so much bloody rubbish?' was just extraordinary.

Twenty-odd years ago, Katie's head had been filled with all that feminism rubbish and she'd rarely worn a bra, which would be why she had such saggy breasts now. Cynthia kept telling her to wear a bra, but the silly girl never listened. It was too late now; her boobs were twice the size and needed all the support they could get. She shook her head. Katie may have had her fair share of men while she was in London, but she was not so lucky in the bedroom department these days, which was undoubtedly due to her size.

She despaired of her daughter, but it wasn't too late for her to find someone to marry, though she would seriously have to do something about her appearance now that she had got so fat. It would have been so easy for her to find Katie a wealthy husband years ago when she was still slim, and quite pretty, but the silly girl was never interested. Trying to find her a husband at forty would be difficult, if not impossible, now she had allowed herself to succumb to that infernal middle-aged spread.

It was barely believable that Katie had turned down her only marriage proposal on her twenty-second birthday when she was old enough to know better. Tom Feral might not have been the catch of the year, but at least he asked.

Then she thought about Katie as a baby and sighed. Sadly, it was not an emotive sigh of a mother recalling those precious times during a child's first few months of life. She was thinking how chubby Katie was then, with her flaming rosy cheeks. Forty years on and nothing much seemed to have changed. How unalike they both were on many levels.

She sat up straight, pulling out the muscles in her back, then stretched out her neck from side to side. She crossed her slim, bronzed, stocking-less legs, stretching them out like a cat in front of her, admiring them as she did so. Once again, she smoothed her, now dyed but not a hair out of place, blonde bob elegantly behind her ears. A blonde bob that framed her bronzed, unblemished skin; how sad it was that Katie had inherited her father's looks.

'Hugh!' Cynthia broke the silence and made him jump to attention as his head popped up over the top of his paper, looking like a rabbit caught in the headlights.

'Yes, my love,' came the singsong response.

'You can get me that gin and tonic now!'

She stopped reading. A wheezy crackle was coming from inside Arthur's chest, as his shoulders heaved. His gnarled fingers covered his mouth as he struggled to stem the flow of laughter.

'Arthur! I didn't think it was *that* funny. Do you need some water?'

He made a last-ditch attempt to clear the sputum from the back of his throat, took a breath, holding a tissue to his mouth and forced a cough.

'No, sit, sit, sit… water's not what I need. Glenmorangie, in my opinion, is the best medicine.' He lifted his glass and took a swig. 'My dear, Lisa, we both know you can write fluently on most subjects, but that is very funny. If you can keep that up for ninety-thousand words give or take, you may well be on to something. I just have one question before you read me some more.'

'And what would that be?'

'Your mother.'

'Ah, yes, my procreator and main protagonist....'

'Although she is completely oblivious to what goes on around her most of the time, won't she figure out that you're writing about her?'

'I have thought about that, Arthur...'

'And...'

'I don't believe she has ever read anything I've written, so it's unlikely she would start now. Even when I was at *Focal Point,* she took great delight in telling me the only magazine she ever read was *Vogue,* but I intend to write it under a pseudonym. So, she will never know.'

'Okay... and have you given any thought as to what your nom de plume will be?'

'I have, yes, my alter ego will be... Lisa Dear.'

'Well, then... let us drink to the success of your book, Lisa Dear, then, please, read me some more.'

Finty Follow Up

'They Always Look at the Mother First is about the tenuous relationship between a narcissist mother and her altruist daughter. Doc Martens takes on Dior as workaholic daughter finally rebels against mollycoddled mother. After forty years of verbal incontinence, will the two ever see eye to eye? Will the twain ever meet?'

'Bodder and Baunton, good morning. Finty Sharp speaking, how may I help?'

'Finty?'

'Yes...'

'Are you sitting down? Because today, Finty Sharp, I am going to be your blast from the past!'

'Oh, my God! Lisa! Lisa Grant! I'd recognise that voice anywhere!'

'Oh, dear, after all those years I've spent trying to modulate my public school accent to accommodate my political leanings, I hope my vocal cords haven't succumbed to my genes, and I sound like my mother. Big booming, Foghorn-Leghorn, I'm-extremely-posh voice.'

'Oh, Li! You're not still hung up about your mother, are you? Mind you, she was a force to be reckoned with. I thought she was the reason you were never going to speak to me again after I gave her your mobile number the day your house was burning down.'

'Ah, I had momentarily forgotten that *you* were the one that gave her that sensitive information!'

'I take it she's still alive then?'

'Alive? Finty, my mother will see me out! Her young and beautiful regime is ongoing. She denies any Botox intervention, but I'm bloody sure she's had it.'

'It's so good to hear from you! How are you?'

'Well… not too bad considering I made a rash and ridiculous decision to stay in the country and give up *Focal Point* after the fire. I had this rather naïve idea that I could rebuild Silkwoods by myself.'

'Rebuild? It must be rebuilt by now, isn't it? If it's not, you *seriously* need to look at changing your insurers.'

'You see, Finty… that's the unfortunate thing. My mother had forgotten to pay the insurance premium, so I've blown all my savings on a bottomless pit called Silkwoods. Anyway… life goes on, but… I am getting bogged down in the country, and I'm beginning to stagnate a bit. So, I'm thinking about moving on, probably to Portugal. You might remember my dad has a vineyard out there. He would like me to be 'more involved in the family business' and, I have to say, the climate is very appealing. I've also got some freelance projects going on. Another possible Portuguese project is running Writers' Retreats, and I immediately thought of you. I thought you might like to host one with me.'

'Sounds like a great plan, and yes, of course I'd be up for it.'

'I'm a way off yet, but I will be in touch as soon as I've nurtured my suntan!'

'I feel jealous already, just give me a call,' Finty enthused, 'We've got so much to catch up on. *Focal Point* wasn't the same after you left, then Anna left and I got to the stage where I needed a change, so when I was offered the job here, I grabbed the opportunity. How did you find me?'

'Oh, I still have my spies around and about,' Lisa giggled, 'No, not really. I got my information from Mr Complete and Utter Shit…'

'Rory Collins?

'Yes, the one and only! He emails me from time to time, when the mood takes him, and, sometimes I respond. I'm sure he does the same with you.'

'Mm, only I never respond!'

'Anyway, he said he'd heard on the grapevine that you had moved to Bodder and Baunton.' There was a pause.

'Naughty boy, that one. I can't believe we both fell for his irresistible charm. Have you met Mr Right in the Shires yet, Li?'

'You've got to be joking. The only unattached males around here fall into three categories. Category One: those I've known all my life who still haven't realised that, for oh so many reasons, they are destined to live their lives as solitary males. Category Two: those who are new to the area, who have been around the relationship block more than once and have glazed looks on their faces giving away the weight of the emotional baggage they are carrying around on their backs, and finally, Category Three: The widespread, predatory males who frequently forget they are married. Like my lecherous landlord. How about you, Finty? Have you found your significant other yet?'

'Nope but given that I spend all my time reading manuscripts, I don't have time to meet anybody *at all,* let alone anyone significant. Oh Li, it's so good to talk to you. You always made me laugh, which reminds me, I had a good laugh a few weeks ago. I was sent the first few chapters of a debut novel, which I read and laughed out loud - which doesn't often happen. It's about a tenuous relationship between a narcissist mother and her altruist daughter. Then I thought, hang on a minute, this all sounds strangely familiar. The envelope was postmarked Cirencester, and the author's name is Lisa Dear. I don't suppose you've heard of her, have you? It's such a coincidence really, when I've heard nothing from you for three years, and you just happen to ring me out of the blue…'

'Busted! I knew you would see through the guise.'

'It was all too much of a coincidence, Li, and I'm so sorry we haven't got back to you yet. I say *we* because I passed it on to one of my colleagues, Neville Shufflebottom.'

'Shufflebottom? Is he for real?'

'He most certainly is. Shufflebottom is a good ye-old English name, apparently, and he's much more experienced than I am, as well as being very supportive of debut authors. I also thought it would be best to pass it on to someone who doesn't know you quite as well as I do!'

'It is a work of fiction, though.'

'Yes, but I would still be seeing you as the antagonist and your mother as her nemeses.'

'Are you actually taking on any newbies right now?'

'We're always on the lookout for new voices, but it always depends on what they are offering us. If they've conjured up a *Harry Potter*, or a *Bridget Jones*, or even a...'

'Cynthia Baskerville-Clifford? Narcissist, serial liar, and debutante of the year for 1958?' A laugh puffed its way down the phone.

'Leave it with me, Li. I will find out where Neville is with it and, don't forget when you move to Portugal, I'm coming, okay?'

Life-Changing Decision

Apart from a few fleeting catch-up telephone calls, Lisa hadn't seen oldest friend, since her fortieth birthday, so was delighted when Adele asked her around for supper one evening. 'It's great to see you Della, I'm sorry I've been such a bad friend recently.' Adele added a couple of cans of tuna to the already frying onions and garlic, stirring furiously.

'It's good to see you too, and I forgive you! Any news on your book?'

'Nope, but I've had a few more knockbacks, and a bit of feedback from an agent who remembered I used to write for *Focal Point…* while she was still at school. She said the title was a bit 'on the nose' and that I should amuse, rather than bludgeon the reader with witty lines.'

'Really? What does a little pipsqueak know anyway?'

'More than we think, I imagine.'

'What about Finty? Hasn't she got back to you yet?'

'I honestly felt a bit cheeky sending it to her, even though I submitted it under the name of Lisa Dear. Anyway, I spoke to her yesterday, and she'd guessed I'd written it.'

'Really, and?'

'I think she felt it was all a bit incestuous, so she passed it on to a colleague, Neville Shufflebottom.'

'That's a good old-fashioned English surname!'

'So I'm told. Well, if Neville's not interested, I've decided that, if

I don't get anywhere with it, I've got an idea for another one. I can only get better at it.'

'Don't be so negative, Lisa Grant! Margaret Mitchell had *Gone with the Wind* rejected umpteen times.'

'That's what Arthur said, but *They Always Look at the Mother First* is not exactly an epic historical romance. Mind you, no doubt my mother would put herself in the same looks department as Vivien Leigh, but there the similarity ends.'

'No, but it's funny, and Bodder and do dah would be a perfect fit. If they don't offer you a deal, I'm sure somebody else will.'

'I wish I had your faith, Della. That reminds me, I ran you off your very own copy today.' She dipped both hands into her tote bag and heaved the bulky manuscript onto the kitchen table.

'I had the office to myself this afternoon, so I made use of our super-fast printer.'

'Ah, thank you! That's great timing because I've just finished reading Helen Fielding's *Bridget Jones: The Edge of Reason.'*

'Erm, well, I hope you don't find it too much of a disappointment after that.'

'Oh, come on! I'm your biggest fan. You know that! Plus, I've already read bits of it and, I love it!' The smell of burning tuna diverted Adele's attention. She whipped it off the heat and gave it a good stir.

'We go back a long way, don't we? You and I.'

'Don't we just? Do you realise I've been married for fourteen years? And I was with the old sod for four years before that?'

'And you were very fortunate to find an old sod like Mike. You don't come across many Mikes in this life.'

'Yeah, we've had our ups and downs, but I can't imagine life without him and our two beautiful, although occasionally stroppy, teenagers.'

'Adele, here's something I really need to tell you.'

'Heavens, that sounds deep. Do I need to sit down?'

'I've been giving my life some serious thought recently.'

'I think I will sit down, but your life's been making such positive progress in such a short space of time. You've finished your book; you've lost so much weight. Running over three miles to raise loads of money for the Hop Skip and Jump charity was a brilliant achievement. You couldn't have done that last year, or any other year, come to that. Seriously though, you are much more positive and happier than you've *ever* been since you came back to Gloucestershire.'

'I know, but it's more about where, and more importantly, who I am going to be with for the rest of my life. That's what has been bugging me. I've dug myself into a bit of a rut since being back here, and I've allowed myself to stagnate.' Her words, fuelled with emotion, made her voice quiver.

'Go on...'

'Job-wise, and relationship-wise, my life isn't going anywhere. I feel like I need a complete change.' Lisa ran both hands over her head, clamping them tightly to her skull as if trying to squeeze out a pounding headache. 'I need to move on. No, I *have* to move on… for my own sanity, and now seems like the right time. I have made two shockingly bad decisions in my life, Della. Giving up *Focal Point*. I know a job's a job; it's not the be-all and end-all. But it was for me, and I know I can never get *Focal Point* back, but I can move on job-wise, and I will. But, saying no to Jack…' There, she had said it. After eighteen years of studiously avoiding mentioning Jack in front of Adele, she had said his name while looking at her directly in the eye. It was time to lose the façade and pour out her emotions. 'I will *never* forgive myself for that, Del, and I'm not sure I will ever be able to move on emotionally from it. When I said no to Jack, I broke my own heart, as well as his. I might be able to bury my head in my work and pretend everything's all right, but it's not. I don't think I can ever get over what I did to him. I'm so, so sorry I hurt him so badly. I said no for all the wrong reasons. I loved him with all my heart, but I just couldn't say it to his face. I don't know why I couldn't. I *still* love him, even though I know he's happily married and living in America. I was so ridiculously screwed up about my bloody mother at the time, convinced I was going to turn into her one day. I allowed that fallacy to override what my heart was telling me.'

Adele reached across the table, taking Lisa's hands in her own. 'Oh, Li, why do you *always* have to bottle things up?'

An involuntary tear slid down Lisa's cheek and splashed onto the table.

'I don't know, and you are the only person I would ever want to talk to about Jack. But I felt that I couldn't, because when I hurt him, I hurt you as well. The two people I really cared about, and still do. I don't understand how I could ever have done that. So yes, I've been blotting stuff out by immersing myself in work, so I don't have to face up to the mistakes I've made.'

'Why didn't you tell me any of this before?' There was a trace of frustrated annoyance in Adele's voice. She let go of Lisa's hands, slapping the palms of her hands onto the table.

'Because I only made up my mind this morning.'

'To do what? Tell me about how you felt and still feel about my brother? Or to finally come clean and let it all out? You're an idiot, Lisa Grant! For what it's worth, I forgave you years ago for dumping Jack, and I've struggled to forgive *him* too, because he didn't handle the situation with a great deal of maturity either. Stomping off, leaving you alone in Paris, flying back to London and heading straight for the Flying Duck, where he got completely legless before spending the night with Brenda, the tart-in-law, which he can't even remember doing! Then he compounded his error by believing the lying little cow when she told him he was responsible for getting her up the duff! The mere fact he was so bloody drunk tells me he wouldn't have been capable of impregnating the ginger-haired trollop anyway, and everyone knows she'd slept with half of London! She latched onto Jack because he had been offered a job in New York.' She slid across to the chair next to Lisa's and hugged her. 'I'll tell you something,

Lisa Grant, if I ever get the chance to bang both your heads together, I will do it. I don't know about you, but I need a drink.' She got up and poured two large glasses of *Monte das Uvas Branco.*

'Here, that'll cheer you up. Have a few more and stay the night because I sense there is more you need to tell me, and it will give you a break from another night inhaling mould spores at dingy bloody dell.'

'It's a bit like all those years ago when I finally made the decision to join you and Connie in London. I prevaricated a bit, then made the leap and never looked back. Moving to London opened all sorts of doors for me. I'm really hoping that making a clean break now will open new doors for me before I end up turning into a grumpy, lonely old woman.'

'You will never turn into a *lonely* old woman! I will be there with you, and we can be grumpy old fossils together, but I sense this clean break is taking you somewhere.'

'You know that my dad has always wanted me to live and work in Portugal?'

'I do. It's been on the cards since you left *Focal Point.* You bought yourself a *Teach Yourself Portuguese in Three Months* tutorial, which didn't work, so you decided against it…'

'Well, I've changed my mind.'

Adele took a short sharp intake of breath and sat bolt upright. 'So, you're going then?'

'I gave in my notice at work today, and because I am owed so much time off, they are letting me leave at the end of the week. I expect they've already compiled a shortlist of young, dynamic graduates to replace me anyway.'

'What about Silkwoods? What about Arthur, who will be keeping an eye on him? Because that bloody mother of yours never goes anywhere near him.'

'I haven't told Arthur or anyone yet. Dad still thinks I'm arriving on Christmas Eve and leaving just before New Year. Leaving Arthur will be a huge wrench, but he'd hate to think he was the only reason I was stagnating in Gloucestershire. I've approached an estate agent about selling what is left of the house. I think my father will actually cry when I turn up on his doorstep with more than one suitcase.'

'I think I'm going to cry now. I'm speechless. But mostly about you selling Silkwoods. I secretly hoped that one day you'd accept Arthur's offer of financial help and rebuild it, because I know how much you love the place. I should have realised that would never happen because you're so bloody stubborn.'

'I never thought I would sell it either. But you know me, I could never borrow money from anybody, especially Arthur. I've never wanted to be a drain on anyone's resources.'

'I do know! You've always lived up to your teenage mantra of being a fiercely independent woman.'

'The thing is, I just can't bring myself to go to Silkwoods anymore. I find it too upsetting, and apart from anything else, can you really see me rattling around in that great big place on my own?'

'Oh Li, you *should* have told me you were stressing about all this.'

'I just feel I've reached the stage in my life when I don't want to be on my own anymore. I think… No, I know I *need* a significant other in my life. You have a significant Mike; Connie has a significant Danny; even my mother has a significant Jeremy, and I don't even have a significant cat! There are no Mr Remotely Rights in Gloucestershire, not for me anyway, and I've had my time in London, so I thought I would give Portugal a try.'

'I understand, really I do, and I'll always support you with whatever it is you decide is right for you. I'm just sad you won't be here for our Millennium party, and I've no idea how I'll survive without our regular wine-drinking-putting-the-world-to-right sessions. Still, Portugal isn't a million miles away, but I'm really going to miss you. I hope you're not planning to drive all that way in your old Land Rover?'

'Of course, I am.'

'Well… you better crank it into gear now if you are going to make it in time for Christmas.'

'It's never let me down yet.'

Starting Over

The sun was beginning to fade as, with the hint of a tear in her eye, Lisa watched her old Land Rover being towed away into the sunset with steam pouring out from under its bonnet. She had ignored both Adele and Jim's concerns about a thirty-five-year-old vehicle making the trip, now their words had come back to bite her. She shouldn't have been quite so dismissive and regretted telling them, *'my trusty old steed has got me everywhere so far... next stop, the Algarve!'*

It did get her as far as the ferry terminal, where its engine coughed and spluttered for the last time. Cirencester to Portsmouth was a big ask. Santander to Guia would have been a motorway too far. She consoled herself with the thought that breaking down in an English-speaking port was preferable to breaking down in the heart of the Basque country, but this was not a good start to her new life.

She stood in the middle of the car park, surrounded by all her belongings as the ferry staff argued about how they were going to board all her luggage, and the trickier problem of where they would stow it all for the sailing.

The commotion attracted attention from fellow passengers sitting smugly inside their sturdy sets of wheels. Her luggage contained her sifted out wardrobe of age-appropriate clothing suitable for a forty-year-old, as well as all of her boxed manuscripts, and her Dell computer and printer, which were both looking out of sorts on the tarmac.

She was beginning to panic. There wasn't time to buy another car in Portsmouth, so she would have to buy one when she arrived at Santander, but how would she get all her stuff off the boat and to the nearest car dealer?

A sleek-looking motorhome drew alongside her and pooped its horn. '*Cheeky sod,' she thought.* What was left of the evening sun was shining directly onto the windscreen, making it impossible for her to see the driver's face.

The driver got out of the vehicle and waved. His physique and *Top Gun* sunglasses looked vaguely familiar as he sauntered towards her, smiling, in a slow-motion *take-my-breath-away* moment.

'Lisa? Lisa Grant?'

'Um, yes…'

'Of all the gin joints in all the towns in all the world, she walks into mine. What are you doing here?'

The words, *oh, hell*, flashed through her mind.

'It's me, Rory! Rory Collins! You *must* remember *me?* I know it's been a while, but I haven't changed *that* much. Look,' he said, holding his arms out wide. 'I'm still as irresistible as ever.'

Lisa's cheeks flushed, much to her irritation. 'Rory… of course, I remember. How could I forget about your suspect Humphrey Bogart impersonations? I'm sorry. I was miles away.' *Why am I apologising? And how could I forget you, you complete and utter shit?* 'I've just had a bit of a disaster.'

He ignored what she was saying and clasped his slim bronzed fingers around her upper arms, pulling her close. Wrapping both his arms about her, he kissed her on the lips, more firmly than she would have liked, as their uninvited audience erupted into applause and wolf whistles.

He smelt good, a combination of sandalwood and musk. Feeling an involuntary surge in her loins, she scolded herself for it. He had *dumped* her, for God's sake.

Rory surveyed Lisa's belongings scattered around her. 'So, and I don't wish to presume when it comes to the feminist I know and love, but you look a bit like a damsel in distress to me.'

'I had a trusty steed half an hour ago. A 1963 Land Rover, but it just died and is being towed away to the scrapyard in the sky as we speak.'

'That's awful! Where are you headed?'

'My father's place in the Algarve.'

'What a *fantastic* coincidence! And that's just made my day. I'm doing a shoot at Vale do Lobo. So, my trusty steed and I can take you and your goods and chattels all the way. It's just as well I travel light.' Inwardly, she heaved a huge sigh of relief.

'That would be amazing, Rory, thank you. Monte das Uvas is only about thirty minutes from Vale do Lobo.'

'I couldn't be happier! You never answer my emails, so it will be great to have you as a captive audience between here and Portugal, so we can catch up properly. It's so good to see you, Li, and you are looking *fantastic!*'

Ha! all those sweaty runs on the Gloucestershire roads and tracks, covered in mud splatter and cow pats, had paid off. And there could be no better judge than Rory Collins.

Later that evening, they sat down to eat aboard the MV Cap Finistère as she began to roll in the swell.

'Whoa! I've never been on a ferry before,' Lisa said, blocking her plate with her hand to stop it from sliding off the table. 'I hope, for your sake, I don't get seasick.'

'I'm very pleased you booked a cabin,' Rory responded with what Lisa thought was a hopeful glint in his eye. 'Something I forgot to do, but I can reciprocate tomorrow night because I've booked a very nice-looking B and B, La Balbina; it's about twenty miles outside Santander. I thought I would stay in a few nice places on the way down, and I'll sleep in the motorhome on the way back. I'm planning a bit of a road trip after the shoot. Europe is always photographed in the summer sunshine, so I thought I would capture it during the winter months. So, it's just as well I'm driving a house on wheels. Do you always travel with so much stuff?'

'No! I've just said goodbye to dear old Blighty, for good. I felt I was due a complete change. My life has got a bit dull recently. So, I'm starting a new life in Portugal.'

'You? Dull? Never. Still no wedding ring, I see...' He grasped her left hand and leaned in for a closer inspection. 'I see you still bite your nails, though.'

She snatched her hand away. 'You know me, Rory, I've always been allergic to weddings, my own anyway. My mother has been a kept woman all her life, and that is never going to happen to me.'

'Ah yes, Elizabeth… I remember her well.'

'I'm sure you do. You carried my mother off on your Harley Davidson, with your knight-in-shining-armour helmet on.'

'Honda …'

'Whatever it was, she was very taken with your engine.'

Rory looked irritated. 'Li… I gave your mother a lift to the theatre, and that is all! I don't know what *she* told *you*. You said she had a penchant for being economical with the truth. Anyway, I'm sorry you and I lost touch when I left London.'

'Yes, you never told me you were leaving, you sod, but best not get shitty with you now and dig up old dirt as you've just offered to drive me 1,320 odd miles.'

'I heard you left *Focal Point* because of something to do with your mother. Was she ill?'

'Ill? No, she burnt the bloody family home down! My house, as it happens, my dad had put it in my name when I was born. There'd been a power cut, and she 'accidentally' dropped a candle in the attic. And, to add insult to injury, she'd forgotten to pay the insurance premium.'

'No, shit?'

'No shit, indeed.'

During the night, in true Collins' style, Rory had shown signs of affection, which might have led to something more intimate if given any encouragement. Then, somewhere around Roscoff, Lisa's sea legs capsized, and she lost the contents of her stomach. She continued to retch across the Bay of Biscay, with Rory standing over her.

'I *told* you not to drink so much red wine. You might have got away with one glass, but the best part of a bottle? That was pushing it.'

'It's nothing to do with the sodding wine! It's gale-force bloody ten out there!'

Taking It Slow

Twenty-four hours after leaving Portsmouth, the ship docked in Santander just as the sun was beginning to fade. The campervan bounced as it clattered over the exit ramp, and still feeling poorly, Lisa sat slumped in the passenger seat of the Mercedes Sprinter with her eyes closed.

'Feeling better?' Rory asked, placing a concerned hand on her knee.

Lisa opened one eye, grabbed the offending hand, and placed it firmly back on the steering wheel. 'Keep your hands on the wheel, Rory. I'm not sure I am feeling *better*; the swaying motion of the campervan isn't exactly helping.'

'Don't worry, Li. You'll be soaking in a nice, hot bath at La Balbina before you know it.'

An hour later, they were still driving around in the dark. 'Rory, stop! I cannot believe that a) you didn't bring a map, and b) you refused to pull over and ask for directions.'

'Well, I don't speak Basque.'

'Neither do I! What is it about men and asking for directions?' She pulled a map from her bag. 'From now on I will be doing the map reading. At this rate we won't reach the Portuguese border by Christmas!'

'Ah, so glad to see you are still the feisty Lisa I know and love.'

*

Dear Diary

Salamanca – 4th December 1999

It's a liberating feeling, finally breaking free of the ridiculous workaholic life I've been living forever. I'm filled with boundless energy, probably a combination of not working, not getting enough sleep, and losing a stone in weight. Whatever it is, I hope it lasts!

This is our third night in a plush hotel in Salamanca, at Rory's expense. Okay, so I am breaking my own 'strong, independent woman who likes to pay her own way' rules,' but hey!

Had 'Drover' not died on the quayside at Portsmouth, the plan was to keep driving and have one sleepover here, in a tiny B and B, on the outskirts of town. So, just this once I will allow myself to be pampered. Rory is not exactly strapped for cash, so I don't feel too guilty about it.

We are in a family-sized room with two king-size beds, but I've been playing it cool. I know Rory is keen - no change there - which is good for my ego, but I'm not a slut. We may have lived together, on but mostly off, so he cannot expect to pick up exactly where we left off.

As fond as I am of Rory, I need to keep reminding myself about what he did. Here today, gone tomorrow, arriving every evening for about a week, then, like the Scarlet Pimpernel, he would disappear for weeks until he finally buggered off for good. So, whatever happens on this trip, it won't be permanent. I don't want it to be anyway. He could see a Spanish senorita any day now, and I won't see him for the dust from Rocinante's hooves. In fact, Rory reminds me of Don

Quixote; he's always looking for his next adventure. Anyway, fate has thrown us together, and so far we seem to be getting on well. Cautionary reminder to self: a leopard never changes its spots!

We did have a bit of a spat the other day, although, to be fair, it was me who instigated it - shame on me!

I asked him how long he thought it had been since we last saw each other. He looked up from his plate of pata negra, otherwise known as Iberian pig's leg, and slowly shook his head from side to side, squeezing his eyes together as if trying to solve a cryptic crossword clue. He had no idea.

'Okay, let me remind you. The last time I saw you, you were squashed inside the same compartment of the revolving doors leaving Giuseppe's, with my mother. That morning, you left my bed, reminding me we'd made our plans for the weekend. That weekend came and went, and I heard nothing from you. I was about to file a missing person's report when Finty just happened to drop into conversation that you'd gone to Australia. indefinitely.'

He hadn't been able to look at me. He just sucked the air in through his teeth - one of his many irritating habits - and something he always did when he knew he was in the wrong. He sighed heavily before looking at me again, smiling and fluttering his eyelashes.

'Ah, so you do remember.' I said. 'It was almost a decade ago... not that I'm counting... well, I'm not anymore.'

'Oh, Li... I'd like to think I'm a little more mature these days. And, I am genuinely sorry, but I always stayed in touch. Didn't I?' As if

being genuinely sorry and staying in touch had made things all right. They didn't. Then he compounded his attempt at saying sorry by following it up with, 'I can't believe you are still on your own. I'm just surprised nobody's snapped you up, that's all.'

'Snapped me up?' That really ignited my fuse, so I let him have it. 'I'm not a bloody commodity waiting to be snapped up! Clearly, during the last ten years, you have forgotten everything about me, including my allergy to weddings. I am, and always have been, a fiercely strong, independent woman.'

'Hmm… looks can always be deceptive in my experience. I thought that being allergic to marriage was a bloke thing anyway.'

'Well, it's not just a bloke thing.' I retaliated, taking a sip of wine, and thumping the glass back on the table. 'It's so good to see you again,' he had muttered, reaching out to hold my hand. 'You're still the same feisty but completely irresistible, Lisa Grant. You haven't changed a bit. I asked you to marry me once. Do you remember?'

'Yes, I do, and you were pissed!'

'So were you!'

'Well, thank goodness I wasn't pissed enough to have said yes, otherwise I would have ended up as nuts as Miss Havisham waiting for you to rock up on our wedding day.'

'Okay, let me put it this way. I am amazed that you're still on your own… with no significant other in your life. That's sad, Li, especially now you're forty.'

'Oh, for goodness sake, Rory! You sound just like my mother.' He

backed off at that point, and, hopefully, he will stay off the subject. It's difficult to be angry with Rory for long. The combination of his off-the-Richter-scale good looks and charm makes him irresistible. Unfortunately, he has the same effect on every woman on the planet as well.

For now, I am enjoying spending time with him again. Still, there will be no straying across the platonic friendship boundary on either side. This journey is the start of my new life. I bumped into Rory purely by chance, and we've teamed up only because we're travelling in the same direction. He is not a part of my future.

There's so much to explore in Salamanca, the Golden City, so-called because of its Medieval sandstone buildings. We spent a long time in the cathedral, absorbing its history and culture. It was built in 1513 and is full of artistic treasures, some of which brought tears to my eyes. I had Rory fooled for a while when I showed him the stone carving of the spaceman, enthusing about the breakthroughs in space travel that the Spanish made in the 16th century. Perhaps I should have been an actress. I did eventually come clean and told him that the spaceman was carved during the renovations in 1992, but he can be so gullible. I love churches. There is something very calming about them, although I have never been very religious. I wonder when the last time I said any prayers was? Probably my first night at Coln Castle! But I did say one today, for Arthur, while I was in the cathedral. I feel bad about leaving him.

Rory thinks he may be all cultured out and wants to spend a few days chilling and drinking Rioja. I said he can do as much wine tasting as he likes when we get to Monte das Uvas for free. We are off to Cáceres tomorrow. It was built by the Romans, so it should warm up his interest in culture again. He always had a soft spot for Aphrodite.

Dear Diary

Parador de Cáceres – December 6th, 1999

Not a lot of sightseeing today. We had a long, leisurely lunch, followed by a stroll around the town. I'm back in our sumptuous bedroom now. Another fine hostelry at Rory's expense; it's a double bed, though.

Rory has gone to get us a nightcap, and after a few days on the road I am feeling very uninhibited... in many ways. I don't feel tired, and I don't feel I want to play hard to get. YOLO! What was it I said the other day about Rory not being a part of my future? One night isn't going to turn us into an 'item.'

The door swung open, and Lisa snapped her diary shut. Rory propped himself up with one hand against the doorframe, with a red carnation between his teeth and a bottle of champagne and two glasses in the other. She couldn't help but laugh, but in that instant, Rory morphed from an itinerant and often irritating photographer, into a hot Don Juan! The thought of unbridled sex was suddenly overwhelming. After all, bed-rattling sex was the one thing she knew he could be relied on to provide.

'Champagne for the senorita!' he announced, slamming the door behind him with his foot. 'Well, it's Cava, actually, but when in Spain and all that. What are you writing? Another book?'

'No... I started a diary in Salamanca.'

'I hope I'm being recorded in a favourable light. Knight in shining armour rescues a damsel in distress in Portsmouth.' He filled both glasses and offered one to Lisa. 'We're having a great time, aren't we? We seem to be getting on just as well as we used to. Here's to us.'

Lisa got to her feet, and they chinked their glasses together.

'Here's to us.'

They took a sip, and Rory bent his head and kissed her firmly on the mouth. Putting down his glass, he pulled her closer to him.

'You know what, Lisa Grant? Things between us could get a little hotter if we...'

'If we... added a little Spanish paprika?' she interrupted. 'That's exactly what I was thinking...'

Dear Diary

Parador de Cáceres—7th December 1999

Missed breakfast! Ha! Ha! There's nothing like a liberating big bang before you go to sleep, and again when you wake up. I can't believe I just wrote that, but I think I'm still quite nifty between the sheets, although I say it myself. And Rory, despite his dubious powers of memory, seems to have remembered where my G-spot is. I just feel a bit sorry for the couple next door.

He has gone out with his spear to find food before we move on to

Badajoz today to see the ancient walled city, then we're off to Evora, which will be our first stop in Portugal. From there we will visit Lisbon and Estoril, then on to Dad's. We've only spent a short time together, but it's been great, and I will miss the old sod when he goes.

*

Will stood in his office window watching a campervan climbing slowly up the hill in the fading light.

'We're not expecting anybody in a campervan, are we, Tommy?' Will and Thomas were catching up on paperwork in the office, despite it being well past 6 o'clock.

'A lost tourist, I expect. I'll go and put them right.'

'No, no, it's okay. I'll go. I'll be popping a cork as soon as I get in, so I'll expect to see you shortly.'

Will felt drawn to the campervan. As he left the office, he walked briskly towards the front door, watching the campervan draw closer. A disembodied arm started waving frantically out of the passenger side window.

'Lisa?'

As soon as the campervan stopped, Lisa got out and ran towards her father with her arms outstretched.

'Hello, Dad,' she said, wrapping her arms around him.

'How wonderful to see you, my darling, two weeks early too! The best early Christmas present I could ever have hoped for. What a fantastic surprise!'

'And I've got a bigger one for you, Dad...'

Christmas Day

When Lisa awoke on Christmas day, Rory was propped up on one elbow watching her.

'Happy Christmas, sleeping beauty… It's a beautiful, sunny day… It will probably be pissing down in the UK… if not snowing.'

She stretched from head to toe. 'Happy Christmas to you too. What time is it?'

Rory reached for his watch on the bedside table. 'Just before ten. I think your dad said something about a spot of brunch at ten-thirty which, knowing Will and Thomas, will be a full-on breakfast buffet.'

'I'd better get moving then. There's loads that needs doing for today's main gourmet event and, as the only female in this male-dominated household, now I'm outnumbered by 5-1 since Henry and Charles arrived, I feel I should be flaunting my domestic goddess skills, not that I've got any to boast about.'

'Hang on a minute, Li, there's something I been wanting to ask you. I've been thinking.'

'Oh, God! That sounds dangerous!'

'Very funny. I just thought that, as we got on so well travelling down here, and there were no fallings-out or anything…'

'Yes, we had a great time.'

'Well, how about we take it a step further… you and me?'

'Oh Christ, Rory! You're not going to propose again, are you?'

'No, of course not. Like you, getting married is not at the top of my list. But I do have a proposal of sorts to make. Why don't we travel around the world together? Just take a couple of backpacks and go! You can write about our adventures, and I can take photos. I bet you *Focal Point,* among others, would pay us for a blow-by-blow account of our trip.'

'You've got to be joking! At least I hope you are? If you'd asked me twenty years ago, I would have gone with you like a shot, and I wasn't into camping then, let alone now. I really can't see myself trekking across a cow pat splattered field in the middle of the night to get to the nearest latrine.'

'I wouldn't make you camp, exactly…'

'I should bloody well hope not. Not at my age anyway…'

'Glamp, perhaps?

'You're serious, aren't you?'

'Deadly! I've wanted to do it for a long time, and I can't think of anyone else I would rather do it with.'

'Rory… I've only just got my head around coming here. I honestly don't know if it will stretch to going any further afield… not right now anyway.'

'I'm not going to push you into making a decision, but as you know, the shoot at Vale do Lobo finishes on Millennium Eve when I'm planning to push off and drive around Europe. You could come with me, and we could just keep going. Just give it some thought anyway.'

'I promise you, I will *think* about it, but it would be a huge deal for me. You've been taking off here, there and everywhere for years, and often forgetting to tell those you're closest to you're going anywhere!'

'Yes well, I was a feckless youth then. But I've told you this time, and more importantly, I'm asking you to come with me.'

'I'm not making any promises, Rory, but I will think about it.' She kissed him lightly on the lips and headed for the shower. As the water pounded down on her head, she revisited the day Rory met her mother, as well as the day Finty told her he had gone to Australia.

Stepping out of the shower, she studied her reflection in the mirror.

'Fourteen days with Rory does not mean you are joined at the hip. It's been fun; you've been flattered by his attention. He's boosted your ego, but that is it. You know he's habitually unreliable; he disappeared to another continent and didn't even bother to tell you. He's fickle, and he fancied your mother, for God's sake! A few days travelling with him from Santander to Monte das Uvas hasn't suddenly turned him into Mr Reliability. Rushing around the world with him would be a reckless and foolish thing to do, and you bloody well know it!' She dressed and joined Rory and the others in the dining room.

After such a late brunch, it surprised Lisa to find she still had room for their delicious evening meal. Her father and Thomas had done them proud.

Rory sat back with a satisfied grin. 'I don't think I have eaten so much in my entire life,' He clutched his lean stomach with both hands. 'I think I will always want Christmas dinner Portuguese-style! Thank you so much, Will and Thomas. It has been a great day.'

Lisa got to her feet, 'I think I'm going for a breath of fresh air and walk some of our amazing meal off before it gets dark. Who's coming with me?' The animated conversation suddenly fell silent at the suggestion of a walk.

Will scanned the room. 'What a lazy bunch! Come on, Lisa, your old father, will go with you.'

Three hundred feet up the path above the house, her father and Thomas had cleared a small area of scrubland and built a patio area. They had used Mediterranean bricks to create a barbecue, and large granite blocks for seating and a table. Sheltered by the lee of the rockface, it was the perfect place to view the thriving vineyard, house, and outbuildings, as well as the orange groves scattered around the slopes down to the Atlantic Ocean beyond. It was also a great place to view the night sky, so it was affectionately known as the Planetarium.

'You've done such a good job up here, Dad.'

'We love it! We often come here with a bottle or two of wine to gaze at the stars.'

'You chose well when you bought this place.'

Will laughed, scraping his sun-bleached floppy fringe away from his eyes. 'It was more luck than good judgment. We really didn't know what we were letting ourselves in for, but we have been happy here once we'd made it habitable. When you came back into my life, I didn't think it could get any better. But now I have you here all the time... well, it's something I never allowed myself to dream could ever happen. Come on, let's walk for another twenty minutes, then go back. It will be dark soon. Did you ring Arthur, by the way?'

'Yes, I did, and he was pleased with my Christmas present, a set of audiobooks. I confess I felt bad about leaving him, but he has always been keen for me to spread my wings.'

'How is he?'

'He's okay, very frail, but he's always upbeat, so uncomplaining, given his medical history. He's eighty-five, but his brain is as sharp as it ever was.'

'Rory seems like a nice chap?' her father said, placing a protective arm around Lisa's shoulders.

'He made a great travelling companion on the way down here. He's fun, and he really looked after me. Thank you for including him in our Christmas, by the way. He was very pleased to be asked.'

'You don't have to *thank* us, Lisa. Anybody who is genuinely fond of you is always welcome here.

'And I am very fond of him, Dad…'

'Then, why is it that I feel there's a *but* coming?'

'Being in a relationship with Rory is never going to be a relaxing one. Wanderlust is in his DNA. He's happiest when he's on the move. Travel consumes him. The time he has spent here with us, he has been the most relaxed I've ever seen him.'

'And that would have something to do with you, I think.'

Lisa sighed and turned to face her father. 'I would never presume to tie anybody down in a relationship, but, as you know, I've been here before with Rory. We were, loosely, together in London, and he used to disappear for days, sometimes weeks. I knew he had a girl in every magazine in London, Finty too apparently. But my life back then was so hectic, I kind of turned a blind eye to what he was doing behind my back. Then he disappeared off to Australia and didn't even tell me he was going. He always kept in touch... for what it is worth. But, as fond of him as I am, a commitment to Rory would be reckless. I don't know, Dad. I'm hopeless at long-term relationships, but for the first time in my life, I would like to have a significant other in my life. I just don't think it's Rory. He put me on the spot when I woke up this morning, asking me to travel around the world with him.'

'Good heavens, and you've only just arrived here! I hope you will give this proposal some considered thought before giving him your answer?'

'Of course, I will. I've made two foolish and rash decisions in my life, dumping Jack, and giving up my career after the fire. I'm not planning to make any more.'

'And I'm very confident that you won't. Come on, it's time to go back. I'll race you down the hill.'

When they walked through the front door, Henry was on the phone in the hall.

'She's here now... hang on a sec, and I'll put her on. Happy Christmas, love to everybody, and I look forward to seeing you when I get back. It's Adele,' he said, handing the phone to Lisa.

'Hi! Happy Christmas!'

'And a... Happy Christmas... to you too!' Lisa puffed.

'You sound out of breath…'

'I am! I've just run down the hill from the Planetarium, and my dad outsprinted me. I'll get my own back on the flat.'

'Thanks for emailing me to let me know you got there safely. My heart really went out to you when you told me about the death of poor old 'Rover', but I did warn you! Hope you've all had a good day?'

'Brilliant, thank you. As you know, my dad and Thomas are brilliant cooks, so I think I've eaten the equivalent of my bodyweight today!'

'I've got a bit of interesting news for you, but first I'm dying to find out who your knight in shining armour is.'

'News? Good, I hope. My knight was Rory Collins, of all people. He just happened to be heading for Vale do Lobo in a great big campervan.'

'Rory?'

'Yes, you must remember him?'

'Li! How could I possibly forget about Rory? You were always on the phone, wanting a shoulder to cry on after he dumped you.'

'He didn't exactly *dump* me…'

'It depends on what your definition of dumping is, but going to work and never coming back would be classified as dumping in my book. So, you travelled down in a campervan… together?'

'Yes, we didn't sleep in the van though; we stayed in a few very nice paradors on the way, at Rory's expense.'

'In the same room?'

'Adele! I hate it when you go all prudish on me. I thought you would be pleased for me, and it's been such a long time since I crushed the bedsprings. He's still pretty irresistible. He's been working in Africa, so he's all bronzed and gorgeous!'

'My goodness me, Lisa Grant, how quickly things change. A few weeks outside Gloucestershire where everything is doom and gloom, to everything in the Portuguese garden being wonderfully rosé.'

Lisa laughed and, cupping her hand around the mouthpiece of the phone, whispered, 'I am just so relieved and very pleased to report that having abstained for so long that all parts seem to be in good working order! Forty and still functioning.' Her remark was followed by silence. Adele never approved of Rory. 'Della?'

'Sorry, I was a bit distracted for a minute.'

'What's your news then?'

'My news?' She sounded huffy. 'Oh, nothing much really, Jack arrived a couple of days ago'

'Jack?'

'Big brother Jack!' Adele snapped.

'Yes, I know who you mean! I knew he was spending Christmas and New Year with you.'

'It's the first Christmas we've spent together since he went to live in New York.' Her tone changed from huffy to sharp.

Lisa felt a pang of guilt. It was entirely her fault that he had taken the job in the States, which meant that they never saw a great deal of each other.

'He is very disappointed he is not going to see you. He's got something for you, apparently.' Lisa's racing heart skipped a beat, as the words 'How's Brenda, and the twins? And how are Amy and Josh getting on with their cousins?' forced their way out of her mouth. She instantly regretted saying them.

A whoosh streamed down the telephone as Adele sighed. 'No, Li... no Brenda, or the twins,' came the dismissive response. 'Enjoy the rest of your Christmas Day, and we're all very sorry not to be seeing you on New Year's Eve. Never mind. Give my love to your dad...'

Lisa was being cut short. 'Will do. Love to you all...' She put the phone down and walked through to the sitting room where Henry was asleep on the sofa. One of her father and Thomas's most inspired ideas when they restored the house at Monte das Uvas was to install a large sliding glass door separating the sitting room from the veranda. So, when the temperatures cooled during the winter months, the aesthetically perfect view down to the sea could still be seen from the sitting room as the log-burning fire crackled and spat inside.

She silently slid the glass door open just wide enough to let herself out onto the veranda and stood with her arms folded, gazing towards the horizon.

Adele had been short with her. She had been expecting something along the lines of, *I miss you so much,* she hadn't bargained for snappy. Maybe she was just jaded. Christmas can be exhausting, especially when you're the one doing the entertaining.

It was odd that Jack was over for both Christmas and the New Year without Brenda and the twins. It couldn't be for financial reasons, surely? Jack had been CEO of Harkness for ten years. She thought Adele would have been pleased to have him to herself for Christmas, and the New Year, given that she couldn't stand her sister-in-law.

Jack had something for her. What on Earth could it be? As she thought about Jack, Peter Frampton popped into her head singing *Baby I Love Your Way.* Then her thoughts turned to Rory's proposal, and Peter Frampton's gentle love song faded away, replaced by Bruce Springsteen's *Born to Run.* Her brain flooded with images of running around the African bush with Rory, being chased by her mother in the guise of a hungry lioness shouting, 'Rory! You're supposed to look at me first!'

With Rory, there would never be any commitment. Perhaps that was why they always got on so well together in the past? There was a time when she thought she never wanted someone to share every day of her life with, but she had changed. Now, she needed a significant other. A soul mate, someone she could share the rest of what was left of her life with. Someone she could put down roots with. Someone who would always be there when she turned out the light at night and would reciprocate when she would roll over and say, 'I love you,' and they would fall asleep in each other's arms. A few nights of unbridled passion with Rory were never to bind them together forever. She'd been there before! She was forty and had just started a new life in Portugal. Being seduced into a trip around the world with someone so easily distracted by the opposite sex was farcical; he could dump her at any time. It was the nature of the beast.

*

After putting the phone down to Lisa, Adele stormed into the sitting room and threw herself onto the sofa, folding her arms across her chest.

'Whatever's the matter?' asked Mike. 'You look like you've just had a conversation with Ice Queen Elizabeth, not Lisa.'

Jack looked away from the TV. The rerun of an old comedy classic wasn't holding his attention anyway. 'Have you finished talking to Li already, Adele? I told you I wanted to wish her a Happy Christmas.'

'I know you did, Jack, but when she told me who her knight in shining armour was, I wound the conversation up. I just can't believe it!'

Mike gave his wife a cheeky grin. 'Who? Brad Pitt? Leonardo DiCaprio…'

'No, Mike, you're so not funny. It was that manipulative little paparazzi prick… Rory Collins! I mean, what are the odds? Li takes off to start a new life in Portugal, and she just happens to bump into Rory, bloody Collins on day one. He'll do exactly what he did to her last time. Buoy her up, give her a good time and then dump her.'

'Ah, that's not good! Wait a minute, I have an idea. We'll turn Jack into Saint George, and he can go out there, rescue the damsel in distress and slay the paparazzi dragon!' Mike slapped his brother-in-law heartily on the back.

Adele gave Mike an exasperated look. 'Don't be so ridiculous. Jack can't just rock up there unannounced.'

'I don't see why not!' Jack exclaimed. 'I thought Lisa would be here on New Year's Eve. I need to see her, and now I have the perfect excuse.'

'She might not want to see you.'

About to pop another lager can, Mike looked at Jack, then to Adele. 'Of course, she will. She's been miserable for eighteen years without Jack; she'll be delighted to see him.'

Josh pressed the stop key on his Walkman. 'Mum, did I just hear that right? Is Uncle Jack… like… really going to … slay a dragon?'

Adele rolled her eyes and sighed. 'You heard right, Josh, but I think your dad and Uncle Jack are a bit over-Christmas-ed.'

The Surprise Visit

After Christmas, Lisa put any travel plans to the back of her mind and threw herself into building the Monte das Uvas website. Rory was focused on finishing the gig at Vale do Lobo, complaining he had never worked so hard and would be relieved when New Year's Day finally arrived.

'I really appreciate you doing this for us.' Will straightened a mess of paperwork and snapped it into a box file. 'What should we call the new website?'

She looked up from the desk opposite her father's. 'I'm more than happy to do it, Dad. I love doing it. I'll build the site first, then we can apply for a domain name and hosting, but I was thinking along the lines of *Monte das Uvas* with the tagline, *Vinho da Vida.*'

Will's face lit up. '*Wine of Life*. I like the sound of that!'

'Hmm, just an idea. I've always been addicted to writing, but these days, anything to do with computers comes a very close second. There's always so much to learn.' She knew Will was enjoying having her around and that she'd found Rory's proposition unsettling. He only wanted her to be happy and wouldn't try to influence her decision.

'Come on,' Will said, getting up. 'It's lunchtime. We're a fine pair of workaholics, you and me. Thomas is also very conscientious, but he's always getting cross with me because sometimes, I find it hard to switch off. You've been staring at that screen since eight this morning. Let's go and grab something to eat.' As he got up, he looked out of the window. 'Ah, I see we've got another visitor. I wonder who that could be? There's a hire car parked next to the campervan.'

'Another tourist wanting to get their hands on a few boxes of *Monte das Uvas*, I expect, Dad.'

'Well, let's go and find out.'

As they walked towards the front door, a pissed-off looking Rory emerged, cameras dangling from both shoulders.

'Who's arrived?' her father asked.

'Jack!' came the petulant response.

'Jack, who?' Lisa asked.

'Jack Wilde!' he snapped, glowering at her. A look that said, *And I bet you knew he was coming.* 'He says he's here to personally deliver something to Lisa. I'm off to Vale de Lobo!'

She wanted to say, 'Rory wait, I had no idea he was coming,' but she seemed to be at a loss for words.

'Lisa? Are you alright?' her father asked softly, as Rory sped off down the hill leaving a wake of scattered gravel and dust behind him.

She was rooted to the spot, focusing on the hire car with Jack-related thoughts racing through her head, along with a Peter Frampton soundtrack.

'I… er…' She was trembling. 'Dad… I really don't think I can do this. I haven't seen him since I told him I didn't want to marry him.'

She felt close to tears and wanted her father to say, *'There, there, everything's going to be okay.'* She might have fantasized about this moment for the past eighteen years, but having been presented with it, all she felt capable of doing was falling apart. She had never fainted before, but now would be a good time, and she wouldn't have to face it all.

'Come on, Lisa,' her father gave her a hug, 'everything will be okay, I promise. I'll scoop everybody up, and we'll all quietly disappear into the kitchen and sort something out for lunch, so you two can have the sitting room to yourselves. Give me a couple of minutes and then come in.'

Lisa waited by the front door, taking deep breaths, for precisely five minutes, before going in. She slipped silently in through the door of the sitting room, and all she could hear was her heart pounding. Jack had his back to her, looking out to the veranda, a glass of Vino Branco in his hand. His hair was still jet-black, but his curls were a little shorter. He spun around, spilling a little wine as he did so, which broke the ice.

He smiled at her, and his Bambi-Esque eyes made her feel woozy. Fishing out a handkerchief from his jacket pocket, he dabbed his hand and the glass.

'As you can see, even after all these years, Lisa Grant, you still make me feel a little jittery, but in a good way.' She smiled but didn't know what to say or do next. Her throat felt like it had been clamped by an invisible vice. If she tried speaking, she thought she would choke. All she wanted to do was cry. He put down his glass and gently wrapped her in his arms.

'It's been such a long time, Li… way too long…'

She instantly relaxed in his embrace, breathing in the scent of him, and *Baby I Love Your Way* popped back into her head. He had once made her feel so secure, so loved, and she had turned him away. Feeling the warmth of his body against her own, she began to relax as eighteen years of repentance and silent tears began to slip away.

Rory returned to Monte das Uvas late that night, and Lisa was already in bed. His mood seemed to have improved since he grumped off earlier in the day, and the J word was never mentioned. He seemed upbeat, telling Lisa he would be staying for the millennium party at Vale do Lobo and that he had met a delightful Portuguese reporter called Célia. He was gone by the time Lisa woke up the next day.

A New Millennium

Will and Thomas started preparations for their millennium party early the following morning and continued throughout most of the day. Thomas, Charles, and Lisa sorted out the food while Jack and Henry helped Will set up his impressive stash of fireworks, which promised a spectacular display.

As midnight approached and the party was in full swing, Lisa took her father to one side and wished him a *Happy New Year.* She had asked him earlier in the day if he would mind if she slipped away from the party to take Jack up to the Planetarium, to watch the fireworks and the stars.

'Of course, I don't mind. I think it's an excellent idea, but you can't see in a new year, let alone a new Millennium, without taking some champagne up there with you. Leave it with me. I've got to go out in the Mini Moke later; I'll take a bottle or two up there and leave them in a cool box.'

But Will had done more than just take a couple of bottles up to the Planetarium.

Jack's stared in disbelief. 'Wow! So this is the famous Planetarium. It's… amazing. Cushions and blankets, even torches to light, and logs in the barbecue pit, too. Your dad never did things by halves.' He peered into the cool box. 'Two bottles of, *Monte das Uvas Champanhe Lisa.* And it looks like there's enough party food for ten people, not just the two of us!'

'It's actually made me feel quite emotional. I had no idea Dad was going to go to quite so much trouble. Being without him for such a large chunk of my life has made me realise just how precious our relationship is.' Lisa lit a match and threw it into the fire, which whooshed into the night sky.

Jack rubbed his hand comfortingly, up, and down Lisa's upper arm. The way he always used to. 'Noo Year's Eve always brings out everybody's emotions. It's a good time for everyone to stop and think, as well as hope that the noo year will give us the chance to get things right.'

'Noo year...? You're a bona fide New Yawker now, aren't you Jack?'

'Occupational hazard, I guess, given I've been surrounded by millions of 'em for eighteen years.' He checked his watch. 'It's very nearly midnight.' He grabbed the champagne from the cool box, and Lisa placed two glasses on the table.

There was a chorus of animated voices from below counting down the seconds to the start of the new millennium, culminating in cries of *'Happy New Year'* and *'Feliz Ano Nova,'* as Jack popped the champagne cork and filled their glasses, the first of her father's rockets powered into the clear dark night, exploding in a cascade of a thousand colours. Fireworks began exploding up and down the coast as far as the eye could see. They clinked their glasses together, as Jack leant forward, kissing her lightly on her cheek, his lips brushing the corner of her mouth. She felt a ripple of giddy excitement rush through her body as her father let off another rocket. Whatever he had as a young man, he certainly hadn't lost. When he looked at her, he still took her breath away.

'Happy Noo Year, Lisa. It's so good to see you again.'

'Happy Noo Year to you too, Mr Yorkles.'

'Yep, that would be me, Mr Yorkles of Lawn-Guyland.' He smiled, and the honesty in his Bambi-esque eyes transported her back to Paris and the vision of him on bended knee in front of her. As the fireworks popped and banged around them, she felt she wanted to plead with him for forgiveness and tell him she was sorry.

They took another sip of the champagne, giggling as it fizzed and bubbled up their noses.

'*Mm,* this tastes good. It's been a long time since I last tasted *Champagne Lisa.*'

'I can't believe we've got so old, Jack. How did that happen?'

'Life has a nasty habit of slipping past without you noticing. One minute we are looking at our whole lives stretched out before us, then we blink and, suddenly, twenty years have shot by.'

She put her glass down as her father, Thomas and Henry simultaneously let off rockets, which hissed and hummed as they soared into the sky.

'Jack... I never meant to hurt you. I have no idea what on Earth was going through my head all those years ago. I was immature and stupid.'

'Who knows what was going on inside both our heads? I'm sorry about the way I behaved, too. I should never have left you in Paris, on your own.'

'I should have followed you and tried to salvage things. Instead, I bought a bottle of Pernod and drank far too much of it sitting underneath the Eiffel Tower. It wasn't my finest hour, and I don't even *like* Pernod. I was so sick; I couldn't go anywhere for two days.' They laughed, watching Henry lighting the fuse of a Catherine Wheel. It spun and twirled in a frenzy of mesmerising colour.

'The insanity of youth, hey? But this is nice. You and I, together again for the first time after much too long, and on such a spectacular occasion.'

'Older… wiser…' she mused. 'Actually, the latter doesn't apply in my case. World-weary and battle scarred might be more appropriate. Adele, no doubt, told you that I've only just moved out here to start a new life and I feel bad because she arranged her millennium party around you. And you… are here.'

'I think she arranged it around you as well, but don't feel bad. I'm here with her blessing. Adele is one of the most forgiving people I know.'

'I know she is…. How come you're over without Brenda and the children?'

'There is no more Brenda and me, Li. Not anymore. We've just come to the end of an acrimonious divorce.'

An involuntary sigh escaped her lips. Was that why he was in Portugal with her?

'While you were drinking Pernod in Paris that night, I bumped into

Brenda in the Flying Duck. Apparently, I was crying into a glass of Southern Comfort on ice while trying to sing, *Baby I Love Your Way*. When I started sliding off the bar stool, she volunteered to take me home. You do know the only reason I went to bed with her was to get back at you for turning me down? How stupid and immature was that? Not that I have any recollection of it. It's hard to believe I was capable of doing anything more than passing out. And I've been miserable for eighteen years as a result, which serves me right. I have no idea how Brenda and I managed to stick together for so long. For the children's sake, I suppose, and they blame me for everything. They've got very curly hair, by the way, so I'm guessing they probably are mine, despite what Adele has to say.'

'Our parents have a lot to answer for, Jack, but I'm sure you make a great dad and don't forget, the teenage years are not the easiest. Ask your sister. She could write a thesis on the subject.'

'Do you regret not having children, Li?'

Jack's question was blunt and sensitive, but it didn't faze her. 'Well, yes and then no... you know how paranoid I've always been about my genes, and that one day I would turn into my mother. I still might, God forbid! Anyway, passing on her emotionless genes to my children, I wouldn't want to inflict that on anyone. Then, of course, I have never really found anybody I wanted to have children with.' The last few words caught in her throat, and she took a sip of champagne.

'There has never been anything emotionless about you, Li. I told you years ago you would never be like Elizabeth and, maybe, it's just a question of allowing your heart to believe that the right person has been there all along?'

As she was trying to get her head around what he had just said, he asked another thought-provoking question.

'So, what does the future have in store for you and I, Li? How many more years must we regret going our separate ways? That's why I came over to the UK. To work out where I want to be for the rest of my life. I haven't exactly been a mover and shaker as far as my career is concerned, and it's about to go full circle. I'm still with Harkness who, you will remember, I started working for twenty-odd years ago, and because they don't want this old stalwart to leave them, they've asked me to run their London office. Which means I really will be back where I started.' When Lisa chuckled, he nodded affectionately. 'I've really missed that infectious giggle, Lisa Grant.'

She smiled, feeling her cheeks flush. 'I think we're both having a mid-life crisis.' She leaned into him playfully with her shoulder. 'I've been wondering where I'm going to be spending the rest of my life too. At least I've managed to get myself as far as Portugal. Dad has been trying to persuade me to come and live here for years, and the climate has always made it very appealing. I can help them around the vineyard, and I've kickstarted my freelance work, then there's the book. Did Adele tell you I finally finished writing *that* book?'

'Oh, my God. I'm so sorry... I've been a little side-tracked since I saw you... Just hang on a minute; I need to get something out of the car.'

She watched him run down the hill and puff his way back. *Yes indeed, Jack Wilde. What about our future?*

When he returned to the Planetarium, he slumped onto the chaise-longue beside her, exhausted. I'm not as fit as I was twenty years ago.' He handed her an A4-size envelope. 'Apart from wanting, more than anything, to watch the millennium sunrise with you, this is my *official* excuse for coming to see you... to give you this. It's from Finty. I arranged to meet her for a coffee when I arrived in London. I'd never met her before, but I promised a mutual friend I'd look her up. We started talking about *Focal Point*, and your name inevitably popped up. She asked me if I was going to see you over Christmas and New Year. At that point, I thought you would be at Adele and Mike's party. I promised Finty I would deliver this in person. So here I am, and here it is. It's from a colleague of hers, Neville Shuffle... something.'

She took the envelope from him and held it in both hands. 'Bottom... Shufflebottom. You might remember that spoofy novel I started writing about my ex-umbilical attachment when we were all in London?'

'I remember it very well, actually! You read some of it to me sitting cross-legged on your bed, stark naked and as drunk as a skunk. It's a vision that's always stayed with me.' His lips cracked open into a broad smile.

Her cheeks flushed, and a warm sensation flooded through her whole body as the hazy memory of cavorting stark naked around her bedroom at the flat at Notting Hill singing *Honey Bun* flashed into her mind.

'Well, I eventually finished it, and I've been pitching it to various publishers and agents. I have quite a collection of rejection letters. I expect this is another one. Look.' She held up her right hand and spread out her fingers. 'I've bitten my nails to the quick waiting to hear back. Anyway, here goes…' When she opened the envelope, she gasped with excitement. 'This is excellent news, Jack.' She held up a letter for him to see. 'Neville Shufflethingie likes my book. This, is my author badge of honour… it's a - ***Representation Contract.***

'Congratulations!'

'Oh, my God! What a way to start the New Year! Did you know what was in it?'

'I kind of guessed from the size of the envelope that it wasn't a rejection letter.'

There was a bonus as well - thanks to an inspirational idea of Finty's. Bodder and Baunton were prepared to offer her an advance to produce a compilation of updated interviews with the people she had interviewed during her journalistic career.

'We think most of them are still alive, so we would expect you to re-interview them and see how far they have come or how far they have fallen since you first interviewed them.'

'This is just bloody brilliant, Jack. I can't believe my luck. I wonder if Maggie Thatcher would be up for it. I know what I am going to call it too… *Straight Talk - My Life in Interviews.* Maybe they would go for a *Curtain Up - My Life in Reviews.* I did hundreds of theatre reviews while I was at *Focal Point*. Anyway, I must ring Arthur first thing tomorrow, I mean today. He'll be so pleased for me.'

'You deserve it. Now you can work from anywhere in the world you want.'

Rory suddenly popped into Lisa's head. She could work from anywhere in the world where she chose to put down roots, but trailing around the world with feckless Rory while trying to put a book together was never going to work.

'And Rory...' Jack must have read her mind. 'Does he feature in your life plan? Will you be putting down roots together?'

She plumped up the pillows on the chaise longue and lay back against them. 'I think Rory finds the concept of putting roots down too claustrophobic. Anyway, let's not talk about him. I want to hear about everything that has happened to you over the last eighteen years, but first of all, we should do a bit of stargazing. Just look at that... isn't it the Milky Way?'

*

The following morning, Lisa woke to the sound of a solitary seagull leaving its roosting place. Peering out from under the blanket her father had thoughtfully provided, she realised Jack was watching her, smiling. Looking up into his warm brown eyes, she felt relaxed and happy, a feeling that had eluded her since she last woke up with him in Paris all those years ago.

'I was about to wake you. The sun's just about to come up.'

'At what point did I drop off?'

'Oh, somewhere between my stimulating account of me catching Brenda in our bed with my gym buddy, Barnaby Tyler, and the twins' seventeenth birthday.'

'Oops… Sorry. I hope I didn't snore?'

'Just a little, but I've really missed the Lisa Grant snore.'

She sat up as the first rays of sun burst above the horizon. Jack pulled her close and responding to his touch, she felt an adrenalin rush surge through her body as, mesmerised, they watched the luminous glow of deep oranges, bright yellows, and flame reds, spread across the sky.

Jack turned to face Lisa, stroking her cheek with the tips of his fingers. 'Pretty special, huh?'

Nestling into his arms, she looked at him and whispered, 'Yes, it's… truly amazing.'

Emotional Overload

Lisa felt more relaxed and happier than she could remember for the last eighteen years. Jack was back in her life and a free man, which made his comment about *'What are we both going to be doing for the rest of our lives'* doubly exciting, and one that would be receiving the full focus of her attention.

With the rising sun boosting their sagging energy levels, they took off down the hill to the house. But they hadn't run far when Lisa stopped abruptly and caught Jack's arm. 'There's another hire car next to yours. It looks like we have more visitors.' Shielding her eyes to see more clearly. 'What on earth? Oh, God. What's he doing here!'

'Even after eighteen years, I still remember what Jeremy Jermayne looks like and if *he's* here…'

'Yes, *she* will be here, too. They never go anywhere without each other. It's a bit odd, though. My mother never shows up anywhere without letting everyone know in advance because she likes to receive the red carpet treatment wherever she goes. Jack, I honestly don't think I can face her at this time of the morning.'

'Come on, be brave.' Jack took Lisa's hand, and they started down the hill again. 'I'd doubt even your mother would come all this way at such an ungodly hour unless it were important, would she?'

'You're right, of course. Look, Jeremy's waving, I ought to be nice to him at least.' Lisa waved back, and when they came closer, she greeted him, 'Jeremy. What a surprise, Happy New Year. Are you planning on… staying?'

'Happy New Year to you, Sweet Pea,' Jeremy kissed her on both cheeks. 'And a Happy New Year to you too, Jack. It's been a long time since you tried to knock me out, but I haven't forgotten. You won't do it again, I hope. I'm sixty now; I might not come round.'

Jack gave Lisa a sideways glance before shaking Jeremy's hand. 'I was much younger then, but I'm still as protective.'

Forcing a laugh, Lisa caught Jack's arm. 'Yes, it was all such a long time ago, and Jack's never hit anyone again. So, no need to worry, Jeremy, Jack's punching days are over. Anyway, I take it my mother is here, too?'

'Yes, she's already gone inside. I was getting her make-up bag out of the car just in case she wants to freshen up a bit.'

'It's a good job her make-up bag is on wheels, given the size of it.' Lisa quipped, 'You must have got a very early flight?'

'We arrived on the 6 o'clock flight from Heathrow and were lucky to find a hire car office open when we landed at Faro airport. Your mother hasn't been up this early for years, but I'm afraid she has some bad news for you, Sweet Pea, and she wanted to tell you in person rather than over the phone.'

Lisa's bubble of buoyed exuberance burst; could it be that after forty years of their volatile relationship, her mother had arrived out of the blue to tell her some devastating illness had struck her? She ran towards the house, closely followed by Jack and Jeremy. As she opened the heavy pine front door, Lisa could hear her mother's sonorous Foghorn-Leghorn voice reverberating around the house.

'It's quite a nice view from here to the sea, Will, although I'm not sure that I would want to look at it all the time, and I would put some curtains or blinds up if I were you, you never know who might be looking in at you when it's dark.'

When Lisa stepped into the room, Thomas, Henry, Charles, and Will were standing in a line, bleary-eyed in their dressing gowns, together with a dishevelled Rory, still dressed in his crumpled linen suit, looking in dire need of a hair of the dog.

'*Er...* look who I found in reception at Vale do Lobo this morning?' Rory said, trying to be cheerful but knowing Elizabeth would be the last person anybody would want to see. 'I'd, er, just finished having breakfast at Spikes with this charming Portuguese feature writer I've met called Célia, when I overheard Elizabeth asking for directions to Monte das Uvas.'

Lisa ignored Rory, eager to know the purpose of her mother's unannounced appearance. 'Happy New Year, Mother, this is such a surprise! I hope everything is okay?'

Elizabeth scrutinised her daughter's body. 'You've lost a bit of weight, I see, Lisa dear. *What* an improvement. You're almost down to an acceptable size now.'

Lisa was about to respond, but what was the point?

'I'm afraid I have news for you, which you might find distressing.'

'Oh dear, Mother, it must be bad news if you both felt the need to fly to Portugal to tell me on New Year's Day.'

'Arthur's dead, dear.'

Her mother had delivered the news without an ounce of warmth. She might as well have thrown a brick at her head. 'I don't believe you! I only spoke to him two nights ago, and he was fine! If this is another of your sick lies, Mother, you honestly have excelled yourself this time!'

'It's true, I am afraid. The nursing home called me late last night to say he had passed away peacefully in his sleep. I rang you straight away, only to find out your number was disconnected. I had to suffer the indignity of finding out from Adele that you'd left the country. Out of interest, when were you going to tell *me* you had forsaken the country of your birth? Anyway, Jeremy and I discussed it, and we thought the decent thing to do would be to come out here to tell you personally, and I would be killing two birds with one stone. I've always wanted to see Portugal for myself and see what the fuss was all about.'

Lisa slumped onto the sofa, her mother's words fading to a distant echo. All she could hear now was Arthur's softly spoken voice whispering in her head, *'I've been fortunate to have you as a stepdaughter, Lisa Grant.'* She dipped her head, staring blankly at her knees as tears trickled down her cheeks. Jack sat next to her and held her close.

Elizabeth glared at Jack. 'Oh, you're back on the scene, are you?' I thought she'd sent you packing years ago. She gave Rory a stare. 'No boyfriends for years, and then suddenly, two of you show up at once, just like buses.'

297

'And a Happy Noo Year to you too, Elizabeth!' Jack growled.

'Mother!' Lisa sobbed. 'You have the emotional capacity of a gnat.'

'Oh, for goodness sake, Lisa. Arthur was eighty-five! He'd had a good innings. His time was up!'

'And how would you know if he'd had a good innings or not? He was your husband, for God's sake, and you never spent any time with him. All you were ever interested in was his bloody money!'

Lisa watched as her father gesticulated to Thomas, and in his very best, reassuring everything's-going-to-be-alright voice, he said, 'Why don't you take everybody through to the kitchen and organise brunch?'

Elizabeth gave Lisa a haughty look. 'Anyway, I need you to go back to Gloucestershire and sort everything out. The funeral and so on. I'm sure you will be the first to agree that you are the best person for the job. Okay, Jeremy, now that I have seen Lisa, we can go back to Vale do Lobo and enjoy their facilities.'

'But what about brunch?' Jeremy whined. 'I could murder a glass of that pink champagne.'

'Jeremy! Vale do Lobo, now! And you're driving anyway. You can get completely blotto once you've got us safely back there.'

'Yes, my love.' He paused to place a comforting hand on Lisa's shoulder. 'And I don't want you to worry about your poor mother, Sweet Pea; I will be making an honest woman of her. I've asked her to marry me.'

Saying Goodbye

'You look terrible,' Lisa said, clapping Rory on the back as he stowed several boxes of Monte das Uvas in the back of the campervan.

'I confess I feel as bad as I look. My hangover is worse today than it was yesterday.'

'A good New Year's Eve bash, was it?'

'It was an excellent evening, as I am sure you will all have had at Mont das Uvas.'

'At least you got to know Célia better.'

'I did, she works for the Portuguese magazine *Exame*. Her name means *heavenly,* apparently...'

'And is she?'

'I think she might be...'

'Rory... I...'

'Li, you don't have to say anything.' He clasped her to his chest, talking into a mouthful of hair, 'I do understand. Travelling around Europe, let alone the world, with me, is not what you need right now.'

'But it might be what Célia needs, though?' Lisa whispered in Rory's ear.

'Yes, I think it could well be, but whatever happens, I will be there for Arthur's funeral, okay? As soon as you have a date, just email or text it to me. I won't stray far from a ferry port.'

'Of course, I will, and I am very touched that you want to be there. I really hope things work out for you and the heavenly Célia. Let her do the map-reading, okay?'

He hugged her tightly, then picked her up, spun her around, and planted a kiss on her lips. 'I'll see you at the funeral.'

The following day, Will dropped Lisa and Jack off at Faro Airport to catch a flight to London. 'Just let me know what date the funeral will be, although Thomas and I can come over any time to give you support.'

Once the aircraft reached cruising height, Jack fell asleep, and Lisa gazed out of the window watching the passing clouds, when the realisation that Arthur had died alone began to sink in. A sudden surge of guilt churned her stomach. If she had been in Gloucestershire for Adele and Mike's Millennium party, as initially planned, she would have been there for Arthur.

*

While Adele waited in the arrivals hall at Heathrow airport, she felt apprehensive. She had spoken on the telephone to Lisa and Jack early that morning, but neither gave any indication of a renewed relationship. She'd hoped that four days in the Algarve together had been long enough for them to realise that the one thing they were looking for was each other. Arthur's death would had had a devastating effect on Lisa's emotions, and dealing with his funeral arrangements would be her priority now.

For the umpteenth time, Adele glanced up at the arrivals board, but she already knew that the flight from Faro had landed forty minutes ago. As a new batch of suitcase wheeling passengers came through the gate, she gripped the separator rail and scanned each weary face.

At last, Lisa appeared looking fraught, with Jack's arm around her shoulders. But when she spotted Adele, her face lit up.

'I'm so, so sorry about Arthur, Lisa. Not a great start to your New Year or your new life in Portugal. Come here.'

'Don't be too nice to me, Adele. You'll get me going again. It may have only been five weeks, but I've really missed you.'

'I've missed you too, Li. Come on, let's get you home, then we have some catching up to do.'

Soon after Adele slipped onto the M4 motorway heading for Gloucestershire, she glanced in her rear-view mirror to see Lisa fast asleep on the back seat.

Jack turned to see what Adele was grinning at. 'I caught up with my sleep on the plane, but Lisa told me she couldn't sleep. Thank you for picking us both up at such short notice.'

'I've moved all your stuff out of the spare room into Josh's room. He's gone to stay with a mate for a few days. I hope that's okay? I assume you and Lisa haven't...'

'No, Adele, we haven't. The only time I got to spend with her, alone, was after we went up to the Planetarium at midnight on Millennium Eve and stayed up there to watch the sunrise. She was so upbeat when we came down in the morning, only to find Elizabeth there to tell her about Arthur. So, if I was hoping to relight the spark between us, it was bad timing, and then there was Rory.'

'Well, he's not here now, is he? You and Li will be living under the same roof for the time being, so you'll have plenty of time to get to know each other again. The question is, do *you* still feel the same about Lisa?'

'I do, yes. There was never any doubt in my mind that I would. I've never stopped loving Lisa.'

'Well then, don't be put off by Rory, Jack. It's irritating that he turned up when he did. Rory's a fly-by-night. Lisa would be the first to say he's about as reliable as a chocolate fireguard. No, I think what she actually said was, *he's a complete and utter shit.*'

'Apparently, he's coming to the funeral, so perhaps he's more reliable than people think, and from what I saw, they seem to be very fond of each other.'

'Yes, fond, Jack. I am bizarrely *fond* of Elizabeth, but I don't *love* her.' Jack raised his eyebrows and sighed.

'You know she wants to do the eulogy? I'm not sure it's a great idea; it will be a highly charged and an emotionally draining day for her.'

'Jack... I know you two haven't been together for years, but, and you *must* remember, when Lisa sets her mind to do something, however fragile she may be feeling, there is no changing her mind.'

*

Dressed in a black suit, Lisa sat in the front pew of St. James' church between her father and Nellie, her pink and puffy eyes shielded by sunglasses. She was taking slow, deep breaths through her nose and blowing the air out silently through her mouth, trying to concentrate on her breathing and not her fluttering heart.

Will slipped an arm around her shoulders, gently pulling her towards him and whispered in her ear. 'It's time, darling. Are you sure you want to do this? I am more than happy to step in if you would like me to.'

She looked at her father and nodded, 'I'll be fine.' Will got to his feet and stepped into the aisle to let Lisa out of the pew. Smiling, he gave her one last reassuring nod before she stepped up to the pulpit to give the eulogy.

'Thank you for coming here today. Arthur would have been very touched to see so many of you.' Lisa looked over the congregation, managing a smile for all those genuinely grieving and her mother, whose attention appeared to be focussed elsewhere; the reading of Arthur's will would be at the forefront of her mind, Lisa surmised.

'He met and married my mother when I was seven, so I am very proud to have been able to call him my stepfather for thirty-three years.' Her voice wobbled, so she stopped, and looked down at her notes, drew a deep breath, held it for a few seconds, then let it go. 'Arthur knew he could never replace my father, and he never tried.' She looked at her father, who smiled, nodding encouragingly.

'Arthur and I shared a passion. Books. Arthur had an amazing collection of books at Silkwoods, which was tragically lost in the fire.' She paused to glower at her mother, who looked away from her, adjusting the brim of her Justin Smith hat.

'Arthur was born in New York in 1915. He contracted polio when he was very young and spent much of his childhood in an iron lung, but Arthur never spoke about it, nor did he ever complain about his health. He embraced his life and the people in it.

'He was a great influence in my life in many ways, especially during my formative years. He was always so enthusiastic and encouraging of my love for writing, which started after reading my Blue Peter Badge winning poem to him, not just once, but hundreds of times.

'He was determined that I should do well at school and was a tremendous support throughout my O and A-level years. I honestly believe he knew my A-level English Literature syllabus better than I did.' Soft, muffled laughter echoed around the church.

'More recently, I told him I had finished writing my first book, which I read to him before leaving Gloucestershire to live in Portugal. He was so excited about it, but I only heard on New Year's Day that it's going to be published. He was the first person I wanted to tell, but he died before I could and, I will always feel sad about that.

'But, beyond the horizon, wherever you are, Arthur, whichever Utopia you have arrived at,' her voice cracked and petered to a breathy whisper, 'I am sure you will know, and I hope you're reading Molière and all the other volumes of great writing that your heart desires. As Molière said, and because you and I were such suckers for bouncing quotes off each other… *It is a fine seasoning for joy to think of those we love.*'

She looked down, watching a single, silent tear splatter on to her notes and smear the ink. Holding her index finger to her nose, she sniffed, the sound amplified by the tiny microphone in front of her. Closing her eyes, she composed herself before delivering her final words.

'Even though we can never be together in the same room again, Arthur, you will be with me wherever I go because you will always be in my heart.'

Relieved, she stepped down from the pulpit as the organist started pumping the pedals of the ancient organ, as the packed congregation rose to their feet to sing *And Did Those Feet in Ancient Times,* with heartfelt emotion. Lisa took her place between her father, who took her hand in his, and Nellie, who passed her a wad of tissues.

'That was a wonderful eulogy, darling,' her father whispered. 'Arthur would be proud of you, as am I.'

After a few readings and another hymn, Lisa and her mother followed Arthur's coffin outside. Carried by six burly but emotional members of the Silkwoods Estate workforce. Arthur was laid to rest in the churchyard under a horse chestnut tree in the plot he had reserved for himself and Elizabeth in 1966. Lisa watched the coffin being lowered into the ground with an aching heart and sucking back the tears. There was a slight thud as it hit the bottom, which made Elizabeth gasp before hissing in Lisa's ear, 'whatever you do, don't you dare think about popping me in there. Not that I am planning to go anywhere for a very long time yet.'

Lisa had arranged for the wake to be held at a hotel a short drive away from the church, extending an invitation to everyone who came to the funeral service. It allowed Lisa to talk to those who had known, loved and respected Arthur, which she found comforting. She was surprised when so-called members of Arthur's family introduced themselves to her because she'd never known they existed.

When Rory slipped away from the wake, Lisa went to say goodbye to him in the car park.

'You were fantastic today, Li.'

'I hope so. I held it together, okay, didn't I? Sort of.' Rory's response was to wrap his arms around her and hold her close.

'You were amazing. You know me, sentimentality is not my thing, but you even managed to get me going. Nellie had to pass me a tissue at one point. So… will you stay here, or go back to Portugal?'

'I'll be going back, once I've sorted everything out. My mother is super excited about the reading of Arthur's will, so I will stay around for that, just to make absolutely sure things go smoothly and exactly as Arthur wanted, then I'll go back.'

'And Jack?'

'I've made too many mistakes in my life, Rory, and I now know I made the worst mistake ever when I was twenty-two, and I let him go. I've always known, deep down, that Jack was *the one,* and I think he feels the same. But since I heard about Arthur, I haven't given him much attention.'

'Well, now you have the rest of your lives to give each other your full attention.'

'I've decided I'm going to ask him to be with me for the rest of my life if he'll have me.'

'Of course, he'll have you! Life is too short not to be with the one you love. You ask him. I'll always be your knight in shining armour, Li, remember that, but I've always known I could never win your heart. Right! Before I get uncharacteristically sloppy for a second time today, I must go. I have several meetings in London over the next week or so, and then I'm meeting Célia at Heathrow for the start of our world trip. First stop, New York'

'Enjoy the rest of the world, and don't forget to email me!'

'I won't! And I'll be expecting a response! Parting is such sweet sorrow. One for the road, sweet Lisa Grant!'

Lisa staggered backwards, throwing her arms in the air, then around his neck, before whispering in his ear, 'Now bugger off, sweet Romeo! Go and find your heavenly Celia.'

Arthur's Revenge

A shaft of sunlight splayed across the room through an old sash window highlighting the unsettled dust hanging in suspended animation over the sparse furnishings. A Victorian mahogany table, pushed against a wall, with copies of *Country Life* and *Inside Gloucestershire* fanned across its surface. A few excruciatingly uncomfortable wooden chairs lined up in front of a gnarled wooden desk, with a well-worn leather top. The austere solicitor's chambers in Cirencester seemed to have forgotten to move with the times. It had a Dickensian feel about it, and the smell of musty, well-thumbed-through books clung to the air. A place where Bob Cratchit might trundle in and say, *'Two shillings and a halfpenny, Sir,'* with a timeworn edge to his voice. Not the place to be howling with laughter.

Hot salty tears streamed down Lisa's face, and her shoulders heaved as she clasped her belly with both hands in a futile attempt to stop her muscles from contracting. The solicitor glowered at her from behind the desk after she snorted unattractively. Looking around her, she found the reactions of everyone else in the room completely hysterical. The outraged look on her mother's face, her cheeks bereft of colour, and her mouth contorted into the shape of an O. The angry faces of several members of Arthur's so-called family, who had introduced themselves at the funeral service for the first time, who Lisa assumed only crawled out of the woodwork at times such as this. Jeremy, voicing incomprehensible words of disbelief. What a nerve. *He* had no right to be there.

Everyone assumed that Arthur's will would be straightforward and that he would dutifully leave his fortune to his grieving widow, Elizabeth, the focus of Lisa's irritation, as usual. She'd arrived late, dressed like her namesake, the Queen, about to meet a head of state but, thankfully, not wearing a hat. Elizabeth waited for the solicitor to pull up a chair for her and sat in wide-eyed anticipation, waiting for the reading to start and stifling the odd theatrical tear.

Her mother should be ashamed of herself. She was Arthur's wife in name only, and she had to convolute that by hyphenating Goldsworthy with Grant. She barely saw or communicated with him during their married life and, like the rest of the people in the room, dipped in and out of his life when it suited her. He was someone they never made the time to go and see. All they saw was his wealth, not his intelligence, wit, and wise counsel, just some of the things that Lisa learned to love about him from a very early age, but wily old Arthur made sure he had the last laugh.

'There is a substantial amount of money…' The solicitor kicked off the proceedings gravely, peering at Lisa and the silently baying hyenas over the top of his bifocals. Everybody, except Lisa, sat to attention. Visibly squirming in their chairs with excited anticipation, and a little sigh escaped Elizabeth's lips. Lisa couldn't bear to watch or listen as, eyes closed, she recalled watching the Millennium sunrise with Jack, imagining him making love to her again, and the way he always whispered, 'I love you so much,' just before he—

'As most of you will know…' The solicitor's voice boomed,

bringing her thoughts back down to earth with a feeling of total irreverence. How she hoped that the dear departed could not read the thoughts of the living. '…the manor house at Silkwoods is owned by Miss Lisa Grant, a building of significant historical interest which, sadly, was almost destroyed by fire in 1997.' Lisa flashed her mother an inflammatory look. Elizabeth responded by tipping her head back slightly, closing her eyes and pointing her nose in the air as the legal monologue continued.

'Mr Goldsworthy purchased the farm from Mrs Goldsworthy-Grant when they married in 1966. Since then, the price of the land has risen to around ten thousand pounds per acre. The estate consists of one thousand acres of prime farmland, so one can expect to receive a substantial amount of money if indeed it were to be sold.

The pedigree Dairy Shorthorn herd at Silkwoods is one of the largest in the country and, Mr Goldsworthy's homebred bull, Sir William of Silkwoods, better known as Billy, is a super grand champion. The reputation of the Silkwoods pedigree Dairy Shorthorns' is well known among the bovine community, and offers to buy the entire herd have already been received.

'Because Mr Goldsworthy lived a relatively meagre existence in his later years, there are over a million pounds in the bank, and a similar amount in stocks and shares…' It was Lisa's turn to squirm as she watched Jeremy excitedly clawing his fingers around the arm of his chair to steady himself as the solicitor cleared his throat before dolefully delivering his following words with awkward resolution.

'The Estate of the late Mr Arthur Goldsworthy has been left, in its entirety to his stepdaughter, Miss Lisa Grant. With the proviso that she spends it as *she* chooses, and not as her mother, Elizabeth Goldsworthy-Grant, commands.'

There were gasps from around the room, followed by an eerie silence. You could have heard a pin drop, and something did; Elizabeth's jaw. The solicitor soldiered on with a tinge of embarrassment creeping into his voice.

'To the rest of you…' there were synchronised gasps. 'To the rest of you… Mr Arthur Goldsworthy leaves a crate of whisky, in Mrs Goldsworthy-Grant's case… gin.' A hint of solemnity once again crept into his voice, lowering his tone as he said the word, gin. He stopped momentarily to peer over the top of his bifocals to look at her mother, who was fanning herself with a stray copy of *Inside Gloucestershire,* before continuing, 'to remind you all of the times you chose *not* to take the time to have a drink with him.'

At that point, Lisa's bewilderment exploded into uncontrollable laughter brought on by the expressions on the faces of everyone else, which had so quickly changed from eager anticipation to total disinterest. Arthur had the last laugh, but he knew Lisa would do the right thing. He knew she would slice up her inheritance wisely and discerningly.

'Why?' Her mother started repeatedly slamming the copy of *Inside Gloucestershire* onto the table. Her voice sounding like two invisible hands were clasped around her throat and applying pressure. 'Why?'

311

she repeated, pushing herself up unsteadily on the arms of her chair while glowering at the solicitor.

Jeremy, too, jerked out of his chair as if half expecting to catch her, should she fall.

'I mean… I was Arthur's *wife*, for God's sake! Why on Earth would he do *that?*' her mother demanded.

Lisa later learned from the solicitor that Arthur had pre-warned him that her mother would react with a display of histrionics, and the solicitor had no intention of losing his composure.

'Mrs Goldsworthy-Grant, I am simply conveying the wishes of your late husband.'

'Well, he can't possibly have been in full possession of his faculties when he made *that* will. When did he make it?' Elizabeth demanded.

'It was on, let me see, the 8th of October 1987, Mrs Goldsworthy-Grant.'

'What? On Lisa's birthday?'

Lisa dabbed her eyes with the cuff of her slightly fraying shirt, having managed to compose herself.

'My twenty-first birthday, actually, Mother.'

'Your twenty-first? So, you *knew* about this, Lisa?' her mother snapped. 'It is an outrage! I will contest it.'

Lisa watched her distraught mother shed a few 'real' tears, then rose to her feet to face them all. After delivering Arthur's eulogy, she had found a new level of self-confidence. She knew the words she was about to say would not only come out in the proper order but that she would say them with a degree of authoritative calm.

'No, Mother, you are quite wrong. I had absolutely no idea. But why on Earth would you *want* to contest it? What possible justification could you have for doing so? You were his wife in name only. You never loved him. You never spent any time with him. You rarely bothered to ask how he was. You fell in love with his bank balance and nothing else.' For the first time in forty years, Lisa noticed her mother's cheeks flush, *guilty as charged.* 'It was the same when you, allegedly, fell for my father, and there is no doubt in my mind that you were well aware of his sexual preferences, but it didn't put you off seducing him to get your hands on *his* money. Using me as the embryonic pawn, I believe. How could you stoop so low? So... surely, even you, as someone who has been in an extra-curricular relationship with Jeremy since before I was born, can understand why Arthur chose me as his sole beneficiary? Because, and let's face it, Mother, it's pretty elementary. I was the *only* one who loved him, that's why.'

Her mother gasped, then rendered speechless. Her eyes, although wide open, appeared to glaze over as she made a clumsy attempt to support herself on the table in front of her. She missed and fell to the floor with a thud.

'Elizabeth, my love, come back to me.' Jeremy panicked, picking up the copy of *Inside Gloucestershire* and wafting it over Elizabeth's face. 'This has been such a terrible shock for us, my love, I mean for you!'

Lisa headed to the exit, texting Jack.

'Lisa! Your mother!' Jeremy whined. 'I think we should take her to A&E.'

'She'll be all right, Jeremy. That sort of thing happens when you are emotionally overcome… for the first time in sixty years.'

Lisa glanced back at the jug of water on the solicitor's desk. Pouring its contents over her mother to revive her was very tempting, but she thought better of it. 'Jeremy, sit her up, and put her head between her legs, then offer her a glass of water.'

As someone who always snapped to attention when asked to do something, Jeremy put his hands under Elizabeth's shoulders and started pulling her up.

'Get *off* me, Jeremy. Stop fussing. I'm fine! The last thing I want to do is go to bloody A&E, and I certainly don't want a glass of water. You can take me to The Fleece for a gin and tonic, which will be much more beneficial, and we can discuss what monthly allowance I shall be expecting Lisa to pay me!'

Jeremy managed to get her dazed mother to her feet, brushing off the Dickensian dust from her Stella McCartney suit.

'Honestly, Mother, the way you talk, anybody would think you were on the poverty line, but you never know…' she said, feeling the collar of her mother's suit, 'you might have to cut your cloth a bit, and start shopping in the high street… like the rest of us! Now I must go, I have various entrepreneurial projects I must attend to, and as you may know, Mother, time is money. I will be in touch, in due course.'

'In due course, what the hell are you talking about? Jeremy and I could have starved to death by then. I will email you what our requirements are.' Her mother left the solicitor's office holding on to Jeremy for support and muttering, 'I don't believe this, beholden to my daughter. How dreadful, I never thought it would come to this.'

Lisa laughed out loud as she skipped up the Market Square in sync with the beat of *Crazy Little Thing Called Love,* beaming at everyone in her path and rejoicing the return of her va va voom and general lust for life. How quickly and dramatically her fortunes had changed - from stony-broke to a bloody millionaire.

She felt emancipated and in control, not only of the purse strings but also of her life. Her inheritance had been an unexpected bonus and the icing on the cake in her rebuilt world with Jack, who hadn't responded to her text.

She rang Adele, and Amy answered the phone.

'Hi, Amy, it's only me.'

'Oh hi, Auntie Li. Dad's at work, and Mum's had to go to the shops.'

'Oh, okay, it was Uncle Jack I wanted to speak to, actually.'

'Um, you've just missed him. He's gone.'

'Gone where?'

'To Heathrow. He ordered a taxi about half an hour ago and just took off. He said he was going back to New York. Mum will be furious when she finds out. She spent all morning cooking his favourite… spag bol. Li… hello?'

Going the Wrong Way

Jack was holding the neck of an empty miniature bottle of Bombay Sapphire Gin between his thumb and forefinger, tapping it against the tray table in front of him. He was in a foul mood, questioning his reasoning for going back to New York.

The woman sitting next to him was reading. She cleared her throat and glowered at his tray table. He stopped tapping, shrugged and said, 'I'm very sorry… I was miles away.' She nodded curtly and went back to her book. Jack glanced at the cover, Julia Quinn's *The Viscount Who Loved Me,* and Elizabeth flashed into his mind. The bloody woman had a great deal to answer for. Lisa would have married him years ago if it hadn't been for Elizabeth. Her twisted obsession with finding Lisa a husband, when she was incapable of being faithful to either of hers, poisoned Lisa's views on marriage. It was not too surprising Lisa crossed marriage off her list of lifetime goals from a very early age.

He squeezed his eyes tightly together, recalling the painful memory of stomping off down the Champs de Mars, like an overgrown schoolboy who'd just had his conker annihilated. Jumping into the first taxi he saw and commanding the driver to *'Take me to Charles de Gaulle airport, tout suite!'* The blurry recall of sitting on a barstool at the Flying Horse in the Tottenham Court Road, with Brenda all over him. His alcohol-fuelled brain triggering the words, *'Brenda, you are the most beautiful woman I have ever seen.'* It was a blatant lie and the most ridiculous thing he had ever said in his life.

The following morning disorientated, brought on by the hangover from hell, he had struggled to open his eyes, reaching out his arms, anticipating Lisa's sylph-like image to emerge from the bathroom. Instead, the outline of a much fuller figure, with a mane of red, pre-Raphaelite hair, approached him on the bed. Her lips overwhelmed him, his whole head smothered in a bright auburn thicket. It was the most dismal morning of his life, which turned into 6,570 dreary mornings after she told him she was pregnant, and as Will had done before him, he did *the right thing*. So now, why, after seventeen years of married misery in New York City, was he going back there? If Jack thought it was his subconscious that told him to return to see his children, he was deluding himself because they didn't want to see him. Brenda had screwed him for everything he had and was still screwing Barnaby Tyler as she had been doing long before the divorce. Workwise, he had cleared his desk in New York, and the position of CEO in the London office was his if he wanted it, but now he wasn't sure.

He had been travelling around the world like some lovelorn puppy, wondering if his first and only love still had feelings for him. After watching the millennium sunrise with Lisa, he felt sure that she did. Nothing about her had changed. She was still the person he had loved with all his heart. Her confident exterior betrayed a degree of vulnerability lurking beneath its surface, which she always attempted to hide with her sense of humour. Eighteen years on, his feelings hadn't changed. All he had ever wanted to do was to wake up next to

Lisa.

He had only spent a few days in the Algarve but had fallen in love with the country and had allowed himself to fantasise about living there. Thanks to the magic of Google, he had earmarked a property in need of renovation just off N125, which would be perfect, not only as a home but as a writers' retreat. He knew that hosting writers' retreats was something Lisa was thinking about doing, and he could be a great help to her. This property would be the perfect place. The outbuildings already converted into self-catering units; there was a pool, plus it had the bonus of being in spitting distance of Playa do Trafal, Lisa's favourite beach. He had even started drawing parallels between himself and Will. He had married someone he didn't love because she was pregnant before creating a new life with the love of his life in Portugal after the divorce. But, unlike Will, he had lost his nerve at the hint of a bit of competition. He swilled his gin and tonic. He wasn't sure about anything anymore.

From his window seat, the 747 was eating up the miles in cruise mode, every second taking him further away from Lisa. The only person he had ever wanted to be with. And why was he doing it? Because he felt she'd been ignoring him after they arrived in Gloucestershire. Then, when he'd stepped out of the wake, he'd seen her kissing Rory. Not just a casual goodbye, but full-on and passionate! Now on his second double gin and tonic, it didn't seem such a big deal. She hadn't been *ignoring* him. She had been busy dealing with Arthur's funeral arrangements.

As a young man, he enjoyed staying at Silkwoods with Lisa. He would always fondly remember the evenings they spent with Arthur, soaking up his wit and wisdom. What would Arthur have said to him now? After throwing a Moliere quote at him, *Hearts are often broken; when words are left unspoken,* he would follow with, *'Have the courage of your convictions, man! Tell her how you feel!'* But he couldn't get the image of Lisa kissing that philandering photographer out of his head. The sound of giggling made Jack look up. A man and woman were walking up the aisle, his hands all over her like an octopus. Jack tut-tutted disapprovingly. They were old enough to know better. The lean, dishevelled figure in a crumpled, linen suit looked very familiar. *'Rory? What the hell is he doing here with his arms wrapped around a brunette?'* He mumbled, Rory raised an arm in Jack's direction, and the woman reading next to him looked up. Jack closed his eyes as the enormity of his misconception sank in. His stomach lurched, his intestines reeling from what felt like a Lennox Lewis punch in the solar plexus.

'Bloody hell, Jack! You are the very last person I expected to see up here! Did Lisa's proposal scare you off so much you felt the need to escape? Why aren't you tucked up in a cosy little love nest somewhere?

'Her what?'

'Her proposal! When I said goodbye to her, she said she was planning to ask you to be with her for the rest of her life, as her soul-mate and lover, rather than a lawfully wedded husband. You know how bloke-ish her views on marriage are? Oh, this is gorgeous Célia, by the way. We are off on the first leg of our round-the-world trip. I will be taking stunning photographs of the world at large, and Célia will be writing deliciously seductive pieces to accompany them. All funded by *Focal Point,* would you believe?'

'Pleased to meet you, Jack,' Célia purred.

Jack wasn't listening; he was staring out of the window. Bailing out at 38,000 feet over the Atlantic Ocean was not an option. 'He's not rude, Célia. It's just dawned on him what a tosser he is. Am I right, Jack? Rory persevered, raising his voice, which made the woman sitting next to Jack shift in her seat, glowering from Rory to Jack.

'If your facial expressions are telling me anything, mate, I think you just might have made the biggest mistake of your life. Jack, are you listening to me?'

Jack was still staring out of the window, so the woman sitting next to him elbowed him in the ribs.

'Oh, for goodness sake! Listen to what he has to say, then I can get on with my book,' then nodded to Rory to continue.

'Lisa needs *you*. She always has. She's always loved you, Jack. I might have caused a distraction for a while when she thought she would never get you back, but it's *you* she wants to spend the rest of her life with. She told me the biggest mistake she'd ever made was saying no, to you.'

Jack rested his elbows on the tray table and put his head in his hands. A frustrated groan escaped his lips.

320

'You see, Célia, the penny's finally dropped! He realises what a knob head he's been.'

'I saw you two together after the wake, and I drew all the wrong conclusions.'

'Shame on you, Jack, and you a publishing man! Never judge a book by its cover. Isn't that what they say? Ah, well, good luck, Jack. We were just stretching our legs a bit, back here in cattle class. Let's go back and have more champagne in Club and drink *Focal Point's* health.' He turned Célia around by her shoulders and leaned over to Jack. 'We should arrive at JFK in about four hours and, if you have any hope of salvaging this mess, I suggest you get yourself booked on the first flight back to London. Better still, book Concorde - she might just save your life.'

Pernod in Paris

'If you want my opinion…'

'*No, actually Elizabeth, I don't,*' Adele thought, gritting her teeth while wishing she'd never picked up the telephone in the first place. Still, she was so worried about Lisa not having been in touch, she'd snatched the phone off the hook after the first ring, in the hope it was her, but it wasn't.

'I think she's gone stark raving mad, Adele, dear. Do you realise that she's planning to give *all* Arthur's money away? It's quite shocking. Her good deeds are plastered all over the *Evening Standard* tonight. The last I heard was that she had given the go-ahead for the restoration work to start at Silkwoods, and you're never going to believe this, but she's donated the bloody place to the National Trust. They're very cock-a-hoop about it and plan a re-enactment of an Oliver Cromwell skirmish in the garden. All those years I spent cultivating my perennials. You cannot imagine how *I* feel!'

'Elizabeth! I'm sorry, but I can't chat right now. I *have to* pick up Josh,' she lied and being so heavily focussed on Lisa, she crossed her fingers. 'If I hear *anything*, I'll call you, okay*?*' Adele closed her eyes as Elizabeth drew a prolonged intake of breath. '*Oh, God! Please, not a monologue*! Elizabeth! I'm sorry, but I do need to go,' but Elizabeth wasn't listening, as usual, and droned on.

'And she's set up an annual literary prize, the *Arthur Goldsworthy Memorial Prize for Fiction*. Twenty thousand pounds a year! I could do with that. I've got bills to pay you know. My annual Ascot Royal

Enclosure fee is due, and one has to have Wimbledon debenture seats, as one only watches matches from the Centre Court.' Then lowering her voice. 'I don't think she's mentally stable.'

'Elizabeth! I…'

'You probably don't know this, and I do try to keep it quiet because some people might think it's a little odd, but Jeremy is a huge Blue Peter fan. Unbelievably, Matt Baker was waxing lyrical about Lisa this afternoon as well. 'Blue Peter Badge winner at seven and a philanthropist at forty!' You know, all that sort of nonsense. Where will it all end? I think she needs to see a psychiatrist. Someone needs to stop her before she gives the whole lot away!'

'Elizabeth! I'm sure there's enough of *Lisa's* inheritance to go around. She is generous to a tee, and she's far from stupid! I'm more concerned that she's gone missing!'

'Oh, don't worry, Adele, dear. Agatha Christie went off the radar for a while and turned up luxuriating at the Old Swan Hotel in Harrogate. Writers are funny like that. Lisa will materialise when she feels like it, no doubt to announce who she's giving the rest of the money to!'

Adele's patience had run out, which only left one option. 'Elizabeth, Josh will think I have abandoned him, I have to go. I'll ring you if I hear *anything*,' and hung up. She redialled Jack's number, which was still on divert to voicemail. This time, she left a message. 'Where the hell are you? You should be back in NYC by now. Ring me ASAP. Lisa's gone missing, and it's your bloody fault!'

*

In the departure lounge at Heathrow Airport, a constant, swirling throng of cosmopolitan humanity milled around the concourse buying duty frees before taking to the skies in hundreds of different directions across our ever-shrinking world. People-watching had always been one of Lisa's favourite pastimes, but not today. She was drinking coffee without tasting it and staring into the sea of faces without seeing any of them.

She'd never taken off on her own before without telling anybody. She would tell Arthur, and she ought to tell her father. Adele had rung her six times and sent four messages, and she'd ignored them all. She should respond, to a text, at least. She pulled her phone out of her pocket as another message pinged in.

'For goodness sake, Li, please get in touch! Disappearing off the radar like this is so unlike you. We're all worried, even your mother's called me. It's just a matter of time before she involves Interpol!'

Hearing her flight called over the intercom, she looked up from her phone. Sighing heavily, she texted Adele before turning it.

'I'm sorry, Adele, but I'm fine. Really, I am. Please don't worry about me, but with everything that's been going on, I felt I needed to be alone for a while, so I thought I would spend a few days at this great little place I stayed at 18 years ago, to give myself some thinking time. Speak soon. Lots of love. XX

*

'Adele?'

'Jack! Where the hell have you been? I thought you were going to New York, not Tristan da bloody Cunha. Anyway, I forwarded Lisa's text to you.'

'You did…'

'Well, when Li says, 'I'm *fine*,' it's always meant the exact opposite, and I don't think she should be alone right now. I think I know where she's gone, and I am going to find her. Mike's just dropped me off at Heathrow, and I'm checking in for a flight to Charles de Gaulle as we speak.'

'I know you are. Flight AB1554.'

Adele stared at her phone, confused. 'How do you know?'

'Because, if you look to your left, you might just spot me. I checked in a few minutes ago.'

Adele spun around to see her dishevelled looking brother. 'You look absolutely shocking!'

'This is what you look like when you've crossed the Atlantic twice, in a short space of time, even if the second leg was on Concorde.'

'Concorde? I thought your ghastly ex-wife had bled you dry?'

'She has, but she didn't know about my *Get Lost Brenda Fund*. I think I know where Lisa's gone, too.'

'I don't know why I'm even talking to you. Why did you flounce off like that? You didn't say goodbye to any of us, apart from Amy.'

Jack regaled his lovelorn story to his sister as they boarded the aircraft.

Adele wasn't impressed. 'You're an idiot and a pretty immature one at that. I'd honestly thought by the time we all reached our forties; we'd have grown into sensible adults! Clearly not!'

Onboard the aircraft, there was a copy of the *Evening Standard* on every seat, and the headline on the front page jumped out at them. *New Author and Ex-Columnist for Focal Point Magazine, Lisa Grant, inherits a Fortune from Stepfather and Turns Philanthropist,* along with an image of a smiling Lisa outside the Barbican Centre, with Anna Lockwood and Finty, after a performance of *Les Misérables*.

'I was there too, you know?' Adele mused. 'It was Li's twenty-sixth birthday, and I was pregnant with Josh. I was as stately as a galleon and couldn't get comfortable in my seat. It was really embarrassing as we were sitting in the front row.'

Jack held the paper closer to his face. 'It looks like Li had been bawling her eyes out.'

'She had! By the time Fantine finished singing, *I Dreamed a Dream*, she was in tears, and by the end of the second half, she was inconsolable. I can't believe he cut me out of the photo. I was standing next to Lisa when Rory took this.'

'Rory?'

'Yes, that night was the first time they met. Probably because of my size, he decided to cut me out.'

'What a rat! Never trust photographers.'

'Oh, grow up, Jack! I can't believe you bailed out at the slightest hint of any competition. That's the second time you've left Lisa in the lurch. Now, I seem to remember that Vue de Champs was the name of the hotel you stayed at? Am I right?'

*

It was early afternoon when Adele and Jack checked in at Vue de Champs, and Jack told the concierge they were meeting Lisa there. The Frenchman, who spoke perfect English, was polite but frosty, viewing them both with a degree of suspicion, rattling away on his keyboard. He kept looking up at them furtively as if he was running their details through a security check.

'Mr Wilde and Mrs Maxwell from the UK?' He eyed Jack with suspicion.

'Yes, that's right. I stayed here once before, with Lisa Grant.'

'And you are staying here now with Mrs Maxwell?' The concierge cocked one eyebrow.

Jack sighed, trying to keep his cool. 'Yes, Mrs Maxwell is my *sister,* and we are meeting *Lisa Grant* here. Please could you confirm that she has checked in?'

The concierge screwed up his nose. 'Non! I am sorry, monsieur, madame, but I cannot. The confidentiality of our guests is of paramount importance to us, so I am afraid I cannot divulge that sort of information.'

Adele and Jack hung around the hotel lobby for a while, hoping for a sighting, but nothing.

'She'll come back here at some point, to eat, or something…'. Jack said, stifling a yawn.

'But we don't even know she *is* here, for sure, do we?' Adele lowered her voice sensing the concierge was trying to overhear their conversation, 'and why would she come back here to *eat*? Do you know how ridiculous that sounds, Jack? Paris is the capital of fine dining, and the clue is that this is a B and B. You need to get some serious sleep.'

Jack shrugged. 'Well, that's not happening until we find her.'

'We can't sit around here all day. Why don't we go for a walk? When we get back, I'll resume surveillance of the lobby area so that you can get your head down.'

Ambling in the direction of the Eiffel Tower, they could hear something loosely disguised as singing. An English woman singing *Non, je ne regrette rien* in appalling French. 'Shush!' said Adele, and they stopped to listen. 'Oh, God. Tell me it's not.'

'I think it is, Della.'

Adele sighed, 'It's so difficult to criticise how Brits behave abroad when you know the Brit in question. Come on, let's go.'

Lisa had managed to climb up the stone structure at the base of the east leg of the Eiffel Tower and was sitting perched on a ledge about twelve feet above the ground, clutching a bottle of Pernod. She had attracted quite a crowd.

'Je ne regrette rien!' She bellowed at the top of her lungs, thrusting the bottle of Pernod triumphantly in the air. Two gendarmes were standing below her with a ladder as Jack and Adele approached.

'Mademoiselle… pleeeze come down, before you' urt yourself.'

Lisa bent her head, looking down at them. 'Aww, you both remind me of Officer Crabtree. You know, the English policeman in 'Allo 'Allo, and non, I don't want to come down! It's a free country, isn't eet, monsieurs? France? Liberté, égalité, fraternité, and all zat? I want to ztay 'ere! I like it up 'ere, and I'm not going to 'urt myself. So, s'il vous plaît, pleeeze go away. I vant to be like Marlene Deitrich, alone.'

'Lisa!' Jack pushed between the gendarmes. 'Excusez moi, messieurs. Lisa, please do as you're told, for once. Come down immediately! Or I will have to come up and get you.' He added lamely.

'Oh, goodness! Do I know you? You look very familiar. If only I could see you properly, you are zooming in and out a bit, but you *sound* very familiar. You sound like someone I once knew who went crawling into bed with a red-haired trollop after leaving me alone 'ere. Right 'ere! At zee Eiffel Tower, in 1981!'

The assembled crowd muttered their displeasure, 'Quel bâtard, what a bastard!'

'She's got all your money now, hasn't she, Jack? The ginger-haired trollop. I've got money too now. You'd have been okay if you'd stayed with me. I'm a great catch now. I'm rich! Woohoo! I sent you a text telling you I'd just become a bloody millionaire. You know, the one you didn't reply to because you just went away and left me, again.'

'Lisa, I know you're loaded, but I'm not in New York, am I? I'm right here.'

'Oh! But are you *quite* sure you're not *right here* because of my money, Jack? Even that creepy little man who sat next to me on the plane wanted me for my money. He followed me to the hotel place, but the very nice man at the desk didn't like the look of him and told him to go away. 'Sur votre vélo, on your bike! Allez off, go off, bog off!' he said. And these nice gendarmes down there have been following me around too. They want me to get down, and I don't want to. Tell them, Jack, I don't want to get down.' She stood up, wobbling her way to a standing position. 'I like it up 'ere.'

'Lisa! Get down! Now! Before you fall.'

'Jack!' Adele scolded. 'Shouting isn't going to help.'

'Oh, Deli, you're here too. Formidable! How wonderful. We can all have a party! I don't actually like Pernod, so you can have it. Here, catch!' Lisa dropped the bottle of Pernod, and one of the gendarmes shouted 'Oh, la, la,' and lunged forward to catch it.

Jack moved directly underneath where Lisa was standing. 'Listen to me, Lisa. I'm here at the foot of the Eiffel Tower because I want to be with you, and love you, for always and forever, just like I always did.' There was a ripple of applause from the gathered crowd. 'I was a bleedin' dolt eighteen years ago.' The assembled cosmopolitan crowd looked at each other confused, unfamiliar with the term *bleedin' dolt*, as Jack continued. 'And I was a bleedin' dolt again today, yesterday, whenever it was; I should never have gone anywhere. From now on, I promise, hand on heart, I will never leave you again, and I will never mention the marriage word again. Marriage is an outdated institution anyway, and I'm not very good at it.' Bending down on one knee, he continued. 'I, Jack Wilde, would like to take you, Lisa Grant, to be my un-lawful, unwedded, significant other, now, in your inebriated state, and for the rest of our lives.'

There were cheers from the crowd, and somebody shouted. 'That's Lisa Grant, the philanthropist!'

A few paparazzi photographers were pushing their way towards the front of the crowd, snapping their shutters.

Adele elbowed her way forward. 'Nice speech, Jack, but you need to get the pissed philanthropist down before she hurts herself. Oh God, Lisa's about to get full media coverage. A TV crew has just arrived, as well. She's going to be plastered all over the front pages in the morning. Come on, Lisa, please get down, sweetie.'

'Of course, I'll come down, Deli, as you've asked me so nicely! But I want to say something to you first!' She pointed an uncoordinated finger at Jack. 'Jack Wilde. I've always wanted to be your un-lawful, un-wedded wifey-thingy. I never wanted just any old soulmate, wuvver, and thignificant other! I've always wanted you!' Then, shouting at the top of her lungs. 'I've never told you this before, but I love you, Jack Wilde! I do. I do. I do, with all my heart, I'm going to fly to you, my darling!' She held out both arms and launched herself into the air.

'Li, no wait,' Jack protested as the crowd gasped. A woman screamed, and there was a thud as Lisa landed on top of Jack, who collapsed on impact. Adele pulled Lisa up off Jack's chest, holding her under her arms so he could get up.

'She's out cold,' he said lamely.

Adele glowered at him, shaking her head. 'No shit, Sherlock. Pick her up then! You're going to have to carry her back to the hotel.' Then turning to the crowd, Adele shouted, 'The show's over, folks… Le spectacle a terminé tout le monde.' Then to the gendarmes, 'Thank you for your help, but we've got things under control now, Monsieurs l'agents.'

*

'Jeremy! I'm getting fed up, waiting for Adele to ring me back. Let's watch the Ten O'clock News on the BBC to take our minds off our money worries. Where's the remote control?'

'I've got it, my love. Here we go…'

Elizabeth pushed back into her reclining chair, kicked off her shoes and stretched her legs. 'Oh, good, it's Michael Buerk. I like him, and I much prefer the news at this time of day.'

'After the fuel protests were resolved, support for the Labour Party has been restored. The latest MORI opinion poll suggests Labour are now thirteen points ahead of the Conservatives.'

'Oh heavens! We don't want *them* sneaking into power, do we?' Elizabeth groaned as Michael Buerk continued reeling off the headlines.

'Sven-Göran Eriksson, the fifty-two-year-old Swedish coach of Italian side Lazio, has accepted an offer from the Football Association and will take charge of the England football team for five

years commencing next July.'

'Bloody football. It's never off the television. I would have thought better of the BBC. Surely, they can find something more interesting to report on, and why on Earth can't they find an Englishman to do the job?'

'Lisa Grant, the ex-columnist for Focal Point magazine who recently inherited a fortune from her stepfather, has been hitting the headlines recently after giving away sizeable chunks of her inheritance to worthy causes. Today, she received a very public proposal at the foot of the Eiffel Tower and was completely overwhelmed.'

There was a loud mechanical crunching noise as Elizabeth forced her recliner into the upright position as she stared, open-mouthed, at the television as an airborne Lisa fell into the crowd.

'Good Lord, Elizabeth! It looks like you'll live to see your daughter's wedding day after all,' Jeremy guffawed. 'I wonder who proposed? Whoever it was, this is cause for a celebration. I've got a bottle of Veuve Clicquot chilling in the fridge in anticipation of our next celebration. I'll go and get it.'

'Jeremy! I don't want bloody champagne! Can't you see I'm in shock? You can pour me a very large gin and tonic! And as for *seeing* my only daughter get married, Lisa once told me that, if she ever did get married, it would be on a beach, and I wouldn't be getting an invitation.'

Contentment

Despite the new Millennium getting off to a shaky start, Lisa was feeling the happiest she had ever been. Her skin glowed a healthy bronze, one of the many benefits of permanently living in the Algarve, at their home just off the N125, she and Jack had bought together. The perfect place to host writers' retreats, and they had already hosted two, with Finty, which had been deemed a success among the attendees.

Nothing fazed Lisa anymore. With Jack back in her life, she'd dropped the self-imposed barricade around her heart, ready to embrace everything life had to throw at her. The pain of losing Arthur was still there, but part of Lisa's grieving process was an obsession with finding out everything about the first nineteen years of her mother's life, up to when she gave birth to Lisa in October 1959.

'Nature v nurture. Our childhood years are a fundamental part of our journey toward becoming a well-balanced adult. Those years are our foundation stones upon which we build the person we become. They deeply affect our future physical, cognitive, emotional, and social development.

She was reading aloud from her computer screen as the balmy warmth of the Portuguese evening flooded through the open double doors of her office, along with a calming chorus of cicadas.

Shifting in her chair, she slid both hands behind her and stretched her aching back. 'At least I'm not feeling sick twenty-four-seven anymore,' she thought before continuing.

Silver spoon, or hand to mouth, it is during a child's formative years that they cultivate an unbreakable bond with their parents. A relationship that is so strong it binds them together for the rest of their lives. Sometimes there is a glitch in the system, and the parent-child bond is never established.

She sat back, sighing heavily. There was a time when she believed the past should stay in the past, but now she felt that nobody, especially family, should be left behind. Being a part of a loving, close-knit family was the most important thing in the world. Deep down, she had always felt that some sort of childhood trauma was responsible for her mother's astonishing indifference, and she'd been right. Now she knew the heart-rending truth, she better understood, although she was amazed her mother had managed to keep such sensitive information to herself for almost sixty years.

Hearing Jack's bare feet slap across the tiled floor behind her reminded her she had been grouchy with him earlier in the day. She'd felt bad about it, even if he had laughed it off, shaking his head and saying, '*just another five months to go!*'

Standing behind her, Jack reached round and stroked Lisa's stomach. 'How's my favourite grumpy, expectant mother? I read somewhere that at four months, your uterus is the size of a cabbage!'

She put her hands on top of his. 'I'm sorry I was spiky earlier. I blame it on my hormones. Oh, and lack of sleep, things are starting to feel a little squashed down there.'

Nobody had been more surprised than Lisa when she found out she was pregnant; she'd imagined her ovaries were shrivelled prunes. But after her hangover had worn off, she conceived before they left Paris. At the time, Jack had joked that it might have been something to do with their mutual magnetic attraction, or the after-effects of a Pernod overdose.

'Anyway, do you remember it's Friday? It's gone 7.15, and I booked our favourite table at Temperus for 8. So, if we're walking, we need to leave soon.'

'Of course, I haven't forgotten! I'm eating for two, remember? I'm starving.'

Jack craned his head over her shoulder, scanning what was on her computer screen. 'That's deep! Are those the thoughts of Lisa Grant or Lisa Dear?'

Lisa laughed, 'I'm just playing around with a few ideas, that's all. Now I've finally fitted the last piece of the jigsaw of my mother's life, well, up to her giving birth to me. I am confident that we will be enjoying many more years of her scintillating wit and charm.'

He swivelled her chair around to face him.

'When are you going to tell her?'

'That I know everything she's been hiding from us forever? Or about the baby?'

'About everything!'

Lisa thought for a second. 'Picking the right time to tell her will be crucial. I don't want her launching herself at me, saying I'd no business going behind her back but, I'll tell her the truth. I wanted to find out so I could understand better why she never allowed me to enjoy a proper mother-daughter relationship with her. And, it's my way of offering her an olive branch because I'm hoping we can at least *try* to enjoy each other while we still can. But the biggest thing I've learned from all this is that *my* childhood, compared to my mother's, was like a stroll in the park with Mary Poppins. Give me five minutes. I need to change… If I can find anything that still fits around my waist. So, how about I tell you everything I've found out over dinner? Then, perhaps you can help me decide when the best time to tell her might be.'

Forebears

Elizabeth was born into an uncertain world on the 1st January 1940, the day Britain called up 2,000,000 young men for military service, including her nineteen-year-old father, Edward. Her seventeen-year-old mother, Gertrude Clemmens, was alone in her parents' cottage on Viscount Rutherford's Ditton Hall Estate in Cambridgeshire, when her waters broke. She panicked, but to her relief, her mother, Evelyn, came home from her work in the hall kitchen just as the baby's head began pushing its way into the world.

For a first time mother, giving birth to Elizabeth wasn't as difficult as Gertrude had imagined. In the weeks leading up to the birth, her mother had painted a somewhat painful picture about what to expect. But contrary to what she'd said, her contractions were not unbearably painful, and Elizabeth had slipped into a towel held by Gertrude's mother without complications. After Evelyn cut the cord and gently wiped the baby's face, she wrapped Elizabeth in the swaddling blanket she'd used for the births of both Gertrude and her younger sister, Clara.

When little Elizabeth gave her first cry, Gertrude gave her mother a glowing smile. 'Thank you, mam. Now I know what it feels like to be a mother, too,' she said, stroking her baby's downy head. 'You are the most beautiful baby in the whole world, my lovely Lizzie,' she whispered. 'Just you wait 'til your dad sees you… He'll be cock-o-hoop.'

Edward Campbell was Viscount Rutherford's only son, heir to the

Rutherford title and the Ditton Hall Estate. Edward and Gertrude were poles apart on the social scale, but bound together by a love so strong that nothing could tear them apart.

As a caring and thoughtful young man, Edward was very different from his father in both looks and personality. He'd started his first year at Emmanuel College, Cambridge, the last Michaelmas term to study Classics and, so far, it hadn't been the university experience he'd anticipated. His studies frequently disrupted by air raid precaution drills following Neville Chamberlain's declaration on 3rd September 1939 that Britain was at war with Germany. Edward was looking forward to starting his second term at Cambridge, but it was looking more unlikely with each day that passed.

The morning Elizabeth was born, Edward was deep in thought in the Baroque chapel at Ditton Hall, agonising over his future. He was no coward but, the concept of war appalled him, but it was the thought of leaving his beloved Gertrude behind that he found terrifying because God forbid, what if he didn't come back? And now, there was his unborn child to think about.

Gertrude's father, Ben Clemmens, was Rutherford's gamekeeper, and when he found out Gertrude was pregnant with Edward's child, he had delivered him an ultimatum. 'You've got our Gertie up the duff, so I expect you to do right by her.' Ben was a man of few words, but his words were well chosen and to the point when he spoke. He was a skilled user of most firearms, including a Purdey shotgun, a gift from Lord Rutherford. Ben always had the Purdey tucked under his arm, and he'd threatened to use it on Edward if he didn't 'do right' by Gertie.

More than anything, Edward wanted to marry Gertrude and live quietly in a cottage on his father's estate, but he knew his parents would never allow it. Edward's mother had compiled a long list of young debutantes she planned to introduce him to. Introductions that were now on hold because of the threat of war, much to his relief.

Edward had been putting off having the 'Gertrude conversation' with his parents, particularly his father, as he knew what his reaction would be. A tirade about the fatuous social class system and the scandal, as well as the shame that 'marrying a servant' would bring upon the family name. His father had never given a second thought about all the young men in the village, most of them employed by the Ditton Hall estate, who had already signed up to fight for King and Country. But Edward wondered, now he was facing the same fate as his peers, whatever their social standing, whether his father might think again. Now, about to become a father himself, he must have that conversation with his parents without further delay because time was not on his side.

He was also agonising over the other conversation he needed to have with Gertie. He hadn't told her he'd signed up, but consoled himself with the thought that, as Gertie knew him better than anybody else, she would understand that he would want to do his duty. The potential of going to war and leaving his parents meant nothing to him, but the thought of leaving Gertrude had become unbearable. If he died in action, what would fate hold in store for his beloved and their child without his protection?

The entrance door to the chapel groaned open, and Edward's face lit up to see Evelyn walking towards him, with a broad smile on her face. His heart skipped a beat as she sat down next to him in anticipation of what she was about to tell him.

'You have a beautiful, healthy daughter, Edward,' she whispered.

He sprang to his feet, kissed Evelyn on both cheeks, and rushed outside. He ran across the manicured lawns, along the banks of the River Cam that meandered its way through the sweeping formal gardens at Ditton Hall, lorded over by towering oaks and magnificent elms. He crossed the bridge shaded by cascading weeping willow trees, startling a pair of mute swans who flapped their wings in feeble protest at the sound of his feet pounding across the wooden slats.

His breath became laboured, his lungs burning with the exertion as he sprinted along the leaf-strewn path he had taken so many times before, which wound its way through the woods to the Clemmens' cottage. He took the stairs three at a time, catching his breath at the top, before going into the bedroom Gertrude shared with her sister, Clara. Gertie was sitting up in bed, looking radiant as she breastfed Elizabeth. Clara was sitting on the side of the bed, chattering excitedly, and Ben, as dour as ever, stood a few feet away, the Purdey tucked under his arm.

Still, out of breath, Edward looked at his daughter in awe, panting out the words, 'she's… So… Beautiful. Just like her mother. Oh,

Gertie, this is the best and proudest moment of my life. I love you so much, and I love our little girl. You've made me the happiest man alive.'

Gertie passed the swaddling child to Edward, whose tears overwhelmed him when Elizabeth's tiny fingers touched his nose as Ben Clemmens looked on.

Born a hard-nosed ruralite, who had served in World War I, Ben had seen things many men could not endure. Edward's display of emotion took him by surprise, making him feel uncomfortable. Clearing his throat, he mumbled under his breath, '*Young men of today 'ave gone bloody soft.*'

During the next few days, it was inevitable that Edward allowed the euphoria of becoming a father to be eclipsed by the haunting reality that he would have to leave to join his regiment the following week. He still hadn't spoken to his parents about Gertrude. It was a conversation Edward never wanted to have because he knew they would make it impossible for him to marry his one true love. He still hadn't told Gertie that he had signed up either. After Elizabeth was born, she had been as happy as he had ever seen her, so he hadn't had the heart to tell her. The thought of leaving them both had become unbearable and, in his heart, he knew he couldn't do it.

One morning, he arrived at the Clemmens' cottage asking if he could take Gertrude for a spin in his MG TA Midget.

At first, Gertie was reluctant to leave her baby daughter for the first time. 'I don't know if I can bear to be apart from my beautiful baby for one second,' she protested.

'There's always got to be a first time, Gertie,' Evelyn said. 'I left you with Mrs Crittall at the post office when you were only two days old so that I could get back to work. You go and have a nice time. I'll always look after Lizzie with my life, I promise.'

Edward's heart was pounding during the short drive to Granchester Meadows. He parked the car, and they walked to Gertie's *special place*, accessed only by farm tracks and footpaths from the road. Hand in hand, they sauntered through kissing gates and wooden footbridges to a secluded area on the banks of the River Granta, a tributary of the River Cam, the place they had first made love.

'You haven't forgotten this is my *special place* then?' Gertie planted a kiss on Edward's cheek. 'You're a bit of an old romantic at heart, aren't you, my Eddie? It's so pretty and quiet here. I love it so, but not as much as I love you, my handsome Edward Campbell.'

He turned to face her and smiled. 'I love you too, Gertrude Clemmens, you know that. Whatever happens with this dreadful war, I will always love you. You and I should never part, and we won't be.'

A cautious smile slid across Gertie's face. 'And there was me thinking you were bringing me here to tell me you'd signed up and were leaving.'

'I have signed up, Gertie, with the Cambridgeshire Regiment, and I have to report at 08.00hrs next Friday.'

Gertrude held his stare. 'Oh, Edward. I knew you would. Out of all the boys I ever knew, you are the bravest and most fearless. I'm so proud of you, but I'm not sure if Lizzie and I can bear to let you go.'

As silent tears slid down Gertie's cheeks, Edward's heart lurched inside his chest. Leaning over, he wrapped both arms tightly around her, and whispered in her ear. 'And, I can't bear the thought of leaving you, my beautiful Gertie, or our little Elizabeth. You both mean the world to me. So, I've decided… I'm not going. I won't let this bloody awful war, or my parents, take away the only two things that I hold most dear. Come away with me, Gertie, please!' He held her at arm's length, his eyes pleading.

'What?'

'Your father has said he will shoot me if I don't do right for you, and I *want* to do the right thing.'

'He doesn't mean that, silly! He's all bark and no bite, my old dad.'

'No, I am serious! I want to marry you, with all my heart, and then we can go away! We can just disappear. Just you, me and Elizabeth.'

'Disappear? Where to, Edward? We can't just go!'

'We can, Gertie, don't you see? Ben will give us his permission for you to marry me, and we will go to Scotland. I know of a croft in a remote area, somewhere no one will ever find us. We'll keep in touch with Ben and Evelyn, of course, but only them.'

'But Edward, you can't! You are the heir to Ditton and everything that goes with it. What will his Lordship say?'

'I don't care what *he* says, Gertie! Don't you see? I don't want any of it. I don't *want* Ditton Hall, and I certainly don't want his bloody title! All I want is for you and me to live somewhere our baby will grow up knowing she is loved, and we will be happy, every single minute of each day.'

Gertie looked away from him, wringing her hands and shaking her head. 'You've not thought this through, Edward. I'm not going to be held responsible for you being shamed and disinherited by your parents, and not only that, won't you be hounded as a deserter if you don't turn up on Friday? They used to shoot young lads for desertion in the Great War. No, Edward, I won't run the risk of that.'

Blinkered to the reality, Edward wasn't listening. 'Oh, come on, Gertie. Let's go, let's get away from here. Just the three of us.'

'Edward, no! Lizzie's so little, and I don't think I want to be stuck in the arse end of nowhere either. What if any of us get sick? And, I think I would struggle to cope with Lizzie without having my mam close by.'

Edward looked at Gertie in amazement. He'd been so confident that she would instantly agree to his plan, but he hadn't thought it through, he'd blindly allowed himself to get carried away, and now he felt foolish. 'You're right, Gertie. You always are. You have such a sensible head on your young shoulders. Come on. I will take you home and ask Ben for his permission for us to marry. Then, I will tell my father that I intend to marry you, whether he likes it or not.'

Once on the road back to Ditton, Edward put his foot down hard on the accelerator.

'Slow down, Eddie! More haste, less speed, my love!'

Taking his left hand off the steering wheel, he took her hand in his. 'I'm anxious to do everything I should have done months ago! Whether you come away with me or not, Gertie, I still want you to be my wife.'

'I love you so much, Edward Campbell.'

He turned to smile at her, momentarily losing concentration, as he looked into her eyes, as the words, 'I love you, always and forever,' escaped his lips. Turning to face the road again, a herd of cattle was spilling out of a field onto the lane. He swerved to avoid them but couldn't avoid ploughing his vehicle headlong into a five-hundred-year-old oak tree. They both died instantly.

Edward's parents were devastated to lose their only son but were inconsolable, as well as appalled when they found out that Edward and Gertrude had a daughter. Compassion was not something Viscount Rutherford was well-known for, so he quickly spread the rumour that Edward had merely been giving Gertie a lift into the village. Rutherford paid Ben and Evelyn Clemmens a handsome amount, which would set them up for life, to leave his employment, provided they agreed to all Rutherford's terms, including a heart-breaking proviso - they had to leave the infant Elizabeth behind.

Despite Evelyn's emotional protestations, Ben believed his lordship intended to raise Elizabeth at Ditton Hall, which he thought would give his granddaughter the best start in life.

Viscount Rutherford, however, had a different plan. Raising Elizabeth at Ditton Hall had never crossed his mind. Her mother was their gamekeeper's daughter, so it would be considered an outrage to have her under the same roof; the scandal would cast a cloud over the family name, which would be too much to bear. So, he delivered his self-absorbed, emotionless spinster sister, Sarah, an ultimatum, to provide a home for Elizabeth.

'I have set up a more than generous trust fund for the child's welfare, her upbringing, education and so on, which will see her through until she finds herself a husband. I am prepared to be a joint-legal guardian, along with your good self, but I want nothing to do with this child. If the idea unsettles you, Sarah, dear, I suggest you tell the world at large that you are doing this as a kindness to someone less fortunate than yourself.'

Sarah was far from impressed, as this arrangement would disrupt her modus vivendi for the next seventeen years, so she too would need an incentive, but Rutherford had already thought of that.

'As I shall now die without an heir, I have rewritten my will, and I have left Ditton Hall to you, so it stays in our family. In the event of my dear wife outliving me, I would expect her to have full use of the west wing, as we do now. As soon as you have made suitable preparations to bring the infant into your home, employ a wet nurse, and so on, I would like you to collect the child from the Clemmens' cottage. Of course, it's not too late for you to marry and to have children of your own Sarah if you ever decided to show a little more interest in the opposite sex.'

'Don't you think you have inflicted enough on me, dear brother?

You can collect the child yourself! And, as for your suggestion that I have little interest in men, I have always preferred my own company, having grown up with someone as disagreeable as yourself.'

The Viscount and Lady Rutherford carried out the heinous act themselves. The fewer people who knew, the better. They arrived at the Clemmens' cottage unannounced, the Viscount pulling up his Lagonda drophead coupe by the door. Ben had seen their car approach and ran back to the house.

'Get out of the car and take the child,' Rutherford instructed, and his wife dutifully obeyed.

Breathless, Ben appeared, bending his head to plead with Rutherford through the driver's window. 'My Lord, we were hoping you were going to give us a bit more time with our Lizzie. She's barely a month old, and it's breaking all our hearts to give her up.'

Irritated, Rutherford wound the window down. 'Gone soft, have we, Clemmens?'

Evelyn was standing in front of the crib as Lady Rutherford walked into the bedroom. 'I'll not let you take her, My Lady! I promised our Gertrude I would look after our Lizzie with my life. She's our flesh and blood. How can you do this to us? We will raise her, and love her as our own, just like we raised her mother.'

Lady Rutherford peered into the crib. Elizabeth was fast asleep. She leaned in and calmly picked her up, holding her at arm's length while studying her face. 'There is absolutely no proof that this child is Edward's anyway, but my husband has chosen to give you the benefit of the doubt and has made what I believe to be a most generous offer not only to you and your husband, but to provide the child with a proper education.'

'Her name is Elizabeth!' Evelyn's voice quivered with emotion.

Elizabeth started grumbling, realising she had been picked up. She blinked her eyes open to face her paternal grandmother's cold stare and started to cry. Viscountess Rutherford showed no emotion as she carried the screaming child to the car.

'No, no, no, My Lady, please don't take her.' Evelyn became hysterical, and Ben had to forcibly restrain her from banging her fists on the Lagonda's closed windows before falling to her knees sobbing. Ben dropped to his knees and held his wife in his arms. He, too, broke down and wept as the Lagonda moved away. Clara, who had witnessed the whole heart-breaking scenario from her bedroom window, threw herself onto her sister's bed and cried herself to sleep.

With the infant Elizabeth safely behind closed doors at her Great-Aunt's home, Hauxton House, a short drive from Ditton Hall, Viscount Rutherford took it upon himself to arrange the legalities. He and his sister, Lady Sarah Campbell, became Elizabeth's legal guardians, providing for her financially until she turned twenty-one. Between them, they quickly spread the falsehood that Elizabeth's parents, distant relations of the Rutherford family, had succumbed to Malaria while visiting South Africa, and Lady Sarah Campbell had shown incredible selflessness by taking in their orphaned child, Elizabeth, to raise as her own, with the blessing of the Rutherford family.

Great-Aunt Sarah was a crusty stick insect of a woman who, by choice, had always lived an uninspired, dull, and celibate life. Affection was something she considered frivolous and unnecessary because nobody had ever afforded her any.

Throughout her childhood, Elizabeth was raised by a succession of cold and emotionless Victorian nannies and governesses, deprived of the most important of all human needs, love. To compensate for the lack of emotional stability, Elizabeth was never short of material things - what she demanded she got. So it was inevitable that, in the absence of anyone to steer towards a more compassionate approach to life, she became a spoilt and petulant child who, not knowing any better, would take her querulous behaviour into adulthood.

Great-Aunt Sarah sent her away to boarding school at eight, and Elizabeth had known since that time that her rite of passage would be finishing school at seventeen, the time Great-Aunt Sarah's stint in loco parentis came to an end.

Evelyn and Clara never gave up on Elizabeth. They visited many times, and always on her birthday, despite Ben's dour view that 'it's best to leave the child alone!' Year after year, they persisted, but Great-Aunt Sarah turned them away, fobbing them off with some excuse as to why they couldn't see her. For seventeen years, the Clemmens family continued sending Elizabeth presents and letters in the post about her parents and how much she was loved, but Elizabeth never saw any of them.

Great-Aunt Sarah kept them locked in a cupboard, only deciding to liberate them a few days before Elizabeth was due to leave London to become a debutante. While searching for a pair of gloves Elizabeth thought she'd dropped in the boot room, she discovered the cupboard, usually hidden by an old greatcoat of Great-Aunt Sarah's. Curious, Elizabeth looked inside. At first, she was confused. Why would Great-Aunt Sarah keep a hoard of papers and photographs, as well as wrapped presents, locked away in a cupboard? She was about to close the door when she spotted her own name on a gift tag, *To my beautiful niece, Elizabeth, with all my love, Clara.* And another from 'grandparents' called Evelyn and Ben. Who were these people? There was a birth certificate among the papers for someone called Elizabeth Clemmens. Looking at it more closely, she realised they shared the same birthday. It was an uncanny coincidence, were these presents supposed to be for Elizbeth *Clemmens* or for her? Was it some mistake? This discovery warranted further investigation, but fearing being discovered rooting through Great-Aunt Sarah's, until now, private cupboard, she grabbed a handful of the most important looking documents, including the birth certificate, and closed the door.

After a sleepless night, during which Elizabeth's curiosity got the better of her, she told her aunt she was going for a walk. The mother's name on the birth certificate was, Gertrude Clemmens, who lived at the Gamekeeper's Cottage at Ditton Hall, the home of her elusive guardian, Viscount Rutherford, who she'd only ever seen from a distance, but never met.

Elizabeth arrived at the entrance of the impressive Ditton Hall. As the gates were closed, she knocked on the door of the lodge. The door opened, releasing the tantalising, mouth-watering smell of freshly baked bread. A woman wearing a pinafore, with tell-tale traces of flour smeared across her rosy face, looked at her quizzically.

'Can I help you, darlin''?'

'Yes, I'm Lord Rutherford's ward, and I'm looking for Gertrude Clemmens, who lives at the Gamekeeper's cottage. I wondered if you could be so kind as to give me directions.' An incredulous look washed across the woman's face.

'If you are His Lordship's ward, why are you knocking on my door?'

'Because I, er, simply, don't want to trouble him.' Elizabeth forced a haughty smile.

'Hmm, if you are who you say you are, and you sound posh enough to be related to the old bugger, why 'aven't you got a chauffeur to drive you around?'

'Well, one needs to exercise, from time to time.'

'One does, eh? Look, young Miss, I can tell you that the Clemmens family has long since gone.'

'Gone? Gone where?'

'I've no idea, my love, they came, and they went before I came to Ditton, but if you want to find out about them, I suggest you speak to old Mrs Crittall at the post office. She and Gertie's mum were friendly-like, so she might know where they went.'

Elizabeth walked up the short, paved path to the Post Office and opened the door. A woman sitting behind the counter got to her feet. Her grey hair was wound into a bun, and she patted it a couple of times to make sure it was in place.

'Mrs Crittall?'

'Yes.'

'I am hoping to find Gertrude Clemmens, who used to live at the Gamekeeper's Cottage at Ditton Hall, and the lady at the lodge told me you might know where she is as you and Gertrude's mother were friends.'

Frowning, Mrs Crittall asked. 'Why would a fine young lady like you be looking for Gertrude Clemmens?'

'Because, I think I might have found some things that belong to an Elizabeth Clemmens.', who is her daughter, I believe.'

Mrs Crittall sniffed suspiciously. 'And who wants to know?'

'Well, I do.' Elizabeth tilted her head quizzically. 'My name is Elizabeth Campbell. I'm Viscount Rutherford's ward. I live in Hauxton, with his sister.'

'Heavens to Betsy!' Mrs Crittall came out from behind the counter and stood in front of Elizabeth. Mrs Crittall's look was unnerving. It was like she'd just seen a ghost. 'I never thought I'd see this day. I've kept this secret to myself for seventeen years because Evelyn, Gertie's mum, made me swear never to say anything, and I never 'ave.'

'What secret?'

'You? You are Gertie's little Lizzie. *You* are Elizabeth Clemmens.'

353

Elizabeth was stunned. Rendered speechless, she sank into a chair by the counter looking up at Mrs Crittall.

'Oh, no, I think you are mistaken Mrs Crittall, both my parents died while on holiday in South Africa, when I was a baby.'

'Hmm, is that what the Rutherfords told you? Your parents were a love match made in heaven, and neither of them ever ventured further than Cambridge, as far as I know. Your mam, Gertrude Clemmens, and Mr Edward, the Viscount's only son, were childhood sweethearts. Everyone knew that, except for Rutherford, of course, and when he did find out, the miserable old bugger never accepted that his only son worshipped the ground your mother stood on. Their deaths were felt so deeply by everyone who'd known them.' Mrs Crittall told Elizabeth was still in touch with Evelyn Clemmens. 'She lives in the hope that one day you might better understand and try to find your grandparents and aunt. Never a day goes by without them thinking about their Lizzie.'

Elizabeth never cried, but a silent tear trickled down her cheek.

'My goodness, you look just like your mam.'

A surge of emotion washed through Elizabeth's body. She got to her feet and ran out of the Post Office. She was incensed. How could the Rutherford family have lied to her for seventeen years, allowing her to grow up never knowing who she really was? She could never forgive them.

Returning to Hauxton, she went straight to her room, struggling to fathom what Mrs Crittall had told her, while looking at the photographs of the people she had just found out were her parents. Her maternal grandmother lived in the hope that one day she might try to find her, but her new life in the upper echelons of society was about to begin. What would she have in common with these people now, anyway? Finding her maternal grandparents and aunt was never going to happen. She was sure of one thing though, she would never understand, and learning to trust anybody ever again would be a challenge, if not impossible.

1957

Marriageable Material

Two days later, Elizabeth walked through the Italianate portico at Cambridge Railway Station giddy with excitement. Heads turned as she made her way onto the platform. She knew she was a beautiful young woman, a technicolour ray of light illuminating a black-and-white world still recovering from the vice-like grip of post-war austerity.

On the platform, the Fenton Flyer was waiting to continue its journey to King's Cross Station. Elizabeth leaned forward, pursing her lips, and kissed the air, her smooth cheek grazing the dry, wrinkled jowls of her Great-Aunt Sarah. It was the first and last time they made physical contact. Elizabeth jerked her head away; she hated the woman with a vengeance. She knew the feeling was mutual.

Great-Aunt Sarah was one of the last bastions of conventional upper-class Victorian respectability. As such, she would consider it unbecoming for a lady to raise her voice, but on this occasion, she made an exception and, throwing convention to the wind, she balled. The ear-piercing whistles coming from the front and the back ends of the train abated, drowned out by the sheer volume of Great-Aunt Sarah's booming voice, fortified by her aristocratic accent. 'Go to the city and find yourself a husband, Elizabeth dear, and one with some money. The last thing any woman wants in this life is a beastly job, and the Debutantes House is the best place to mould you into marriageable material.'

'*You're quite wrong!*' Elizabeth thought, staring her great-aunt in the eye. *'The last thing I want is to spend one moment longer with you!'*

The guard was striding towards them, slamming the carriage doors shut. Elizabeth resisted the urge to throw herself onto the train. Instead, she smiled serenely, kept her composure, and stepped aboard the first-class carriage as would be deemed fit for someone of noble birth. Once on the train, she turned to wave goodbye to Great-Aunt Sarah, but she had already left the platform.

'Good riddance, you old battle-axe! I'm *finally* getting away from you.'

She watched the guard blow his whistle, his red cheeks puffed out and an arm raised towards the driver. The train whistled its response and slowly chuffed out of the station. As the Fenton Flyer picked up speed, a broad smile rippled across Elizabeth's face. She was leaving Cambridgeshire for good without a backward glance and no emotional ties, intent on making a new life, she would never return.

She had the carriage to herself, so relieved her small suitcase of half its weight, before putting it on the rack above her head. Sitting down, she rested her head against the padded seating covered with brocade-style upholstery. Her life was now her own, with a bank account to go with it. She had plans to go to Harrods to buy a wardrobe of clothes, more appropriate for her exciting new life in London.

Looking down at the 1957 edition of *Burke's Peerage, Baronetage, Knightage, and Landed Gentry* she'd taken out of her suitcase, she hoisted it onto her knee, running the palm of her hand across its cover.

Listed somewhere in this illustrious tome, she would find the name of her future husband. Closing her eyes, she visualised images of her future self, linking arms with the young man she would marry after her year at the Debutantes House. He would be as handsome as Prince Philip, Duke of Edinburgh, but a little younger. They would start their married lives together living in a mansion in Knightsbridge or Belgravia, where they would host parties for London's elite. As they grew older, he would inherit his father's country seat, and Elizabeth would appear in full-length features in *Country Life*. Provided her husband-to-be had a well-stocked bank account, it would be a marriage made in heaven.

By March 1958, Elizabeth was in her element. The London debutante 'season' was in full swing. Elizabeth relished being a part of the non-stop social soirées, endless charity events, and quintessentially English sporting events, such as Ascot and Henley Royal Regatta. All excellent opportunities for her to show herself off to the crème de la crème of eligible young men, with a view to marriage.

Along with the other polished young ladies from the Debutantes House, Elizabeth now had her eyes on the main prize, apart from reeling in a husband. She was counting the days to the highlight of their year as debutantes, Queen Charlotte's Ball. Founded by George III, the ball first waltzed its way into the debutante's social calendar in 1780 as a birthday celebration in honour of his wife Charlotte of Mecklenburg-Strelitz.

In 1958, Elizabeth joined the procession of four hundred fresh-faced young women from the Debutante's House and other finishing schools, including the Cygnets House and the Monkey Club, and waiting her turn to be presented to Queen Elizabeth II. Curtseying to the Queen was the highlight of her life so far. Elizabeth knew that the tradition would not survive the 20th century or the next twelve months. Princess Margaret believed *every tart* in London was doing 'the Season', and the Duke of Edinburgh thought the event was *bloody daft*. Their combined opinions must have influenced the young Queen Elizabeth II because she decided to abolish future ceremonies. So, Elizabeth was doubly delighted as she was guaranteed a place in history, along with the other 1958 debutantes, as they would be the last aristocratic ingénues to be presented to a reigning monarch at court during the 178th Queen Charlotte's Ball.

The Debutantes House taught Elizabeth the social graces and upper-class cultural etiquette to prepare her for entry into society. The platform from where she would snare the man of her dreams, someone whose bank account would provide her with the privileged lifestyle she so craved. A union that would guarantee Elizabeth never having to contemplate that nasty four-letter word 'work' or the equally ghastly three-letter word 'job', but she needed to move fast. Eighteen and husband-less would be a concern. Nineteen and husband-less was unthinkable.

On the eve of Queen Charlotte's Ball, the housemistress zipped up Elizabeth's coming-out-into-society dress. It was a snug fit around her svelte form.

'You could never possibly look more beautiful than you do tonight, Elizabeth dear. You will be snapped up as a blushing bride-to-be before you know it!' Elizabeth was in no doubt.

Standing at the top of the stairs at the Debutantes House having her photograph taken, Elizabeth knew she looked radiant in her virginal white satin décolleté dress. The ultimate coming out accessory complemented the look, white leather gloves up to her elbows, with three small pearl buttons at the wrist, which one would undo to drink or eat.

'The camera loves you, Elizabeth!' The photographer was in his element, bouncing around her like a Labrador puppy, deliberately taking his time before falling to his knees to get a shot from another dimension. Elizabeth knew the other young ladies of the Debutantes House were queuing on the curling Georgian staircase in their long white frocks, waiting for their turn in the limelight. Still, Elizabeth didn't care that they were becoming impatient. She was loving every second of being the centre of attention.

'What's going on up there? Why on earth is it taking so long?' Someone shouted up the stairs.

Lady Penelope Lindsay, at the head of the queue, hissed her response down the stairwell. 'Slapper Campbell is enjoying being centre stage, as usual. She's fluttering her eyelashes at the photographer and giving him her best come-hither look.'

Elizabeth smiled inwardly when the photographer flashed Lady

Penelope a smile, arching his eyebrows as he jumped to his feet.

'Look at me, Elizabeth! Give me that insatiable come-to-bed eyes look of yours!' She obliged, pouting.

'Oh, yes! Now, look to the left, please.'

Elizabeth caught a glimpse of herself in a full-length mirror, and her reflection confirmed what she already knew. She was beautiful. Her honey-blonde hair softly curled just above her shoulders, her make-up was subtle, au naturel, with a little rouge, red lipstick, and mascara. Her defined eyebrows accentuated her large, smouldering, brown eyes. Around her neck, she wore a diamond-and-sapphire necklace, which had been delivered earlier in the day. 'A gift from Viscount Rutherford, Elizabeth,' the headmistress had said.

There had been no note with it, which was no surprise. Elizabeth barely knew what Rutherford looked like because the miserable old sod had kept a low profile during the last seventeen years. The necklace was the very least he could have done. Triggered by a twinge of guilt, perhaps? If it was, he hadn't given this final gesture too much thought because Elizabeth would have preferred a tiara.

Footloose

Will Grant was elated as he came out of London's Drury Lane Theatre, flying over the steps to the pavement in one single bound. He had just seen a performance of *My Fair Lady* with Rex Harrison as Henry Higgins and twenty-three-year-old Julie Andrews as Eliza Doolittle. Members of the equally ecstatic audience leaving the theatre behind him applauded when his feet touched the ground. Turning around, he bowed to the assembled crowd before striding away in the direction of Shaftesbury Avenue singing, 'Just you wait, 'enry 'iggins, just you wait!'

Ripping off his black tie, he stuffed it into the pocket of his dinner jacket and danced through the streets, his lean nineteen-year-old body bursting with energy. On the brink of his adult life, he was free to go wherever the whim would take him. Tonight, he was on his way to Old Compton Road and the 2i's Coffee Bar, the in-place for emerging British pop music culture. He needed to get a move on because, after umpteen curtain calls at Drury Lane, he was running late. Breaking into a run, he tried to recall the lyrics of *I'm an Ordinary Man.* The tune was in his head, but the words escaped him, although he remembered the last line. 'Never let a woman in your life!' he yelled at the top of his lungs.

'Too bloody right, mate!' a man responded from the other side of the street. 'Once you let 'em in, you'll never get rid of 'em!'

The woman on the man's arm recoiled, snatching the flat cap off his head and beating him with it as she yelled at him, 'I've been trying to get rid of you for years, you old battle cruiser! But you won't go! Look at the state of you compared to that young dish over there.' Will laughed and carried on chasseing along the pavement.

He was popular amongst his peers, unaware he oozed charisma and charm. Gregarious by nature, his natural magnetism and sense of humour made it easy for him to make friends. Despite his love for country life, living in London fed his love of fashion; he was always immaculately dressed, turning heads wherever he went. He was oblivious to his good looks, his features a mix of masculine and feminine characteristics, which intrigued and attracted. A shock of golden-blond hair, with a heavy quiff that flopped across his brow, through which he habitually ran his fingers to scrape it away from his large, oval-shaped green eyes. He thought it highly amusing when a total stranger mistook him for Robert Wagner in The Flamingo Club.

He knew from an early age he was destined to take over the reins of running the family farm, Silkwoods, in Gloucestershire, and he relished the challenge. Even as a boy, he was always at his father's side learning everything he could about mixed-crop and livestock farming. He wasn't put off by the hard work it entailed. Seeing the land flourish from efficient crop rotation and the animals living off it thrive was a passion.

His other great love was playing polo, aspiring to a plus handicap at the age of seventeen. He could have become one of the UK's finest players, but as much as he loved the sport, he knew it was nothing more than an indulgent hobby. During his last term at Stowe School, he looked forward to spending the summer working on the farm and playing polo. But his father, Alistair, had other ideas and had found him a job in the city.

'All young men should experience the city.' His father delivered the words with upbeat certainty. 'Find yourself a girl... or two while you're there. I'm not about to drop off my perch just yet, so take this opportunity to enjoy London life for a while. Well, for the next five years or so.'

Will was very close to his father. After his wife died, Alistair brought Will up by himself, investing as much time as possible in his young son, something Will hoped to do with his own children one day. He always felt the need to please his father, so although the thought of experiencing the city *for five years or so* sounded a little galling, he agreed to Alistair's suggestion. To Will, the productive diversity farming offered, plus the added attraction of polo ponies on the doorstep, far outweighed the potential moneymaking opportunities London currently offered. Socially, however, London offered many eye-opening opportunities. The endless round of parties, especially during 'the Season', and London's vibrant nightlife never failed to disappoint.

He arrived at the 2i's Coffee Bar and squeezed his way through the crowd making his way downstairs to where the live music was happening. He had arranged to meet an old school friend, Charlie Lyons, and was already half an hour late.

Charlie had rung Will at work to tell him he had a friend staying from Gloucestershire for a couple of days. 'His name is Thomas Cahoon, and you're neighbours, apparently, but he says your paths have never crossed.'

'What an amazing coincidence! His family does indeed farm the land next to ours. I think I remember Dad saying he recently got married.'

'Well, not that recently. I was one of the ushers at his wedding. He's got two children now, would you believe? Two boys, one is three, and the other is eighteen months. I feel sorry for the poor sod. I couldn't cope with having any snotty little brats at this stage of my life. Two children at twenty, it's like he's signed his life away, and his wife, Anna, is enormous!'

'Charlie Lyons! I can't believe even you would say a thing like that! I'm sure she is charming.'

'When I say enormous, I mean enormously tall! She's an excellent polo player. She was brought up in India and has played since she could straddle a pony. So maybe that's what drew them together because he plays as well.'

'Really?'

'Not as good as you, I don't suppose, but yes, they both play. Another reason why I'm surprised you haven't met. Anyway, as tomorrow is Friday, I plan to take Thomas for a wild night out in the Big Smoke. You know, get him drunk, smoke a few cigars, and if we get lucky, pick up some girls and have the whole of Saturday to recover from our hangovers, and I would like you to join us.'

Will felt ambivalent about meeting Thomas. Despite being neighbours, they were unlikely to have anything in common, apart from exchanging anecdotes on the ingredients of silage, until he found out they shared a passion, polo.

'I'm booked to go to Drury Lane tomorrow night. You know I'm a sucker for the musical theatre, but...'

'Oh, come on, Will, you can meet us afterwards. The night will still be young, and I want to make sure Thomas lets his hair down before he goes back to changing his brats' nappies. I can't think of anyone better qualified than you to make sure he does.'

Now wedged on the narrow staircase at the 2i, unable to move up or down, Will wished he had left the theatre and headed straight for the nearest pub. 'Charlie Lyons! Why do I ever listen to you?' he bellowed, but the skiffle band drowned out his voice. 'Oh shit!' He was stuck with his back pressed flat against the wall. The atmosphere was stifling, the air polluted with the combined smell of stale sweat and perfume as the constant stream of bodies wormed their way up and down the stairs. The back of a man's neck pushed up against his face, and Old Spice replaced the fetid air.

'If I could turn around and introduce myself, I would. But I'm stuck. I'm Thomas Cahoon, and I'm guessing you must be Will Grant. I lost Charlie over half an hour ago. If we both push at the same time, we can shoulder our way out of here. I've never felt so close to suffocation in my life, and I could murder a drink.'

Loose Ends

Despite Will's deep affection for the country, he enjoyed London life until the day he received a call in his office late one afternoon. 'Will?' The low pitch of a Scottish accent was instantly recognisable.

'Dr Gladstone! What a surprise, is everything alright?' He immediately regretted asking the question as a feeling of impending doom swept over him. Why would the family doctor ring him out of the blue and at work?

'Will, there is no easy way to tell you this, and I am so sorry to have to be the bearer of bad news, but your father died this afternoon.'

Contemplating what had been said, Will felt the back of his throat tighten but managed to squeeze out the words, 'What? How? I only spoke to him last night. He said he was getting an early night because he was going out with the hounds this morning as the hunt were meeting at the house.'

'They did meet at Silkwoods, and your father went out with them. Young Thomas Cahoon was out as well and said your father was going hell for leather all morning. Around midday, the fox went to ground at Upper Chilcott, and Thomas noticed your father wasn't there. Sensing something was wrong, he retraced his steps. From the top of Chittlegove Rise, Thomas could see your father's old cob standing stock-still, with your father slumped over his neck. As Thomas galloped across the field to help him, your father slid out of the saddle. Thomas tried to resuscitate him, but he'd had a cardiac arrest and would have been dead when he hit the ground… Will?'

Short stuttering intakes of breath forcing back tears prevented Will's reply, but at last, he breathed the word, 'Badger.'

'Badger?'

'My father's cob…'

'Ah, yes, Badger. Well, Badger stayed with your father while Thomas went to get help.'

'Thank you for letting me know, Dr Gladstone.'

'Will, I hate being the bearer of such bad news, and, as a doctor, I probably shouldn't recommend a good stiff whiskey, but it might help. If there is anything you need when you come home, Mrs Gladstone and I would be happy to help.'

After saying goodbye to Dr Gladstone, Will gingerly got to his feet and went through to his boss's office. 'I'm sorry to bother you, Sir, but I've just heard that my father died earlier today.' Unable to make eye contact with his superior, he stared at the floor, his fringe flopping over his eyes. 'I would like to hand in my notice because I need to go back to Gloucestershire and run the farm.'

'I'm very sorry to hear that, Will, but you are contracted to work a three-month notice.'

'Yes, I knew that, but I was hoping, under the circumstances, that you might let me go a little sooner.'

'The problem is, Will, that we need to find someone to replace you, which I confess is not going to be easy. You have been doing such a terrific job for the company, and we will miss you… very much. However, I understand your predicament and would be prepared to grant you two weeks compassionate leave so you can go home and sort things out, *pro tem,* until we can release you at the beginning of February 1959. If you leave now, you should have enough time to go back to your flat, pack a suitcase, and make the last train to Kemble.'

Waking up alone at Silkwood for the first time, Will felt drained after a night of fitful sleep. In his post waking moments, his thoughts were jumbled. Apart from arranging his father's funeral, there was a great deal for him to do. This year's calves needed to be weaned and brought back into the barn before the temperature started to drop. Ewes would need to be dipped to avoid infections, and their wool clipped from around the tail area in readiness for the mating season. His father did so much of the work around the farm, he would need to employ more farmhands, but he also felt lucky. Silkwoods already had an experienced farm manager, Jim Liddington, who had worked alongside Alistair for most of his life. Leaving the farm in Jim's capable hands until he worked out his notice in London made him feel a little more relaxed.

He rolled out of bed, scratching his mop of blond hair and looked out of the bedroom window. Thomas was hacking up the drive. A whole gamut of emotions rushed through his body as he threw his clothes on and ran downstairs to meet him. During his initial meeting with Thomas, Will discovered they had a great deal in common. He found him so easy to spend time with and felt he could talk to him about anything. Silkwoods without his father was going to be painful, but with Thomas only a ten-minute ride through the woods, he knew he would be able to cope much better.

He opened the heavy oak front door and watched Thomas dismount and tie the bridle reins to one of the iron rings hammered into the Cotswold stone wall opposite. Thomas walked towards him with his arms outstretched. Will's heart lurched. He had never felt so happy to see anyone in his life. Thomas wrapped his arms around him.

Will reciprocated, holding on tightly, sucking back the tears. 'Thank you for being with my father when he died and for doing all you could for him.'

'I'm so sorry I couldn't have done more, Will. Your father was a wonderful man, and he will be a significant loss to the whole community. I saw Jim at the Post Office in Colesbourne earlier. He said you were home, so I wanted to come over to offer you my condolences, and I thought you might need a friend right now. So, I'm here to help in any way I can.'

They spent most of the day together overseeing what needed to be done on the farm, and in the early evening, they shared a drink together.

'So that's settled then, Will. I will help Jim with the horses and anything else I can do until you get back.'

'Are you absolutely sure you want to do this, Thomas? After all, you've got your own farm to think about.'

'Don't worry, I have plenty of time to help out. My father prefers to be in control. He refuses to let me take the reins, and don't forget, we are running a much smaller operation than you are here.'

'My father always said that farm managers didn't come any better than Jim, but I know he will appreciate your help.'

'And I'm more than happy to give it.'

'I still can't believe he's gone, Thomas.' Will sighed. I thought he would go on forever. At least he died doing something he loved, and during the thrill of the chase, too.' They both laughed. 'Dear Badger, my dad loved that horse. Of all the thoroughbreds we have in the yard, he would choose that old cob with his stout build and docked tail over all of them. We're not sure quite how old he is, but he is well into his twenties and still goes like the clappers!'

'Ah, well, you can't tie a good horse down. Here's to Alistair!' Thomas stood up, raising his glass.

Will followed suit, and they chinked their glasses. 'Here's to you, Dad.'

Closing In

Despite still not having found a husband, Elizabeth finished her year at the Debutantes House on a high, after being crowned Debutante of the Year for 1958. A coveted title, which she believed was an excellent addition to her marriageable material curriculum vitae. Elizabeth was now sharing a flat with two other young ladies from the Debutantes House. She had selected Katherine and Antonia carefully, confident that they would be less competition in the looks department, as they were all on the hunt for a husband.

Elizabeth couldn't understand why she hadn't been showered with proposals, and she needed to find a husband soon because her Rutherford-funded bank account was beginning to run dry, but she wasn't too worried. If things got desperate, she could always sell the diamond and sapphire necklace. She was sure about one thing though, crawling back to old-man-Rutherford to ask for more money was never going to happen.

A young man called Jeremy Jermayne, who fell into the tall, dark and handsome category, was always there to offer Elizabeth his arm. He was impeccably spoken. His upper class received pronunciation, flawless. Every inch the 'deb's delight', and he could so easily have been *the one*. He had told Elizabeth she was the most beautiful woman he had ever seen, boosting her already fully inflated ego, but despite Jeremy's perfect pedigree, there was a problem.

Elizabeth's initial attraction to Jeremy had been purely physical, but before she allowed herself to get to know him properly, she had done her research. The surname Jermayne first appeared around the Battle of Hastings, starting a lineage of well-heeled upstanding pillars of society; Lawyers, Members of Parliament, and High Sheriffs. Although none of them ever received a knighthood, the family had lorded over Suffolk for hundreds of years from their substantial family seat, Saxmundham Hall, until Jeremy's philandering grandfather, Ambrose, broke the mould.

Elizabeth read that Ambrose's life had been one of drunken debauchery, fuelled by a gambling addiction. Jeremy's father salvaged what he could after Ambrose's death. Saxmundham Hall's sale paid off most of his inherited debts before he tragically succumbed to a hail of German bullets during the D-Day Landings. Jeremy's mother sold everything, including the much scaled-down family home, before moving into a one up, two down in Little Wallop. The noble Mrs Jermayne managing to keep a stiff upper lip as she sacrificed her own home comforts to pay for Jeremy to be educated at Eton.

So, despite Jeremy being out of the right drawer and having all the right connections, he was no good to Elizabeth without money, and there was little sign he was ever going to make any. His work prospects were nil. At best, he was workshy; at worst, he was incredibly lazy and looking for the same thing as Elizabeth but in reverse. Jeremy was looking for a wealthy woman to live off. Elizabeth made it quite clear to Jeremy that she couldn't allow herself to marry someone whose only inheritance would be a semi-detached cottage. He quite understood, provided she continued with their relationship. 'For escort and recreational purposes at least, my love. Until we find someone more suitable for you.'

Jeremy was fortunate to be living an expense-free existence just off Berkeley Square with his old school friend and son of a millionaire, Tarquin Montague. Tarquin received invitations to all the social soirées hosted by the London's elite, so Jeremy was always included as an appendage of the Montague household.

*

At breakfast one morning, whilst planning their day around hair appointments and manicures, as usual, Elizabeth and her flatmates discussed marriage prospects.

Elizabeth announced with a sullen expression, 'I hear Tarquin Montague has popped the question to a rather plain-looking girl.'

Antonia reached for another Fortnum and Mason's croissant. 'Ah, but she is the daughter of a Duke, so a Lady in her own right.'

'Well, I'm the granddaughter of a Viscount!' Elizabeth snapped.

'Have you heard about Will Grant?' Katherine asked.

'No, he's a bit of dish, isn't he? With all that floppy blond hair,' Antonia giggled.

'Definitely not my type,' Elizabeth chipped in, 'I prefer them tall, dark and handsome. I don't think I know him anyway.'

'I'm surprised because not only is he a bit of a dish, but he is quite delightful, thoughtful and funny. Anyway, his father recently suffered a massive heart attack, or something, whilst out hunting and died while he was still in the saddle.'

'Oh, dear,' Elizabeth proffered, 'if one will persist in taking part in barbaric country sports…'

Katherine continued. 'It might well be barbaric, Elizabeth. But the point is that his father's death has left Will quite parentless, and a very wealthy young man, as well as the proud owner of Silkwoods.'

'Silkwoods?' Elizabeth and Antonia responded in unison.

'Yes, it's a 1000-acre estate in Gloucestershire, with an enormous Grade II listed manor house to go with it.'

'I love Gloucestershire!' Antonia squealed with delight.

'So do I,' Elizabeth added enthusiastically, even though she'd never been there. 'What do you say, girls? Let's organise a drinks party. We said we were going to have one soon, and let's ask Will.'

Tying the Knot

While Antonia and Katherine started drawing up a list of potential guests, Elizabeth undertook a little research. She tutted. Will's name did not appear in either Burke's Peerage or Debrett's, which was disappointing. Maybe a title wasn't so important if he'd just become one of the most eligible bachelors in the country.

Later that day, Elizabeth just 'happened' to bump into him outside his office in the City, her perfectly exfoliated body melting into his as they collided.

'Oh! I'm so sorry,' stammered Will, scraping the quiff back from his brow. 'I wasn't looking where I was going! Are you alright?'

She fixed him with her very best limpid-pool stare and smiled seductively, batting her eyelashes three or four times before feigning a faint into his arms.

After their worlds *accidentally* collided, Elizabeth made sure she was everywhere he went. But despite all her efforts, he wasn't showing much interest. She had turned down invitations from most of his peers who would have given a great deal to have her on their arm, but it seemed as though she was not what Will was looking for.

Undeterred, Elizabeth continued to pursue him around London, eventually corralling him into a quiet corner at a party. 'I've never met anybody quite like you before, Will. I think I'm falling in love with you,' she purred, while batting her Lana Turner eyelashes with hypnotic effect. If she were expecting him to respond by scooping her up in his arms and proclaiming his undying love for her – as Jeremy would have done – she was wrong. But she hadn't expected him to laugh.

'Elizabeth! I've never met anybody quite like you before either, but you can't possibly *love* me because you barely even *know* me.' She was disgruntled at the time, but she didn't give up. The stakes were too high. So, she waited patiently until an opportunity presented itself for her to seal the deal. She didn't have to wait long. At a drinks party they both attended, she learned that Will was leaving London permanently to run Silkwoods. When she spotted him leaving without so much as an au revoir, she grabbed her coat and ran after him.

'Will, wait!' He had just flagged down a cab and was getting into it. 'Can I share?' He turned around and stepped back on to the pavement. With just a hint of irritation in his voice, he uttered, 'Sure. No problem. Mine's the first stop.' He held open the cab door for her.

'You're leaving early?' Elizabeth said, running her hand down his arm from his shoulder.'

'Yes, well, I've got work in the morning, and I haven't eaten yet, so I'm feeling extremely pissed. The champagne cocktails went straight to my head!'

Elizabeth had to move fast. If she didn't do something now, she might never see Will again. 'I haven't eaten either. We could have a bite to eat somewhere together.' But her hopes were quickly dashed.

'That would be nice, Elizabeth, but I haven't had an early night for weeks. Ah, here we are now. Just here will be fine, Cabbie.' When the taxi pulled into the curb, Will got out. 'Perhaps we can catch up another time, Elizabeth?'

'Oh, Will. Can't I come up for a nightcap? I haven't seen your flat before.'

'What's it to be, mate?' The cabbie asked. 'It sounds like you might be on a promise to me.'

Elizabeth giggled. 'Yes, come on, Will. What's it going to be?'

*

Disgruntled but not wanting to appear rude, Will had relented and invited Elizabeth in for a nightcap. His mind raced with ways to get rid of her in the shortest possible time. 'I've only got whiskey, I am afraid,' he said, unscrewing the bottle.

Elizabeth fluttered her heavily mascaraed eyelashes. 'Whiskey will be perfect, thank you.'

He poured her drink and flopped on to the sofa next to her. But before he could protest, she threw her leg across him and straddled his lap, and as she covered his mouth with hers, he felt he couldn't breathe. Feeling himself inside her, a wave of disgust washed over him as he realised he was actually enjoying it. Resigned to his situation, he gritted his teeth and let her get on with it; the quicker it was over, the sooner she would be gone.

In the foggy waking moments of a hangover the following day, he dismissed what had happened between them for what it was, drunken sex. It would never happen again. He only had a few weeks left in London, and he would make sure he kept a low profile.

When the press started reporting assignations between the

glamorous Elizabeth Campbell and the handsome Duke of Grandborough, Will breathed a sigh of relief. Photographs of a smiling Elizabeth and the Duke were plastered across all the broadsheets; one with her handling the Duke's twelve bore on the grouse moor at his family's estate in Yorkshire, another with their arms linked at a highbrow wedding, and 'à deux' during a romantic candlelight dinner. Now she had a more high-ranking assignation going on, Will assumed he was safe, but he was wrong. Twenty-four hours before he was due to leave London for good, his heart sank when Elizabeth arrived on his doorstep wearing a pair of pussycat sunglasses.

'Why, Elizabeth, how *lovely* to see you! A late-night was it, last night? The sunglasses, I mean. A bit hung-over, are we?'

'I need to speak to you urgently, Will.' She pushed past him and slumped onto the sofa. 'There's no easy way of telling you this, but I'm pregnant.'

He sat down next to her, putting a reluctant arm around her shoulders. 'That's, err, wonderful news Elizabeth. I'm very pleased for you and Jeremy. Or is it His Lordship? Whichever one it is, I'm sure they are falling over themselves to marry you.'

She pushed him away roughly, snatching the sunglasses away from her face. 'Jeremy? Grandbo? No! It was you, you idiot! You're the one I had that ridiculous one-night stand with! You were all over me like a rampant stallion. There is no question; you are the father. It's you who needs to marry me!'

Even though he was drunk at the time, his recollection of the event differed somewhat from Elizabeth's rampant stallion description. He pulled away from her. 'Why me? Why do you automatically assume I'm the father? It's common knowledge you and Jeremy have been *at it* for months. And what about the Duke? I assume you've slept with him as well. Your reputation goes before you, my dear! I'm going back to Gloucestershire to run the family farm and play polo, not tie myself down with the most insufferable woman in London!' He stopped his tirade and got up to pour himself a stiff whiskey. With a trembling hand, he knocked it back in one.

'Damn you, Will! If we are going to make our marriage work, the least you can do is be civil to me. You're widely regarded as being exceedingly bright, so you should be able to work it out.'

'Work out what?' He turned to glower at her and hissed, 'insane as well as insufferable,' before slamming his glass down on to the drinks tray and pouring himself another one.

'The dates, Will, they don't add up. Not with Jeremy anyway, and Grandbo only wants to walk a virgin up the aisle. He told me to get out when he discovered I wasn't.'

'How did he find out? I don't suppose for one moment you told him.'

'That bow-legged bitch, Penelope Lindsay, spilled the beans. I'd told Jeremy, who as it turns out, couldn't keep his mouth shut.' Elizabeth started to sob. 'Grandbo was about to put his grandmother's engagement ring on my finger as well. A sapphire... the size of a

380

quail's egg. Oh, Will, I really thought he was the one, but unfortunately, he's not interested in marrying a woman with a desecrated hymen, let alone one carrying a developing foetus. I never wanted children. My life is ruined, and it's all your fault!'

Will wondered how he could have been so stupid? Despite being way out of his comfort zone, he had made little, or no, attempt to resist being pounced upon by an eighteen-year-old siren with the sexual appetite of a tigress. Will angst over things for a few days, wishing his father was still alive. He would have known what the best thing to do would be. He confided in Charlie Lyons, whose only comment, which in hindsight, was to be expected.

'Will Grant! You, of all people! Getting into the knickers of the Debutante of the Year for 1958! You sly old dog, who would have thought it?'

Will knew eyebrows would be raised when they married at Westminster Register Office in secret, their friends describing their courtship as a 'bit of a whirlwind romance', as well as the age-old and uncannily correct assumption: shotgun wedding.

Settling In

When Elizabeth first arrived at Silkwoods, it was not what she had been expecting. Will had so often waxed lyrical about the home he loved so much she had envisaged a building of similar stature as Studley Castle. Somewhere she could throw herself into the role of the lady of the manor and open a wing or two to the public a few times a year if she felt like it.

Every morning Elizabeth woke to the musty smell of old bricks and mortar. There were spiders the size of her fist in the sink, and the old plumbing groaned when she ran a bath. The taps spewed out russet-coloured water with slivers of rust in it. What made matters worse was the house was miles away from anywhere, so she couldn't step outside and hail a taxi.

'It's like living in the dark ages!' she complained to Jeremy over the telephone. 'I half expect to come downstairs in the mornings and find Benedictine monks helping themselves to the contents of the bloody drinks cupboard.'

Will's father had made some attempt to modernise the house over the years but had lost interest after his wife died, so, as Elizabeth soon found out, it was way past needing a woman's touch. Silkwoods was in dire need of total refurbishment. Will gave Elizabeth free rein to do what she wanted to the house. After an initial burst of enthusiasm, when she employed a carpenter to build a walk-in wardrobe in the master bedroom, Elizabeth gave up.

Housework, in a debutante's vocabulary, is defined as *a tedious but necessary task which one employs staff to do.* Cookery classes formed a part of the finishing school syllabus, but Elizabeth never went to any lessons as she couldn't bring herself to touch uncooked food.

Fortunately for Elizabeth, Nellie, farm manager Jim's wife, was looking for work as both her children were now at school. Elizabeth wasted no time in employing her as a full-time cook/housekeeper. It was an ideal arrangement. Elizabeth would have nothing to do with the house she wasn't interested in. Instead, she spent her days shopping in Cheltenham. But the pleasure of buying clothes and make-up stopped when her bump started to show.

Living a Lie

It was early spring, and Silkwoods was alive with the sound of birdsong, from a chorus of blackbirds to a lone crowing pheasant. The mosses and lichens of the woodland floor, submerged in a carpet of spring flowers, including daffodils, snowdrops, and early flowering purple orchids. Will was hacking along a footpath through the woods with Thomas behind him. There was a rustling in the undergrowth, which spooked the horses, as a female fallow deer took off at speed, twigs snapping under her hooves as she took flight.

'When's the baby due?' Thomas asked. 'It's the end of September, isn't it?'

Will's mind was elsewhere. He had woken up that morning with an uneasy tension in the pit of his stomach, which hadn't gone away. He thought exercising the horses with Thomas would shake off his general malaise. He had been unusually silent while they were saddling up and wondered if Thomas sensed he was feeling out of sorts.

'Anna's offered to pop round to talk to Elizabeth anytime. She thought it might be helpful to chat to someone about what to expect when giving birth for the first time.'

This time, Will reacted, digging his heels into the sides of the bay mare he was riding and galloped off down the track. By the time Thomas caught up, Will had dismounted by a wooden bridge over the river Churn, his horse's neck stretching down into the water drinking. Will was sitting on the bank, his knees drawn up to his chin, and he was crying.

Thomas hitched both horses' reins to the bridge and sat down next to Will, putting an arm around his shoulders, rubbing his upper arm with his hand.

Will pulled a handkerchief from his jacket pocket and wiped his eyes. 'Oh, Christ! I never used to cry when I was a child. I think I've gone soft in adulthood.' He blew his nose and took a deep breath. 'I'm sorry, I don't know what came over me.'

'I do! You've very recently lost your father, you've taken over the reins of running one of the largest estates in Gloucestershire, and you've just got married. Three pretty grown-up and stressful things to deal with, one after another. Getting married young comes as a shock to the system, as it does when you're expecting your first child.'

'I now know why they say marriage is for better or for worse.' Will gave Thomas a hopeless look. 'Mine is definitely erring towards the latter!'

'Well, it has to be said, Elizabeth is a force of nature.'

'She doesn't even *like* me, Thomas. And if I were honest, I don't like her very much either. I should never have married her, but when she told me she was pregnant, I felt I had to do the right thing. I know I let her seduce me, and I should have tried to show a degree of self-control and, for what it's worth, we haven't slept together since. I've been such a fool because I know now, the only reason she married me was for my money, and she used the baby as bait. Bobby Grandborough was going to marry her until he found out she wasn't a virgin. What a mess I've got myself into. And the last thing I would ever want to do is bring a child into a loveless marriage, and yes, in answer to your question, the baby's due in September. And I don't think I am ready to be a father.'

Thomas reached into his pocket and pulled out a hip flask. 'Have a swig of this. Whiskey always makes me feel better when I'm feeling down. You'll cope, I did.'

Will tipped his head back and took a slug. 'I envy you and Anna.'

'Why?'

'Well, you married when you were both eighteen. You must have been very much in love.'

Thomas moved his arm away from Will's shoulders, a soft sigh escaping his lips. 'I wish it were true and, don't get me wrong, I have a deep affection for her, but… if I tell you the real reason why Anna and I married, I need you to promise you will never tell a living soul.'

'Thomas… I honestly think I would trust you with my life. I swear on my parents' grave, I won't breathe a word.'

'During my last term at boarding school, one of the masters caught me in flagrante with another boy, and we were both expelled. Most boys' schools turn a blind eye, but not mine. My father was so ashamed of me he couldn't bring himself to look at me. Sometimes, he still can't. So, it was my father's idea. He *arranged* for me to marry Anna. It was a marriage of convenience for everybody, except for me, of course. Anna's father is a tea planter in Assam, and he and my father were in the same regiment during the war. After the war, he went back to India with his wife. When Anna finished boarding school, they thought she would be better off staying in the UK to find a husband rather than going back to India. Her parents couldn't afford to let her do 'The Season,' so my father volunteered me as the ideal husband. It was such a sham, the big society wedding and everything. Your father came, you were away at school. My father honestly believed that, as soon as I had a woman in my bed, I would forget about having sex with men.'

Will looked up, flicking his fringe to the side with a shake of his head. He hadn't noticed Thomas' dark brown eyes before, nor his full, slightly pink lips framed with a hint of five o'clock shadow, and, for a few seconds, the world stood still. The only sound was the rustling leaves on the majestic Silkwoods trees towering above them, gently buffeted by the breeze and the beating heart inside his chest. The spring sunshine streaming through the canopy flickered across Thomas' face like cine film footage.

'And have you? Have you forgotten about having sex with men?' Will asked.

Thomas bit his bottom lip and closed his eyes, then opened them to return Will's gaze. 'I hadn't allowed myself to think about it until I met you.' Stretching out his hand, he slid his fingers down Will's cheekbone, then snatched them away.

'It's okay,' Will reached for Thomas' hand and held it to his cheek. 'I've known for some time, well before my drunken sexcapade with Elizabeth, that I wanted to make love to men, not women and, after meeting you, I was sure.'

'But I can't, Will, as much as I want to. I have a wife and two children now. And my father would not only disinherit me, but he'd probably shoot me after having us both publicly flogged if he found out there was more going on between us than the accepted backslapping, ale drinking kind of friendship. Rural Gloucestershire really doesn't tolerate poofs.'

'But nobody else needs to know… apart from you and me.'

'The thing about secrets, Will, is they have a nasty habit of coming back to bite you. There are so many other people to consider, including your unborn child. It's not just about us.'

A kit of pigeons took flight behind them, making them jump.

'I'm not sure I can live a lie, Thomas.'

'Sometimes, dear Will, we have no choice.'

New Life

Elizabeth stood with her knees slightly bent, and her hands clawed tightly around the drying rail of the Aga cooking stove when suddenly an audible pop gushed amniotic fluid down both her legs. 'Oh God, it's happening… Nellie,' she yelled at the top of her voice.

Nellie bustled into the room. 'Oh, good, your waters have broken. It's about time. I'll go and call the midwife.'

A glazed expression spread across Elizabeth's face. 'Don't leave me,' she whimpered.

'I'll only be a jiffy, Mrs Grant. I'm going to call the midwife, Jim too, so he can find Will and make sure he's here for the birth. He's ever so excited about it.'

'It's all very well for Will! He doesn't have to squeeze the thing out of a vagina,' Elizabeth mumbled.

As Nellie left the kitchen, Elizabeth burst into tears. The involuntary burst of waterworks took her by surprise. She never cried about anything. She tried to stop, but she was still snivelling when Nellie came back into the room.

Nellie put an arm around Elizabeth's shoulders. 'There, there, Mrs Grant, it's been a long do for you, but you'll be holding your beautiful baby in your arms very soon now.'

Elizabeth's glassy expression turned to one of surprise, and, pulling away from Nellie, she looked down at the puddle on the floor. 'Baby? What about my beautiful Rayne shoes? It's the first time I've worn them.'

'Right! Let's get you upstairs before Phyllis, the midwife, arrives, shall we?'

By the time Nellie half pushed Elizabeth up the grand Jacobean staircase to her en-suite bedroom, Phyllis had arrived bristling with efficiency.

'How are we doing, Elizabeth?'

'How does it look like we are doing? We are in bloody agony. I need you to get this thing out of me!'

'That's why I'm here, my lovely.'

'I'm not *your* lovely!' Elizabeth moaned. As her contractions intensified, she became hysterical.

'There, there, Elizabeth. Take some nice, slow, deep breaths for me,' Phyllis encouraged.

'But I'm in pain! Can't you see that? Everything hurts. I knew I should have stayed in London and had it delivered by a proper Harley Street physician, not a tin pot provincial midwife.'

Phyllis gasped. 'I'll have you know, Mrs Grant, I've delivered hundreds of babies in my time. Breech and all sorts, and I will be delivering yours very shortly.'

'Nellie! Go and call the bloody doctor!' Elizabeth groaned.

Phyllis was undeterred. 'I delivered my first babber when I was fourteen. My auntie Pat was caught short at the greengrocers.'

'Well, you won't be delivering this one!'

'If Doctor Gladstone is still doing morning surgery, you're not going to have a choice.'

As her contractions became longer and the time between them shorter, Elizabeth became more and more anxious, 'Nellie! Where's the bloody doctor? My Harley Street physician could have got here quicker.'

'He's on his way, Mrs Grant.'

'I expect he'll come in his Armstrong-Siddeley Hurricane as it's a nice day.' Phyllis was doing her best to carry on regardless. 'He calls it his indulgent fair-weather motor. He only uses his sturdy Land Rover to reach his patients who live off the beaten track. He always manages to get to them, whatever the weather.'

'Whatever he's driving, he better put his bloody foot down. I need to get this thing out of me!'

'Breathe, Elizabeth, breathe. There's a good girl,' encouraged Phyliss. 'Open your legs for me so I can see what's happening down there.'

'I'm not opening my legs for you or anybody else!'

'Well, you're going to have to, if that baby's ever going to see the light of day!'

'Where's the bloody doctor!'

'I'm here, Elizabeth.' Dr Gladstone strode into the bedroom, took off his fedora, and placed his bag on a chair by Elizabeth's bed.

'Hello, Doctor.' Phyllis and Nellie chorused in relieved unison.

Dr Gladstone took Elizabeth's hand, and to his surprise, she snatched it away. Undeterred, he leaned over her, giving instructions in his deep, reassuring Scottish accent. 'Now, Elizabeth, I would like you to breathe in through your nose to the count of three. And then breathe out through your mouth, to the count of four.'

'Just get this thing out of me!' Elizabeth pleaded.

'Elizabeth, your baby's doing fine.'

'Well, bully for the baby, I'm not!' She watched, appalled, as Dr Gladstone, brow furrowed, peered up at her vagina. His squinting eyes, magnified by the lenses of his round, metal-framed spectacles.

'The baby's head is crowning, Elizabeth,' Phyllis enthused as both she and Nellie leaned in for a closer look.

'Oh, for God's sake! This is all so undignified,' Elizabeth wailed. 'I feel like one of Will's prize heifers giving birth with everybody gawping at my pudenda.' In between the panting, she was vaguely aware that the grandfather clock in the hall was striking noon. A deep-throated groan escaped her lips as she kicked out her right leg.

The heel of her foot impacted with the bridge of the good doctor's nose, and, with one last almighty groan, Lisa Elizabeth Grant shot out of her vagina coated in a mix of amniotic fluid, blood, and vernix. Lisa's barely audible cries were drowned out by Elizabeth's blood-curdling screams.

'That's the last time I'm ever bloody well going to go through all this! Do you hear me, Will Grant? You can keep your trousers on in future!'

'You have a beautiful baby girl, Mrs Grant,' Phyllis announced with pride as she cut the cord before wrapping Lisa in a dusky pink towel. Making cooing noises, she clasped Lisa to her bosom as

Elizabeth closed her legs with a groan.

'Don't worry, Elizabeth. You will start feeling better down there… in six to twelve weeks, give or take. Holding your baby for the first time will make you feel like all that pushing and shoving has been a labour of love.'

Elizabeth wasn't convinced, frowning as Phyllis leaned forward, gently placing Lisa in the crook of her right arm. Feeling the warmth of her daughter's tiny body against her skin for the first time, she stiffened. Of all the things she had wanted in her life, a child wasn't one of them. She viewed the swaddling child with suspicion, wondering which way was up. She separated the towel with her thumb and forefinger and peered inside.

'She has a full head of hair too,' Phyllis chirped. 'Most babies are born with precious little hair. Both of mine looked like Yul Brynner when they popped out, especially our little gal.'

'A full head of hair?' Elizabeth repeated robotically.

Lisa's soft gurgling turned into a full-on bellow as she eyeballed her mother for the first time.

Elizabeth recoiled, holding her at arm's length. 'It's much too loud! And it's *covered* in hair!'

'Some babies are born with a full head of hair, Elizabeth. It's perfectly normal.' Dr Gladstone, still recovering from Elizabeth's right heel jab, reasserted himself. He approached the bed, holding a bloodied white handkerchief to his nose with one hand. He placed his other hand on Elizabeth's shoulder as a gesture of reassurance, but when she flinched at his touch, he withdrew it.

'Yes, overdue babies can often have a full head of hair, and your gorgeous girl was more than just a trifle late in arriving. And it's also perfectly normal for babies to cry when they are born. I always worry when they don't.' He exchanged knowing nods with the midwife.

Despite the doctor's soothing tone, Elizabeth's face scrunched into a scowl. 'Well, not only is this one *covered* in hair, it's also horribly greasy, and it sounds more like a wild banshee than a baby! Take it away and wash it!' she commanded, handing *it* back to a dumbstruck Phyllis. 'And cut all its hair off! It can't *possibly* be normal.'

Just then, Will burst through the door. 'I swear if anybody touches one single hair on my child's head, they will have me to answer to!'

'You have a daughter, Will. Many congratulations.' Dr Gladstone slapped him heartily on his back, his steely grey eyes twinkling.

'Would you like to hold her?' Phyllis asked.

Will's face lit up as he took the tiny bundle in his arms. Lisa immediately stopped crying, reaching out a minute hand towards his face in slow, uncoordinated movements. As her tiny fingertips brushed against his chin, he smiled and held her closer, his eyes overflowing with tears of joy. 'You're *so* beautiful,' he whispered. 'I'm going to take great care of you… always.'

'Oh, for God's sake, Will! What about *me?* I've just forced that great big head out of my vagina!'

2000 - 2002

The Rutherford Legacy

Lisa could no longer put off telling her mother about the baby or what she had found buried in a solicitor's chambers in Cambridge, so she lost no time in booking a flight to London.

Once the aircraft gained cruising speed and levelled off over the Bay of Biscay, the flight attendant brought drinks and snacks.

Jack gripped Lisa's hand. 'It will be emotional meeting with your mother, especially as it will be the first time you've seen her since Arthur's funeral.'

'I know, but I'm ready to make my peace with her. Now I know the whole story.'

'You told me all about Elizabeth's upbringing with her grandfather's sister Sarah, and I know about your mother's cousin Rose, but how did you find her?'

'I didn't. Rose found me. She stumbled across Arthur's obituary in *The Times*, then contacted the undertakers asking them to pass on a letter to me. I already knew my great aunt, Clara Clemmens, had a daughter called Rose. I couldn't believe it. My mother had a first cousin she had no idea about! As soon as I received Rose's letter, I rang her. She wrote to me because she wasn't sure if my mother wanted to hear from her, given that she's never tried to contact them herself. Embarrassingly, Rose saw me flying through the air in Paris on the News at Ten. I told her that was not my finest hour.' Lisa hesitated and gripped Jack's hand a little tighter, 'I meant my Pernod spectacle, not the days we spent there afterwards.'

Jack laughed, 'I hoped that's what you meant!'

'So, it was Rose who filled in all the pertinent bits. The motor car accident and my infant-mother being taken away from her maternal grandparents and growing up with her stony-hearted great aunt. I don't think it was a coincidence that Great Aunt Sarah left the cupboard door open; she *wanted* my mother to find its contents.'

Jack gave a sympathetic nod. 'It sounds to me like she crumbled under the weight of seventeen years of guilt. Not allowing Elizabeth's heartbroken grandparents and aunt Clara to have any communication with her was outrageous.'

'Yes, given they were the only people who loved her. Losing both their daughters must have been tough for my great-grandparents; Gertrude at seventeen and Clara at twenty-nine. Rose said Ben and Evelyn both died in the late 1980s, but they never forgot about my mother. Mrs Crittall at the post office told them that Elizabeth had visited her before moving to London, so Evelyn lived the rest of her life hoping that my mother would contact her, but as she didn't, I imagine Evelyn must have died heartbroken.'

'No wonder your mother is like she is.' Jack cocked his head to one side, 'but she should never have taken it out on you.'

'I know, there is no excuse but, now I know what happened, I can understand.'

'What's Rose like?' Jack asked.

'She's lovely. Very caring, unassuming and, fortunately for me, a solicitor, who happens to be well-versed in inheritance disputes.

Together, we took on the legal challenge to establish Rose's theory that my mother was the rightful heir to Ditton Hall, which turned out to be less of a battle than I had anticipated. Surprisingly, the Rutherford family lawyers knew about her.'

Jack looked puzzled. 'So why didn't the Rutherford's solicitor contact Elizabeth after Aunt Sarah died?'

'Because her father's name wasn't on the birth certificate, they had no proof that she was Edward Campbell's daughter. After Edward's death, a letter he wrote to his parents was found among his personal effects. Written the day my mother was born, he poured his heart out about his undying love for Gertrude and his new-born baby, how much he wanted to marry her, and the pride he felt having become a father. He ended the letter with a plea to his parents to provide for both Gertrude and Elizabeth, should he become a casualty of war.'

Jack was incensed. 'But surely, there would have been sufficient evidence in that letter for the solicitors to contact your mother then!'

'Ah, but, for some reason, too painful perhaps? The Rutherfords chose not to open it, but Rose insisted it should be. So, there is no question. My mother is the sole heir to Ditton Hall.'

From Gatwick airport, they caught a train to Charing Cross station, then by taxi to an imposing-looking property in Lisa and Jack's old stamping ground, Notting Hill, where Elizabeth had moved following Arthur's death.

Jack got out to pay the cabbie as Lisa stepped on to the pavement. She looked up at the gleaming white three-story stucco-fronted property, accessed through a wrought-iron gate.

'I might have guessed something as huge as this would be my mother's idea of downsizing.'

Jack laughed, putting his hands on her shoulders. 'I'll meet you in what used to be our' old coffee shop, okay? I hope it goes well.'

'It will be fine!' She kissed him on the lips, 'I love you.'

'I love you more, Lisa Grant,' he responded, walking away, 'call me if you need back up.'

Taking a deep breath, she rang the doorbell, and Jeremy opened the door.

'Good God, Lisa! What a surprise, Sweet Pea!' Stepping forward, he kissed her on both cheeks before stopping to look at her. 'How wonderful to see you. You're looking positively glowing. Come on in!'

Lisa looked around the entrance hall. 'This is very nice.'

'Yes, well, thanks to your allowance, it's had the full Elizabeth Goldsworthy-Grant make-over since we moved in.'

'I take it she's here?'

'Yes, she's in the garden, deadheading her petunias.'

'Her petunias?' Lisa chuckled, 'I didn't think my mother was interested in gardening. Not doing it herself anyway.'

'She's taken to it like a duck to water since we moved here. I think she finds it therapeutic.'

'Really? Well, that's great. I thought you two were supposed to be getting married?'

'We were, but your mother seems to have gone off the idea. She seems a bit out of sorts at the moment, but I'm sure seeing you will cheer her up.'

Lisa bit her tongue. That would be a first.

'Come on through. Elizabeth will be thrilled to see you.'

They walked through into the garden to see Elizabeth with her back to them perched on a garden kneeler, head bent, scrutinising each petunia carefully before snipping the dead bits off.

'Sugarplum, we have a surprise visitor!'

Elizabeth started to get up. 'Oh God, I hate surprises. Ouch! My bloody knees are stiff. Help me up, Jeremy!'

As Jeremy jumped to it, Lisa shook her head and mouthed the words, 'I'll do it.' She went over to her mother and took hold of her outstretched hand, helping Elizabeth to her feet.

Her mother looked shocked. 'Heavens, Lisa. What a surprise. You've caught me in my gardening gear. Goodness, I must look a fright.' Elizabeth leant forward and air-kissed Lisa. 'If you'd told me you were coming, I would have looked halfway decent.'

'Hello, Mother. You look great just as you are. Very elegant for a gardener, I would say, and anyway, you never have to dress up for me.' Anticipating her mother's usual once over, Lisa had deliberately worn a cotton dress that emphasised her bump.

Elizabeth's eyes slowly moved up from Lisa's middle until, with a knowing grin, she made eye contact. 'You've put on weight again, Lisa, dear!'

'You're not going to say I need to cut down on carbs, are you, Mother?'

Elizabeth shook her head. 'Don't be silly! Of course, I'm not! I have to say it's a surprise, though. I never thought it would ever happen. How far along are you?'

Lisa put both hands on her belly, 'nearly five months.'

'Whose is it?'

'It's Jack's, of course! I can't believe you just said that.' Lisa tried hard to curb her irritation. 'I'm here because I need to talk to you about something really important. Can we sit down?' She motioned to a curved garden bench under a tulip tree. 'Over there, perhaps? Your garden looks lovely, by the way.'

As they made their way across a well-manicured lawn, Elizabeth beamed with satisfaction and plumped up her bob with both hands. 'Thank you. Who would ever have guessed I had green fingers?' She sat down and patted the bench inviting Lisa to sit down. Now then, what is so important that you need to turn up on my doorstep unannounced, apart from letting me know you are pregnant, which I would have thought would have been a priority.'

'I've always wondered why you and I have never shared a loving relationship.'

'Oh, goodness, Lisa, where are you going with all this?'

'Where am I going with it? I'm going right back to the beginning, to the Gamekeeper's Cottage at Ditton Hall.'

Elizabeth got up, 'I think you should leave. I've no wish to start digging up the dirt at this stage of my life!'

'Please sit down, Mother. I *need* to have this conversation with you. We should have had it years ago but, because I already feel such love for my baby before he or she has even been born, I needed to know why you chose to disassociate yourself from me from the day I popped out.'

Elizabeth rested her head against the chair back. 'It's a long story, Lisa, and it's not a very pretty one.'

'Yes, and it's one you've somehow managed to keep to yourself your entire life. I cannot imagine what life was like for you growing up.'

'You couldn't possibly know.'

'Actually, I do have a pretty good idea. I know about your parents, I know about Ben and Evelyn Clemmens, and that you have a first cousin called Rose, who is lovely, and can't wait to meet you. I'm sorry I went behind your back, but I made it my business to find out because I wanted to understand why we've never enjoyed a proper mother-daughter relationship.'

Elizabeth seemed at a loss for words for once. Her look of disbelief gave way to despair as her eyes overflowed with tears that rolled silently down her cheeks.

Seeing her mother cry for the first time, Lisa felt choked and instinctively put both arms around Elizabeth's shoulders, pressing her cheek against hers. 'It's okay, Mother. I want us to be friends. I want you to be more of a part of my life and my baby's.'

'I'm so sorry, Lisa,' Elizabeth sniffled, 'one should try and keep a stiff upper lip at all times.'

'It's okay, don't be sorry, and to hell with stiff upper lips. They never worked for me anyway. Just let it all go. You'll feel so much better when you do, I promise.'

'When I realised who I was, I couldn't tell anyone,' Elizabeth sobbed. 'It was the shame of it all, you see, being betwixt and between. I was someone, and yet I was no one. I had no real identity. I could have chosen to find my mother's parents, but I chose the life I knew, and there was no going back.'

Lisa turned to face her mother. 'Look, no more secrets between you and I, ever again. I don't know how you've carried all this around with you for sixty years.'

'Excuse me, I'm not quite sixty yet, Lisa dear.'

'Oops, no, you're not, quite, are you? We're going to have so much fun getting to know each other properly. Oh, and this might cheer you up. Rose is a lawyer, and between us, we've discovered you are the sole heir to Ditton Hall.'

In shock, Elizabeth shot up, then fell back into her chair. After taking a moment to compose herself, she gave Lisa a satisfied smile. 'I always thought I should be entitled to the estate! Jeremy!' Elizabeth shouted, 'that bottle of champagne you've been keeping in the fridge for a special occasion. You can open it now!' Then turning back to Lisa, 'What about the title? I hope I get that too. Lady Elizabeth has a very nice ring to it, don't you think?'

Commitment

A warm, gusty south-westerly blew off the sea at Praia do Trafal. Lisa linked her arm with her father as they walked barefoot across the sand towards the sea. Will looked effortlessly suave in a pair of white linen trousers and a pale pink linen shirt, which complemented Lisa's knee-length, pink linen dress.

'Ah, look. There's your mother, standing out from the crowd, resplendent in fuchsia pink. What on earth has she got on her head?'

'It looks like a floral skyscraper!'

'You did send her an invitation, didn't you? The one that clearly states *Beach Celebration*, and not Westminster Abbey?'

'Of course, but she rang me to say she'd already bought *a splendid Giorgio Armani* for the occasion and was determined to wear it with her Jimmy Choos. I did try to explain you get sand between your toes when you go on the beach.'

Will gave a wry smile. 'I thought wedding bells were going to ring for Elizabeth. Didn't Jeremy pop the question after Arthur died?'

'He did. But after reading Arthur's will, nothing was mentioned again until the day I told my mother she was the heir to the Rutherford estate. He got down on both knees to re-propose before I'd even left the house. I do have serious reservations about the pair of them rattling around Ditton Hall in their dotages. It's miles away from anywhere, but they are too blinkered to realise it. It will be a shock after living in London for years. You can't just pop outside and hail a cab in the remotest part of Cambridgeshire.'

Elizabeth, Jeremy, and Rose were sitting in the front row of a handful of spindly gilt chairs on the beach facing the sea and a flower-strewn archway, quivering in the breeze. A smiling celebrant stood underneath the arched halo of flowers. Her long blonde hair was blowing in her face as she laughed as she shared a joke with Jack and Mike, who stood patiently with their hands laced behind their backs.

'Where is she? Talk about keeping the bridegroom waiting.' Elizabeth's exasperated voice fluttered on the breeze.

'Elizabeth, you *know* this is not a wedding, per se.' Jeremy was feeling brave. 'It's about two people who have always been in love, who want the people closest to them to witness them pronounced soulmates for life. And to celebrate the birth of your grandson.'

'Such an *extraordinary* idea. And look at the groom and the best man! They're wearing shorts. At least they've got nice, brown legs. As for my grandson, it's almost two years since Lisa gave birth to him while giving a group of tourists a conducted tour of Mont das Uvas. It was just as well one of them turned out to be a gynaecologist. It's outrageous! Not only was that child born out of wedlock, but they haven't even bothered to have him christened!'

'Lizzie!' Rose interjected, 'you and I were both born out of wedlock! If you must use such an outdated expression. Little Artur was born out of love, as we were.'

Elizabeth pursed her lips. 'If you say so, Rose, dear.'

'I do say so, Mrs Hoity-Toity.'

'Hoity-what?'

'Toity! Bloody hell, Lizzie, you were sent away to a posh school. You *must* know what it means. You, Mrs Hoity-Toity, need some of your rough edges knocked off!'

'I beg your pardon?'

'You heard! I'll make you into a caring soul yet. Lisa's more like our side of the family, though. She's lovely.'

'Yes, well, of course, I brought her up rather well on my own after putting up with all the dreadful business with Will. And one prefers to be addressed as Elizabeth, not Lizzie if you don't mind.'

Rose sighed. 'And telling all these porky pies has got to stop, *Lizzie*!'

Elizabeth, giving the impression she wasn't listening, tapped one of her Jimmy Choos against the leg of Jeremy's chair, trying to get rid of the sand.

The knocking noise made Mike turn around. 'Have you seen your significant other's mother this morning, Jack?'

'No. But I can *hear* the Debutante of the Year for 1958 loud and clear, even though the wind should be carrying her voice north towards the hills of Loulé.'

'Well, she's all trussed up for a society wedding, wearing a shocking pink suit and a hat guaranteed to win Best in Show at Chelsea.'

As Peter Frampton's *Baby I Love Your Way* floated on the breeze, Lisa and her father walked up the sandy aisle between the two rows of gilt chairs.

'You look beautiful, Piglet.'

'And you look very handsome yourself, Pooh. And Roo there,' she said, pointing her bouquet at her son, 'is going to keep us all young.'

Artur was standing on Adele's knee, looking over her shoulder, watching his mother and grandfather walked towards him.

Will waved at his grandson. 'He may have got his father's black curls, but he's the spit of his mother.'

'He's my greatest achievement, Dad. I can't believe it was only such a short time ago I was living in a bloody awful cottage near Silkwoods, convinced my ovaries were wrinkled prunes.'

'Thank God, she's here!' Elizabeth fanned herself with a handkerchief, 'It's about bloody time! I'm ready for a gin and tonic! I've never been to a wedding with a female vicar before. Quite extraordinary.'

Jeremy rolled his eyes. 'Elizabeth! For the umpteenth time, this is not a wedding! And she's a celebrant, not a vicar.'

'Goodness knows what the Almighty would have to say about it all. It's enough to make his halo curl.'

As Lisa walked past her mother, she realised Elizabeth was watching her. Turning to smile at her, Elizabeth reciprocated, and much to her delight, her mother's face radiated happiness, her eyes glistening in the sunshine.

Rose reached for Elizabeth's hand. 'Lizzie, are you alright, darling? You look like you are about to pass out!'

'I'm alright, I think, thank you. One is a little overwhelmed. It must be the heat.'

'Nothing to do with Lisa, then? Your only daughter, who is looking radiant and floating on cloud nine on her way to making a lifetime commitment to the love of her life.' Rose pulled out a handful of tissues from her bag. 'I'm feeling a little emotional myself. Would you like one?'

'Oh, no, Rose dear. One never cries in public.'

'Get over yourself, Lizzie! Release all that pent up emotion. It's no sin to cry! You're surrounded by family anyway. Nobody's going to think any less of you if you shed a tear or two or bawl your bloody eyes out.' She nodded towards Jeremy in the next seat. 'Just look at the state of him!'

Elizabeth gasped. Jeremy was sobbing into a monogramed handkerchief. 'Jeremy! You're letting the side down!'

'But I've never seen Lisa look so happy before, my love.'

'Welcome, everyone,' the celebrant began. 'We are all here today to celebrate the love Lisa and Jack share.'

Lisa turned to Jack and looked into his eyes. His adoring expression told her everything she needed to know. Jack was all she had ever wanted in her life, but she'd been too blind to see it at twenty-two. Now they would share the rest of their lives together and raise their beautiful son in a world filled with love, encouraging him to go out into the world to achieve whatever his heart desired. They would watch spectacular sunsets and inhale the heady scent of moonlit lavender and pine under a canopy of stars.

After the ceremony and before a sumptuous Portuguese sit-down celebratory meal at the Temperus Beach Bar, Rory organised group photographs at the water's edge. As temperatures soared, some had stripped down to swimsuits and played in the surf, while others simply paddled.

While Jack enjoyed a cold beer and light-hearted banter with Will and Thomas, Lisa strolled along the water's edge with Artur on her hip, watching all the people she cared about splashing around in the sea, including her mother.

'Now, that's a sight I thought I would never see, Artur. Look at your grandma.'

Knee-deep in the sea, a shoe-less, tights-less Elizabeth, with her Giorgio Armani dress tucked into her knickers, howled with laughter as Rose dunked her hat in the ocean. Lisa couldn't help grinning, but it was a sign her mother was beginning to throw off the shackles of her loveless childhood and starting to enjoy life with her family.

For all her mother's faults, she'd always known she could never cut their umbilical tie. Her heart had been telling her for years. She was ready to *forgive* Elizabeth for her lack of compassion because those feelings of indifference, hurt and betrayal had gone.

'Lisa!' Elizabeth emerged from the sea, pulling down the hem of her drenched silk-lined cotton dress. 'Hang on a minute.'

Lisa stopped walking, feeling the wind-driven waves lap over her feet. There was something different in the tone of her mother's voice. It was softer, more caring. She looked relaxed and happy, especially with seawater dripping from her face and hair. Another sign she was letting go of the past.

'Are you having a nice time, Mother? Your poor dress, though. Let me have it in the morning, and I'll hand wash it for you.'

'Don't be silly, darling!'

'Darling? Did she just call me darling? She never calls anybody, darling. Least of all me, and she hasn't even had a drink yet.'

'I'll have it dry cleaned! One doesn't *hand-wash* anything! It ruins your hands. I just wanted to say. You were quite right.'

'Right? Me? I'm never right in your eyes.'

'I'm having a wonderful time, but I should buy some beach clothes. What do you say we go shopping tomorrow? Perhaps we could make a day of it and go to Porches? Their pottery is to die for, and then we could do lunch somewhere. If not tomorrow, any day soon will be fine. We're enjoying our stay here so much that Jeremy and I have decided to rent the Vale do Lobo villa for another month. As money is no longer an object, we might even buy one, so we can spend more time here.'

'Hmm… Fun? Spend more time here? Is this my mother talking?'

'Perhaps we can do it the day Jeremy goes for another wine tasting at Mont das Uvas?'

Lisa was sceptical. 'This is a bit of a revelation, Mother. Are you really thinking about buying a property over here? I didn't think you were a great fan of the heat, let alone the beach, and…'

'No, on the contrary, it's just that our lives have always been such a social whirl, we've never had time for holidays. Jeremy's even taken up paragliding. He's a bit of a natural, actually.'

Lisa stifled a giggle as an image of Jeremy dangling under a parachute flashed through her mind. 'And you, mother, what about you? What will you be doing while Jeremy is enjoying his new found freedom aloft?'

'I will be spending more time with you and Artur. You said you wanted me to,' Elizabeth beamed, pulling down the clinging wet fabric of her dress and wringing it out.

Artur started wriggling around in Lisa's arms, and she put him down gently. After stamping his feet playfully in the wet sand, he wrapped his tiny arms around Elizabeth's legs.

'Well, Mother, it looks like your grandson is happy about you spending more time here.'

'And, what about you, Lisa? Are you happy?'

Lisa grinned at Artur, now imitating his grandmother by trying to wring out her hat. 'Mother, today I am ecstatically happy. Having all the people I care about around me is wonderful. And, if you do decide to buy over here, I can't think of anything nicer. Right, let's go and find you something dry to wear before we have lunch. I put loads of clothes in the back of the car for such an eventuality, although I didn't think it would be you who would need them, and you'll have to change using a beach towel poncho.'

'Oh, that's okay, whatever a poncho is.'

'Then, after you've changed, we'll find you a gin and tonic, and we will enjoy a drink together. Right! You hold Artur's other hand, and we'll swing him up the beach. He'd love that.'

'Swing him?'

'Yes, Mother. Artur and I will show you how we do it!'

'Wing, wing, wing, whee!' Artur squealed.

Lisa stepped away from Elizabeth, struggling to change inside the towelling poncho, and watched her family and friends coming off the beach. Her thoughts turned to the one person who wasn't there, and, whispering into the breeze, she hoped somehow, he might hear.

'Life will never be the same without you, Arthur. I miss you terribly, especially on this, the happiest day of my life. I wish you'd met your namesake, my beautiful boy, Artur; you would have made a brilliant grandpa. Wherever you are, Arthur, I hope you know I love you so very much. You will forever be in my heart.'

***

About the author

Tessa Barrie was born in Yorkshire on the UK Mainland and now lives in the beautiful British Channel Island of Jersey.

As well as mentor to the feisty canine blogger *Cassie the Blog* Dog, Tessa writes her own blog at *My Alter Ego and Me*, where she entertains readers with her forgetfully funny *Dotage Diaries* and a series of squibs under the heading of *My Life to Date and How I've Survived It*.

Since receiving her first writing gong aged seven, a Blue Peter badge for poetry, Tessa has contributed articles, poetry, and short stories to magazines and anthologies. Her song-writing phase lasted many years after writing her first and last musical at fifteen.

On a more serious note, Tessa has co-written one non-fiction book, *Brian Trubshaw - Test Pilot*, under the name of alter ego, Sally Edmondson.

After working in the insurance industry for many years, redundancy allowed her to concentrate on her writing. Since then, Tessa has been long-listed in several writing competitions, including Fiction Factory, Flash 500, and Retreat West. She has also finished writing her first novel.

It is of paramount importance to Tessa that all her writing is knitted together with a degree of humour. However, feedback on the early drafts of her firstborn book delivered a stark warning. 'Make sure you amuse, rather than bludgeon, the reader with witty lines.' So, realising less is more when it comes to comic writing. After many agonising rewrites and several lengthy eye-watering edits, her debut novel *Just Say It* has finally hit the electronic shelves. Novel number two, a murder mystery spoof, is in the pipeline.

Thank you for choosing to read my book. If you'd like to know more about me and my writing, or just to say hello, you can contact me on these platforms.

My Alter Ego and Me www.tessabarrie.com
Twitter - TessaBarrie
Instagram - tessa_barrie
Facebook - TessaBarrieAuthor